BINTI

THE COMPLETE TRILOGY

BINTI

THE COMPLETE TRILOGY

BINTI

BINTI: SACRED FIRE

BINTI: HOME

BINTI: THE NIGHT MASQUERADE

NNEDI OKORAFOR

DAW BOOKS, INC.

DONALD A. WOLLHEIM, FOUNDER

1745 Broadway, New York, NY 10019

ELIZABETH R. WOLLHEIM

SHEILA E. GILBERT

PUBLISHERS

www.dawbooks.com

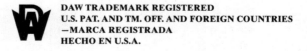

BINTI

Dedicated to the little blue jellyfish I saw swimming the Khalid Lagoon that sunny day in Sharjah, United Arab Emirates

I powered up the transporter and said a silent prayer. I had no idea what I was going to do if it didn't work. My transporter was cheap, so even a droplet of moisture, or more likely, a grain of sand, would cause it to short. It was faulty and most of the time I had to restart it over and over before it worked. *Please not now, please not now*, I thought.

The transporter shivered in the sand and I held my breath. Tiny, flat, and black as a prayer stone, it buzzed softly and then slowly rose from the sand. Finally, it produced the baggage-lifting force. I grinned. Now I could make it to the shuttle. I swiped *otjize* from my forehead with my index finger and knelt down. Then I touched the finger to the sand, grounding the sweet smelling red clay into it. "Thank you," I whispered. It was a half-mile walk along the dark desert road. With the transporter working, I would make it there on time.

Straightening up, I paused and shut my eyes. Now the weight of my entire life was pressing on my shoulders. I was defying the most traditional part of myself for the first time in my entire life. I was leaving in the dead of night and they had no clue. My nine siblings, all older than me except for my younger sister and brother, would never see this coming. My parents would never imagine I'd do such a thing in a million years. By the time they all realized what I'd done and where I was going, I'd have left the planet. In my absence, my parents would growl to each other that I was to never set foot in their home again. My four aunties and two uncles who lived down the road would shout and gossip among themselves about how I'd scandalized our entire bloodline. I was going to be a pariah.

"Go," I softly whispered to the transporter, stamping my foot. The thin metal rings I wore around each ankle jingled noisily, but I stamped my foot again. Once on, the transporter worked best when I didn't touch it. "Go," I said again, sweat forming on my brow. When nothing moved, I chanced giving the two large suitcases sitting atop the force field a shove. They moved smoothly and I breathed another sigh of relief. At least some luck was on my side.

———

Fifteen minutes later I purchased a ticket and boarded the shuttle. The sun was barely beginning to peak over the horizon. As I moved past seated passengers far too aware of the bushy ends of my plaited hair softly slapping people in the face, I cast my eyes to the floor. Our hair is thick and mine has always been *very* thick. My old auntie liked to call it "ododo" because it grew wild and dense like ododo grass. Just before leaving, I'd rolled my plaited hair with fresh sweet-smelling *otjize* I'd made specifically for this trip. Who knew what I looked like to these people who didn't know my people so well.

A woman leaned away from me as I passed, her face pinched as if she smelled something foul. "Sorry," I whispered, watching my feet and trying to ignore the stares of almost everyone in the shuttle. Still, I couldn't help glancing around. Two girls who might have been a few years older than me, covered their mouths with hands so pale that they looked untouched by the sun. Everyone looked as if the sun was his or her enemy. I was the only Himba on the shuttle. I quickly found and moved to a seat.

The shuttle was one of the new sleek models that looked like the bullets my teachers used to calculate ballistic coefficients during my A-levels when I was growing up. These ones glided fast over land using a combination of air current, magnetic fields, and exponential energy—an easy craft to build if you had the equipment and the time. It was also a nice vehicle for hot desert terrain where the roads leading out of town were terribly maintained. My people didn't like to leave the homeland. I sat in the back so I could look out the large window.

I could see the lights from my father's astrolabe shop and the sand storm analyzer my brother had built at the top of the Root—that's what we called my parents' big, big house. Six generations of my family had lived there. It was the oldest house in my village, maybe the oldest in the city. It was made of stone and concrete, cool in the night, hot in the day. And it was patched with solar planes and covered with bioluminescent plants that liked to stop glowing just before sunrise. My bedroom was at the top of the house. The shuttle began to move and I stared until I couldn't see it anymore. "What am I doing?" I whispered.

An hour and a half later, the shuttle arrived at the launch port. I was the last off, which was good because the sight of the launch port overwhelmed me so much that all I could do for several moments was stand there. I was wearing a long red skirt, one that was silky like water, a light orange wind-top that was stiff and durable, thin leather sandals, and my anklets. No one around me wore such an outfit. All I saw were light flowing garments and veils; not one woman's ankles were exposed, let alone jingling with steel anklets. I breathed through my mouth and felt my face grow hot.

"Stupid stupid stupid," I whispered. We Himba don't travel. We stay put. Our ancestral land is life; move away from it and you diminish. We even cover our bodies with it. *Otjize* is red land. Here in the launch port, most were Khoush and a few other non-Himba. Here, I was an outsider; I was outside. "What was I thinking?" I whispered.

I was sixteen years old and had never been beyond my city, let alone near a launch station. I was by myself and I had just left my family. My prospects of marriage had been 100 percent and now they would be zero. No man wanted a woman who'd run away. However, beyond my prospects of normal life being ruined, I had scored so high on the planetary exams in mathematics that the Oomza University had not only admitted me, but promised to pay for whatever I needed in order to attend. No matter what choice I made, I was never going to have a normal life, really.

I looked around and immediately knew what to do next. I walked to the help desk.

═══

The travel security officer scanned my astrolabe, a full *deep* scan. Dizzy with shock, I shut my eyes and breathed through my mouth to steady myself. Just to leave the planet, I had to give them access to my *entire* life—me, my family, and all forecasts of my future. I stood there, frozen, hearing my mother's voice in my head. "There is a reason why our people do not go to that university. Oomza Uni wants you for its own gain, Binti. You go to that school and you become its slave." I couldn't help but contemplate the possible truth in her words. I hadn't even gotten there yet and already I'd given them my life. I wanted to ask the officer if he did this for everyone, but I was afraid now that he'd done it. They could do anything to me, at this point. Best not to make trouble.

When the officer handed me my astrolabe, I resisted the urge to snatch it back. He was an old Khoush man, so old that he was privileged to wear the blackest turban and face veil. His shaky hands were so gnarled and arthritic that he nearly dropped my astrolabe. He was bent like a dying palm tree and when he'd said, "You have never traveled; I must do a full scan. Remain where you are," his voice was drier than the red desert outside my city. But he read my astrolabe as fast as my father, which both impressed and scared me. He'd coaxed it open by whispering a few choice equations and his suddenly steady hands worked the dials as if they were his own.

When he finished, he looked up at me with his light green piercing eyes that seemed to see deeper into me than his scan of my astrolabe. There were people behind me and I was aware of their whispers, soft laughter and a young child murmuring. It was cool in the terminal, but I felt the heat of social pressure. My temples ached and my feet tingled.

"Congratulations," he said to me in his parched voice, holding out my astrolabe.

I frowned at him, confused. "What for?"

"You are the pride of your people, child," he said, looking me in the eye. Then he smiled broadly and patted my shoulder. He'd just seen my entire life. He knew of my admission into Oomza Uni.

"Oh." My eyes pricked with tears. "Thank you, sir," I said, hoarsely, as I took my astrolabe.

I quickly made my way through the many people in the terminal, too aware of their closeness. I considered finding a lavatory and applying more *otjize* to my skin and tying my hair back, but instead I kept moving. Most of the people in the busy terminal wore the black and white garments of the Khoush people—the women draped in white with multicolored belts and veils and the men draped in black like powerful spirits. I had seen plenty of them on television and here and there in my city, but never had I been in a sea of Khoush. This was the rest of the world and I was finally in it.

As I stood in line for boarding security, I felt a tug at my hair. I turned around and met the eyes of a group of Khoush women. They were all staring at me; *everyone* behind me was staring at me.

The woman who'd tugged my plait was looking at her fingers and rubbing them together, frowning. Her fingertips were orange red with my *otjize*. She sniffed them. "It smells like jasmine flowers," she said to the woman on her left, surprised.

"Not shit?" one woman said. "I hear it smells like shit because it *is* shit."

"No, definitely jasmine flowers. It is thick like shit, though."

"Is her hair even real?" another woman asked the woman rubbing her fingers.

"I don't know."

"These 'dirt bathers' are a filthy people," the first woman muttered.

I just turned back around, my shoulders hunched. My mother had counseled me to be quiet around Khoush. My father told me that when he was around Khoush merchants when they came to our city to buy astrolabes, he tried to make himself as small as possible. "It is either that or I will start a war with them that I will finish," he said. My father didn't believe in war. He said war was evil, but if it came he would revel in it like sand in a storm. Then he'd say a little prayer to the Seven to keep war away and then another prayer to seal his words.

I pulled my plaits to my front and touched the *edan* in my pocket. I let my mind focus on it, its strange language, its strange metal, its strange feel. I'd found the *edan* eight years ago while exploring the sands of the hinter deserts one late afternoon. *"Edan"* was a general name for a device too old for anyone to know it functions, so old that they were now just art.

My *edan* was more interesting than any book, than any new astrolabe design I made in my father's shop that these women would probably kill each other to buy. And it was mine, in my pocket, and these nosy women behind me could never know. Those women talked about me, the men probably did too. But none of them knew what I had, where I was going, who I was. Let them gossip and judge. Thankfully, they knew not to touch my hair again. I don't like war either.

The security guard scowled when I stepped forward. Behind him I could see three entrances, the one in the middle led into the ship called "Third Fish," the ship I was to take to Oomza Uni. Its open door was large and round leading into a long corridor illuminated by soft blue lights.

"Step forward," the guard said. He wore the uniform of all launch site lower-level personnel—a long white gown and gray gloves. I'd only seen this uniform in streaming stories and books and I wanted to giggle, despite myself. He looked ridiculous. I stepped forward and everything went red and warm.

When the body scan beeped its completion, the security guard reached right into my left pocket and brought out my *edan*. He held it to his face with a deep scowl.

I waited. What would he know?

He was inspecting its stellated cube shape, pressing its many points with his finger and eyeing the strange symbols on it that I had spent two years unsuccessfully trying to decode. He held it to his face to better see the intricate loops and swirls of blue and black and white, so much like the lace placed on the heads of young girls when they turn eleven and go through their eleventh-year rite.

"What is this made of?" the guard asked, holding it over a scanner. "It's not reading as any known metal."

I shrugged, too aware of the people behind me waiting in line and staring at me. To them, I was probably like one of the people who lived in caves deep in the hinter desert who were so blackened by the sun that they looked like walking shadows. I'm not proud to say that I have some Desert People blood in me from my father's side of the family, that's where my dark skin and extra-bushy hair come from.

"Your identity reads that you're a harmonizer, a masterful one who builds some of the finest astrolabes," he said. "But this object isn't an astrolabe. Did you build it? And how can you build something and not know what it's made of?"

"I didn't build it," I said.

"Who did?"

"It's . . . it's just an old, old thing," I said. "It has no math or current. It's just an inert computative apparatus that I carry for good luck." This was partially a lie. But even I didn't know exactly what it could and couldn't do.

The man looked as if he would ask more, but didn't. Inside, I smiled. Government security guards were only educated up to age ten, yet because of their jobs, they were used to ordering people around. And they especially looked down on people like me. Apparently, they were the same everywhere, no matter the tribe. He had no idea what a "computative apparatus" was, but he didn't want to show that I, a poor Himba girl, was more educated than he. Not in front of all these people. So he quickly moved me along and, finally, there I stood at my ship's entrance.

I couldn't see the end of the corridor, so I stared at the entrance. The ship was a magnificent piece of living technology. Third Fish was a Miri 12, a type of ship closely related to a shrimp. Miri 12s were stable calm creatures with natural exoskeletons that could withstand the harshness of space. They were genetically enhanced to grow three breathing chambers within their bodies.

Scientists planted rapidly growing plants within these three enormous rooms that not only produced oxygen from the CO_2 directed in from other parts of the ship, but also absorbed benzene, formaldehyde, and trichloroethylene. This was some of the most amazing technology I'd ever read about. Once settled on the ship, I was determined to convince someone to let me see one of these amazing rooms. But at the moment, I wasn't thinking about the technology of the ship. I was on the threshold now, between home and my future.

I stepped into the blue corridor.

So that is how it all began. I found my room. I found my group— twelve other new students, all human, all Khoush, between the ages of fifteen and eighteen. An hour later, my group and I located a ship technician to show us one of the breathing chambers. I wasn't the only new Oomza Uni student who desperately wanted to see the technology at work. The air in there smelled like the jungles and forests I'd only read about. The plants had tough leaves and they grew everywhere, from ceiling to walls to floor. They were wild with flowers, and I could have stood there breathing that soft, fragrant air for days.

We met our group leader hours later. He was a stern old Khoush man who looked the twelve of us over and paused at me and asked, "Why are you covered in red greasy clay and weighed down by all those steel anklets?" When I told him that I was Himba, he coolly said, "I know, but that doesn't answer my question." I explained to him the tradition of my people's skin care and how we wore the steel rings on our ankles to protect us from snakebites. He looked at me for a long time, the others in my group staring at me like a rare bizarre butterfly.

"Wear your *otjize*," he said. "But not so much that you stain up this ship. And if those anklets are to protect you from snakebites, you no longer need them."

I took my anklets off, except for two on each ankle. Enough to jingle with each step.

I was the only Himba on the ship, out of nearly five hundred passengers. My tribe is obsessed with innovation and technology, but it is small, private, and, as I said, we don't like to leave Earth. We prefer to explore the universe by traveling inward, as opposed to outward. No Himba has ever gone to Oomza Uni. So me being the only one on the ship was not that surprising. However, just because something isn't surprising doesn't mean it's easy to deal with.

The ship was packed with outward-looking people who loved mathematics, experimenting, learning, reading, inventing, studying, obsessing, revealing. The people on the ship weren't Himba, but I soon understood that they were still my people. I stood out as a Himba, but the commonalities shined brighter. I made friends quickly. And by the second week in space, they were *good* friends.

Olo, Remi, Kwuga, Nur, Anajama, Rhoden. Only Olo and Remi were in my group. Everyone else I met in the dining area or the learning room where various lectures were held by professors onboard the ship. They were all girls who grew up in sprawling houses, who'd never walked through the desert, who'd never stepped on a snake in the dry grass. They were girls who could not stand the rays of Earth's sun unless it was shining through a tinted window.

Yet they were girls who knew what I meant when I spoke of "treeing." We sat in my room (because, having so few travel items, mine was the emptiest) and challenged each other to look out at the stars and imagine the most complex equation and then split it in half and then in half again and again. When you do math fractals long enough, you kick yourself into treeing just enough to get lost in the shallows of the mathematical sea. None of us would have made it into the university if we couldn't tree, but it's not easy. We were the best and we pushed each other to get closer to "God."

Then there was Heru. I had never spoken to him, but we smiled across the table at each other during mealtimes. He was from one of those cities so far from mine that they seemed like a figment of my imagination, where there was snow and where men rode those enormous gray birds and the women could speak with those birds without moving their mouths.

Once Heru was standing behind me in the dinner line with one of his friends. I felt someone pick up one of my plaits and I whirled around, ready to be angry. I met his eyes and he'd quickly let go of my hair, smiled, and raised his hands up defensively. "I couldn't help it," he said, his fingertips reddish with my *otjize*.

"You can't control yourself?" I snapped.

"You have exactly twenty-one," he said. "And they're braided in tessellating triangles. Is it some sort of code?"

I wanted to tell him that there *was* a code, that the pattern spoke my family's bloodline, culture, and history. That my father had designed the code and my mother and aunties had shown me how to braid it into my hair. However, looking at Heru made my heart beat too fast and my words escaped me, so I merely shrugged and turned back around to pick up a bowl of soup. Heru was tall and had the whitest teeth I'd ever seen. And he was very good in mathematics; few would have noticed the code in my hair.

But I never got the chance to tell him that my hair was braided into the history of my people. Because what happened, happened. It occured on the eighteenth day of the journey. The five days before we arrived on the planet Oomza Uni, the most powerful and innovative sprawling university in the Milky Way. I was the happiest I'd ever been in my life and I was farther from my beloved family than I'd ever been in my life.

I was at the table savoring a mouthful of a gelatinous milk-based dessert with slivers of coconut in it; I was gazing at Heru, who wasn't gazing at me. I'd put my fork down and had my *edan* in my hands. I fiddled with it as I watched Heru talk to the boy beside him. The delicious creamy dessert was melting coolly on my tongue. Beside me, Olo and Remi were singing a traditional song from their city because they missed home, a song that had to be sung with a wavery voice like a water spirit.

Then someone screamed and Heru's chest burst open, spattering me with his warm blood. There was a Meduse right behind him.

———

In my culture, it is blasphemy to pray to inanimate objects, but I did anyway. I prayed to a metal even my father had been unable to identify. I held it to my chest, shut my eyes, and I prayed to it, *I am in your protection. Please protect me. I am in your protection. Please protect me.*

My body was shuddering so hard that I could imagine what it would be like to die from terror. I held my breath, the stench of *them* still in my nasal cavity and mouth. Heru's blood was on my face, wet and thick. I prayed to the mystery metal my *edan* was made of because that had to be the only thing keeping me alive at this moment.

Breathing hard from my mouth, I peeked from one eye. I shut it again. The Meduse were hovering less than a foot away. One had launched itself at me but then froze an inch from my flesh; it had reached a tentacle toward my *edan* and then suddenly collapsed, the tentacle turning ash gray as it quickly dried up like a dead leaf.

I could hear the others, their near substantial bodies softly rustling as their transparent domes filled with and released the gas they breathed back in. They were tall as grown men, their domes' flesh thin as fine silk, their long tentacles spilling down to the floor like a series of gigantic ghostly noodles. I grasped my *edan* closer to me. *I am in your protection. Please protect me.*

Everyone in the dining hall was dead. At least one hundred people. I had a feeling everyone on the ship was dead. The Meduse had burst into the hall and begun committing *moojh-ha ki-bira* before anyone knew what was happening. That's what the Khoush call it. We'd all been taught this Meduse form of killing in history class. The Khoush built the lessons into history, literature, and culture classes across several regions. Even my people were required to learn about it, despite the fact that it wasn't our fight. The Khoush expected everyone to remember their greatest enemy and injustice. They even worked Meduse anatomy and rudimentary technology into mathematics and science classes.

Moojh-ha ki-bira means the "great wave." The Meduse move like water when at war. There is no water on their planet, but they worship water as a god. Their ancestors came from water long ago. The Khoush were settled on the most water-soaked lands on Earth, a planet made mostly of water, and they saw the Meduse as inferior.

The trouble between the Meduse and the Khoush was an old fight and an older disagreement. Somehow, they had agreed to a treaty not to attack each other's ships. Yet here the Meduse were performing *moojh-ha ki-bira.*

I'd been talking to my friends.

My *friends.*

Olo, Remi, Kwuga, Nur, Anajama, Rhoden, and Dullaz. We had spent so many late nights laughing over our fears about how difficult and strange Oomza Uni would be. All of us had twisted ideas that were probably wrong . . . maybe partially right. We had so much in common. I wasn't thinking about home or how I'd *had* to leave it or the horrible messages my family had sent to my astrolabe hours after I'd left. I was looking ahead toward my future and I was laughing because it was so bright.

Then the Meduse came through the dining hall entrance. I was looking right at Heru when the red circle appeared in the upper left side of his shirt. The thing that tore through was like a sword, but thin as paper . . . and flexible and easily stained by blood. The tip wiggled and grasped like a finger. I saw it pinch and hook to the flesh near his collarbone.

Moojh-ha ki-bira.

I don't remember what I did or said. My eyes were open, taking it all in, but the rest of my brain was screaming. For no reason at all, I focused on the number five. Over and over, I thought, *5–5–5–5–5–5–5–5–5*, as Heru's eyes went from shocked to blank. His open mouth let out a gagging sound, then a spurt of thick red blood, then blood frothed with saliva as he began to fall forward. His head hit the table with a flat thud. His neck was turned and I could see that his eyes were open. His left hand flexed spasmodically, until it stopped. But his eyes were still open. He wasn't blinking.

Heru was dead. Olo, Remi, Kwuga, Nur, Anajama, Rhoden, and Dullaz were dead. Everyone was dead.

The dinner hall stank of blood.

———

None of my family had wanted me to go to Oomza Uni. Even my best friend Dele hadn't wanted me to go. Still, not long after I received the news of my university acceptance and my whole family was saying no, Dele had joked that if I went, I at least wouldn't have to worry about the Meduse, because I would be the only Himba on the ship.

"So even if they kill everyone else, they won't even *see* you!" he'd said. Then he'd laughed and laughed, sure that I wasn't going anyway.

Now his words came back to me. Dele. I'd pushed thoughts of him deep into my mind and read none of his messages. Ignoring the people I loved was the only way I could keep going. When I'd received the scholarship to study at Oomza Uni, I'd gone into the desert and cried for hours. With joy.

I'd wanted this since I knew what a university was. Oomza Uni was the top of the top, its population was only 5 percent human. Imagine what it meant to go there as one of that 5 percent; to be with others obsessed with knowledge, creation, and discovery. Then I went home and told my family and wept with shock.

"You can't go," my oldest sister said. "You're a master harmonizer. Who else is good enough to take over father's shop?"

"Don't be selfish," my sister Suum spat. She was only a year older than me, but she still felt she could run my life. "Stop chasing fame and be rational. You can't just leave and fly across the *galaxy*."

My brothers had all just laughed and dismissed the idea. My parents said nothing, not even congratulations. Their silence was answer enough. Even my best friend Dele. He congratulated and told me that I was smarter than everyone at Oomza Uni, but then he'd laughed, too. "You cannot go," he simply said. "We're Himba. God has already chosen our paths."

I was the first Himba in history to be bestowed with the honor of acceptance into Oomza Uni. The hate messages, threats to my life, laughter and ridicule that came from the Khoush in my city made me want to hide more. But deep down inside me, I wanted . . . I *needed* it. I couldn't help but act on it. The urge was so strong that it was mathematical. When I'd sit in the desert, alone, listening to the wind, I would see and feel the numbers the way I did when I was deep in my work in my father's shop. And those numbers added up to the sum of my destiny.

So in secret, I filled out and uploaded the acceptance forms. The desert was the perfect place for privacy when they contacted my astrolabe for university interviews. When everything was set, I packed my things and got on that shuttle. I come from a family of *Bitolus*; my father is a master harmonizer and I was to be his successor. We *Bitolus* know true deep mathematics and we can control their current, we know systems. We are few and we are happy and uninterested in weapons and war, but we can protect ourselves. And as my father says, "God favors us."

━━━━━

I clutched my *edan* to my chest now as I opened my eyes. The Meduse in front of me was blue and translucent, except for one of its tentacles, which was tinted pink like the waters of the salty lake beside my village and curled up like the branch of a confined tree. I held up my *edan* and the Meduse jerked back, pluming out its gas and loudly inhaling. *Fear*, I thought. *That was fear.*

I stood up, realizing that my time of death was not here yet. I took a quick look around the giant hall. I could smell dinner over the stink of blood and Meduse gases. Roasted and marinated meats, brown long-grained rice, spicy red stews, flat breads, and that rich gelatinous dessert I loved so much. They were all still laid out on the grand table, the hot foods cooling as the bodies cooled and the dessert melting as the dead Meduse melted.

"Back!" I hissed, thrusting the *edan* at the Meduse. My garments rustled and my anklets jingled as I got up. I pressed my backside against the table. The Meduse were behind me and on my sides, but I focused on the one before me. "This will kill you!" I said as forcibly as I could. I cleared my throat and raised my voice. "You saw what it did to your brother."

I motioned to the shriveled dead one two feet away; its mushy flesh had dried and begun to turn brown and opaque. It had tried to take me and then something made it die. Bits of it had crumbled to dust as I spoke, the mere vibration of my voice enough to destabilize the remains. I grabbed my satchel as I slid away from the table and moved toward the grand table of food. My mind was moving fast now. I was seeing numbers and then blurs. Good. I was my father's daughter. He'd taught me in the tradition of my ancestors and I was the best in the family.

"I am Binti Ekeopara Zuzu Dambu Kaipka of Namib," I whispered. This is what my father always reminded me when he saw my face go blank and I started to tree. He would then loudly speak his lessons to me about astrolabes, including how they worked, the art of them, the true negotiation of them, the lineage. While I was in this state, my father passed me three hundred years of oral knowledge about circuits, wire, metals, oils, heat, electricity, math current, sand bar.

And so I had become a master harmonizer by the age of twelve. I could communicate with spirit flow and convince them to become one current. I was born with my mother's gift of mathematical sight. My mother only used it to protect the family, and now I was going to grow that skill at the best university in the galaxy . . . if I survived. "Binti Ekeopara Zuzu Dambu Kaipka of Namib, that is my name," I said again.

My mind cleared as the equations flew through it, opening it wider, growing progressively more complex and satisfying. $V - E + F = 2$, $a^2 + b^2 = c^2$, I thought. I knew what to do now. I moved to the table of food and grabbed a tray. I heaped chicken wings, a turkey leg, and three steaks of beef onto it. Then several rolls; bread would stay fresh longer. I dumped three oranges on my tray, because they carried juice and vitamin C. I grabbed two whole bladders of water and shoved them into my satchel as well. Then I slid a slice of white milky dessert on my tray. I did not know its name, but it was easily the most wonderful thing I'd ever tasted. Each bite would fuel my mental well-being. And if I were going to survive, I'd need that, especially.

I moved quickly, holding up the *edan*, my back straining with the weight of my loaded satchel as I held the large food-heavy tray with my left hand. The Meduse followed me, their tentacles caressing the floor as they floated. They had no eyes, but from what I knew of the Meduse, they had scent receptors on the tips of their tentacles. They saw me through smell.

The hallway leading to the rooms was wide and all the doors were plated with sheets of gold metal. My father would have spat at this wastefulness. Gold was an information conductor and its mathematical signals were stronger than anything. Yet here it was wasted on gaudy extravagance.

When I arrived at my room, the trance lifted from me without warning and I suddenly had no idea what to do next. I stopped treeing and the clarity of mind retreated like a loss of confidence. All I could think to do was let the door scan my eye. It opened, I slipped in and it shut behind me with a sucking sound, sealing the room, a mechanism probably triggered by the ship's emergency programming.

I managed to put the tray and satchel on my bed just before my legs gave. Then I sunk to the cool floor beside the black landing chair on the fair side of the room. My face was sweaty and I rested my cheek on the floor for a moment and sighed. Images of my friends Olo, Remi, Kwuga, Nur, Anajama, Rhoden crowded my mind. I thought I heard Heru's soft laughter above me . . . then the sound of his chest bursting open, then the heat of his blood on my face. I whimpered, biting my lip. "I'm here, I'm here, I'm here," I whispered. Because I was and there was no way out. I shut my eyes tightly as the tears came. I curled my body and stayed like that for several minutes.

═══════

I brought my astrolabe to my face. I'd made the casing with golden sand bar that I'd molded, sculpted, and polished myself. It was the size of a child's hand and far better than any astrolabe one could buy from the finest seller. I'd taken care to fashion its weight to suit my hands, the dials to respond to only my fingers, and its currents were so true that they'd probably outlast my own future children. I'd made this astrolabe two months ago specifically for my journey, replacing the one my father had made for me when I was three years old.

I started to speak my family name to my astrolabe, but then I whispered, "No," and rested it on my belly. My family was planets away by now; what more could they do than weep? I rubbed the on button and spoke, "Emergency." The astrolabe warmed in my hands and emitted the calming scent of roses as it vibrated. Then it went cool. "Emergency," I said again. This time it didn't even warm up.

"Map," I said. I held my breath, waiting. I glanced at the door. I'd read that Meduse could not move through walls, but even I knew that just because information was in a book didn't make it true. Especially when the information concerned the Meduse. My door was secure, but I was Himba and I doubted the Khoush had given me one of the rooms with full security locks. The Meduse would come in when they wanted or when they were willing to risk death to do away with me. I may not have been Khoush . . . but I was a human on a Khoush ship.

My astrolabe suddenly warmed and vibrated. "Your location is 121 hours from your destination of Oomza Uni," it said in its whispery voice. So the Meduse felt it okay for me to know where the ship was. The virtual constellation lit up my room with white, light blue, red, yellow, and orange dots, slowly rotating globes from the size of a large fly to the size of my fist. Suns, planets, bloom territories all sectioned in the mathematical net that I'd always found easy to read. The ship had long since left my solar system. We'd slowed down right in the middle of what was known as "the Jungle." The pilots of the ship should have been more vigilant. "And maybe less arrogant," I said, feeling ill.

The ship was still heading for Oomza Uni, though, and that was mildly encouraging. I shut my eyes and prayed to the Seven. I wanted to ask, "Why did you let this happen?" but that was blasphemy. You never ask why. It was not a question for you to ask.

"I'm going to die here."

━━━

Seventy-two hours later, I was still alive. But I'd run out of food and had very little water left. Me and my thoughts in that small room, no escape outside. I had to stop crying; I couldn't afford to lose water. The toilet facilities were just outside my room so I'd been forced to use the case that carried my beaded jewelry collection. All I had was my jar of *otjize*, some of which I used to clean my body as much as possible. I paced, recited equations, and was sure that if I didn't die of thirst or starvation I'd die by fire from the currents I'd nervously created and discharged to keep myself busy.

I looked at the map yet again and saw what I knew I'd see; we were still heading to Oomza Uni. "But why?" I whispered. "Security will . . ."

I shut my eyes, trying to stop myself from completing the thought yet again. But I could never stop myself and this time was no different. In my mind's eye, I saw a bright yellow beam zip from Oomza Uni and the ship scattering in a radiating mass of silent light and flame. I got up and shuffled to the far side of my room and back as I talked. "But suicidal Meduse? It just doesn't make sense. Maybe they don't know how to . . ."

There was a slow knock at the door and I nearly jumped to the ceiling. Then I froze, listening with every part of my body. Other than the sound of my voice, I hadn't heard a thing from them since that first twenty-four hours. The knock came again. The last knock was hard, more like a kick, but not near the bottom of the door.

"L . . . leave me alone!" I screamed, grabbing my *edan*. My words were met with a hard bang at the door and an angry, harsh hiss. I screeched and moved as far from the door as my room would permit, nearly falling over my largest suitcase. *Think think think*. No weapons, except the *edan* . . . and I didn't know what made it a weapon.

Everyone was dead. I was still about forty-eight hours from safety or being blown up. They say that when faced with a fight you cannot win, you can never predict what you will do next. But I'd always known I'd fight until I was killed. It was an abomination to commit suicide or to give up your life. I was sure that I was ready. The Meduse were very intelligent; they'd find a way to kill me, despite my *edan*.

Nevertheless, I didn't pick up the nearest weapon. I didn't prepare for my last violent rabid stand. Instead, I looked my death square in the face and then . . . then I *surrendered* to it. I sat on my bed and waited for my death. Already, my body felt as if it were no longer mine; I'd let it go. And in that moment, deep in my submission, I laid my eyes on my *edan* and stared at its branching splitting dividing blue fractals.

And I saw it.

I *really* saw it.

And all I could do was smile and think, *How did I not know?*

—————

I sat in the landing chair beside my window, hand-rolling *otjize* into my plaits. I looked at my reddened hands, brought them to my nose and sniffed. Oily clay that sang of sweet flowers, desert wind, and soil. *Home*, I thought, tears stinging my eyes. I should not have left. I picked up the *edan*, looking for what I'd seen. I turned the *edan* over and over before my eyes. The blue object whose many points I'd rubbed, pressed, stared at, and pondered for so many years.

More thumping came from the door. "Leave me alone," I muttered weakly.

I smeared *otjize* onto the point of the *edan* with the spiral that always reminded me of a fingerprint. I rubbed it in a slow circular motion. My shoulders relaxed as I calmed. Then my starved and thirsty brain dropped into a mathematical trance like a stone dropped into deep water. And I felt the water envelop me as down down down I went.

My clouded mind cleared and everything went silent and motionless, my finger still polishing the *edan*. I smelled home, heard the desert wind blowing grains of sand over each other. My stomach fluttered as I dropped deeper in and my entire body felt sweet and pure and empty and light. The *edan* was heavy in my hands; so heavy that it would fall right through my flesh.

"Oh," I breathed, realizing that there was now a tiny button in the center of the spiral. This was what I'd seen. It had always been there, but now it was as if it were in focus. I pushed it with my index finger. It depressed with a soft "click" and then the stone felt like warm wax and my world wavered. There was another loud knock at the door. Then through the clearest silence I'd ever experienced, so clear that the slightest sound would tear its fabric, I heard a solid oily low voice say, "Girl."

I was catapulted out of my trance, my eyes wide, my mouth yawning in a silent scream.

"Girl," I heard again. I hadn't heard a human voice since the final screams of those killed by the Meduse, over seventy-two hours ago.

I looked around my room. I was alone. Slowly, I turned and looked out the window beside me. There was nothing out there for me but the blackness of space.

"Girl. You will die," the voice said slowly. "Soon." I heard more voices, but they were too low to understand. "Suffering is against the Way. Let us end you."

I jumped up and the rush of blood made me nearly collapse and crash to the floor. Instead I fell painfully to my knees, still clutching the *edan*. There was another knock at the door. "Open this door," the voice demanded.

My hands began to shake, but I didn't drop my *edan*. It was warm and a brilliant blue light was glowing from within it now. A current was running through it so steadily that it made the muscles of my hand constrict. I couldn't let go of it if I tried.

"I will not," I said, through clenched teeth. "Rather die in here, on *my* terms."

The knocking stopped. Then I heard several things at once. Scuffling at the door, not toward it, but *away*. Terrified moaning and wailing. More *voices*. Several of them.

"This is evil!"

"It carries shame," another voice said. This was the first voice I heard that sounded high-pitched, almost female. "The shame she carries allows her to mimic speech."

"No. It has to have sense for that," another voice said.

"Evil! Let me deactivate the door and kill it."

"Okwu, you will die if you . . ."

"I will kill it!" the one called Okwu growled. "Death will be my honor! We're too close now, we can't have . . ."

"Me!" I shouted suddenly. "O . . . Okwu!" Calling its name, addressing it so directly sounded strange on my lips. I pushed on. "Okwu, why don't you talk to me?"

I looked at my cramped hands. From within it, from my *edan*, possibly the strongest current I'd ever produced streamed in jagged connected bright blue branches. It slowly etched and lurched through the closed door, a line of connected bright blue treelike branches that shifted in shape but never broke their connection. The current was touching the Meduse. Connecting them to me.

And though I'd created it, I couldn't control it now. I wanted to scream, revolted. But I had to save my life first. "I am speaking to you!" I said. "Me!"

Silence.

I slowly stood up, my heart pounding. I stumbled to the shut door on aching trembling legs. The door's organic steel was so thin, but one of the strongest substances on my planet. Where the current touched it, tiny green leaves unfurled. I touched them, focusing on the leaves and not the fact that the door was covered with a sheet of gold, a super communication conducter. Nor the fact of the Meduse just beyond my door.

I heard a rustle and I used all my strength not to scuttle back. I flared my nostrils as I grasped the *edan*. The weight of my hair on my shoulders was assuring, my hair was heavy with *otjize*, and this was good luck and the strength of my people, even if my people were far far away.

The loud bang of something hard and powerful hitting the door made me yelp. I stayed where I was. "Evil thing," I heard the one called Okwu say. Of all the voices, that one I could recognize. It was the angriest and scariest. The voice sounded spoken, not transmitted in my mind. I could hear the vibration of the "v" in "evil" and the hard breathy "th" in "thing." Did they have mouths?

"I'm not evil," I said.

I heard whispering and rustling behind the door. Then the more female voice said, "Open this door."

"No!"

They muttered among themselves. Minutes passed. I sunk to the floor, leaning against the door. The blue current sunk with me, streaming through the door at my shoulder; more green leaves bloomed there, some fell down my shoulder onto my lap. I leaned my head against the door and stared down at them. Green tiny leaves of green tiny life when I was so close to death. I giggled and my empty belly rumbled and my sore abdominal muscles ached.

Then, quietly, calmly, "You are understanding us?" this was the growling voice that had been calling me evil. Okwu.

"Yes," I said.

"Humans only understand violence."

I closed my eyes and felt my weak body relax. I sighed and said, "The only thing I have killed are small animals for food, and only with swift grace and after prayer and thanking the beast for its sacrifice." I was exhausted.

"I do not believe you."

"Just as I do not believe you will not kill me if I open the door. All you do is kill." I opened my eyes. Energy that I didn't know I still had rippled through me and I was so angry that I couldn't catch my breath. "Like . . . like you . . . killed my friends!" I coughed and slumped down, weakly. "My friends," I whispered, tears welling in my eyes. "Oooh, my friends!"

"Humans must be killed before they kill us," the voice said.

"You're all stupid," I spat, wiping my tears as they kept coming. I sobbed hard and then took a deep breath, trying to pull it together. I exhaled loudly, snot flying from my nose. As I wiped my face with my arm, there were more whispers. Then the higher pitched voice spoke.

"What is this blue ghost you have sent to help us communicate?"

"I don't know," I said, sniffing. I got up and walked to my bed. Moving away from the door instantly made me feel better. The blue current extended with me.

"Why do we understand you?" Okwu asked. I could still hear its voice perfectly from where I was.

"I . . . I don't know," I said, sitting on my bed and then lying back.

"No Meduse has ever spoken to a human . . . except long ago."

"I don't care," I grunted.

"Open the door. We won't harm you."

"No."

There was a long pause. So long that I must have fallen asleep. I was awakened by a sucking sound. At first I paid no mind to it, taking the moment to wipe off the caked snot on my face with my arm. The ship made all sorts of sounds, even before the Meduse attacked. It was a living thing and like any beast, its bowels gurgled and quaked every so often. Then I sat up straight as the sucking sound grew louder. The door trembled. It buckled a bit and then completely crumpled, the gold plating on the outside now visible. The stale air of my room whooshed out into the hallway and suddenly the air cooled and smelled fresher.

There stood the Meduse. I could not tell how many of them, for they were transparent and when they stood together, all I could see were a tangle of translucent tentacles and undulating domes. I clutched the *edan* to my chest as I pressed myself on the other side of the room, against the window.

It happened fast like the desert wolves who attack travelers at night back home. One of the Meduse shot toward me. I watched it come. I saw my parents, sisters, brothers, aunts, and uncles, all gathered at a remembrance for me—full of pain and loss. I saw my spirit break from my body and return to my planet, to the desert, where I would tell stories to the sand people.

Time must have slowed down because the Meduse was motionless, yet suddenly it was hovering over me, its tentacles hanging an inch from my head. I gasped, bracing myself for pain and then death. Its pink withered tentacle brushed my arm firmly enough to rub off some of the *otjize* there. *Soft*, I thought. *Smooth.*

There it was. So close now. White like the ice I'd only seen in pictures and entertainment streams, its stinger was longer than my leg. I stared at it, jutting from its bundle of tentacles. It crackled and dried, wisps of white mist wafting from it. Inches from my chest. Now it went from white to a dull light-gray. I looked down at my cramped hands, the *edan* between them. The current flowing from it washed over the Meduse and extended beyond it. Then I looked up at the Meduse and grinned. "I hope it hurts," I whispered.

The Meduse's tentacles shuddered and it began to back away. I could see its pink deformed tentacle, part of it smeared red with my *otjize*.

"You are the foundation of evil," it said. It was the one called Okwu. I nearly laughed. Why did this one hate me so strongly?

"She still holds the shame," I heard one say from near the door.

Okwu began to recover as it moved away from me. Quickly, it left with the others.

=====

Ten hours passed.

I had no food left. No water. I packed and repacked my things. Keeping busy staved off the dehydration and hunger a bit, though my constant need to urinate kept reminding me of my predicament. And movement was tricky because the *edan*'s current still wouldn't release my hands' muscles, but I managed. I tried not to indulge in my fear of the Meduse finding a way to get the ship to stop producing and circulating air and maintaining its internal pressure, or just coming back and killing me.

When I wasn't packing and repacking, I was staring at my *edan*, studying it; the patterns on it now glowed with the current. I needed to know how it was allowing me to communicate. I tried different soft equations on it and received no response. After a while, when not even hard equations affected it, I lay back on my bed and let myself tree. This was my state of mind when the Meduse came in.

"What is that?"

I screamed. I'd been gazing out the window, so I heard the Meduse before I saw it.

"What?" I shrieked, breathless. "I . . . what is what?"

Okwu, the one who'd tried to kill me. Contrary to how it had looked when it left, it was very much alive, though I could not see its stinger.

"What is the substance on your skin?" it asked firmly. "None of the other humans have it."

"Of course they don't," I snapped. "It is *otjize*, only my people wear it and I am the only one of my people on the ship. I'm not Khoush."

"What is it?" it asked, remaining in the doorway.

"Why?"

It moved into my room and I held up the *edan* and quickly said, "Mostly . . . mostly clay and oil from my homeland. Our land is desert, but we live in the region where there is sacred red clay."

"Why do you spread it on your skins?"

"Because my people are sons and daughters of the soil," I said. "And . . . and it's beautiful."

It paused for a long moment and I just stared at it. Really looking at the thing. It moved as if it had a front and a back. And though it seemed to be fully transparent, I could not see its solid white stinger within the drapes of hanging tentacles. Whether it was thinking about what I'd said or considering how best to kill me, I didn't know. But moments later, it turned and left. And it was only after several minutes, when my heart rate slowed, that I realized something odd. Its withered tentacle didn't look as withered. Where it had been curled up tightly into itself, now it was merely bent.

———

It came back fifteen minutes later. And immediately, I looked to make sure I'd seen what I knew I'd seen. And there it was, pink and not so curled up. That tentacle had been different when Okwu had accidently touched me and rubbed off my *otjize*.

"Give me some of it," it said, gliding into my room.

"I don't have any more!" I said, panicking. I only had one large jar of *otjize*, the most I'd ever made in one batch. It was enough to last me until I could find red clay on Oomza Uni and make more. And even then, I wasn't sure if I'd find the right kind of clay. It was another planet. Maybe it wouldn't have clay at all.

In all my preparation, the one thing I didn't take enough time to do was research the Oomza Uni planet itself, so focused I was on just *getting* there. All I knew was that though it was much smaller than earth, it had a similar atmosphere and I wouldn't have to wear a special suit or adaptive lungs or anything like that. But its surface could easily be made of something my skin couldn't tolerate. I couldn't give all my *otjize* to this Meduse; this was my *culture*.

"The chief knows of your people, you have much with you."

"If your chief knows my people, then he will have told you that taking it from me is like taking my soul," I said, my voice cracking. My jar was under my bed. I held up my *edan*.

But Okwu didn't leave or approach. Its curled pink tentacle twitched.

I decided to take a chance. "It helped you, didn't it? Your tentacle."

It blew out a great puff of its gas, sucked it in and left.

It returned five minutes later with five others.

"What is that object made of?" Okwu asked, the others standing silently behind it.

I was still on my bed and I pushed my legs under the covers. "I don't know. But a desert woman once said it was made from something called 'god stone.' My father said there is no such . . ."

"It is shame," it insisted.

None of them moved to enter my room. Three of them made loud puffing sounds as they let out the reeking gasses they inhaled in order to breathe.

"There is nothing shameful about an object that keeps me alive," I said.

"It poisons Meduse," one of the others said.

"Only if you get too close to me," I said, looking straight at it. "Only if you try and *kill* me."

Pause.

"How are you communicating with us?"

"I don't know, Okwu." I spoke its name as if I owned it.

"What are you called?"

I sat up straight, ignoring the fatigue trying to pull my bones to the bed. "I am Binti Ekeopara Zuzu Dambu Kaipka of Namib." I considered speaking its single name to reflect its cultural simplicity compared to mine, but my strength and bravado were already waning.

Okwu moved forward and I held up the *edan*. "Stay back! You know what it'll do!" I said. However, it did not try to attack me again, though it didn't start to shrivel up as it approached, either. It stopped feet away, beside the metal table jutting from the wall carrying my open suitcase and one of the containers of water.

"What do you need?" it flatly asked.

I stared, weighing my options. I didn't have any. "Water, food," I said.

Before I could say more, it left. I leaned against the window and tried not to look outside into the blackness. Feet away from me, the door was crushed to the side, the path of my fate was no longer mine. I lay back and fell into the deepest sleep I'd had since the ship left Earth.

━━━━

The faint smell of smoke woke me up. There was a plate on my bed, right before my nose. On it was a small slab of smoked fish. Beside it was a bowl of water.

I sat up, still tightly grasping the *edan*. I leaned forward, and sucked up as much water from the bowl as I could. Then, still holding the *edan*, I pressed my forearms together and worked the food onto them. I brought the fish up, bent forward and took a bite of it.

Smoky salty goodness burst across my taste buds. The chefs on the ship fed these fish well and allowed them to grow strong and mate copiously. Then they lulled the fish into a sleep that the fish never woke from and slow cooked their flesh long enough for flavor and short enough to maintain texture. I'd asked the chefs about their process as any good Himba would before eating it. The chefs were all Khoush, and Khoush did not normally perform what they called "superstitious ritual." But these chefs were Oomza Uni students and they said they did, even lulling the fish to sleep in a similar way. Again, I'd been assured that I was heading in the right direction.

The fish was delicious, but it was full of bones. And it was as I was using my tongue to work a long, flexible, but tough bone from my teeth that I looked up and noticed the Meduse hovering in the doorway. I didn't have to see the withered tentacle to know it was Okwu. Inhaling with surprise, I nearly choked on the bone. I dropped what was left, spat out the bone and opened my mouth to speak. Then I closed it.

I was still alive.

Okwu didn't move or speak, though the blue current still connected us. Moments passed, Okwu hovering and emitting the foulsmelling gasp as it breathed and me sucking bits of fish from my mouth wondering if this was my last meal. After a while, I grasped the remaining hunk of fish with my forearms and continued eating.

"You know," I finally said, to fill the silence. "There are a people in my village who have lived for generations at the edge of the lake." I looked at the Meduse. Nothing. "They know all the fish in it," I continued. "There is a fish that grows plenty in that lake and they catch and smoke them like this. The only difference is that my people can prepare it in such a way where there are no bones. They remove them all." I pulled a bone from between my teeth. "They have studied this fish. They have worked it out mathematically. They know where every bone will be, no matter the age, size, sex of the fish. They go in and remove every bone without disturbing the body. It is delicious!" I put down the remaining bones. "This was delicious, too." I hesitated and then said, "Thank you."

Okwu didn't move, continuing to hover and puff out gas. I got up and walked to the counter where a tray had been set. I leaned down and sucked up the water from this bowl as well. Already, I felt much stronger and more alert. I jumped when it spoke.

"I wish I could just kill you."

I paused. "Like my mother always says, 'we all wish for many things,'" I said, touching a last bit of fish in my back tooth.

"You don't look like a human Oomza Uni student," it said. "Your color is darker and you . . ." It blasted out a large cloud of gas and I fought not to wrinkle my nose. "You have *okuoko*."

I frowned at the unfamiliar word. "What is *okuoko*?"

And that's when it moved for the first time since I'd awakened. It's long tentacles jiggled playfully and a laugh escaped my mouth before I could stop it. It billowed out more gas in rapid succession and made a deep thrumming sound. This made me laugh even harder. "You mean my hair?" I asked, shaking my thick plaits.

"*Okuoko*, yes," it said.

"*Okuoko*," I said. I had to admit, I liked the sound of it. "How come the word is different?"

"I don't know," it said. "I hear you in my language as well. When you said *okuoko* it is *okuoko*." It paused. "The Khoush are the color of the flesh of the fish you ate and they have no *okuoko*. You are red brown like the fish's outer skin and you have *okuoko* like Meduse, though small."

"There are different kinds of humans," I said. "My people don't normally leave my planet." Several Meduse came to the door and crowded in. Okwu moved closer, blasting out more gas and inhaling it. This time I did cough at the stench of it.

"Why have you?" it asked. "You are probably the most evil of your people."

I frowned at it. Realizing something. It spoke like one of my brothers, Bena. I was born only three years after him yet we'd never been very close. He was angry and always speaking out about the way my people were maltreated by the Khoush majority despite the fact that they needed us and our astrolabes to survive. He was always calling them evil, though he'd never traveled to a Khoush country or known a Khoush. His anger was rightful, but all that he said was from what he didn't truly know.

Even I could tell that Okwu was not an elder among these Meduse; it was too hotheaded and . . . there was something about it that reminded me of me. Maybe its curiosity; I think I'd have been one of the first to come see, if I were it, too. My father said that my curiosity was the last obstacle I had to overcome to be a true master harmonizer. If there was one thing my father and I disagreed on, it was that; I believed I could only be great if I were curious enough to seek greatness. Okwu was young, like me. And maybe that's why it was so eager to die and prove itself to the others and that's why the others were fine with it.

"You know nothing of me," I said. I felt myself grow hot. "This is not a military ship, this is a ship full of professors! Students! All dead! You killed everyone!"

It seemed to chuckle. "Not your pilot. We did not sting that one."

And just like that, I understood. They would get through the university's security if the security people thought the ship was still full of living breathing unmurdered professors and students. Then the Meduse would be able to invade Oomza Uni.

"We don't need *you*. But that one is useful."

"That's why we are still on course," I said.

"No. We can fly this creature ship," it said. "But your pilot can speak to the people on Oomza Uni in the way they expect." It paused, then moved closer. "See? We never *needed* you."

I felt the force of its threat physically. The sharp tingle came in white bursts in my toes and traveled up my body to the top of my head. I opened my mouth, suddenly short of breath. *This* was what fearing death truly felt like, not my initial submission to it. I leaned away, holding up my *edan*. I was sitting on my bed, its red covers making me think of blood. There was nowhere to go.

"That shame is the only reason you are alive," it said.

"Your *okuoko* is better," I whispered, pointing at the tentacle. "Won't you spare me for curing that?" I could barely breathe. When it didn't respond, I asked, "Why? Or maybe there is no reason."

"You think we are like you humans?" it asked, angrily. "We don't kill for sport or even for gain. Only for purpose."

I frowned. They sounded like the same thing to me, gain and purpose.

"In your university, in one of its museums, placed on display like a piece of rare meat is the stinger of our chief," it said. I wrinkled my face, but said nothing. "Our chief is . . ." It paused. "We know of the attack and mutilation of our chief, but we do not know how it got there. We do not care. We will land on Oomza Uni and take it back. So you see? We have purpose."

It billowed out gas and left the room. I lay back in my bed, exhausted.

———

But they brought me more food and water. Okwu brought it. And it sat with me while I ate and drank. More fish and some dried-up dates and a flask of water. This time, I barely tasted it as I ate.

"It's suicide," I said.

"What is . . . suicide," it asked.

"What you are doing!" I said. "On Oomza Uni, there's a city where all the students and professors do is study, test, create *weapons*. Weapons for taking every form of life. Your own weapons were probably made there!"

"Our weapons are made within our bodies," it said.

"What of the current-killer you used against the Khoush in the Meduse-Khoush War?" I asked.

It said nothing.

"Suicide is death on purpose!"

"Meduse aren't afraid of death," it said. "And this would be honorable. We will show them never to dishonor Meduse again. Our people will remember our sacrifice and celebrate . . ."

"I . . . I have an idea!" I shouted. My voice cracked. I pushed forward. "Let me talk to your chief!" I shrieked. I don't know if it was the delicious fish I'd eaten, shock, hopelessness, or exhaustion. I stood up and stepped to it, my legs shaky and my eyes wild. "Let me . . . I'm a master harmonizer. That's why I'm going to Oomza Uni. I am the best of the best, Okwu. I can create harmony *anywhere*." I was so out of breath that I was wheezing. I inhaled deeply, seeing stars explode before my eyes. "Let me be . . . let me speak for the Meduse. The people in Oomza Uni are academics, so they'll understand honor and history and symbolism and matters of the body." I didn't know any of this for sure. These were only my dreams . . . and my experience of those on the ship.

"Now you speak of 'suicide' for the both of us," it said.

"Please," I said. "I can make your chief listen."

"Our chief hates humans," Okwu said. "Humans took its stinger. Do you know what . . ."

"I'll give you my jar of *otjize*," I blurted. "You can put it all over your . . . on every *okuoko*, your dome, who knows, it might make you glow like a star or give you super-powers or sting harder and faster or . . ."

"We don't like stinging."

"Please," I begged. "Imagine what you will be. Imagine if my plan works. You'll get the stinger back and none of you will have died. You'll be a hero." *And I get to live*, I thought.

"We don't care about being heroes." But its pink tentacle twitched when it said this.

———

The Meduse ship was docked beside the Third Fish. I'd walked across the large chitinous corridor linking them, ignoring the fact that the chances of my returning were very low.

Their ship stank. I was sure of it, even if I couldn't smell it through my breather. Everything about the Meduse stank. I could barely concentrate on the spongy blue surface beneath my bare feet. Or the cool gasses Okwu promised would not harm my flesh even though I could not breathe it. Or the Meduse, some green, some blue, some pink, moving on every surface, floor, high ceiling, wall, or stopping and probably staring at me with whatever they stared with. Or the current-connected *edan* I still grasped in my hands. I was doing equations in my head. I needed everything I had to do what I was about to do.

The room was so enormous that it almost felt as if we were outside. Almost. I'm a child of the desert; nothing indoors can feel like the outdoors to me. But this room was huge. The chief was no bigger than the others, no more colorful. It had no more tentacles than the others. It was surrounded by other Meduse. It looked so much like those around it that Okwu had to stand beside it to let me know who it was.

The current from the *edan* was going crazy—branching out in every direction bringing me their words. I should have been terrified. Okwu had told me that requesting a meeting like this with the chief was risking not only my life, but Okwu's life as well. For the chief hated human beings and Okwu had just begged to bring one into their "great ship."

Spongy. As if it were full of the firm jelly beads in the milky pudding my mother liked to make. I could sense current all around me. These people had deep active technology built into the walls and many of them had it running within their very bodies. Some of them were walking astrolabes, it was part of their biology.

I adjusted my facemask. The air that it pumped in smelled like desert flowers. The makers of the mask had to have been Khoush women. They liked everything to smell like flowers, even their privates. But at the moment, I could have kissed those women, for as I gazed at the chief, the smell of flowers burst into my nose and mouth and suddenly I was imagining the chief hovering in the desert surrounded by the dry sweet-smelling flowers that only bloomed at night. I felt calm. I didn't feel at home, because in the part of the desert that I knew, only tiny scentless flowers grew. But I sensed Earth.

I slowly stopped treeing, my mind clean and clear, but much stupider. I needed to speak, not act. So I had no choice. I held my chin up and then did as Okwu instructed me. I sunk to the spongy floor. Then right there, within the ship that brought the death of my friends, the boy I was coming to love, my fellow Oomza Uni human citizens from Earth, before the one who had instructed its people to perform *moojh-ha ki-bira*, also called the "great wave" of death, on my people—still grasping the *edan*, I prostrated. I pressed my face to the floor. Then I waited.

"This is Binti Ekeopara Zuzu Dambu Kaipka of Namib, the one . . . the one who survives," Okwu said.

"You may just call me Binti," I whispered, keeping my head down. My first name was singular and two syllabled like Okwu's name and I thought maybe it would please the chief.

"Tell the girl to sit up," the chief said. "If there is the slightest damage to the ship's flesh because of this one, I will have you executed first, Okwu. Then this creature."

"Binti," Okwu said, his voice was hard, flat. "Get up."

I shut my eyes. I could feel the *edan*'s current working through me, touching everything. Including the floor beneath me. And I could *hear* it. The floor. It was singing. But not words. Just humming. Happy and aloof. It wasn't paying attention. I pushed myself up, and leaned back on my knees. Then I looked at where my chest had been. Still a deep blue. I looked up at the chief.

"My people are the creators and builders of astrolabes," I said. "We use math to create the currents within them. The best of us have the gift to bring harmony so delicious that we can make atoms caress each other like lovers. That's what my sister said." I blinked as it came to me. "I think that's why this *edan* works for me! I found it. In the desert. A wild woman there once told me that it is a piece of old old technology; she called it a 'god stone.' I didn't believe her then, but I do now. I've had it for eight years, but it only worked for *me* now." I pounded my chest. "For *me*! On that ship full of you after you'd all done . . . done that. Let me speak for you, let me speak to them. So no more have to die."

I lowered my head, pressing my *edan* to my belly. Just as Okwu told me. I could hear others behind me. They could have stung me a thousand times.

"You know what they have taken from me," the chief asked.

"Yes," I said, keeping my head down.

"My stinger is my people's power," it said. "They took it from us. That's an act of war."

"My way will get your stinger back," I quickly said. Then I braced myself for the rough stab in the back. I felt the sharpness press against the nape of my neck. I bit my lower lip to keep from screaming.

"Tell your plan," Okwu said.

I spoke fast. "The pilot gets us cleared to land, then I leave the ship with one of you to negotiate with Oomza Uni to get the stinger back . . . peacefully."

"That will take our element of surprise," the chief said. "You know nothing about strategy."

"If you attack, you will kill many, but then they will kill you.

All of you," I said. "Ahh," I hissed as the stinger pointed at my neck was pressed harder against my flesh. "Please, I'm just . . ."

"Chief, Binti doesn't know how to speak," Okwu said. "Binti is uncivilized. Forgive it. It is young, a girl."

"How can we trust it?" the Meduse beside the chief asked Okwu.

"What would I do?" I asked, my face squeezed with pain. "Run?" I wiped tears from my face. I wiped and wiped, but they kept coming. The nightmare kept happening.

"You people are good at hiding," another Meduse sneered. "especially the females like you." Several of the Meduse, including the chief, shook their tentacles and vibrated their domes in a clear display of laughter.

"Let Binti put down the *edan*," Okwu said.

I stared at Okwu, astonished. "What?"

"Put it *down*," it said. "You will be completely vulnerable. How can you be our ambassador, if you need that to stay safe from us."

"It's what allows me to hear you!" I shrieked. And it was all I had.

The chief whipped up one of its tentacles and every single Meduse in that enormous room stopped moving. They stopped as if the very currents of time stopped. Everything stopped as it does when things get so cold that they become ice. I looked around and when none of them moved, slowly, carefully I dragged myself inches forward and turned to see the Meduse behind me. Its stinger was up, at the height of where my neck had been. I looked at Okwu, who said nothing. Then at the chief. I lowered my eyes. Then I ventured another look, keeping my head low.

"Choose," the chief said.

My shield. My translator. I tried to flex the muscles in my hands. I was greeted with sharp intense pain. It had been over three days. We were five hours from Oomza Uni. I tried again. I screamed. The *edan* pulsed a bright blue deep within its black and gray crevices, lighting up its loops and swirls. Like one of the bioluminescent snails that invaded the edges of my home's lake.

When my left index finger pulled away from the *edan*, I couldn't hold the tears back. The *edan*'s blue-white glow blurred before my eyes. My joints popped and the muscles spasmed. Then my middle finger and pinky pulled away. I bit my lip so hard that I tasted blood. I took several quick breaths and then flexed every single one of my fingers at the same time. All of my joints went *CRACK*! I heard a thousand wasps in my head. My body went numb. The *edan* fell from my hands. Right before my eyes, I saw it and I wanted to laugh. The blue current I'd conjured danced before me, the definition of harmony made from chaos.

There was a soft *pap* as the *edan* hit the floor, rolled twice, then stopped. I had just killed myself. My head grew heavy . . . and all went black.

═══

The Meduse were right. I could not have represented them if I was holding the *edan*. This was Oomza Uni. Someone there would know everything there was to know about the *edan* and thus its toxicity to the Meduse. No one at Oomza Uni would have really believed I was their ambassador unless I let go.

Death. When I left my home, I died. I had not prayed to the Seven before I left. I didn't think it was time. I had not gone on my pilgrimage like a proper woman. I was sure I'd return to my village as a full woman to do that. I had left my family. I thought I could return to them when I'd done what I needed to do.

Now I could never go back. The Meduse. The Meduse are not what we humans think. They are truth. They are clarity. They are decisive. There are sharp lines and edges. They understand honor and dishonor. I had to earn their honor and the only way to do that was by dying a second time.

I felt the stinger plunge into my spine just before I blacked out and just after I'd conjured up the wild line of current that I guided to the *edan*. It was a terrible pain. Then I left. I left them, I left that ship. I could hear the ship singing its half-word song and I knew it was singing to me. My last thought was to my family, and I hoped it reached them.

═══════

Home. I smelled the earth at the border of the desert just before it rained, during Fertile Season. The place right behind the Root, where I dug up the clay I used for my *otjize* and chased the geckos who were too fragile to survive a mile away in the desert. I opened my eyes; I was on my bed in my room, naked except for my wrapped skirt. The rest of my body was smooth with a thick layer of *otjize*. I flared my nostrils and inhaled the smell of me. Home . . .

I sat up and something rolled off my chest. It landed in my crotch and I grabbed it. The *edan*. It was cool in my hand and all dull blue as it had been for years before. I reached behind and felt my back. The spot where the stinger had stabbed me was sore and I could feel something rough and scabby there. It too was covered with *otjize*. My astrolabe sat on the curve of the window and I checked my map and stared outside for a very long time. I grunted, slowly standing up. My foot hit something on the floor. My jar. I put the *edan* down and picked it up, grasping it with both hands. The jar was more than half-empty. I laughed, dressed and stared out the window again. We were landing on Oomza Uni in an hour and the view was spectacular.

═══════

They did not come. Not to tell me what to do or when to do it. So I strapped myself in the black landing chair beside the window and stared at the incredible sight expanding before my eyes. There were two suns, one that was very small and one that was large but comfortably far away. Hours of sunshine on all parts of the planet were far more than hours of dark, but there were few deserts on Oomza Uni.

I used my astrolabe in binocular vision to see things up close. Oomza Uni, such a small planet compared to Earth. Only one-third water, its lands were every shade of the rainbow—some parts blue, green, white, purple, red, white, black, orange. And some areas were smooth, others jagged with peaks that touched the clouds. And the area we were hurtling toward was orange, but interrupted by patches of the dense green of large forests of trees, small lakes, and the hard gray-blue forests of tall skyscrapers.

My ears popped as we entered the atmosphere. The sky started to turn a light pinkish color, then red orange. I was looking out from within a fireball. We were inside the air that was being ripped apart as we entered the atmosphere. There wasn't much shaking or vibrating, but I could see the heat generated by the ship. The ship would shed its skin the day after we arrived as it readjusted to gravity.

We descended from the sky and zoomed between monstrously beautiful structures that made the skyscrapers of Earth look miniscule. I laughed wildly as we descended lower and lower. Down, down we fell. No military ships came to shoot us out of the sky. We landed and, moments after smiling with excitement, I wondered if they would kill the pilot now that he was useless? I had not negotiated that with the Meduse. I ripped off my safety belt and jumped up and then fell to the floor. My legs felt like weights.

"What is . . ."

I heard a horrible noise, a low rumble that boiled to an angry-sounding growl. I looked around, sure there was a monster about to enter my room. But then I realized two things. Okwu was standing in my doorway and I understood what it was saying.

I did as it said and pushed myself into a sitting position, bringing my legs to my chest. I grasped the side of my bed and dragged myself up to sit on it.

"Take your time," Okwu said. "Your kind do not adjust quickly to *jadevia*."

"You mean gravity?" I asked.

"Yes."

I slowly stood up. I took a step and looked at Okwu, then past it at the empty doorway. "Where are the others?"

"Waiting in the dining room."

"The pilot?" I asked

"In the dining room as well."

"Alive?"

"Yes."

I sighed, relieved, and then paused. The sound of its speech vibrating against my skin. This was its true voice. I could not only hear at its frequency, but I saw its tentacles quiver as it spoke. And I could understand it. Before, it had just looked like their tentacles were quivering for no reason.

"Was it the sting?" I asked.

"No," it said. "That is something else. You understand, because you truly are what you say you are—a harmonizer."

I didn't care to understand. Not at the moment.

"Your tentacle," I said. "Your *okuoko*." It hung straight, still pink but now translucent like the others.

"The rest was used to help several of our sick," it said. "Your people will be remembered by my people."

The more it spoke, the less monstrous its voice sounded. I took another step.

"Are you ready?" Okwu asked.

I was. I left the *edan* behind with my other things.

━━━━━

I was still weak from the landing, but this had to happen fast. I don't know how they broke the news of their presence to Oomza

Uni authorities, but they must have. Otherwise, how would we be able to leave the ship during the brightest part of the day?

I understood the plan as soon as Okwu and the chief came to my room. I followed them down the hallway. We did not pass through the dining room where so many had been brutally killed, and I was glad. But as we passed the entrance, I saw all the Meduse in there. The bodies were all gone. The chairs and tables were all stacked on one side of the large room as if a windstorm had swept through it. Between the transparent folds and tentacles, I thought I glimpsed someone in the red flowing uniform of the pilot, but I wasn't sure.

"You know what you will say," the chief said. Not a question, but a statement. And within the statement, a threat.

I wore my best red shirt and wrapper, made from the threads of well-fed silkworms. I'd bought it for my first day of class at Oomza Uni, but this was a more important occasion. And I'd used fresh *otjize* on my skin and to thicken my plaited hair even more. As I'd palm rolled my plaits smooth like the bodies of snakes, I noticed that my hair had grown about an inch since I'd left home. This was odd. I looked at the thick wiry new growth, admiring its dark brown color before pressing the *otjize* onto it, making it red. There was a tingling sensation on my scalp as I worked the *otjize* in and my head ached. I was exhausted. I held my *otjize*-covered hands to my nose and inhaled the scent of home.

Years ago, I had snuck out to the lake one night with some other girls and we'd all washed and scrubbed off all our *otjize* using the lake's salty water. It took us half the night. Then we'd stared at each other horrified by what we'd done. If any man saw us, we'd be ruined for life. If our parents saw us, we'd all be beaten and that would only be a fraction of the punishment. Our families and people we knew would think us mentally unstable when they heard, and that too would ruin our chances of marriage.

But above all this, outside of the horror of what we'd done, we all felt an awesome glorious . . . shock. Our hair hung in thick clumps, black in the moonlight. Our skin glistened, dark brown. *Glistened*. And there had been a breeze that night and it felt amazing on our exposed skin. I thought of this as I applied the *otjize* to my new growth, covering up the dark brown color of my hair. What if I washed it all off now? I was the first of my people to come to Oomza Uni, would the people here even know the difference? But Okwu and the chief came minutes later and there was no time. Plus, really, this was Oomza Uni, someone would have researched and known of my people. And that person would know I was naked if I washed all my *otjize* off . . . and crazy.

I didn't want to do it anyway, I thought as I walked behind Okwu and the chief. There were soldiers waiting at the doorway; both were human and I wondered what point they were trying to make by doing that. Just like the photos in the books I read, they wore all-blue kaftans and no shoes.

"You first," the chief growled, moving behind me. I felt one of its tentacles, heavy and smooth, shove me softly in the back right where I'd been stung. The soreness there caused me to stand up taller. And then more softly in a voice that only tickled my ear with its strange vibration. "Look strong, girl."

Following the soldiers and followed by two Meduse, I stepped onto the surface of another planet for the first time in my life. My scalp was still tingling, and this added to the magical sensation of being so far from home. The first thing I noticed was the smell and weight of the air when I walked off the ship. It smelled jungly, green, heavy with leaves. The air was full of *water*. It was just like the air in the ship's plant-filled breathing chambers!

I parted my lips and inhaled it as I followed the soldiers down the open black walkway. Behind me, I heard the Meduse, pluming out and sucking in gas. Softly, though, unlike on the ship. We were walking toward a great building, the ship port.

"We will take you to the Oomza Uni Presidential Building," one of the soldiers said in to me in perfect Khoush. He looked up at the Meduse and I saw a crease of worry wrinkle his brow. "I don't know . . . their language. Can you.. . ."

I nodded.

He looked about twenty-five and was dark brown skinned like me, but unlike the men of my people, his skin was naked, his hair shaven low, and he was quite short, standing a head shorter than me. "Do you mind swift transport?"

I turned and translated for Okwu and the chief.

"These people are primitive," the chief responded. But it and Okwu agreed to board the shuttle.

The room's wall and floor were a light blue, the large open windows letting in sunshine and a warm breeze. There were ten professors, one from each of the ten university departments. They sat, stood, hovered, and crouched behind a long table of glass. Against every wall were soldiers wearing blue uniforms of cloth, color, and light. There were so many different types of people in the room that I found it hard to concentrate. But I had to or there would be more death.

The one who spoke for all the professors looked like one of the sand people's gods and I almost laughed. It was like a spider made of wind, gray and undulating, here and not quite there. When it spoke, it was in a whisper that I could clearly hear despite the fact that I was several feet away. And it spoke in the language of the Meduse.

It introduced itself as something that sounded like "Haras" and said, "Tell me what you need to tell me."

And then all attention was suddenly on me.

"None of you have ever seen anyone like me," I said. "I come from a people who live near a small salty lake on the edge of a desert. On my people's land, fresh water, water humans can drink, is so little that we do not use it to bathe as so many others do. We wash with *otjize*, a mix of red clay from our land and oils from our local flowers."

Several of the human professors looked at each other and chuckled. One of the large insectile people clicked its mandibles. I frowned, flaring my nostrils. It was the first time I'd received treatment similar to the way my people were treated on Earth by the Khoush. In a way, this set me at ease. People were people, everywhere. These professors were just like anyone else.

"This was my first time leaving the home of my parents. I had never even left my own city, let alone my planet Earth. Days later, in the blackness of space, everyone on my ship but the pilot was killed, many right before my eyes, by a people at war with those who view my own people as near slaves." I waited for this to sink in, then continued. "You've never seen the Meduse, either. Only studied them . . . from afar. I know. I have read about them too." I stepped forward. "Or maybe some of you or your students have studied the stinger you have in the weapons museum up close."

I saw several of them look at each other. Some murmured to one another. Others, I did not know well enough to tell what they were doing. As I spoke, I fell into a rhythm, a meditative state very much like my math-induced ones. Except I was fully present, and before long tears were falling from my eyes. I told them in detail about watching Heru's chest burst open, desperately grabbing food, staying in that room waiting to die, the *edan* saving me and not knowing how or why or what.

I spoke of Okwu and how my *otjize* had really been what saved me. I spoke of the Meduse's cold exactness, focus, violence, sense of honor, and willingness to listen. I said things that I didn't know I'd thought about or comprehended. I found words I didn't even know I knew. And eventually, I told them how they could satisfy the Meduse and prevent a bloodbath in which everyone would lose.

I was sure they would agree. These professors were educated

beyond anything I could imagine. Thoughtful. Insightful. United. Individual. The Meduse chief came forward and spoke its piece, as well. It was angry, but thorough, eloquent with a sterile logic. "If you do not give it to us willingly, we have the right to take back what was brutally stolen from us without provocation," the chief said.

After the chief spoke, the professors discussed among themselves for over an hour. They did not retreat to a separate room to do this. They did it right before the chief, Okwu, and me. They moved from the glass table and stood in a group.

Okwu, the chief, and I just stood there. Back in my home, the elders were always stoic and quiet and they always discussed everything in private. It must have been the same for the Meduse, because Okwu's tentacles shuddered and it said, "What kind of people are these?"

"Let them do the right thing," the chief said.

Feet away from us, beyond the glass table, these professors were shouting with anger, sometimes guffawing with glee, flicking antennae in each other's faces, making ear-popping clicks to get the attention of colleagues. One professor, about the size of my head, flew from one part of the group to the other, producing webs of gray light that slowly descended on the group. This chaotic method of madness would decide whether I would live or die.

I caught bits and pieces of the discussion about Meduse history and methods, the mechanics of the Third Fish, the scholars who'd brought the stinger. Okwu and the chief didn't seem to mind hovering there waiting. However, my legs soon grew tired and I sat down right there on the blue floor.

———

Finally, the professors quieted and took their places at the glass table again. I stood up, my heart seeming to pound in my mouth, my palms sweaty. I glanced at the chief and felt even more nervous; its *okuoko* were vibrating and its blue color was deeper, almost glowing. When I looked at Okwu, where its *okuoko* hung, I caught a glimpse of the white of its stinger, ready to strike.

The spiderlike Haras raised two front legs and spoke in the language of the Meduse and said, "On behalf of all the people of Oomza Uni and on behalf of Oomza University, I apologize for the actions of a group of our own in taking the stinger from you, Chief Meduse. The scholars who did this will be found, expelled, and exiled. Museum specimen of such prestige are highly prized at our university, however such things must only be acquired with permission from the people to whom they belong. Oomza protocol is based on honor, respect, wisdom, and knowledge. We will return it to you immediately."

My legs grew weak and before I knew it, I was sitting back on the floor. My head felt heavy and tingly, my thoughts scattered. "I'm sorry," I said, in the language I'd spoken all my life. I felt something press my back, steadying me. Okwu.

"I am all right," I said, pushing my hands to the floor and standing back up. But Okwu kept a tentacle to my back.

The one named Haras continued. "Binti, you have made your people proud and I'd personally like to welcome you to Oomza Uni." It motioned one of its limbs toward the human woman beside it. She looked Khoush and wore tight-fitting green garments that clasped every part of her body, from neck to toe. "This is Okpala. She is in our mathematics department. When you are settled, aside from taking classes with her, you will study your *edan* with her. According to Okpala, what you did is impossible."

I opened my mouth to speak, but Okpala put up a hand and I shut my mouth.

"We have one request," Haras said. "We of Oomza Uni wish Okwu to stay behind as the first Meduse student to attend the university and as a showing of allegiance between Oomza Uni governments and the Meduse and a renewal of the pact between human and Meduse."

I heard Okwu rumble behind me, then the chief was speaking up. "For the first time in my own lifetime, I am learning something completely outside of core beliefs," the chief said. "Who'd have thought that a place harboring human beings could carry such honor and foresight." It paused and then said, "I will confer with my advisors before I make my decision."

The chief was pleased. I could hear it in its voice. I looked around me. No one from my tribe. At once, I felt both part of something historic and very alone. Would my family even comprehend it all when I explained it to them? Or would they just fixate on the fact that I'd almost died, was now too far to return home and had left them in order to make the "biggest mistake of my life"?

I swayed on my feet, a smile on my face.

"Binti," the one named Okpala said. "What will you do now?"

"What do you mean?" I asked. "I want to study mathematics and currents. Maybe create a new type of astrolabe. The *edan*, I want to study that and . . ."

"Yes," she said. "That is true, but what about your home? Will you ever return?"

"Of course," I said. "Eventually, I will visit and . . ."

"I have studied your people," she said. "They don't like outsiders."

"I'm not an outsider," I said, with a twinge of irritation. "I am . . ." And that's when it caught my eye. My hair was rested against my back, weighed down by the *otjize*, but as I'd gotten up, one lock had come to rest on my shoulder. I felt it rub against the front of my shoulder and I *saw* it now.

I frowned, not wanting to move. Before the realization hit me, I knew to drop into meditation, treeing out of desperation. I held myself in there for a moment, equations flying through my mind,

like wind and sand. Around me, I heard movement and, still treeing, I saw that the soldiers were leaving the room. The professors
were getting up, talking among themselves in their various ways.
All except Okpala. She was looking right at me.

I slowly lifted up one of my locks and brought it forward I
rubbed off the *ojtize*. It glowed a strong deep blue like the sky back
on earth on a clear day, like Okwu and so many of the other Meduse, like the uniforms of the Oomza Uni soldiers. And it was
translucent. Soft, but tough. I touched the top of my head and
pressed. They felt the same and . . . I felt my hand touching them.
The tingling sensation was gone. My hair was no longer hair. There
was a ringing in my ear as I began to breathe heavily, still in meditation. I wanted to tear off my clothes and inspect every part of my
body. To see what else that sting had changed. It had not been a
sting. A sting would have torn out my insides, as it did for Heru.

"Only those," Okwu said. "Nothing else."

"This is why I understand you?" I flatly asked. Talking while in
meditation was like softly whispering from a hole deep in the
ground. I was looking up from a cool dark place.

"Yes."

"Why?"

"Because you had to understand us and it was the only way,"
Okwu said.

"And you needed to prove to them that you were truly our ambassador, not prisoner," the chief said. It paused. "I will return to
the ship; we will make our decision about Okwu." It turned to leave
and then turned back. "Binti, you will forever hold the highest
honor among the Meduse. My destiny is stronger for leading me to
you." Then it left.

I stood there, in my strange body. If I hadn't been deep in
meditation I would have screamed and screamed. I was so far
from home.

I'm told that news of what had happened spread across all Oomza Uni within minutes. It was said that a human tribal female from a distant blue planet saved the university from Meduse terrorists by sacrificing her blood and using her unique gift of mathematical harmony and ancestral magic. "Tribal": that's what they called humans from ethnic groups too remote and "uncivilized" to regularly send students to attend Oomza Uni.

Over the next two days, I learned that people viewed my reddened dark skin and strange hair with wonder. And when they saw me with Okwu, they grew tense and quiet, moving away. Where they saw me as a fascinating exotic human, they saw Okwu as a dangerous threat. Okwu was of a warlike people who, up until now, had only been viewed with fear among people from all over. Okwu enjoyed its infamy, whereas I just wanted to find a quiet desert to walk into so I could study in peace.

"All people fear decisive, proud honor," Okwu proclaimed.

We were in one of the Weapons City libraries, staring at the empty chamber where the chief's stinger had been kept. A three-hour transport from Math City, Weapons City was packed with activity on every street and crowded with sprawling flat gray buildings made of stone. Beneath each of these structures were inverted buildings that extended at least a half-mile underground where only those students, researchers, and professors involved knew what was being invented, tested, or destroyed. After the meeting, this was where they'd taken me, the chief, and Okwu for the retrieval of the stinger.

We'd been escorted by a person who looked like a small green child with roots for a head, who I later learned was the head professor of Weapons City. He was the one who went into the five-by-five-foot case made of thick clear crystal and opened it. The stinger was placed atop a slab of crystal and looked like a sharp tusk of ice.

The chief slowly approached the case, extended an *okuoko*, and then let out a large bluish puff of gas the moment its *okuoko* touched the stinger. I'll never forget the way the chief's body went from blue to clear the moment the stinger became a part of it again. Only a blue line remained at the point of demarcation where it had reattached—a scar that would always remind it of what human beings of Oomza Uni had done to it for the sake of research and academics.

Afterward, just before the chief and the others boarded the Third Fish that would take them back to their own ship just outside the atmosphere, upon Okwu's request, I knelt before the chief and placed its stinger on my lap. It was heavy and it felt like a slab of solid water and the edge at its tip looked like it could slice into another universe. I smeared a dollop of my *otjize* on the blue scar where it had reattached. After a minute, I wiped some of it away. The blue scar was gone. Their chief was returned to its full royal translucence, they had the half jar of *otjize* Okwu had taken from me, which healed their flesh like magic, and they were leaving one of their own as the first Meduse to study at the great Oomza University. The Meduse left Oomza Uni happier and better off than when they'd arrived.

═══════

My *otjize*. Yes, there is a story there. Weeks later, after I'd started classes and people had finally started to leave me be, opting to simply stare and gossip in silence instead, I ran out of *otjize*. For days, I'd known it would happen. I'd found a sweet-smelling oil of the same chemical makeup in the market. A black flower that grew in a series of nearby caverns produced the oil. But a similar clay was much harder to find. There was a forest not far from my dorm, across the busy streets, just beyond one of the classroom buildings. I'd never seen anyone go into it, but there was a path opening.

That evening, before dark, I walked in there. I walked fast, ignoring all the stares and grateful when the presence of people tapered off the closer I got to the path entrance. I carried my satchel with my astrolabe, a bag of nuts, my *edan* in my hands, cool and small. I squeezed my *edan* as I left the road and stepped onto the path. The forest seemed to swallow me within a few steps and I could no longer see the purpling sky. My skin felt near naked, the layer of *otjize* I wore was so thin.

I frowned, hesitating for a moment. We didn't have such places where I came from and the denseness of the trees, all the leaves, the small buzzing creatures, made me feel like the forest was choking me. But then I looked at the ground. I looked right there, at my sandaled feet and found precisely what I needed.

I made the *otjize* that night. I mixed it and then let it sit in the strong sunshine for the next day. I didn't go to class, nor did I eat that day. In the evening, I went to the dorm and showered and did that which my people rarely do: I washed with water. As I let the water run through my hair and down my face, I wept. This was all I had left of my homeland and it was being washed into the runnels that would feed the trees outside my dorm.

When I finished, I stood there, away from the running stream of water that flowed from the ceiling. Slowly, I reached up. I touched my "hair." The *okuoko* were soft but firm and slippery with wetness. They touched my back, soft and slick. I shook them, feeling them *otjize*-free for the first time.

I shut my eyes and prayed to the Seven; I hadn't done this since arriving on the planet. I prayed to my living parents and ancestors. I opened my eyes. It was time to call home. Soon.

I peeked out of the washing space. I shared the space with five other human students. One of them just happened to be leaving as I peeked out. As soon as he was gone, I grabbed my wrapper and came out. I wrapped it around my waist and I looked at myself in the large mirror. I looked for a very very long time. Not at my dark brown skin, but where my hair had been. The *okuoko* were a soft transparent blue with darker blue dots at their tips. They grew out of my head as if they'd been doing that all my life, so natural looking that I couldn't say they were ugly. They were just a little longer than my hair had been, hanging just past my backside, and they were thick as sizable snakes.

There were ten of them and I could no longer braid them into my family's code pattern as I had done with my own hair. I pinched one and felt the pressure. Would they grow like hair? *Were* they hair? I could ask Okwu, but I wasn't ready to ask it anything. Not yet. I quickly ran to my room and sat in the sun and let them dry.

Ten hours later, when dark finally fell, it was time. I'd bought the container at the market; it was made from the shed exoskeleton of students who sold them for spending money. It was clear like one of Okwu's tentacles and dyed red. I'd packed it with the fresh *otjize*, which now looked thick and ready.

I pressed my right index and middle finger together and was about to dig out the first dollop when I hesitated, suddenly incredibly unsure. What if my fingers passed right through it like liquid soap? What if what I'd harvested from the forest wasn't clay at all? What if it was hard like stone?

I pulled my hand away and took a deep breath. If I couldn't make *otjize* here, then I'd have to . . . change. I touched one of my tentacle-like locks and felt a painful pressure in my chest as my mind tried to take me to a place I wasn't ready to go to. I plunged my two fingers into my new concoction . . . and scooped it up. I spread it on my flesh. Then I wept.

───

I went to see Okwu in its dorm. I was still unsure what to call those who lived in this large gas-filled spherical complex. When you entered, it was just one great space where plants grew on the walls and hung from the ceiling. There were no individual rooms, and people who looked like Okwu in some ways but different in others walked across the expansive floor, up the walls, on the ceiling. Somehow, when I came to the front entrance, Okwu would always come within the next few minutes. It would always emit a large plume of gas as it readjusted to the air outside.

"You look well," it said, as we moved down the walkway. We both loved the walkway because of the winds the warm clear sea-water created as it rushed by below.

I smiled. "I *feel* well."

"When did you make it?"

"Over the last two suns," I said.

"I'm glad," it said. "You were beginning to fade."

It held up an *okuoko*. "I was working with a yellow current to use in one of my classmate's body tech," it said.

"Oh," I said, looking at its burned flesh.

We paused, looking down at the rushing waters. The relief I'd felt at the naturalness, the trueness of the *otjize* immediately started waning. *This* was the real test. I rubbed some *otjize* from my arm and then took Okwu's *okuoko* in my hand. I applied the *otjize* and then let the *okuoko* drop as I held my breath. We walked back to my dorm. My *otjize* from Earth had healed Okwu and then the chief. It would heal many others. The *otjize* created by my people, mixed with my homeland. This was the foundation of the Meduse's respect for me. Now all of it was gone. I was someone else. Not even fully Himba anymore. What would Okwu think of me now?

When we got to my dorm, we stopped.

"I know what you are thinking," Okwu said.

"I know you Meduse," I said. "You're people of honor, but you're firm and rigid. And traditional." I felt sorrow wash over and I sobbed, covering my face with my hand. Feeling my *otjize* smear beneath it. "But you've become my friend," I said. When I brought my hand away, my palm was red with *otjize*. "You are all I have here. I don't know how it happened, but you are . . ."

"You will call your family and have them," Okwu said.

I frowned and stepped away from Okwu. "So callous," I whispered.

"Binti," Okwu said. It exhaled out gas, in what I knew was a laugh. "Whether you carry the substance that can heal and bring life back to my people or not, I am your friend. I am honored to know you." It shook its *okuoko*, making one of them vibrate. I yelped when I felt the vibration in one of mine.

"What is that?" I shouted, holding up my hands.

"It means we are family through battle," it said. "You are the first to join our family in this way in a long time. We do not like humans."

I smiled.

He held up an *okuoko*. "Show it to me tomorrow," I said, doubtfully.

"Tomorrow will be the same," it said.

When I rubbed off the *otjize* the burn was gone.

———

I sat in the silence of my room looking at my *edan* as I sent out a signal to my family with my astrolabe. Outside was dark and I looked into the sky, at the stars, knowing the pink one was home. The first to answer was my mother.

Binti: Sacred Fire

The fact that the bridge is shaky does not mean it will break.

—*an Enyi Zinariya proverb*

I even missed my sisters.

And it wasn't just because it was one of those nights. You see, there's something that happens to a child of the soil when she leaves her soil. It's a death, then a painful rebirth . . . but first you have to walk around the new world as a sort of ghost. I was a ghost at Oomza Uni. Displaced but still in the place I needed to be. The place where I wanted to be. If only people understood that. Understood *me*.

And I even missed my sisters.

I squatted there in the dirt. This place beside my dorm was a favorite spot of mine because the soil here was dry like back home. There was also a flat green sturdy plant that grew in a crack at the edge of the dorm building's wall. It grew in fives, five leaves on five branches in bunches of five. And the plant smelled nice at this time of day. My mother would have loved these plants as much as I did and my father would have wanted to study them and see if their leaves conducted current. They didn't; I'd tried running a current through them already. Nothing. But the plants knew mathematics, which was even godlier. Praise the Seven for these plants of the fives, my new favorite number.

I shut my eyes and tried to imagine I was with my sisters. Anything to drown out the sight of Heru and his always bursting chest. Over and over, warm blood spattering my face, no sound coming from him. His face frozen with shock. The stinger of one of Okwu's people driven through his back . . . or was it the stinger of Okwu itself? I refused to ask. Never. But I wondered wondered wondered. The one Person on this university planet whom I had a connection with, who was the closest thing I had to family, family through war, may have killed the boy I had a crush on, killed Heru right before my eyes.

I grabbed my *okuoko* and squeezed, knowing I was smearing off some of the *otjize* I'd rolled them with. My *okuoko* had a firm yet almost gelatinous texture and it was still strange to me, but gradually I was getting used to them. As much as I could. They had sensation like any other part of my body, so grasping them was like grasping several long fingers. Shuddering, I let go.

I reached down and picked up a handful of the dry red soil and let it sift through my fingers. This planet wasn't home, but it was a planet. A home. I pressed my palms flat to the ground. Immediately, I felt a little better. My heartbeat slowed, Heru and his shocked face retreated and I sighed.

"Hello? Are you alright?"

I looked up, shielding my eyes with one of my *otjize*-covered hands. I knew this girl, but I didn't know her name. I still barely knew anyone's name at my dorm. Since arriving six earth weeks ago, I'd hidden away from my schoolmates as much as I could. In the dining hall, I collected my food and took it to my room. I didn't like dining halls.

"I'm fine," I muttered, trying to get up. Then I remembered Heru's parents and all my strength left me again. They'd called me yesterday. The holographic image of his mother had simply stared at me, stared so hard that I could practically *feel* her trying to sift through all that was me to find my memories of her son. She only wanted those glimmers of her son, not the surviving Himba girl to whom they belonged. Then she'd burst into tears, unable to say a word to me.

Heru's father had shouted at me from behind her, "How does a beggar survive and my son not? What did you trade?! What filthy charms did you work?!" I thought they'd then break the connection, but they didn't. They'd instead shouted and cried at me for over a half hour. I held my astrolabe, with a shaking hand, listening, gazing back at them into their eyes, quiet, from planets away. When they'd had enough, they finally broke the connection. The whole thing was horrible.

Whimpering, I pressed a hand to my face, wishing the girl whose name I didn't know would leave me to grovel in the dirt alone.

"Don't worry," she said, squatting before me. "I'll come down to you."

My eyes flooded with tears that dropped into the soil at my sandaled feet and onto my long orange red skirt. Heru was dying again. The stinger in his chest. White. But his blood spread on it so easily. So red. I grunted, my heart was racing again.

She put a hand on my shoulder. "Breathe," she whispered.

"Can't."

"You are, though," she chuckled. "If you weren't you'd have passed out by now."

I blinked. *I am alive*, I thought. *I just think I'm dead.* I looked up at her smiling face. She had eyes green like leaves, skin the color of sand flower. She was dark for a Khoush, probably from spending so much time under Oomza's suns. Even now she wore the blue jumpsuit I often saw her jogging about wearing. We both laughed.

"Breathe more," she said, and I did. I felt stronger. The sight of Heru disappeared, for now. She helped me up and for a moment we stood there looking at each other. "My name's Haifa. You're Binti."

"I have nothing to add to that," I said.

"Everyone's been wondering how you can be so together," she said. "You save the university and everyone back home and then turn right around and start the semester without missing a step like some sort of superhero. Today, I think I'm finally convinced you're actually normal and, well, *mostly* human."

I burst out laughing. Oh yes, now I was breathing just fine.

"It's nearly second sunset, best part of the day," she said taking my hand. "Come sit and eat some mini apples with me. I've had a long day, too."

"Okay."

We walked across the dirt to the dorm path and I waited for the question: "Where's your Okwu?" In these first weeks of registration, moving into my dorm, orientation, then classes, whenever I met anyone, this question was never far behind. I was so glad when Haifa didn't ask it now.

We sat on the stone steps. Large and uneven, the fifty steps extended down about a half-mile to the first buildings of Math City. They were made for People with legs of various lengths. Nevertheless, the stone steps were tan and smooth and the sunlight warmed them, making them the perfect place for us to sit at this hour. We simply sat there eating sour mini apples, watching the second sunset. It was always a spectacular scene of orange-pink that softly glowed in the swelling darkness. With most classes having ended by this hour, there was no traffic on the steps.

"Why were you grabbing your hair like that?" she asked.

I shrugged. Then I just said it; I wasn't home anymore. "They're not hair."

"Oh I know that," she said, popping another mini apple into her mouth and rolling it about before biting. "Everyone does."

"They do?"

She rolled her eyes. "Don't you like them?"

I shrugged, "They're mine." I took an apple. I looked at it. Red and soft in flesh, the apples were delicious after you ate a few and your taste buds adjusted. "I was . . . I was having a moment. It's been a lot."

"I know," she said. "What's it been like? You're part Meduse, now."

I looked at her, but she seemed genuinely curious, an openness on her face that made it impossible for me to feel annoyed. "I'm . . . still getting used to it."

"Of course you are. You don't adjust to that kind of thing in a day." She got up and did a graceful dancer's twirl on one of the stones, her hands out. "Look at me," she announced. "I'm fantastic." She sat back down. "It's not the same as your situation, but I was born physically male and when I was thirteen I transitioned to female."

My eyebrows rose. "Oh," I said. Back home, we called people like Haifa *eanda oruzo*, but they weren't so open about it. And we didn't say "transition", we said "align" and once they align, it was never mentioned again. Amongst the Himba, you "were what you knew you were once you knew what you were and that was that", to quote my village's chief Kapika. I wondered if all the people of the Khoush communities were as open about alignment as Haifa.

"All my life, I knew this was who I'd be, but it still took some getting used to after I transitioned," she said. "Well, more everyone around me, than me."

"Did it hurt?" I asked.

"Did it hurt for you?"

"Well, yes . . . I mean . . . I . . . it was . . ."

"I'm joking, Binti," she said, gazing at the sunset. "*You* got stabbed in the back with a Meduse stinger, that's not going to feel good. And you didn't even have a say in what happened to you. Doesn't that bother you?"

I looked at my hands.

"No warning, no nothing, just 'stab', then you wake up and you're part-Meduse. That's really something," she added, more to herself than me. Her words were making me nauseous and I focused on the deepening pink-orange sky. Haifa didn't notice. "My goodness. Maybe we *can't* really compare."

"Maybe," I said, my nausea passing. Still, Haifa had changed, too. And she'd been so clear in what she wanted that she'd done it voluntarily. I certainly would not have chosen to be stung by a Meduse, but would I have gone into that ship and risked everything if I had known what was about to happen? After a moment of thought, I knew I would have. I'd gone in there with the intent to live, but sure that I was going to die.

———

I can never forget the look on my mother's face when I finally contacted home. I was sure everyone at home was livid with me, I couldn't take it anymore. I'd grabbed my astrolabe and messaged home, not knowing who'd respond. Those moments of wait were agony. I'd grasped my edan so tightly that my hand ached. I considered treeing, but I didn't think it was a good idea for my family after so many weeks to finally see me while I was up in the tree. Then there she was. As the hologram bloomed, I could initially see that she was standing in the kitchen. She was lit by a different sun than the one that would rise where I was in a few hours. She stared at me for a long time and I stared back, my eyes filling with tears.

"Binti."

"Mama."

It sounded like we said it at the same time but there probably was some sort of digital lag because of the distance.

"You made it."

"I did." I was weeping.

"Good."

I told her everything. Every detail. Every fear. Every triumph. Everything except about what the sting had done. She listened and gasped with surprise and shock and laughed a few times and listened some more. She told me I was foolish and wise and that I owed her so much because I knew how much I'd hurt her, hurt everyone. Yet my mother still understood. And she reveled in the fact that I was her child. Papa had refused to speak with me this day. And that was like him. I told myself, maybe next time I reach out he'll be the one to respond. I missed my family.

If I were surrounded by family, these first few weeks on Oomza Uni would have been better. I'd have still been tormented, but not so much. But I was there without any of them and the only family I had was often the source of my terror. During nights, I still relived my time on the ship over and over until all that I focused on was fear and . . . "What if Okwu . . . ?".

This night, as I so often did, I eventually rolled over, picked up my *edan* from the shelf beside my bed and held it to my chest like a talisman. I stayed this way all night. I didn't sleep.

———

At second morning, I had individual study with Professor Okpala. This would be our fourth session and I was looking forward to it, despite my lack of sleep. I went to see Okwu first as was my routine. It came out of its dorm as I walked up the path.

"Binti," Okwu said. "You look tired."

"I didn't sleep well. I kept . . ." I looked directly at it. In the sunlight of the second sun, Okwu's translucent blue dome shined like something underwater. "I kept thinking about the ship. And what your people did to everyone onboard except me and the pilot." *And the fact that maybe you yourself killed Heru*, I thought.

"It was war," Okwu said. "You should strengthen yourself with that knowledge. In war there's death."

I frowned at it, sensing that Okwu felt more than its words. Ever since I'd been stung and changed, it was this way. Okwu thought about what happened, too. It wondered. Things didn't sit well for Okwu, even if it didn't feel any guilt or terror over those Third Fish memories.

It began to move and I followed it. "Have you eaten?" it asked.

"I have. Have you?"

"I won't until after class today. My mind is sharper when I want to eat."

We were walking toward the shuttle station.

"Have you spoken with your mother, again?" Okwu asked. "You are better when you do."

"I will," I said.

"What of Heru's brother? Has he left you alone?" It thrummed softly.

I looked at my feet. Heru's younger brother Jabari had contacted me days after that terrible call from Heru's parents. Talking to Jabari was even worse and still I had not disconnected. He'd demanded I recount every detail of his brother's death, having not a care for my own feelings. "No," I said glumly. "Not since that call."

"That's good," it said. "Talking to him is useless."

We stopped on the walkway and looked over the bridge. This walkway that ran over rushing waters that emptied into a strange sea some miles away was a favorite spot of ours. We came here every morning and we often met here. I inhaled the rush of wind that blew both my and Okwu's *okuoko*. Okwu breathed out a burst of gas and I exhaled.

"Whoo!" Grinning, I spread my arms out as I faced the edge of the walkway that dropped down to the rushing water. "I'm awake now!" I exhaled and inhaled again, my eyes closed imagining myself leaping from the walkway toward the water, but then swooping over it as I then flew into the sky, up up into space. My good mood shifted a shade darker. I slowly turned to Okwu and said the first thing on my mind, "Sometimes, I hear you speak and your voice still sounds rough."

After a moment, Okwu replied, "Sometimes I wonder why your voice sounds so smooth to me."

"Oh," I said. "Is that bad?"

"I prefer my language."

I chuckled.

Okwu floated to the edge of the walkway and then hovered in the air over the edge, its *okuoko* dangling in midair. A strong breeze blew Okwu upward and then it slowly floated back to my level, still hovering over the drop. It returned to the walkway, its dome thrumming with pleasure.

We stayed there for a bit, standing side-by-side watching the water rush by. The air was so fresh; we both loved coming here. There was movement, but the area stayed the same and once in a while, there would be a procession of yellow fishlike creatures who were longer than the Root back home and slender like pipes. In the turquoise blue waters, you could see them perfectly wiggling like giant ribbons with large flat heads and big bulbous red eyes. I really loved them.

"Let's go to class," I said.

———

Okwu had a class in Math City so we walked together most of the way. We came to the building where its class was held and it was there that we parted ways. Professor Okpala's office was only a few minutes' walk away, at the center of Math City. I watched Okwu float off toward its building. Then I grasped the strap of my red leather satchel and pulled it closer to me. The straps and other parts of it were already caked with my otjize; no one would ever mistake my things for someone else's. As I walked, I could feel my *edan* in the pocket of my long red skirt. "I am Binti Ekeopara Zuzu Dambu Kaipka of Namib," I whispered to myself.

I walked along the wide street, staying close to the spiraling, coiling, hexagonal glass and cuticle buildings of Math City. A swift transport shuttle zipped through the center of the street, avoiding People who also moved in various ways down the middle of the street. On average, I was quite small compared to most of those around me and I was usually the only humanoid, let alone human. This was why I kept close to the buildings. Haifa had described human walking as "inefficient motion" and compared to almost everyone else, this was fairly accurate. Walking always seemed so slow and graceless compared to all the gliding, zipping, tumbling, creeping, flying, and porting.

Back home, the closest there was to even one of the streets in Math City was the weekend market where everyone was Himba and a few minutes' walk away was open empty desert. As I walked, People stared at me, some talked about me in various languages I didn't have to understand to understand. It wasn't in my head. When I walked down the street, everyone noticed in some way.

"I am Binti Ekeopara Zuzu Dambu Kaipka of Namib," I repeated to myself. But I refused to tree. No one was going to scare me into the tree. I scurried across the busy street, leaping around what looked like a Night Masquerade . . . at least this is what I *heard* they looked like. The Night Masquerade was a mythical creature in Himba culture that only men and boys could see.

"Hello, Himba hero Binti," it said in Meduse, as it strode past me with its long stick-like body. Every move it made was accompanied by the sound of cracking and snapping.

"Greetings," I said over my shoulder. I giggled to myself, knowing there was no way it could be a Night Masquerade. I quickly moved on.

Math City was a grid of hexagons and Professor Okpala's office was at its center in one of the five spiral towers. It was at the very top and I loved going up there. Her office had no walls, so the entire space was open to the elements. It didn't rain much in Math City and the temperature for this time of the year hovered around ninety degrees and this was ideal for a desert girl like me.

This was my tenth session with Professor Okpala since I'd arrived at Oomza Uni. Thus far, all we'd really done were deep treeing exercises where I'd call up the exact current that I now understood activated the *edan*'s strange translation technology. It didn't translate every language, but some of the ones that it did translate surprised me. I'd communicated with a bee-like insect hovering around a flower Okpala had brought in. The insect had been obsessed with the deep orange hue of the flower and the work it planned to do with others of its kind. And it hadn't been interested in talking to me, so it didn't respond to anything I said to it except to tell me, "Go away, I'm busy".

Okpala had later introduced me to one of her graduate students, an Okwu-like Person. It had been angry when it realized I could understand the insults it spoke about me to Professor Okpala. It had been jealous of my closeness to the Meduse and didn't think I deserved the honor, no matter what I'd done to earn it.

"Sit down," Okpala said when I stepped out of the elevator. "You'll need all your strength today . . . if you do this right." The astrolabe she wore clipped to her hip vibrated. "Relax yourself for a few minutes while I talk to this student," she said stepping away.

I slipped my sandals off and stepped onto the densely woven vines that made the floor of her office. I went to the place she called "the classroom", the area in the middle of the open space that was her office. There was a small grey solid stone table here and nothing else. I dumped my satchel beside it and sat down.

Straightening my long red orange skirt, I stretched my legs in front of me and reached into my satchel. I brought out the tiny capture station that I'd brought from home. I carried it with me everywhere because I liked the taste of the water it pulled and formed in its cup-sized bag and because it was a piece of home.

The cool air the capture station blew at me as it pulled condensation from the clear sky felt refreshing in the hot sun. After a few minutes, the bag was full enough to fill a cup. I held the orange bag of fresh cool water to my forehead and then drank deeply from it. When I finished, I rolled up the bag and put everything back in my satchel. In the heat, the *otjize* kept my skin comfortable. I smiled turning my face to the sun. All my nightmares, flashbacks, and loneliness retreated. I put my *edan* on my lap, my astrolabe beside me and waited for Professor Okpala.

She came back to me five minutes later. "Okay, let's see if it's willing to open up to you, share what it knows," she said, clipping her astrolabe back to the cloth hanging from the side of her skintight red and green suit. She sat across from me with a tablet.

"What do you mean?" I asked. "It's not alive. Is it?" I frowned, remembering a lizard egg I'd once found back home. "Is it?"

I'd found what I thought was a dried dead lizard egg in the desert and kept it in my room because I liked its soft blue color. After I'd had it for over four years, it hatched. I'd come into my bedroom that day just in time to see the tiny blue lizard glance at me and then leap from my open bedroom window. I ran over and looked down. There it was, scampering toward the desert.

"Focus, Binti," Professor Okpala said. "All *edan* are different. Settle down. Climb a bit into the tree." She touched her tablet and it glowed a deep transparent purple. I could see what she was writing through the clear tablet: 'Binti: First attempt'.

I allowed myself to drop into the tree by grasping the Pythagorean theorem. I sighed, the world around me fragmenting and then both dimming the slightest bit and clarifying. I focused my attention on my *edan*. Somewhere in the distance my mind still quipped, *But maybe it is alive.* I pushed the distraction away.

"Good," Professor Okpala said. "Now, I'm going to ask something of you."

"Okay," I said. She could ask me anything; I would know the answer.

"Home," she said. The word hit me hard in the chest like a stone, but I didn't feel it. "What do you miss about it?"

"The sand," I said.

Professor Okpala typed something on her tablet as she looked at me with piercing eyes. "We have sand here."

"It's not the same. Different memory."

"Hold your *edan*, call up a current . . . and tell me exactly what you mean by you 'miss the sand'. Do that as you guide the current into the *edan*."

I climbed a little higher into the tree as I thought about it. "In the evening, I would sit outside behind the Root, that's my family's home. I'd be wearing my long skirt over my legs, and I would plunge my hands into the sand. It was cool on the surface, but underneath was warm, like the body of a living thing. Inside, my mother would be in the kitchen cooking pumpkin soup and my father would be walking home from his shop because it was a windy evening and he loved the wind. My brother would be on the roof of the Root making sure the storm analyzer he'd built was secure and my little sister wouldn't be home because she was out with her friends near the lake collecting matured clusterwink snails."

The current I ran over my *edan* entered the grooves and crevices and I gasped. It was doing this without me guiding it. "My friends who were more obsessed with marriage than all other things," I said. "My best friend Dele who always knew the town rules, my classmates laughing about how they didn't understand any of the math problems. But I understood it all and I just . . . sometimes I felt lonely." I don't know when I did it, but I made the current thicker. Stronger. I stared at the blue current, my eyes unfocusing. I could feel the possibility and I went higher and deeper. I stopped talking at Professor Okpala. I went with it. It was like sliding down a sand dune.

"It . . . it wasn't the day I left that I knew I was different. Not really. It was long before that. When I was seven years old. During school. Five, five, five, five. It was only me and I started going into the desert."

I felt a sting in my chest as I caught my breath. That was the moment I jumped the rails. It didn't matter that I was treeing. It didn't matter that I was with my professor, who was watching me closely, typing all that she saw into her tablet. I was far from home. The only Himba on an entire planet. My hair was braided into the tessellating design of my family, and not one person on this planet would be able to decode, read and understand the great weight of its importance. What did I think I was doing?

I was alone. Lost in space. I was in a strange place. So I arrived right back at that moment. Heru's chest. It was exploding. I was there. I grabbed my *edan* and held it to my chest, the blue purple current leaving the edan and rotating around my clenching hands now. It held my hand there, the muscles stiffening. I shut my eyes and I prayed to it, *I am in your protection. Please protect me. I am in your protection. Please protect me.*

The memory opened up and multiplied, a living fractal.

I opened my eyes to my professor. My nostrils flared and I smelled every scent around me—grass, flowers, and I smelled blood. The sky was red, my hands were red. Looking into the eyes of my professor, I opened my mouth wide and screamed so loudly that my throat stung. Professor Okpala jumped, but even this didn't make her drop her tablet. With all my strength, I bashed the *edan* against the stone table. I bashed it again.

"Binti!" my professor shouted, horrified. "Stop it!"

Bash! I was still screaming. "Evil thing! I hate you! Die! Let me die!"

"Binti!"

Bash! "Die!"

Professor Okpala was grabbing me. She'd finally put down her tablet. I cried and shrieked, trying to push her away, trying to smash the *edan* on the stone table some more. But my professor was much stronger than me and she dragged me from the stone table. My hand was bleeding and the sight of the blood made me shriek even louder. She hugged me to her. "Everything is dead!" I screamed, curling up. "Everyone is dead!"

"Then relax, Binti. If everyone is dead, there's nothing left to do," she said, hugging me tighter. "Relax."

═══════

I calmed down. Professor Okpala didn't immediately dismiss me, though she told me I needed to go to the medic and have a nurse look at my hand. She'd picked up her tablet and was typing notes again while I stood near the edge of her office looking out at Math City. Despite all I'd done to it, my *edan* was unharmed. Not a chip or a scratch. As I gazed at the spiraling sand-colored building across from me, I held it now, tightly in my uninjured hand. My injured right hand throbbed dully.

"Did you feel the *edan* open even slightly?" my professor asked.

"What?" I asked, still facing the edge of her office. I looked down at the *edan* in my left hand and quickly said, "I don't know . . . I . . ."

"Were you even trying when . . . it went wrong?"

"Yes," I said. "And a part of me was still focused on getting the *edan* open. How does that happen?"

"*Edans* are tricky powerful things," she said getting up. "Their pull can be wildly intense. And you're a very interesting student. But this was a failure, Binti. Our next session needs to be better."

She sent me on my way ten minutes later, telling me that I'd be expected at the ANE, the Alien Non-Emergency Medic Building. I left her office with a pounding headache. Once downstairs, in the lobby, I paused, feeling the tears coming like a rainstorm. I started walking when I noticed students were looking at me as they passed. I'd nearly died to get to Oomza Uni and already I was a failure.

The moment I stepped into the sunshine, I felt better. I paused on the steps in front of the tower, students walking in and out of the building. A professor who looked like a large slug, slithered around me and muttered, "Go get drunk on the sun in the fields, student hero. This is a place of study."

But I needed my moment, so I dropped my satchel beside me, tilted my face up, and let the sunshine roll over me. I sighed, smiling, "Ah, I miss the desert."

Crack!

I screeched and jumped, stumbling to the side, nearly tripping over my satchel. I smelled smoke, my face prickling with the rush of adrenaline. I reached into my pocket and grabbed my *edan* with my left hand. Smoke was rising from the hem of my skirt! I jumped again, shoved my *edan* back into my pocket and dropped down. I smacked at the black smoking circles in the material, ignoring the pain in my right hand. Coughing, I smacked harder until the flames were out, bits of grey ash floating up.

Snickering.

I looked up. Two Khoush boys were looking down at me, grins on their faces. With my peripheral vision I saw someone step up beside me from behind and grab my satchel. I snatched it back and pulled it to me, looking up. It was a girl, and like the boys and most of the humans at Oomza Uni, she was Khoush. She looked down her nose at me, smirking. I frowned. I couldn't tell who threw the current that singed my skirt, but it was definitely one of these three.

"Stay down," the taller boy said. His hair was black and shiny, reaching his chest in ringlets and he wore the tight green jumpsuit that weapons majors wore if they had humanoid bodies. "You must be used to that position, doesn't the word 'Himba' mean 'beggar'?"

I stood up. "Himba" did mean "beggar" in otjihimba. But that was an ancient coinage no one really cared about anymore. "Why would you do that?" I asked, my voice higher than normal.

"I don't need a reason, traitor," he spat. "Department heads and students who don't know any better celebrate you, but plenty of us detest you. Meduse sympathizer. You're planets away from earth, yet you betray your own homeland. You should be ashamed of yourself."

"Should have died on the ship," the other boy said. "We'd be better off. The pilot would have come up with a better plan." This boy I knew. He was in two of my math classes and he came from one of the few Khoush villages that existed near Himba country. His name was Abd, which meant "servant" in Khoush.

I grabbed my satchel and tried to walk away, but the two boys stepped in front of me. I groaned, looking at the girl who hadn't said a word yet. Deeply irritated, I aimed my question at her. "What do you want?"

"What we want," the tall boy said. ". . . what many of us who know better want is for you to take that Meduse ingrate you brought here back into space."

My left eye twitched and my hands shook, the right one throbbing more because of it. Since I'd arrived, most students, professors and staff had been warm and welcoming to me. There'd even been a party thrown for Okwu and me in the walkways outside my dorm. That day, so many had surrounded Okwu, fascinated to meet a "friendly" Meduse, that Okwu had to stay at the party until it ended. Of course, these students and faculty quickly learned that though Okwu was "friendly", it wasn't exactly nice. I must say, it was entertaining to watch them realize this fact.

However, there were a few who strongly opposed a Meduse presence on Oomza Uni and they made themselves known. These students (Khoush and otherwise) deeply feared Okwu, so they accosted me. It had happened a few times since my arrival on Oomza Uni. These individuals feared and or hated the Meduse; the Meduse were a powerful and principled yet warlike people and so they had many enemies. Just after orientation, in the halls of my dorm, in passing when I was in Central City, when Okwu was not with me, these particular anti-Meduse students let me know what they thought and it was always the hatred, the rage. To an extent, I understood some of them.

For example, Abd's family had been deeply affected by the war, as he'd angrily told me on my fourth day on Oomza Uni, during our second day of Math 101 class. Several of his family members had been killed by Meduse *moojh-ha ki-bara*-style, he'd told me, and how dare I expose him to the presence of one of these monsters. I was a "shameful typical silly foolish lowly Himba girl", according to him. I didn't agree with this, of course, but I felt his pain.

My hand ached as I turned again, trying to step around them. I nearly bumped into a crab-like person side-walking into the building. It clicked its claws at me and then, in Meduse, said, "Leave it be, Himba hero. What's done is done. Stop walking into people."

"I'm sorry," I said, cradling my right hand. Through my tear-blurred eyes, I met the Khoush girl's cold light brown eyes.

"Why didn't you stop them," the girl asked.

"What?"

"You could have asked for *anything* during that meeting, once you got them to listen," she said. "Why would you ask them to admit a Meduse into Oomza?"

"I didn't! It wasn't even my idea. But I . . ." I blinked and shook my head. "Wait, why am I even *talking* to you? Get out of my way!" My head throbbed harder and I could have sworn I felt tingling in the tips of my *okuoko*.

Then the three of them were staring at me with shock, as if I'd roared in the voice of a djinn or sacred snake. They were frozen there like stone. I didn't know what I'd done, but seeing them like this gave me a deep satisfaction so profound that more tears squeezed from my eyes. When the dark wet spot appeared in the crotch of the tall boy's jumpsuit and Abd began to hyperventilate, his mouth hanging open, I understood. I straightened up, my satisfaction deepening.

"What are you called, girl?" Okwu asked in Khoush. It was

hovering directly behind me. Then it exhaled a great puff of gas. I knew to hold my breath, but the others immediately began coughing.

"Zerlin," the girl replied in a high-pitched voice when her fit of coughing subsided.

"Zerlin, Abd, Eyad, walk away from the Binti right now," Okwu said.

The two boys turned and shakily walked off. They didn't run, they walked because Okwu had said to walk. Zerlin stayed. Tears now in *her* eyes, she said, "You shouldn't be at this university! You *killed* my sister's best friend on that ship." She hugged herself, stumbling back. She pointed a finger at Okwu that shook so badly, it was almost comical. "Monster!"

Okwu blew out a puff of gas and said, "It wasn't me specifically. But we are a hive mind. If need be, we are monstrous."

She backed away from Okwu as Okwu floated toward her. Then she turned and ran off. When she was gone, I sat down right there on the concrete, bringing my knees to my chest. It didn't matter if my long skirt got dirty, the hem was already burned.

"What did you do to your hand?" Okwu asked.

"I tried to smash my *edan* against a stone table," I said, resting my head on my knees. "I was really angry and it's more solid than it looks."

"I will go with you to the medic building," Okwu said.

━━━━

Nothing was broken, none of my fingers at least. Just bruised and swollen with one large bleeding cut that required a small flesh knit. The medic building student nurse, who looked like a large flower floating on a cloud of red mist, said I was lucky. *I would have been fine with all five fingers broken if I could have smashed my* edan, I thought, but I didn't really feel this way. What happened on Third Fish wasn't caused by the *edan* and the *edan was* why I was alive.

The first sun was setting by the time I got out of the hospital. "Thanks for waiting, Okwu," I said as we walked to the shuttle.

"There were airborne links in the lobby, so I finished my homework while I waited," Okwu said.

I had my satchel with my tablet, a capture station, some mini apples, lip oil, a palm-size container of my *otjize*. I needed my satchel wherever I went. But Okwu and those like it moved about not needing anything, having everything. I envied this. Okwu liked to say, "People like me are always complete."

I pinched my nose as we approached the shuttle. I was still getting used to these things. The shuttle tracks were made slick with a green oil called "narrow escape" that was secreted from huge black pitcher plants growing near the tracks. The plants stank of fresh blood and that smell triggered my flashbacks. I'd avoided Oomza shuttles for weeks, but swift transport busses weren't made for 500-mile journeys that needed to be made in minutes, so I had to get over myself.

Once on the shuttle, I was glad to easily find a seat made for someone near my size. Okwu hovered beside me with a group of other Meduse-like People. I gazed out the window as the busy sandstone towers and hive-like edifices of Central City began to retreat within moments. Then, we were zipping past the arid lands of purple grasses that surrounded Central City. I glimpsed the Oomza Station where professors met for professor-only meetings and debates, then it was gone.

I sat back and relaxed. Beside me Okwu was chatting with another Meduse-like creature. Okwu and those who hovered and had jelly-fish like domes, filling up the open areas of the shuttle with their gasses and barely substantial bodies, always became talkative when the shuttle was moving at its fastest. I wondered if this had to do with the fact that such People were most comfortable in space and when the shuttle was zipping forth at over 500 miles per hour, this was the closest they got to that while on Oomza.

I looked at my grimy burned skirt and wished I had a way to

feel at home that didn't require squatting in the dirt beside my dorm. I thought about when my mother would take me to the lake at night to look at the clusterwink snails when they spawned. These were my oldest memories. My mother and I had both stood there looking at the snails, and even back, at the age of four, I agreed with my mother that they looked like a galaxy. We counted the snails until the counting became something else for the both of us, from the water to outer space.

"Wish visiting home didn't have to include interstellar travel," I mumbled to myself. *Even as I got older everyone pulled back from me,* I thought. *Even my best friend Dele. I don't think even he realized he was doing it. We were all falling into our roles, our destiny in the community. We were no longer free* . . . and that was when my musings crossed that toxic boundary I'd crossed in Professor Okpala's office earlier in the day. It was like treeing, but it was carrying me instead of me carrying it. *I couldn't get off the ship.* I'd never been in space before and everyone around me was dead and I was only alive because of an intricate old dead device from a mystery metal.

I gasped and pressed my left hand to the shuttle's large round window, my bandaged hand to my chest. My heart was punching at my ribcage.

"Why are you so tense?"

I was still not used to the sound and feel of the Meduse language and, thankfully, its vibration cut right through to me.

"Tense?" I asked. "D-d-do I look tense?"

"Yes" Okwu said. "You've been tense since we left Math City. That's how I knew to come find you near your professor's office."

"I . . . was tense . . . I'm tense . . . I . . ." I giggled nervously, but even as the sound escaped me, I was seeing Heru's chest exploding, yet again. I turned squarely to Okwu and I saw all those Meduse around me only held from killing me because something about my *edan* was poison to them. I resisted the urge to grab my *edan* from my pocket and thrust it at Okwu.

"Binti! Hey!"

I looked around, glad for a reason to pull my eyes from Okwu.

"Back here! Behind you!" It was Haifa. She was sitting several seats back with her roommate, a Person who I only knew as the Bear.

I waved, pushing a smile on my face. "No, no," I said, when I saw her get up to come over to us. "It's too packed."

But Haifa was never one to avoid motion just because it was difficult. I think she actually liked the challenge. The Bear got up, too, though I didn't know why. Over the weeks, I'd run into the Bear several times in the bathroom, in the study room, eating lunch on the steps and not once had she spoken to me. When Haifa got to us, she boldly shoved the two Meduse-like people out of the way to get to my seat. The two People simply floated back to make space for them. I'll never get over the way Oomza Uni people do that on the shuttle. It's considered polite behavior. I dreaded the day someone shoved me aside to pass and I went sprawling to the floor.

"Okwu," Haifa said.

"Haifa," Okwu said.

"You know each other?" I asked.

"We're in all the same classes," Haifa said.

"I find Haifa annoying" Okwu said. "But I suspect she will make great weapons."

Haifa laughed loudly. "Even a Meduse is threatened by me because I'm just that genius. Everything is right in our universe."

Okwu blasted out a large cloud of gas and Haifa and I coughed. The adult human-sized giant bail of rough brown hair that was the Bear merely shuddered. "No Meduse would fear you, Haifa," Okwu said, its dome vibrated with laughter.

I tuned them out for the moment because I was climbing into the tree as I looked out the window. The shuttle was slowing down; we'd reached our stop. My thoughts went inward as I decided. To clear my mind, I worked an equation through my mind, Euler's identity, $e^{i\pi} + 1 = 0$, one of the most gorgeous formulas I knew. An equation that showed the connection between the most fundamental numbers in mathematics. It was the formula that connected all things because everything is mathematics. I slowly turned to Haifa as she said, "Come on, you two, this is our stop. Okwu, we'll see what's what when we get to exams. You know at the end of the year, we get to battle each other with the weapons we built?"

Okwu's dome thrummed harder and the three of them began to move to the front of the train. I didn't move. It was Okwu who stopped first. "Binti," Okwu said. "Come."

"No," I said. I retreated higher into the tree. And from there, I felt a clarity sharp as brittle crystal.

Okwu returned to me, as did Haifa and the Bear. The shuttle was stopping now. "Binti," Okwu said, switching to Meduse. "Get up."

"No."

"It's our stop," Haifa said. "We have to get off. We've all got homework. And you know what the next stop is and *that's* not even for another *hour*."

"No," I said, again. But even from the tree, my eyes welled up with tears. I gasped, wiped them away, but I didn't move.

"Is she alright?" Haifa asked, turning to the Bear. The Bear moved to me, but she still said nothing. The closeness of her hairy body made my right arm feel warm.

"What . . . what are you doing?" I asked. I stared at her.

When she spoke, her voice was muffled because it came through layers of hair. "Red desert is next stop, Himba girl."

"I know!" I said. And I said this from so deep in the tree that my voice must have resonated with it. Everyone getting off at the front of the shuttle stopped and turned to us.

"Okwu, move aside, I'll pick her up," Haifa screeched. "The shuttle's going to leave soon!"

Haifa took only one step toward me before she stopped. The current I called up zinged an inch from the Bear's hairs and both the Bear and Haifa moved back. We were the only ones left on the shuttle now. I held up my *edan* at Okwu, even if Okwu could withstand my current, my *edan* was poison to it. "I'm-not-getting-up," I growled. All that was going through my mind at this point was one word over and over, "Go." I needed to go. Away from my memories, away from my pain, away from my questions, go go go go go. I'd felt this only once in my life, back on the day I found my *edan*, when I felt my life was being controlled by everything but me. I'd wanted to dance and instead everyone else decided that I was not allowed.

"I'm going into the desert," I said, more tears falling from my eyes. Pleading. "I have to go to the desert. I have to. I have to go."

===

They stayed with me on the shuttle. My friends.

As it pulled off, I looked out the window and it was like I was leaving the planet. I watched us pass the Math City buildings and then our dorms. And then we were on our way, the only ones left on the shuttle. No one went to the red desert except those who were doing research and certainly not at this hour. And the final stop on this line was a small Oomza sterile swamp lab that was only active in the first morning because of the plants that used the evening time to digest everything in the area by the morning; no one went *there* at night, not even the shuttle, which stopped and returned an hour's walk away from the swamp.

"Well, what are we going to do in the desert?" Haifa asked.

"You don't have to do anything," I said. "Just stay on the shuttle until it goes back."

"We're not leaving you there," Okwu and Haifa said at the same time.

"You're really going to do this?" Haifa asked.

"Yes."

"You don't have any water," Okwu said.

I shrugged. Plus, I did have a capture station and a few mini apples in my satchel.

———

The shuttle stopped and in several alien languages including Meduse, some that vibrated and lit up the whole cab, it said, "Please exit the Shuttle." I got off before it got to the three human languages. I walked down the walkway on legs that felt like warm rubber. *What am I doing?* I thought. But at the same time, it felt so *good* to do something, to get off the tracks. I paused, flaring my nostrils. One of those pitcher plants that secreted shuttle track oil that smelled like blood was growing on the other side of the tracks. I shuddered, pinching my nose and quickly moving down the red metal walkway. It ended where the sand began. I stopped, looking out at the desert. Behind us, the shuttle zipped away, gone in seconds. The silence it left us in was so complete that it was like wearing noise-cancelling headgear. So much like home.

"This was *not* how I planned to spend my evening," Haifa said, walking past me. She broke into a sprint, jumped with her arms stretched in the air and launched into a series of flips.

"This place has no water," Okwu said, floating past me. "It is a dead place with no goddesses or gods and too many spirits."

The Bear brushed swiftly past me, seeming to run after Haifa who was still doing flips and laughing. "Come, show me what you can do!" Haifa shouted and the Bear began to spin like a top, flinging sand everywhere. Haifa laughed harder, spreading her arms out and letting the sand the Bear flung up hit her squarely in the face, her eyes and mouth closed.

I turned from them all and started walking into the Oomza Red Desert of Umoya. When I had arrived on Oomza Uni, in that

first week when I barely left my room, I'd obsessed over the hologram of the planet Oomza Uni on my astrolabe. I was acclimating
myself. When I saw it with my own eyes on that day when Third
Fish landed, after all that had happened, I'd wanted to know every
detail about the planet.

This desert was not very big, but if you were human you could
still die out here if you tried to cross it unprepared. If you didn't die
from the heat, then from the lack of water or the packs of roaming
dog-like creatures the size of baby camels called cams, though you
had to go in at least fifty miles to get to them.

I removed my sandals and dug my feet into the sand. It was just
like home—cool and soft, but beneath the surface, it became warm
like the flesh of a great beast. "Oh," I sighed, closing my eyes. How
I missed this. I called up a current and let it wash over my body like
a second skin. Then I walked, bits of sand occasionally popping
and sparking from my feet. The others followed.

We left the shuttle port behind. I left behind all the stares and
gossiping, the People that knew I'd been on a ship where everyone
had been killed and I'd been made genetically part of the killers. I
left Professor Okpala behind. I left behind the fact that I was further from home that I had ever been. I kept walking.

Behind me, Okwu and Haifa bickered about whether they
should grab me and risk getting zapped. The Bear's hair near the
bottom of her body grew full of sand and the sound of her gait got
heavier and heavier. Oomza had one large moon and it was lit by
the two suns, so the desert had plenty of white purple light. And
because all deserts have a certain sameness, no matter the planet, I
knew that after walking for what my astrolabe would have mea-
sured as a half earth hour, the land was about to change. My astrolabe would have shown this on its map, too, but I didn't look at
that. I didn't want maps here.

Okwu floated up to me and said, "Remove your current."

"No," I said.

"We are here with you," it said.

"We have no water, though," Haifa said, walking a few yards away. "At least I don't. These two will be fine out here, but you and I are gonna die." I brought out my capture station and tossed it to her. "Oh!" Haifa said. "Well, at least I know you're not completely suicidal."

I kept walking.

———

I stopped walking when I came to a dead and dried bush.

We'd been walking for three hours and I stopped the moment I no longer felt like screaming. I let my current dissipate and then I sat down right there in the sand. "May the Seven keep me sane," I whispered. And in that moment, they did. Haifa sat on the other side of the dried bush, facing me. The Bear, lowering herself beside her. Okwu hovered nearby me.

I threw my satchel to the side, glad to be rid of the weight. Despite the fact that Haifa had eaten most of my mini apples and was now carrying my capture station, my satchel seemed to have grown heavier by the minute as I'd walked. I looked at my arms, the desert air had dried the *otjize* on my skin and some of it was flaking off. I had been so focused on go go going that I hadn't noticed.

I brought out the small washcloth I always carried and my jar of *otjize*.

"Are you alright now?" Okwu asked, hovering close behind me.

I slowly used the washcloth to rub off the dried *otjize* from my arms and then I'd get to my face. Back home, I'd never have done this in front of my parents, let alone my friends. "I've dragged you all out here," I muttered. "Sorry." I touched my *okuoko* and more *otjize* flaked off. I could see the blue of them beneath it in the bright moonlight. I frowned.

"A nice walk usually makes me feel better," Haifa said. Then she laughed loudly and said, "Seriously, though, I hope we don't die out here." She laughed again.

"That would not be a respectable death," Okwu said.

I flaked more *otjize* off my *okuoko*. My left eye twitched and I grabbed one of my *okuoko*. It hurt. "Okwu," I said. "Why'd you do this to me?" I turned to it. I waited, breathing heavily. In the light of the moon, the smoothness of its blue dome perfectly reflected the sand.

"Our chief demanded it," Okwu said.

"But it's *my* body," I screamed at it. "I went into the Meduse ship for peace. Your people, you all just . . . why couldn't you have just *asked*?! Let . . . let *me* choose?!"

"Not everything can be a choice."

Five five five five five five. I calmed. I could see it even in the ripples of the sand. Back home, I'd been born able to tree and I'd been born with the skill to call up current, to harmonize. When I honed that skill, it bloomed with ease and joy because I was moving in the direction of the Seven. And so my family, my people decided my fate. Or so they thought.

I got up, my legs shaking. I stared at the dried bush. I broke the number sixty-four in half, broke it again, then again, then again as I called up a current. I held up my left hand, letting the current circulate in my palm like a tiny burning planet. Then I whipped my hand toward the dried bush and let it shoot right into its center. *Crack!*

"Binti!" Haifa exclaimed, jumping back as the bush burst into flame, lighting the desert around us. Okwu moved away, too. Not far behind Okwu, I saw something skitter away.

"Back home, the Himba view the *okuruwo* as the gateway to the Seven," I said, as the fire grew. The warmth it gave off was nice in the cooling desert air. "*Okuruwo* means 'sacred fire' in my language. The council elders keep it burning so that we are always connected to the Seven. Heat, fire, smoke, it all leads to the Seven." I stepped a few feet to my right so that I was in the path of the smoke as the breeze blew. I let the smoke wash over me. "Centuries ago, Himba women would take smoke baths because they believed it cleaned them more deeply than water," I said. *Yet it's unbreathable, like Okwu's gas*, I thought.

I brought out my *edan* and held it in my bandaged hand. I glared at it, the smoke obscuring me from the others for the moment as the desert night breeze blew. I touched the many points of its stellated cube form. It had saved my life and built a bridge of communication between myself and a prideful murderous tribe and I still didn't know what it was. If I hadn't found it in the desert back when I was eight years old, would I still be home?

A tiny bit of blood had seeped through my bandage, a tiny red flower. Like the red flower on Heru's chest. Instead of casting the thing into the fire, I opened my mouth and inhaled the fire's smoke. My chest felt as if I'd lit it afire and I coughed violently.

"Eeeeeeeeee!!"

I jumped, still coughing, unconsciously putting my *edan* in my pocket. Okwu, who'd been beside me, suddenly was not. I whirled around. Something near the fire was exploding! Haifa was jumping in the flames and tackling it.

The Bear had caught fire! I ran to Haifa who was rolling the Bear this way and that, trying to put out the Bear's hair. "Throw sand! Throw sand!" I shouted. Okwu started whirling around like a top. I'd never seen it do that. Its whirling sprayed the Bear with copious amounts of sand. I scuttled about throwing sand, too. And all through, the Bear continued shrieking, "Eeeeeeeeeeeeee!"

When the fire was out, the Bear was left with a large patch of her hair burned away, revealing a bald spot of black flesh just above one of her thick legs. I saw that the Bear actually had three thick stumpy brown legs, which explained how she moved so agilely.

I lay on the sand beside the Bear as she sighed softly. Haifa lay where the Bear's chest would have been had she had a chest. Okwu hovered beside us. "Fire can be an evil spirit," it said.

"Why'd you have to get so close?" Haifa breathed, looking angrily at the Bear.

"Fire's the gateway to the Seven," I said, staring at the sky.

"It beautiful," the Bear said.

"You should privilege life before beauty," Okwu said.

I rolled my eyes.

━━━━━

The Bear was okay. It turned out that within an hour, her hair began to grow back over the bald spot and the burned flesh, though still tender, was already healing. Her kind of People were hearty. I realized that her foolish behavior wasn't as perilous as it looked, just painful and a bit embarrassing. Even more fascinating, in a pouch near her chest, the Bear carried a sheer cloth-like thing that she could stretch into a large tent. The Bear was of a nomadic people who could sleep anywhere in comfort. With the items in my satchel and dragging my friends along, I'd come far more prepared for a night in one of Oomza Uni's deserts than I could have ever imagined.

It took the Bear minutes to set up what I could only call . . . a flesh tent. It wasn't part of her flesh, but it was made of her flesh, at least according to Haifa. The Bear placed the small square on the ground. It might have been a light purple, but in the firelight this was difficult to tell. The Bear stepped on the square and began to tap at different spots on it with her several toes. With each tap, a part of it unfolded and unfurled like the wings of a butterfly, until eventually the Bear stepped back and it was as if the thing had a life of its own . . . and really *did* become a delicate creature not so unlike a butterfly.

"What is this?" I asked, laughing, as I stepped up to it. The size of my dorm room, it was oval shaped with a sheer texture like a tinted bubble. I poked at it. "It feels like silk. Do you spin silk? That's beautiful!"

The Bear walked around it and then entered through an opening I hadn't noticed before.

"The Bear isn't going to *know* what silk is, Binti," Haifa said, following the Bear inside.

"Ancient Meduse used to carry these," Okwu said, following Haifa. "We called them *tinana*, 'in-body outside-home'."

I stood there for a moment, then grabbed my satchel and went inside. The tent's ground was spongy and I paused, immediately reminded of the Meduse ship. I put my satchel down beside me and sat down. I looked up at the sky, which I could see right through the membrane more clearly than with my naked eye.

"Some sleep then we head back to the shuttle before the sun comes up," Haifa said. "Binti, no arguing."

"I'm not." I turned to gaze at the fire, which was still raging.

"Well, just in case, you better start treeing or something, because if you freak out again, we *will* all definitely die out here," Haifa said.

Okwu was hovering before my satchel. "What are you doing," I asked, twisting to look up at it. Then my satchel twitched and right before my eyes, not four feet from my face, Okwu brought out its stinger. Now I was screaming for a second time in less than 24 earth hours, and I did it so loudly that I tasted blood in my throat. I stared at its stinger in horror as I rolled over and scrambled on my hands and knees to the other side of the tent. The Bear joined me there, hairs on her body shuddering against my arm. Haifa was on her feet, fists raised.

"I am *protecting* you, Binti," Okwu said. Its stinger was still out. White as a giant tooth, sharp because it was not only stinger, but also giant knife. My satchel kept twitching and Okwu leaned toward it.

"Maybe something crawled into it from outside," Okwu said.

"Do you have to have that . . . that thing out?" I asked. I let myself climb into the tree, grasping at the soothing equation of $f(x) = f(-x)$.

My satchel twitched again, this time enough to move the entire thing. "Binti," Haifa said. "You saw Zerlin, correct?"

"And two of her friends, yes . . . I did," I said. "In Math City, just outside the building my professor's office is in."

"Were any of them near your satchel? At any time? Even for a second?"

I thought about it. The clarity of the tree made it easy to play it all back. "Yes, sort of. Zerlin. She came up next to me, when I was trying to put out my skirt. Come to think of it, I thought she was trying to steal my satchel."

Suddenly, Haifa raised her voice in a battle cry. She ran at my satchel, grabbed it and ran then leaped out of the tent. She tumbled and threw the satchel toward the fire. It landed just far enough to not burst into flame.

I ran out. "My *otjize's* in there." Still treeing, I was calm enough to take it all in. Okwu and the Bear came out, too.

"Yeah, well, I still should have thrown it right in the fire because something else is in there, too," Haifa said, still breathing hard. "*Alghaza* . . . invaders. Burrowing Oomza insects who when they get in your dorm room will turn everything upside down when they can't find a way out of the room immediately. Zerlin probably put them in there. It's something students like to do to new students. She deserves to be hit with many shoes."

I blinked with surprise. Then I burst out laughing. Back home, "deserving to be hit with many shoes" was an expression I only heard the elders use.

My satchel twitched violently and then in the firelight, a rip appeared in the side. They were large like scarab beetles and even in the firelight I could see that they were a bright metallic green with golden legs. Six of them emerged from my satchel, all in a line. They moved, then stopped, moved then stopped, all in unison, as if hearing and dancing to some sort of music. Their insectile feet ground on the sand loudly enough to hear from where I stood as they emerged from my satchel one by one.

Crunch crunch crunch . . . crunch crunch crunch . . . crunch crunch

crunch. When the last insect came out, on the third crunch, it hooked its leg to my satchel and with incredible strength for an insect of this size, flipped my satchel over a yard away.

"What'll they do now?" Haifa said. "I saw someone's dorm room infested with these and they went right to turning the place upside down. What if there's nothing to turn upside down?"

The bugs began to trudge around the fire in a strange procession. For over five minutes, they *crunch crunch crunch* stopped *crunch crunch crunch* stopped. Okwu lost interest and went back into the tent where it hovered low, resting.

"Are they going to do that all night?" Haifa groaned. Then eventually she went back into the tent, too. The Bear and I stayed and watched. The Bear, like me, was a mathematics student and I knew she saw it, too. The insects walked and stopped in a series of three walks to one stop. They stayed an exact distance from each other. And they moved around the fire that was so precise that after a while there was a deepening groove of circular perfection.

Then, just like that one of them opened its wings and slowly, very very noisily flew off into the darkness beyond the firelight. The noise was so loud that I could still hear it when another decided to do the same thing. "Haifa, Okwu, look!" Then another one slowly flew off. And another. The last one walked a full circle around the fire and then it too flew off. Judging from the buzzing noise, the others had waited for the last one to join them. Then gradually, their noise faded into the darkness along with their shiny bodies.

"So *that's* what *alghaza* do when out in the open!" Haifa said, looking up off into the darkness of the desert.

"A bird can't fly in a cage?" I said. It was one of my ex-best friend Dele's favorite quotes. The Bear and I looked at the night sky for a little longer and when nothing else buzzed or glinted in the firelight, we went into the tent. I fell asleep minutes after drinking a cup of capture station water. I slept deep and I slept well. The desert always has the answers.

I woke to the sound of my astrolabe buzzing softly from inside my satchel. I opened my eyes to the first sun shining through the sheer material of the Bear's tent. I was resting my head on my satchel and the sound was annoying. "Quiet," I whispered. "I'm up." My astro-labe stopped buzzing.

Feet away, the Bear stood, snoring softly and beside her Haifa was sprawled out, also deep in sleep. I wiped my eyes and rolled onto my back and stretched. Something was on my toe. I gasped when I looked. A sand-colored small bat-like creature with a wide head that reminded me of a camel was looking back at me. In its strange mouth, it carried a golden *alghaza* eggshell it must have fished from my satchel. It snapped it up as it eyed me, its furry body warm on my toe. I grinned, slowly sitting up. "You're an usu ogu!"

Taking care not to move my leg, I slowly reached into my satchel and brought out my jar of *otjize*. The creature cocked its head; it didn't seem to fear me at all, which was no surprise. Usu ogu were said to be quite intelligent and this one clearly understood that none of us were a threat . . . or maybe that eggshell was just that delicious. I opened the jar and dipped a finger inside. I brought my *edan* from my pocket and rubbed the bit of *otjize* on the point of the *edan* with the spiral that always reminded me of a fingerprint. Slow circular motions. I dropped into mathematical trance, a cold stone in cold water; I climbed into the tree, splitting and multiply-ing. I aimed my blue current into the *edan* and on its own, it con-nected with the usu ogu.

It turned to me. "You smell of smoke. You must be a spirit."

"I'm Binti," I said. "Who are you?"

"Usu ogu are usu ogu," it said. "It only matters what I do."

"And what do you do?" I asked.

"I fly."

And with that, it flew into the air, circled the tent once, turned sideways and zipped through the closed tent flap. My current broke from the usu ogu the moment it was outside. The flap opened again, this time wide. "Simple-minded foolish thing," Okwu said, as it entered. "Of course, it matters who you are."

I laughed, got up and shook the rest of the *alghaza* eggshells from my satchel. I gathered them up and took them outside. They glinted beautifully in the sunshine; even the eggs of *alghaza* hinted that the creatures were supposed to be outdoors. No wonder they were so destructive when they hatched in dorm rooms. I paused and looked at the ash of last night's makeshift sacred fire.

Back home on Earth, the sacred fire was never allowed to burn out. It was the burning path to the Seven. Here on the university planet known as Oomza Uni, my path to the Seven had to be different. I touched the tip of my sandal to the ashes. *My sacred fire will be this desert*, I thought. *It never stops burning, even at night the sand is warm beneath the surface. I can always come here when I need to. And my community will be my friends. Who else would come into the desert with me? That is love.*

I dropped the eggshells onto the ash and brought out my *edan*. "Are you alive? Will you hatch and then make trouble for me like an *alghaza*?" I asked it. Then I chuckled and put it back in my pocket. I didn't think about those two questions for a long time.

BINTI
HOME

"Five, five, five, five, five, five," I whispered. I was already treeing, numbers whipping around me like grains of sand in a sandstorm, and now I felt a deep click as something yielded in my mind. It hurt sweetly, like a knuckle cracking or a muscle stretching. I sunk deeper and there was warmth. I could smell the earthy aroma of the *otjize* I'd rubbed on my skin and the blood in my veins.

The room dropped away. The awed look on my mathematics professor Okpala's face dropped away. I was clutching my *edan*, the points of its stellated shape digging into the palms of my hands. "Oh, my," I whispered. Something was happening to it. I opened my cupped palms. If I had not been deep in mathematical meditation, I'd have dropped it, I'd not have *known* not to drop it.

My first thought was of a ball of ants I'd once seen tumbling down a sand dune when I was about six years old; this was how desert ants moved downhill. I had run to it for a closer look and squealed with disgusted glee at the undulating living mass of ant bodies. My *edan* was writhing and churning like that ball of desert ants now, the many triangular plates that it was made of flipping, twisting, shifting right there between my palms. The blue current I'd called up was hunting around and between them like a worm. This was a new technique that Professor Okpala had taught me and I'd gotten quite good at it over the last two months. She even called it the "wormhole" current because of the shape and the fact that you had to use a metric of wormholes to call it up.

Breathe, I told myself. The suppressed part of me wanted to lament that my *edan* was being shaken apart by the current I was running through it, that I should stop, that I would never be able to put it back together. Instead, I let my mouth hang open and I whispered the soothing number again, "Five, five, five, five, five." *Just breathe, Binti,* I thought. I felt a waft of air cross my face, as if something passed by. My eyelids grew heavy. I let them shut . . .

══════

. . . I was in space. Infinite blackness. Weightless. Flying, falling, ascending, traveling through a planet's ring of brittle metallic dust. It pelted my skin, fine chips of stone. I opened my mouth a bit to breathe, the dust hitting my lips. Could I breathe? Living breath bloomed in my chest from within me and I felt my lungs expand, filling with it. I relaxed.

"Who are you?" a voice asked. It spoke in the dialect of my family and it came from everywhere.

"Binti Ekeopara Zuzu Dambu Kaipka of Namib, that is my name," I said.

Pause.

I waited.

"There's more," the voice said.

"That's all," I said, irritated. "That's my name."

"No."

The flash of anger that spurted through me was a surprise. Then it was welcome. I knew my own name. I was about to scream this when . . .

══════

. . . I was back in the classroom. Sitting before Professor Okpala. *I was so angry,* I thought. *Why was I so angry?* It was a horrible feeling, that fury. Back home, the priestesses of the Seven might even have called this level of anger unclean. Then one of my tentacle-like *okuoko* twitched. Outside, the second sun was setting. Its shine blended with the other sun's, flooding the classroom with a color I loved, a vibrant

combination of pink and orange that the native people of Oomza Uni called "ntu ntu." Ntu ntu bugs were an Oomza insect whose eggs were a vibrant orange-pink that softly glowed in the dark.

The sunlight shined on my *edan*, which floated before me in a network of current, a symmetry of parts. I'd never seen it disassemble like this and making it do so had not been my intention. I'd been trying to get the object itself to communicate with me by running current between its demarcations. Okpala claimed this often worked and I wanted to know what my *edan* would say. I had a moment of anxiety, frantically thinking, *Can I even put it back together?*

Then I watched with great relief as the parts of my *edan* that had detached slowly, systematically reattached. Whole again, the *edan* set itself down on the floor before me. *Thank the Seven*, I thought.

Both the blue from the current I still ran around it and the bright ntu ntu shined on Okpala's downturned face. She had an actual notebook and pencil in hand, so Earth basic. And she was writing frantically, using one of the rough thick pencils she'd made from the branch of the tamarind-like tree that grew outside the mathematics building.

"You fell out of the tree," she said, not looking up. This was how she referred to that moment when you were treeing and then suddenly were not. "What was that about? You finally had the *edan* willing to open itself."

"That's what it was doing? That was a good thing, then?"

She only chuckled to herself, still writing.

I frowned and shook my head. "I don't know . . . something happened." I bit my lip. "Something happened." When she looked up, she caught my eye and I had a moment where I wondered whether I was her student or a piece of research.

I allowed my current to fade, shut my eyes and rested my mind by thinking the soothing equation of $f(x) = f(-x)$. I touched the *edan*. Thankfully, solid again.

"Are you alright?" Professor Okpala asked.

Despite medicating with the soothing equation, my head had started pounding. Then a hot rage flooded into me like boiled water. "Ugh, I don't know," I said, rubbing my forehead, my frown deepening. "I don't think what happened was supposed to happen. Something happened, Professor Okpala. It was strange."

Now Professor Okpala laughed. I clenched my teeth, boiling. Again. Such fury. It was unlike me. And lately, it was *becoming* like me, it happened so often. Now it was happening when I treed? How was that even possible? I didn't like this at all. Still, I'd been working with Professor Okpala for over one Earth year and if there was one thing I should have learned by now it was that working with any type of *edan*, no matter the planet it had been found on, meant working with the unpredictable. "Everything comes with a sacrifice," Okpala liked to say. Every *edan* did something different for different reasons. My *edan* was also poisonous to Meduse; it had been what saved my life when they'd attacked on the ship. It was why Okwu never came to watch any of my sessions with Okpala. However, touching it had no such effect on me. I'd even chanced touching my *okuoko* with my *edan*. It was the one thing that let me know that a part of me may now have been Meduse, but I was still human.

"That was isolated deconstruction," Professor Okpala said. "I've only heard of it happening. Never seen it. Well done."

She said this so calmly. *If she's never seen it happen before, why is she acting like I did something wrong*, I wondered. I flared my nostrils to calm myself down. No, this wasn't like me at all. My tentacle twitched again and a singular very solid thought settled in my mind: *Okwu is about to fight.* An electrifying shiver of rage flew through me and I jumped. Who was trying to bring him harm? Staining to sound calm, I said, "Professor, I have to go. May I?"

She paused, frowning at me. Professor Okpala was Tamazight, and from what my father said of selling to the Tamazight, they were a people of few but strong words. This may have been a generalization, but with my professor, it was accurate. I knew Professor Okpala well; there was a galaxy of activity behind that frown. However, I had to go and I had to go now. She held up a hand and waved it. "Go."

I got up and nearly crashed into the potted plant behind me as I turned awkwardly toward my backpack.

"Careful," she said. "You're weak."

I gathered my backpack and was off before she could change her mind. Professor Okpala was not head professor of the mathematics department for nothing. She'd calculated everything probably the day she met me. It was only much much later that I realized the weight of that brief warning.

====

I took the solar shuttle.

With the second sun setting, the shuttle was at its most charged and thus its most powerful. The university shuttle was snakelike in shape, yet spacious enough to comfortably accommodate fifty people the size of Okwu. Its outer shell was made from the molted cuticle of some giant creature that resided in one of the many Oomza forests. I'd heard that the body of the shuttle was so durable, a crash wouldn't even leave a scratch on it. It rested and traveled on a bed of "narrow escape," slick green oil secreted onto a track way by several large pitcher plants growing beside the station.

I'd always found those huge black plants terrifying, they looked like they'd eat you if you got too close. And they surrounded themselves with a coppery stink that smelled so close to blood that the first time I came to the station, I had what I later understood was a panic attack. I'd stood on the platform staring blankly as I held that smell in my nose. Then came the flashes of memory from that time so vivid . . . I could smell the freshly spilled blood. Memories from when I was in the dining room of a ship in the middle of outer space where everyone had just been viciously murdered by Meduse.

I had not ridden the shuttle that day. I didn't ride it for many weeks, opting to take swift transport, a sort of hovering bus that was actually much slower and used for shorter journeys. When I couldn't stand the slowness and decided to try the solar shuttle again, I'd pinched my nose and breathed through my mouth until I got onboard. Once we started moving, the smell went away.

A native operated the scanner and I handed her my astrolabe to scan. She narrowed her wide blue eyes and looked at me down her small nose, as if she didn't see me take this shuttle often enough to know my schedule. She batted one of my *okuoko* with a finger; her hands were bigger than my head. Then she rubbed the *otjize* between her fingers and motioned for me to enter the shuttle's cabin.

I sat where I always sat, in the section for people my size near one of the large round windows, and strapped myself in. The shuttle traveled five hundred to a thousand miles per hour, depending on how charged it was. I'd be in Weapons City in fifteen minutes and I hoped it wasn't too late, because Okwu was planning to kill his teacher.

═══════

The moment the house-sized lift rumbled open I ran out, my sandaled feet slapping the smooth off-white marble floor. The room was vast and high ceilinged with rounded walls, all cut into the thick toothlike marble. I coughed, my lungs burning. Wan, a Meduse-like person, was feet away, engulfed in a great lavender plume of its breathing gas. It didn't have Okwu's hanging tentacles, but Wan still looked like a giant version of the jellyfish who lived in the lake near my home on Earth. Wan also spoke Okwu's language of Meduse. I'd been down here plenty of times to meet Okwu, so it knew me, too.

"Wan, tell me where Okwu is," I demanded in Meduse.

It puffed its gas down the hallway. "There," Wan said. "Presenting to Professor Dema against Jalal today."

I gasped, understanding. "Thanks, Wan."

But Wan was already heading to the lift. I pulled my wrapper above my ankles and sprinted down the hallway. To my left and right, students from various parts of the galaxy were working on their own final projects of protective weaponry, the assignment this quarter. Okwu's was body armor, its close classmate Jalal's was electrical current.

Okwu and Jalal were taught together, stayed in the same dorm, and worked closely together on their projects. And today, they were being tested against each other, as was the way of Oomza Weapons Education. I was fascinated by the competitive push and pull of weapons learning, but I was glad mathematics was more about harmony. Okwu being Okwu—a Meduse of rigid cold honor, focus, and tradition—loved the program. The problem was that Okwu hated its professor and Professor Dema hated Okwu. Okwu was Meduse and Professor Dema, a human woman, was Khoush. Their people had hated and killed each other for centuries. Tribal hatred lived, even in Oomza Uni. And today that hatred, after simmering for a year, was coming to a head.

I reached the testing space just as Okwu, encased in a metallic skin, brought forth its white and sharp stinger and pointed it at Professor Dema. Feet away, Professor Dema stood, carrying a large gunlike weapon with both her hands and a snarl on her lips. This was not the way final exams were supposed to go.

"Okwu, what are you doing?" Jalal demanded in Meduse. She stood to the side, clutching a series of what looked like thick fire-tipped sticks with her mantislike claws. "You'll kill her!"

"Let us finish this once and for all," Okwu growled in Meduse.

"Meduse have no respect," Okwu's professor said in Khoush. "Why they allowed you into this university is beyond me. You're unteachable."

"I've tolerated your insulting remarks all quarter. Let me end you. Your people should not plague this university," Okwu said.

My lungs were laboring from the gas Okwu was copiously

breathing out as it prepared to attack its professor. If it didn't stop doing this, the entire room would be filled with it. I could see Professor Dema's eyes watering as she resisted coughing as well. I knew Okwu. It was doing this on purpose, enjoying the strained look on Professor Dema's face. I only had seconds to do something. I threw myself before Okwu, pressing myself to the floor before its *okuoko*, which hung just below its weaponized casing. I looked up at Okwu; its tentacles were soft and heavy on the side of my face. Meduse immediately understand prostration.

"Okwu, hear me," I said in Khoush. Since arriving at the university, I'd taught Okwu to speak Khoush and my language of Otji-himba and it hated the sound of both. My theory is that this was partially due to the fact that for Okwu the sound of any language was inferior to Meduse. On top of this, Okwu had to produce the words through the tube between its *okuoko* that blew out the gas it used to breathe in air-filled atmospheres, and doing so was difficult and felt unnatural. Speaking to Okwu in Khoush was irritating to it and thus the best way to get its attention.

I called up a current, treeing faster than I ever could have back home. I'd learned much from Professor Okpala in the last year. My *okuoko* tickled, the current touching them and then reaching for Okwu's *okuoko*. Suddenly, I felt that anger again, and some part of me deep down firmly accused, "Unclean, Binti, you are unclean!" I gnashed my teeth as I fought to stay in control. When I could not, I simply let go. My voice burst from me clear and loud; in Khoush, I shouted, "Stop! Stop it right now!" I felt my *okuoko* standing on end, writhing like the clusters of mating snakes I often saw in the desert back home. I must have looked like a crazed witch; I felt like one, too.

Immediately, Okwu brought down its stinger, stopped pluming gas, and moved away from me. "Stay there, Binti," it said. "If you touch my casing, you will die."

Professor Dema brought down her weapon as well.

Silence.

I lay there on the floor, mathematics cartwheeling through my brain, current still touching my only true friend on the planet even after a year. I felt the tension leave the room, leaving myself, too, finally. Tears of relief fell from the corners of my eyes as my strange random anger drained away. My *okuoko* stopped writhing. There were others in the cavernous workspace, watching. They would talk, word would spread, and this would be another reminder to students, human and nonhuman, to keep their distance from me, even if they liked me well enough.

Okwu's close classmate Jalal put down her weapons and hopped back. Professor Dema threw her gun to the floor and pointed at Okwu. "Your casing is spectacular. You will leave it here and download your recipe for it to my files. But if we meet outside this university where I am not your teacher and you are not my student, one of us will die and it will *not* be me."

I heard Okwu curse at her in Meduse so deep that I couldn't understand exactly what it said. Before I could admonish Okwu's crudeness, Professor Dema snatched up her weapon and shot at Okwu. It made a terrible boom that shook the walls and sent students fleeing. Except Okwu. The wall directly to its left now had a hole larger than Okwu's nine-foot-tall five-foot-wide jellyfish-like body. Chunks and chips of marble crumbled to the floor and dust filled the air.

"You didn't miss," Okwu said in Khoush. Its tentacles shook and its dome vibrated. Laughter.

Minutes later, Okwu and I left the Weapons City Inverted Tower Five. Me with ringing ears and a headache and Okwu with a grade of Outstanding for its final project in Protective Gear 101.

━━━

Once on the surface, I looked at Okwu, wiped marble dust and *otjize* from my face, and said, "I need to go home. I'm going to go on my pilgrimage." I felt the air close to my skin; once I got back to my dorm room and washed up, I'd reapply my *otjize*. I'd take extra time to palm roll a thick layer onto my *okuoko*.

"Why?" Okwu asked.

I'm unclean because I left home, I thought. *If I go home and complete my pilgrimage, I will be cleansed. The Seven will forgive me and I'll be free of this toxic anger.* Of course, I didn't say any of this to Okwu. I only shook my head and stepped into the field of soft water-filled maroon plants that grew over the Inverted Tower Five. Sometimes, I came here and sat on the plants, enjoying the feeling of buoyancy that reminded me of sitting on a raft in the lake back home.

"I'll come too," Okwu said.

I looked at it. "You'll land in a Khoush airport, if you're even allowed on the ship. And they'll . . ."

"The treaty," it said. "I'll go as an ambassador for my people. No Meduse has been on Earth since the war with the Khoush. I'd be coming in peace." It thrummed deep in its dome and then added, "But if the Khoush make war, I will stir it with them, like you stir your *otjize*."

I grunted. "No need for that, Okwu. The peace treaty should be enough. Especially if Oomza Uni endorses the trip. And you come with me." I smiled. "You can meet my family! And I can show you where I grew up and the markets and . . . yes, this is a good idea."

Professor Okpala would certainly approve. A harmonizer harmonized. Bringing Okwu in peace to the land of the people its people had fought would be one of the ten good deeds Okpala had insisted I perform within the academic cycle as part of being a good Math Student. It would also count as the Great Deed I was to do in preparation for my pilgrimage.

Humans. Always Performing

Two weeks later, I powered up the transporter and said a silent prayer. The Seven were in the soil of my home and I was planets away from that home. Would they even hear me? I believed they would; the Seven could be in many places at once and bring all places with them. And they would protect me because I was a Himba returning home.

Still, my transporter did nothing. I stood there, out of breath, staring at the coin-sized flat stone. I'd rolled my hard-shelled pod into the lift and then across the dormitory hall to the entrance. The effort had left me sweaty and annoyed. Now this. The shuttle was a half-mile walk down the uneven rocky pathway. I'd been looking forward to the fresh air before the days on the ship. However, the walk wouldn't be so pleasant if I had to push my heavy traveling pod up the pathway. I knelt down and touched the transponder, again.

Nothing.

I pressed it hard, knowing this wouldn't yield any better result. It wasn't the pressure of the touch that activated it, but the contact with my index fingerprint.

Still nothing.

My face grew hot and I hissed with anger. I brought my foot back and kicked the transporter as hard as I could. It shot into the bushes. I froze with my mouth hanging open, astonished by my actions and the deep satisfaction they yielded. Then I ran to the bushes and started pushing the leaves near the ground this way and that, hoping to spot the tiny thing.

"Don't do that, you'll get all dirty before you're even on the ship," someone said from behind me as strong hands grasped my shoulders and gently pulled me back. It was Haifa. "Let me help you."

"All the way to the shuttle station?" I said, with a laugh.

"I've been studying all day," she said. "I need the exercise." She was wearing a tight green body suit made of a material so thin that I could see the bulging muscles on her long graceful arms and legs. Her astrolabe was attached to a clip sewn into her suit. As with the astrolabes of almost every student in my dorm, I'd tuned up its design and performance and now hers shined like polished metal and operated in a way more suited to her meticulous plodding way of thinking.

Haifa was much taller than me and one of those people who found motion so easy that she couldn't resist moving all the time. The day I met her, after asking me many questions about my *okuoko*, she'd told me that though she'd always been female, she'd been born physically male. Later, when she was thirteen, she'd had her body transitioned and reassigned to female. She'd joked that this process took longer than my getting stung in the back with a stinger to become part Meduse. "But it's why I get to be so tall," she'd bragged.

Every morning, she jogged several miles and then lifted logs at the lumberyard up the road. "The better to compete with people from other places," she now said, stepping to my pod. "Not easy being a human in the weapons department; we're so weak. Plus, I owe you," she said, gesturing to her astrolabe.

She started rolling my pod before I could say "yes," her thick black braids bouncing against her back. As she went, I swiped *otjize* from my forehead with my index finger, knelt down and touched the finger to the red Oomza soil, grounding the *otjize* into it. "Thank you," I whispered. I ran to catch up with Haifa, clutching my satchel to the side of my long silky red-orange wrapper.

"You think your family is going to like your new hairstyle?" Haifa asked, as she pushed and rolled the pod over the rocky path. A large succulent plant pulled in one of its branches as we passed it.

"It's not hair," I said. "They're—"

"I know, I know," she said, rolling her eyes. "I'm being obnoxious. How come you're going home so soon, anyway?"

I stepped over a particularly large stone. "It's just time."

She looked over her shoulder at me as she rolled my pod. "Why isn't that monster here to help you? Does he know you're going?"

I rolled my eyes. "I'm meeting Okwu at the launch port."

"How did it score top of the class on the quarter final? I hear it paid off the professor."

I laughed, nearly jogging to keep up now. "Don't believe everything you hear."

"Or just carry a big gun at all times so that people will always tell the truth," she said, giving the pod a push.

About a hundred meters from the shuttle station, Haifa decided to outdo herself by picking up my pod and sprinting with it. When she reached the front of the shuttle station, she put the pod down, did a graceful backflip, and gleefully jumped up and clicked her heels. A few people waiting at the shuttle platform applauded with whistles, flashes of light, and slapping tentacles. Haifa took a dramatic bow for them. "I am amazing," she declared, as I walked up to her.

A person who looked like a two-foot-tall version of a praying mantis clicked its powerful forelegs. In a sonorous voice, it said, "Humans. Always performing."

The shuttle arrived, gliding on the smooth green oil path, and the five people waiting crowded quickly onboard. I was last to board, pinching my nose to avoid the blood smell of the pitcher plants. Haifa loaded my pod inside for me, gave me a tight hug, and leapt through the large round shuttle window near the entrance like a missile. Moments later, the shuttle got moving; it never waited for long. "Tell Okwu I send my insults!" Haifa shouted as the shuttle passed her. She started to run alongside the shuttle and for a moment, she kept up.

"I will," I said.

"Safe travels, Binti! No fear, Master Harmonizer, just as you belonged in the desert that night, you belong in space!" Haifa shouted and then the shuttle left her in its wake of blasted air, which blew her thick braids back. Holding on to the rail beside me, I turned and watched as we sped away from her. She did one more flip and waved enthusiastically. Then she was gone because we'd reached the day's cruising speed of seven hundred miles per hour.

I stood there for a moment, feeling the usual moment of lightheadedness as the shuttle stabilized its passengers, and then I quickly went to my assigned window seat. I had to squeeze past two furry individuals and they protested when my *otjize* rubbed off on their furry feet and one of my *okuoko* brushed one in the furry face.

"Sorry," I said, in response to their growls.

"We've heard about you," one said in gruff Meduse. "You're a hero, but we didn't know you were so . . . soily."

"It's not soil, its—" I sighed and smiled and just said, "Thank you." Both of their astrolabes began to sing. They grabbed them and began another conversation among themselves and four others projected before them in a language I didn't understand. I sat down and turned to the window.

Fifteen minutes later, when we stopped in Weapons City, I met up with Okwu, who was coming from a meeting with its professor; somehow the two hadn't killed each other and I was thankful. *One day the Meduse and the Khoush will get over themselves*, I thought. The treaty was a good start.

An hour later, we arrived at the launch station. And that's when I began to feel ill.

━━━━

The three university medical center doctors who'd examined me said I was suffering from post-traumatic stress disorder because of what happened on the ship last year. For the first few weeks, I was okay, but eventually I started having nightmares, day terrors, I'd see red and then Heru's chest bursting open. Sometimes, just looking at Okwu made me want to vomit, though I never told it this was happening. And then, months later, there were the random instances of intense focused fury that invaded my usually calm mind.

Eventually, Okwu and I were ordered by the departments of mathematics and weapons to see therapists. Okwu never mentioned how its sessions went and I didn't ask. You just don't ask a Meduse about such things. I doubt it told any of its family, either. In turn, Okwu never asked about my sessions.

My therapist was named Saidia Nwanyi. She was a short squat Khoush woman who liked to sing to herself when no one was around. I learned this on my first visit to her office. It was in Math City, so a five-minute walk from my class. I was uncomfortable that day. Similar to the Meduse, in my family, one does not go to a stranger and spill her deepest thoughts and fears. You go to a family member and if not, you hold it in, deep, close to the heart, even if it tore you up inside. However, I wasn't home and the university was not making seeing a therapist a choice, it was an order. Plus, despite the fact that it made me extremely uncomfortable, I knew I needed help.

So I went and as I approached her office, I heard her singing. I stopped and listened. Then the tears came. The song she sang was an old Khoush song the women, Khoush or Himba, sang as they went into the desert to hold conversation with the Seven. I'd heard my mother sing it for weeks whenever she returned. I'd heard my oldest sister sing it to herself, as she polished astrolabe parts for the shop. I'd sung the song to myself whenever I snuck into the desert.

I entered Dr. Nwanyi's office with wet cheeks and she'd smiled, firmly shaken my hand, and closed the door behind me. That first day, we talked for an hour about my family, Himba customs, and the rigid expectations placed especially on girls in both Himba and Khoush families. She was so easy to talk to and I learned more about the Khoush that day than I had in my entire life. In some ways, Himba and Khoush were like night and day, but in matters of girlhood and womanhood and control, we were the same. What a surprise this was to me. That first day, we didn't talk about what happened on the ship at all and I was glad. Afterward, I walked to my dorm room feeling like I'd visited a place close to home.

Eventually, we did go deep into my experiences on the ship and doing so brought up such rawness. Over those months with Dr. Nwanyi, I learned why sleep was so difficult, why my heart would beat so hard for no reason, why I'd walked into the Oomza desert that day, why I had such a tough time at solar shuttle platforms, and why I couldn't bear the thought of boarding a ship. But now, something had shifted in me. I was ready to go home. I needed to go home.

The day after the showdown between Okwu and its professor, I'd made an appointment with Haras, the University Chief. When we met, I told it how urgent my need was and Haras understood. Within a week, the university had given Okwu permission to travel and gained agreement from the Khoush city of Kokure and my hometown of Osemba to allow Okwu to visit as an ambassador. Okwu would be the first Meduse to come to Khoushland in peace.

The swiftness of these arrangements astonished me, but I moved with it all. One does not question good fortune. Home was calling, as was the Earth desert into which I would go with the other Himba girls and women on pilgrimage. Okwu and I were issued tickets to Earth not long after quarter's end. My therapist, Dr. Nwanyi, hadn't wanted me to go so soon, but I insisted and insisted and insisted.

"Just make sure you breathe," she'd said as I left her office hours before the journey. "Breathe."

Launch

I followed Okwu through the enormous entrance to the Oomza Uni West Launch Port. Immediately, my sharp eyes found the doorways to docked ships far beyond the drop-off zone, ticketing and check-in stations and terminals. I opened my mouth to take in a deep lungful of air and instead coughed hard; Okwu had just decided to let out a large cloud of its gas.

When I finally stopped coughing and my eyes focused on the docked ships, my heart began to beat like a talking drum played by the strongest drummer. I rubbed some *otjize* with my index finger from my cheek and brought it to my nose and inhaled, exhaled, inhaled, exhaled its sweet aroma. My heart continued its hard beat, but at least it slowed some. Okwu was already at check-in and I quickly got behind him.

The Oomza West Launch Port was nothing like the Kokure Launch Port back home. The hugeness of it was breathtaking. Since coming to Oomza Uni, I'd seen buildings of a size that I couldn't previously have imagined. The vastness of the desert easily surpassed these structures, but where the desert was a creation of the Seven, these buildings were not.

The great size of the Oomza West Launch Port was secondary to the great diversity of its travelers. Back at Kokure, almost every traveler and employee was human and I had been the only Himba in a sea of Khoush. Here, everyone was everything . . . at least to my still fresh eyes. I was seventeen years old and I had been at Oomza Uni for only one of those years now, having spent the previous all on Earth among my self-isolating Himba tribe in the town of Osemba. I barely even knew the Khoush city of Kokure, though it was only thirty miles from my home.

The launch port was like a cluster of bubbles, each section its own waiting space for those in transit. There were whole terminals that I could not enter, because the gas they were filled with was not breathable to me. One terminal was encased in thick glass and the inside looked as if it were filled with a wild red hurricane, the people inside it flying about like insects.

Just from standing in line and looking around, I saw people of many shapes, sizes, organisms, wavelengths, and tribes here. I saw no humans like me, though. And if I *had* seen a fellow Himba, it was doubtful that I'd see any with Meduse tentacles instead of hair. Being in this place of diversity and movement was overwhelming, but I felt at home, too . . . as long as I didn't look at the ships.

"Binti and Okwu?" the ticketing agent enthusiastically said in Meduse through a small box on her large dome. She was a creature somewhat like Okwu, jellyfish-like and the size of a storage shed, except her dome was a deep shade of black and she had antennae at the center with a large yellow eye. Over the last year, I'd learned (well, brashly been told) that the females of this group of people had the long antenna with the yellow eyes. The males simply had a large green eye on their dome, no antenna. This one used her eye to stare at Okwu and me with excitement.

"Yes," I responded in the language of my people.

"Oh, how exciting," she said, switching to Otjihimba, too. "I will tell all my male mates about today . . . and maybe even a few of my female ones, too!" She paused for a moment looking at her astrolabe sitting on the counter and then the screen embedded in the counter. The screen hummed softly and complex patterns of light flashed on it and moved in tiny rotating circles. As I watched, my harmonizer mind automatically assigned numbers to each shape and equations to their motions. The agent switched back to Meduse, "Today, you'll be—" She paused, letting out a large burst of gas. I frowned. "You will both be traveling on the human-geared ship, the Third Fish. Do you . . ."

The talking drum in my chest began to beat its rhythm of distress, again.

"That's the ship we came in on," Okwu said.

"Yes. She may have experienced tragedy that day, but she still loves to travel."

I nodded. The Third Fish was a living thing. Why should she die or stop flying because of what happened? Still, of all ships for us to travel on, why the same one inside which so much death had happened and we'd both nearly died?

"Is . . . is this alright?" the agent asked. "The university has given you two lifetime travel privileges, we can put you on any ship . . . but the time may . . ."

"I do not mind," Okwu said.

I nodded. "Okay. Me neither. The spirits and ghosts of the dead don't stay where they're freed." I felt my right eye twitch slightly.

"Great," the ticketing agent said. "You've both been given premium rooms near the pilot quarters."

I hesitated and then stepped forward. "Is there any way I can have . . . the room I had on the way here?"

The agent's eye bent toward me and she released a small cloud of gas. "Why? I . . . I mean, are you sure?"

I nodded.

"It's quite small and near the servant quarters," the agent said. "And the security doors are . . ."

"I know," I said. "I want that room."

The agent nodded, looked at her astrolabe and then the screen. "I can get you the room, but I hope you are okay with it being in a slightly different place."

I frowned. "I don't understand."

"The Third Fish is pregnant and will probably give birth when she arrives on Earth. The newborn will be a great asset to the Earth Miri 12 Fleet, of course. What's good for passengers is that her pregnancy means the Third Fish will travel faster. But it also means her inner rooms and chambers shift some and will be a little more cramped."

"Why will she travel faster?" I asked out of pure curiosity.

"The sooner she'll get to Earth to bear her child," the agent said with a grin. "Isn't it fascinating?"

I nodded, also smiling. It really was.

———

"We're honored to have you both aboard," the boarding security guard said to me in Khoush a half-hour later, after our long walk to the gate. He was human and looked about the age of my father. He had a long beard and white Khoush-style robes. My fast-beating heart flipped just seeing him. Few on Oomza Uni dressed like this and, suddenly, home felt closer than ever.

"Thank you, sir," I said, handing him my astrolabe to scan. On Oomza Uni, all humans and many nonhumans used astrolabes and they were scanned so regularly that doing so no longer bothered me as it had that very first time when I'd left home.

I glanced back at Okwu and whispered, "Say thank you or something." But Okwu said nothing. It clearly didn't appreciate the guard not bothering to look at or speak directly to it in its language.

"Meduse are too proud to use astrolabes, so this part of security does not apply to it," the guard said, clearly picking up on Okwu's irritation. He handed back my astrolabe.

As I took it, I looked past him at the entrance to the Third Fish. The hallway leading inside was the same warm blue it had been that fateful day over a year ago. "Sure," I said, with a wave of my hand. "It's fine." *Was it blue when I exited?* I wondered, as I put my astrolabe into my pocket next to my *edan*. I couldn't remember; I hadn't been paying attention. I'd had other things to worry about, like trying to prevent a battle. Something red caught my eye on the security guard's uniform. A breath caught in my chest as I focused on the small red beetle. It walked right over where the man's heart would be. Red point on white. Red point. On white. I frowned, knowing what was coming, but unable to stop it. The flashback that hit me was so strong I twitched.

Heru's narrow chest.

His kaftan was white.

A red dot appeared on it like a cursor on a blank screen.

On the left side.

Left side.

Left side. Where his heart lived.

It had been beating. Calm. Happy.

Then it was a muscle, torn through.

The Meduse stinger was white and blood stained it easily.

That red dot bloomed like a rose on the bushes that liked to grow in the desert.

Heru's blood. Some spattered on my face. As his heart tore, as my mind broke.

Five five five five five five five five five five five five five five five five five five five.

"Binti of Namib?" the guard asked.

I'd spoken with Heru's parents twice. The first time, his mother only gazed at me through the virtual screen and cried. Openly, unflinchingly, she'd stared at me as if she could reach out and touch her son through my eyes. The second time, Heru's brother, only a year younger than Heru, called and demanded I recount every detail. He didn't care that it made me weep or that it would lead to a full week of nightmare-packed nights for me. And neither did I. Heru's brother looked so much like him, same granite black hair and bushy eyebrows. After those two calls, I heard nothing from Heru's people.

"Binti of Namib?" the guard asked, again.

"Oh," I said, looking up. I shook myself a bit. "Sorry."

"You may board the ship."

"Thank you," I said. I turned to Okwu and I had to stare at it for several seconds, as I prevented myself from falling into another nasty flashback, this one involving Okwu and how it had initially tried to kill me. Then I said to it in Meduse, "You first, my friend."

———

Crossing the threshold and stepping onto the ship was easy enough. I felt the talking drum in my chest, but that was all. Okwu floated off to its room on the other side of the ship and I was glad to be alone. I needed to be alone. I needed to experience *this* alone.

I passed a few people in the hallway to the sleeping rooms. It felt strange to be among so many humans again. Too quiet. I clutched my silky shawl closer to my body, feeling people's eyes on my *okuoko* and my *otjize*-covered skin, especially my arms, neck, and face. Even among the many races at Oomza Uni, it had been a long time since I'd felt so alien.

I started my breathing techniques the moment I saw my room's door; if I began treeing, I'd never experience the full effect of my terror and thus wouldn't be able to address it properly. This was one of Dr. Nwanyi's requests, not in this moment (she hadn't wanted me to take this trip), but in the idea. "When you face your deepest fears, when you are ready," she'd said. "Don't turn away. Stand tall, endure, face them. If you get through it, they will never harm you again."

I took deep, lung-filling breaths as I approached the door. Still, a violent shudder ran through my body and I leaned against the golden wall for support. "Everything is fine," I whispered in Otji-himba. I switched to Meduse, "Everything is fine." But everything wasn't fine. I was walking toward the door, my back stiff, my mind full of equations. I was carrying a tray heavy with food from the dining hall, and everyone on the ship was dead. Chests torn open by Meduse stingers; the Meduse had enacted *moojh-ha ki-bira*, the "great wave."

Leaning against the wall, I pushed myself within feet of my room's door. A woman with a staring small child walked by, greeted me, and entered her room doors away. The hallway grew quiet as the woman's door locked behind her. The *shhhhhp* of the door sealing itself seemed to echo all around me. I began to see stars through my watering eyes.

Heru.

He was lovely. I liked him.

Then his eyes changed because a Meduse ripped through his heart. All my friends who should have been in my class. Dead. I am the only human on Oomza of my year because all others are dead. All dead. All dead.

I smelled their blood now. Heard the ripping. No screams, because that required un-torn lungs. Gasps. Spilling. I'd come here. My choice.

I held my *otjize*-covered hands to my nose and tried to inhale the sweet scent, flowers, clay, tree oils. But I couldn't breathe. I pressed my hands to my chest, as if I could cup my own beating un-torn heart, as if I could calm it. For a moment, everything went black. Then my sight cleared. I whimpered.

"Shallow breaths, increased heart rate, you're having a panic attack," a stiff female voice said in Khoush.

"I am," I whispered. I didn't like for my astrolabe to speak, but Professor Okpala had had me set it to speak whenever I had a panic attack. I'd protested back then, but now I understood why.

"I suggest you drop into mathematical meditation." The voice was coming from my pocket, in which my astrolabe was warming and vibrating gently.

"If I . . . do, I learn . . . nothing," I gasped.

"There is time to learn, Binti," the voice said. "This won't be your last panic attack. But there's no one in this hallway but me and all I can do is notify the ship's medics. Help yourself, drop into meditation right now."

Everything went black, again. And when things came back, no matter how hard I tried, I couldn't stop seeing Meduse stingers tearing through bodies with surprised faces. Heru, Remi, Olu . . . I could not force myself to inhale and get air into my lungs. My chest was burning when I finally gave in. I "slipped into the trees" and dropped into meditation.

Ahhhhh . . .

The numbers flew, split, doubled, spun like the voice of the Seven.

And soon they were everywhere and everything.

I grabbed at Euler's identity, $e^{\wedge\backslash'7bi} \times \pi\backslash'7d + 1 = 0$, and I went from plummeting to gently floating down a warm rabbit hole with soft furry walls and landing on a bed of pillows and flowers. When I looked up from this fragrant quiet place, the narrowed telescopic view made things above clearer. I was on the Third Fish, a peaceful giant who was like a shrimp and could breathe in outer space because of internal rooms full of oxygen-producing plants that served as lungs. The violent death of many had happened on this ship, of my teacher, my friends, but not for me. No, not for me. I'd lived. And I'd become family with the murderous Meduse.

"Mmmmm," I said, from deep within my chest. My heart beat slowly. I reached into my pocket and brought out my *edan*. Quietly, I whispered my favorite equation and the blue current etched into the *edan*'s fractals of fine grooves and lines. I still did not know what it was, but after studying with Professor Okpala and studying the *edan* itself, I knew how to make it speak and later sing. I went to my room's door and let the door scan my eyes. It opened and I stepped into the room where I had learned to survive.

———

My first sleeping cycle (for there isn't even any night and day in space, let alone ones that are on Earth time) was full of violent nightmares so sharp that I could barely tolerate being around Okwu the next day. I'd never told it about my panic attacks or nightmares and I didn't tell it now.

Such things did not move Okwu and all it would say was that these would not kill me and I should strengthen myself and push past it all. Meduse don't understand the human condition; my emotional pain would only irritate Okwu when it couldn't make my pain instantly better. So, instead, I kept my distance from it that first day, saying I needed time to think. The ship had a separate gas-filled dining hall for Okwu and it found the food there so delicious that it spent most of that first day there. Being on the ship had no effect on Okwu; it felt right at home and easily reveled in the luxuries the ship and the university provided.

I didn't analyze this too closely. If I went down that desert hare's burrow, I'd find myself in a dark dark place where I asked questions like, "Who did Okwu kill during the *moojh-ha ki-bira*?" I understood that when Okwu had participated in the killing, it had been bound by the strong Meduse thread of duty, culture, and tradition . . . until my *otjize* showed it something outside of itself.

During those first months at Oomza Uni, Okwu had answered my calls and walked for miles and miles with me through Math City during the deepest part of night when I suffered from homesickness so powerful that all I could do was walk and let my body think I was walking home. It had talked me into contacting all my siblings, even when I was too angry and neglected to initiate contact. Okwu had even allowed my parents to curse and shout at it through my astrolabe until they'd let go of all their anger and fear and calmed down enough to finally ask it, "How is our daughter?"

Okwu had been my enemy and now was my friend, part of my family. Still, I requested that my meals be delivered to my room.

By the second day, the flashbacks retreated and I was able to spend time with Okwu talking in the space between our dining halls.

"It's good to be off planet again," Okwu said.

I gazed out the large window into the blackness. "This is only my second time," I said.

"I know," Okwu said. "That's why being on Oomza Uni was so natural for you. I enjoy the university with its professors and students, but for me, it's left me feeling . . . heavy."

I turned to it, smiling. "But you're so . . . light already. You barely weigh . . ."

"It's not about mass and gravity," it said, twitching its *okuoko* in amusement. "It's the way you feel about needing to be near the desert. You don't live in it, but it's where you run to when things get unbearable. It is always there. It is the same with me and space."

I nodded, thinking of the desert on Oomza Uni and the one near my home. "I understand. Is that why you wanted to come with me so badly?"

It puffed out a plume of gas. "I can travel home at any time," it said. "But the timing seemed right. The chief likes the idea of irritating the Khoush with my visit." It shook its tentacles and vibrated its domes, laughter.

"You're coming to make trouble?" I asked, frowning.

"Meduse like war, especially when one isn't allowed to make war." A ripple of glee ran up the front of its dome.

I grunted turning away from it and said in Otjihimba, "There isn't going to be any war."

Three Earth days. When it came time to eat, though I tried, things didn't get any better. I took one step into the dining hall where the Meduse had performed *moojh-ha ki-bira*, looked around, turned and went right back to my room, and again requested my meals to be sent there.

I spent much of my time meditating in the ship's largest breathing chamber. Most were not allowed to enter these spaces for more than a highly monitored few minutes, but my unique hero status got me whatever I wanted, including unlimited breathing room time. Okwu didn't join me here because its gas wasn't good for the plants, plus it didn't like the smell of the air. For me, the fragrant aroma of the many species of oxygen-producing plants and the moist air required to keep them alive was perfect for my peace of mind. And the *otjize* on my skin remained at its most velvety smooth here.

The three days passed, as time always does when you are alive, whether happy or tortured. And soon, I was strapping myself in my black landing chair and watching the earth get closer and closer.

When we entered the atmosphere, the sunlight touched my skin and the sweet familiar sensation brought tears to my eyes. Then my *okuoko* relaxed on my shoulders as I felt the Earth's sun shine on them for the first time. Even being what they were, my *okuoko* knew the feeling of home. After we landed and the ship settled at its gate, I sat back and looked out the window at the blue sky.

I laughed.

At Home

A week ago, Oomza University Relations instructed Okwu and me to wait two hours for everyone to exit the ship before we did when we arrived on Earth.

"But why?" I'd asked.

"So there is no trouble," both of the reps we'd been meeting with had said simultaneously.

It had been over a hundred years since a Meduse had come to Khoush lands, and never had one arrived in peace. The reps told us the launch port would be cleared for exactly one hour, except for my family, representatives, officials, and media from the local Khoush city of Kokure and my hometown of Osemba. A special shuttle would drive Okwu, me, and my family to my village.

The two hours we waited allowed me to shake off my landing weakness. I wore my finest red long stiff wrapper and silky orange top, my *edan* and astrolabe nestled deep in the front pocket of my top. I'd also put all my metal anklets back on. I did a bit of my favorite traditional dance before my room's mirror to make sure I'd put them on well. The fresh *otjize* I'd rubbed on every part of my body felt like assuring hands. I'd even rolled three of Okwu's *okuoko* with *otjize*; this would please my family, even if it annoyed the Khoush people. To Meduse, touching those hanging long tentacles was like touching a human's long hair, it wasn't all that intimate, but Okwu wouldn't let just anyone touch them. But it let me.

Covering them with so much *otjize*, Okwu told me, made it feel a little intoxicated.

"Everything is . . . happy," it had said, sounding perplexed about this state.

"Good," I said, grinning. "That way, you won't be so grumpy when you meet everyone. Khoush like politeness and the Himba expect a sunny disposition."

"I will wash this off soon," it said. "It's not good to feel this pleased with life."

We walked down the hallway and when we rounded a curve, it opened into the ship's exit. For a moment, I could see everyone out there before they saw me. Three news drones hovered feet away from the entrance. The carpeting before the exit was a sharp red. I blinked and touched my forehead, pushing, shoving the dark thoughts away.

I spotted my family, standing there in a group, then another group of Khoush and Himba welcoming officials. I hadn't told my family about my hair not being hair anymore, that it was now a series of alien tentacles resulting from the Meduse genetics being introduced to mine; that they had sensation and did other things I was still coming to understand. I could hide my *okuoko* with *otjize*, especially when I spoke with my family through my astrolabe where they couldn't see how my *okuoko* sometimes moved on their own. *Won't be able to hide them for long now*, I thought.

Any moment, I would exit and they would all see me. I slowed down and took a deep breath, let it out and took in another. I held a hand out behind me for Okwu to wait. Then I knelt down, swiped some *otjize* from my cheek, and touched it to the ship's floor. My prayer to the Seven was brief and wordless but within it, I asked them to bless the Third Fish, too. "This interstellar traveling beast holds a part of my soul," I whispered. "Please give her a safe delivery and may her child be heavy, strong, as adventurous as her mother and as lovely." I wished the Third Fish could understand me and thus understand my thanks and I felt one of my *okuoko* twitch. As if in response, the entire ship rumbled. I gasped, grinning, delighted. I pressed my palm more firmly to the floor. Then I stood and walked to the exit.

I stepped out of the ship before Okwu, so the sound of my mother's scream reached my ears immediately. "Binti!" Then there was a mad rush and I was suddenly in a crush of bodies, half of them covered in *otjize* (only the women and girls of the Himba use the *otjize*). Mother. Father. Brothers. Sisters. Aunts. Uncles. Cousins.

"My daughter is well!"

"Binti!"

"We've missed you!"

"Look at you!"

"The Seven is here!"

When everyone let go, I started sobbing as I clung to my mother, holding my father's hand as he followed close behind. I caught my brother Bena's eye as he flicked one of my *otjize*-heavy locks with his hand. Thankfully, this didn't hurt much. "Your hair has grown a lot," he said. I grinned at him, but said nothing. My sisters started swinging their long thick *otjize*–palm rolled locks side to side and singing a welcome song, my brothers clapping a beat.

And then it all stopped. I stopped in mid-sob. My parents stopped joyously laughing. Bena was looking behind me with wide eyes, his mouth agape as he pointed. I slowly turned around. For a moment, I was two people—a Himba girl who knew her history very very well and a Himba girl who'd left Earth and become part-Meduse in space. The dissonance left me breathless.

Okwu filled the exit with its girth. Its three *otjize*-covered *okuoko* were waving about, as if in zero gravity, one of them whipping before its dome violently, as if signing some sort of insult. Its light blue semitransparent thin-fleshed dome was protected by the clear metal armor it'd created on Oomza Uni. From the bottom front of its dome protruded its large white toothlike stinger.

Behind me, I heard clattering and the sound of booted footsteps rushing into the room. When I turned, one of the Khoush soldiers had already brought forth his gun and fired it. *Bam!* Screams, running, someone or maybe some two were grabbing and pulling at me. I dug in my heels, yanked at my arms. A small burst of fire bloomed in the carpet at Okwu's tentacles. Inches from Okwu, feet from the Third Fish.

"What are you doing?" I shouted. *Oh no,* I thought, a moan in my gut. I felt Okwu's rage flare, a burning in my scalp, a fire igniting in me, as well. The anger. *Not in front of my family! Unclean, unclean,* I thought. *I am unclean.* Okwu made no sound or move, but I knew in moments, every soldier, maybe every *one* in this room would be dead . . . except possibly me. The Meduse do not kill family, but did that include "family through battle?"

I pulled from my mother's grasp, hearing the sleeve of my top rip. I pushed my father aside, grabbed my wrapper, and lifted it above my knees. Then I ran. Past my family, dodging news drones, who turned to watch me. I flung myself in the space between Okwu and the line of soldiers that had flooded in from a doorway on the left. I let go of my wrapper and thrust my hands out, one palm facing the soldiers and the other facing Okwu.

"Stop!" I screamed. I shut my eyes. Okwu was going to strike; would it notice that it was I? Was I Meduse enough to avoid its stinger? Oh, my family. The Khoush soldiers were already shooting, the fire bullets would tear and burn me from inside out. Still, I stood up straight, my mind clear and crisp; I'd forgotten to drop into meditation.

Silence.

Eyes closed, I heard not even a footstep or rustle of someone's garments or Okwu's whipping tentacles. Then I did hear something and felt it, too. *Oh, not here,* I thought, my heart sinking as it drummed too fast and too hard. It had happened once before on

Oomza Uni. I was in the forest digging up clay to make my *otjize* when a large piglike beast came running at me. It was too late to make a run for it, so I froze and looked it in the eyes. The beast stopped, sniffed me with its wet snout, rubbed its rough brown furry rump against my arm, lost interest, and walked off.

As I watched it disappear into a bush, I noticed my long *okuoko* were writhing on my head like snakes, very much like Okwu's were now as he stood in the exit, stinger ready. I could hear my *okuoko* now, softly vibrating and warming. If I created a current while in this state, there would be sparks popping from the tips of each *otjize*-covered tentacle.

"Oh my Gods, is she part Meduse now?" I heard someone ask.

"Maybe she's its wife," I heard one of the journalists whisper back.

"The Himba are a filthy people," the person said. "That's why they shouldn't be allowed to leave Earth." Then there was snickering.

I met my father's eyes and all I saw was intense raw terror. His eyes quickly moved to Okwu and I knew he was looking at its stinger. I saw the faces of my family and all the other Himba and Khoush here to welcome me and I saw the history lessons kick in as they lay their eyes on the first Meduse they had ever seen in real life.

"Okwu is—" I turned from the soldiers to Okwu and back, trying to speak to them all at the same time. "All of you . . . don't move! If you move . . . Okwu . . . calm down, Okwu! You fight now, you kill everyone in here. These are my family, my people, as you are . . . We'll remain alive and there will be a chance for all of us to grow as . . . as people." Sweat beaded through the *otjize* on my face and tumbled down my cheeks. More silence. Then a soft slippery sound; Okwu sheathing its stinger. Thank the Seven.

"I have respected your wishes, Binti," Okwu said coolly in Meduse.

I turned to the Khoush and spoke quickly. "This is Okwu, Meduse ambassador and student of Oomza Uni. The Pact. Remember the *Pact*. Have you forgotten? It's law. Please. He is here in *peace* . . . unless treated otherwise. Please. We're a people of honor, too." As I stared forcefully at the Khoush soldiers, I couldn't help but feel hyperaware of the *otjize* on my face and the fact that they probably all saw me as a near savage.

Still, after a moment, the soldier in front raised a hand and motioned for the others to stand down. I let out a great sigh of relief and lowered my chin to my chest. "Praise the Seven," I whispered. My mother began to clap furiously, and soon everyone else did, too. Including some of the soldiers.

"Welcome to Earth," a tall Khoush man in immaculate white robes said, sweeping in, grabbing my hand and pumping it. He spoke with the gusto of a politician who's just had the wits scared from him. "I am Truck Omaze, Kokure's new mayor. It's a great honor to have you arriving at our launch port on your way home. You're an inspiration to all of us here on Earth, but especially in this part of the world."

"Thank you, Alhaji," I said, politely, straining to control my quivering voice.

"These Meduse," I heard my father tell my mother. "Look how the Khoush are afraid of just one. If I didn't feel I was going to die of terror, I'd be laughing."

"Shush!" my mother said, elbowing him.

"Come, let us smile to everyone." His grin was false and his grasp was tight as he laughingly whirled me toward the news drones, without giving Okwu a single glance. The mayor smelled of perfumed oil and I was reluctant to get too close to him with his white robes. However, he didn't seem to mind the *otjize* stains, or maybe he was so shaken that he didn't care at the moment. He pulled me close as the drones moved in and his grin broadened. I felt him shudder as Okwu moved in behind us to get into the shots. And despite the fact that we'd all nearly been on the verge of death by fire bullet or stinger or both, I somehow grinned convincingly at the camera drones.

━━━━━

We had about forty-five minutes and both Himba and Khoush journalists sat us down right there in a vacated airport restaurant for interviews. From the questions, I gathered what the community most wanted to know.

"We are proud of you, will you stay?"

"You have befriended the enemy. Will you meet with our elders and share your wisdom?"

"What was your favorite food on Oomza Uni?"

"What are you studying?"

"What kind of fashion are you most interested in now?"

"Why did you come back?"

"They let you come back? Why?"

"Why did you abandon your family?"

"What are those things on your head? Are you still Himba?"

"You still bless with *otjize*, why?"

"Mathematics, astrolabes, and a mysterious object, you're truly amazing. Will you be staying now that you've seen Oomza Uni, a place so much greater than your meager Himba home?"

"What was Oomza Uni like for a tribal girl like you?"

"What is that on your head? What has happened to you?"

"No man wants a girl who runs away, are you happy with your spinsterhood?"

I smiled and politely answered all their questions. Then I moved right on to stiff awkward conversations with Khoush and Himba elected officials. Nothing was asked of Okwu and Okwu was pleased, preferring to menacingly loom in the background behind me. Okwu was happiest around human beings when it was menacingly looming.

I was exhausted. My temples were throbbing, my mind wanting a moment to focus on what had nearly happened with Okwu right outside the Third Fish and not getting a chance to do so. On top of all this, I still needed days to recover from the stress of traveling through space for the equivalent of three days and then the physical shift of being on Earth. Finally, when it was all done, we were escorted to the special shuttle arranged for Okwu and me. My family was offered a separate shuttle. I was glad for the solitude. As soon as I was inside, I slumped in my seat and tried not to look at Okwu clumsily squeezing and then bumbling into the shuttle that was clearly not made for its kind.

"Your land is dry," Okwu said, turning to the large bulbous window at the back as we bulleted through the desert lands between Kokure and Osemba. "Its life is not water-based."

"There used to be more water here," I said, my eyes closed. "Then the climate changed and it went underground or dried up and the rains fell elsewhere."

"I cannot understand why my people warred with the Khoush," it said and we were quiet for a while. I too had often wondered why the Meduse fought with the Khoush and not some other tribe inhabiting the wetter parts of the world.

"But the Khoush have many lakes," I said. "It's us Himba who live closest to the deep desert, the hinterland. And even in my village, we have a lake. It's pink in the sunlight because of all the salt in it."

"When I see this god body, my people will know."

I'd once asked Okwu about its planet Omuriro and it had said little. It told me there was no water on Omuriro, but everything was soft, fleshy, and connected. "You can't breathe there without a mask, but you would be adored," Okwu had said. The Meduse worshipped water as a god, for they believed they came from it. This was the root of the war between the Meduse and the Khoush, though the details had long been blasted away by violence and death, and then angry, most likely incorrect, tales of heroism or cowardice depending on the teller.

I briefly wondered what would happen if Okwu swam in the lake, since it'd never been in a body of water. But I didn't ask.

The Root

My family's house has been called "the Root" for over a hundred and fifty years. It's been in our family for longer than the existence of its name. One of the first homes built in the Himba village of Osemba, the Root was made entirely of stone. Even the bioluminescent plants growing on the outside walls and the roof were generations old. The house was passed down through the women, and my mother—being the oldest daughter in her family and the only one born with the gift of mathematical sight—had been the clear inheritor of it when her mother passed.

A huge edifice built in an upward spiral shape stemming from the enormous meeting room on the bottom floor, the Root also had a spacious kitchen, seven bathrooms, and nine bedrooms. As everything was in Himbaland, the Root was solar powered, its grids so well embedded into the sides and roof of the house that their bases had melted and blended with the stone. The Root was old and more like a self-sustaining creature than a house. My father often joked that one day it would sprout a new bedroom next to mine.

The meeting room was open to all extended family members and close friends whenever they needed it, be it day or night. In this way, home was never a quiet place or a private one. There were no locks on any of the doors, not even in the bathrooms, and mealtimes were always grand occasions. So in many ways, the evening of my homecoming was no different from any other. However, in other ways, it certainly was.

Okwu's arrival in Osemba wasn't as spectacular (or terrifying) as its arrival at the launch port. A modest group of people were there to welcome us and gawk at Okwu, but most would arrive later in the evening. My family arrived in the shuttle behind us and most of them quickly headed home to get ready for the dinner that night.

"Okwu," my father said in Himba, stepping up to us. He was shakily grinning as he looked up at it. "Welcome, to our village." Okwu just floated there and my father glanced at me, his smile faltering. I motioned for him to keep talking. "Okay, heh, I am amazed by how you stood up to the Khoush. They don't treat us Himba very well, either. But we are a quiet people, so . . . we tolerate it and work with them. Come see what I've made for you."

We followed my father around the house. I let my sandals dig into the warm red dirt as I walked. It was so so good to be home.

"Oh," my father peeped, turning to walk backward as Okwu and I followed. "I *really* enjoy the way you speak our language. Did my daughter teach you?"

"Yes," Okwu said. "She is a good teacher."

"She's a *true* master harmonizer," my father said, turning around.

I bit my lip and said nothing.

When we rounded the corner into the back, I was glad to have something to change the subject. "You can credit me for this," my father said, turning to us with his arms out. Okwu thrummed with pleasure from deep in its dome.

"Oh, Papa," I said, laughing. "This is amazing."

Okwu moved past him to the large transparent tent. It touched the flap and a doorway sized just larger than Okwu's body opened, lavender gas billowing out. Okwu floated inside, the flap closing behind it.

"I'm a master harmonizer too," Papa said, looking at me and winking. "And a good researcher. Once I knew the components, it was easy to build a machine that creates their breathing gas. It's similar to the gas produced in some of the spouts near the Khoush-land volcanoes."

"This was all your idea?" I asked, grinning.

"Of course," he said. "The enemy of my enemy is my friend . . . even if it's a monster."

"Okwu isn't a monster, Papa."

"It nearly killed you on that ship and it nearly killed us all at the launch port." When I opened my mouth to protest, he held up a hand. "It's the job of the master harmonizer to make peace and friendship, to harmonize. For you to befriend that thing, you've done well."

I gave him a tight hug. "Thank you."

Okwu didn't come out, except to thank my father and say, "I am very comfortable in here. You are Binti's father."

━━━━━━

My bedroom was the same as when I'd left it. My table was messy with astrolabe parts, bits of wire, and sandstone dust; my closet was closed and my bed was made. There was a package on my bed wrapped in thin red cloth. I smiled. Only my mother would wrap a gift with such care, and always with red cloth. I turned it over, rubbing a hand across the smooth coolness of it, and set it back on my bed. I'd open it later, when things were quiet.

I went to my travel pod and brought out the dress I'd bought in Oomza Uni on a rare occasion where I'd gone shopping. Long and flowing, its design was vaguely Khoush, but mostly something else, and it was sky blue, a color Himba rarely wore. I put it on. When I came downstairs to join everyone in the meeting room, I immediately regretted wearing it. *Stupid stupid, stupid,* I thought, looking around. *I've been away too long.* Feeling the burn of everyone's stares, I made a beeline for my mother, who'd just gone into the kitchen.

Two of my mother's older sisters stood over a huge pot full of boiling rice and another bubbling with bright yellow curried goat stew. My mother lifted the heavy lid of a pot full of red stew so she could dump in a large plate of roasted chicken wings. My stomach grumbled at the sight of it all. With all the delicious exotic foods I'd eaten and prepared in my dorm kitchen on Oomza Uni, nothing compared to a simple plate of spiced rice and spicy red stew with chicken.

"Mama," I said, keeping my voice down so my aunties wouldn't hear. "When do this season's group of women leave for pilgrimage? I couldn't calculate the time or access news of the leaves from off planet." I chuckled nervously looking at my mother, whose eyebrows raised. The pilgrimage time was calculated through numbers based on the current composition of local clay and written on three large palm tree leaves. These leaves were passed from home to home over a month until all Himba knew.

"*You* want to go on your pilgrimage?" my mother asked.

I nodded. "I want to see everyone, of course, but this is why I came home, too."

My mother and I said it simultaneously, "It's time." Then we both nodded. She reached out and carefully touched my *okuoko*. She took one in her hand and squeezed it. I winced.

"So they aren't hair anymore," she said.

"No."

I glanced at my aunties' turned backs. I knew they were listening, as they stirred what was in the pots.

"It did this to you?"

"They," I said. "Not Okwu . . . I don't think." I paused, remembering the moment when the stinger was plunged into my back as I knelt before the Meduse chief trying to save my life, those Meduse and the lives of so many others on Oomza Uni. "Really, I don't know if it was Okwu; I didn't see."

"They're a hive mind," she said. "So it doesn't matter." She was rubbing the *otjize* off to reveal the true transparent blue of them with darker blue dots on the tips. I held my breath, as she inspected me with a mother's eye and hand. She whispered softly and I held still. My mother only used her mathematical sight to protect the family. Now she used it to look into me. Deep.

She'll see everything, I thought. Seconds passed, her hand grasping my *okuoko,* her eyes boring into me, her lips whispering simple, but intuitively smooth equations that slipped away from my ears like oil from soap. I shifted from one foot to the other and prayed to the Seven that she wouldn't start calling on Them to "come exorcise her polluted daughter" like some distraught mother in the overly dramatic newsfeed shows my sisters enjoyed watching. Suddenly, my mother let go of my *okuoko* and looked at me with clear eyes. Blinking. She lifted my chin. "The women leave tomorrow."

My eyes grew wide. "Oh no! But . . . but I just got here!"

"Yes. For such a gifted harmonizer, your timing has always been awful."

"My pilgrimage dress. Is that what's in this package?" I asked.

She nodded.

"You knew."

"You're my daughter," my mother said. When she pulled me to her and hugged me tightly, I rested my head on her chest and sighed. "Even if you're wearing these strange blue clothes that make you look like some sort of masquerade."

I burst out laughing.

———

All nine of my siblings came to my welcoming dinner, aunts, uncles, cousins, nieces, and nephews. Chief Kapika of the local Himba

Council came too, as did his second-wife Neeka. Only my best friend Dele remained missing. He hadn't been at the launch port, either. I was disappointed, but I would track him down early in the morning, before I left for my four-day pilgrimage.

"What kind of dress is that?" my sister Vera asked, as I stepped from the last stair into the crowded meeting room. "You look like some kind of mermaid masquerade. Maybe you should go greet Mami Wata at the lake." She laughed at her own words.

I prickled. Vera was eleven years older than me, inches taller, and so beautiful that she'd had her pick of husbands from fifteen amazing suitors five years ago. She'd chosen a man who was handsome like a water spirit and an extremely successful astrolabe seller, to my father's delight. Vera was also the most outspoken about my "irresponsibly selfish choice" to leave. She held her two-year-old son on her hip and he looked at me with wide eyes and a precious grin.

"Little Zu seems to like my dress," I said.

"Zu likes anything strange," she said, putting Zu down. He stepped up to me and grasped the bottom of my dress to look at it more closely. "I'm kidding," Vera said. "Honestly, I expected you to come back wearing a skintight spacesuit or something. This isn't so bad. And we're all relieved that you made it home safely."

She gave me a tight hug.

"Thanks," I said.

And that was how the night began. As expected. I had a chance to catch up with several of my age mates, all of whom were proudly betrothed, boys and girls. I was relieved, though slightly bothered, that none of them asked if I were here to enter a betrothal too. Chief Kapika gave a speech about Himba pride. "And now our Binti Ekeopara Zuzu Dambu Kaipka of Osemba is back with us; now the community can contract back into itself like a self-protecting flower. We are all here. And that is good." When he'd finished talking, everyone applauded. I'd smiled, uncomfortably. I was returning to

Oomza Uni in two months for the beginning of next quarter, but I didn't have to tell everyone this yet.

Eventually, we all sat down to eat and that's when everything went wrong. I was enjoying a second helping of ostrich stew, my stomach stretched beyond its usual point. Back on Oomza Uni, Professor Okpala demanded that all her mathematics students control their daily intake of rich foods. To be full made treeing more difficult, she'd said. She was right. I'd never been one to eat more than what my body required, but I found my mind was sharper when I stayed just a little hungry with every meal. Over the months, I grew used to this not-quite-full sensation. However, today, I indulged.

I felt slow and heavy. And at the moment, to my delight, I was alone. The better to focus on my food. My father stood a few feet away with his two brothers, Uncle Gideon and Uncle Akpe, talking. One moment, Uncle Gideon was laughing raucously at something and then the next, he was struggling to keep my father from toppling over.

"Papa!" I shrieked, jumping up. It was as if my father's fall created a vacuum, for everyone in the room rushed toward him. My brother Bena got to him before me, pushing me aside to do so.

My mother came running. "Moaoogo," she shouted. "Moaoogo, what is the matter?"

Bena and my uncle held him up. "I'm fine," my father insisted, but he was out of breath. "I'm fine." Even as he spoke, he winced, limply holding his hands together. And it was then that I noticed the joints of his fingers were extremely swollen, almost bulbous. When had my father developed arthritis? I frowned as my sister Vera stepped up beside me on one side, her son clasping her skirts, and my oldest sister Omaihi on the other. I am not short, but all of my sisters, even my younger sister Peraa, who is two years my junior, were taller than me. Between Vera and Omaihi, I felt like a child standing between adult giants.

"Papa are you alright?" my sister Omaihi asked.

"Yes, yes, yes," our father insisted, as his brothers helped him to sit down. My brother Bena joined Vera, Omaihi, and me, his arms across his chest and a frown on his face.

"Papa's always overdoing it," he said. "Stands all day in the shop working on the astrolabes and then comes to dinner and *still* doesn't sit down."

"Now you see, Binti," Vera hissed.

I could feel them all glaring at me now. "How long has he been—"

"Since you left, really," Vera said, looking squarely at me. Bena and Omaihi looked at me too.

"What?" I asked. "You think I caused it by leaving?"

Vera scoffed and only continued glaring at me.

I looked to Bena and Omaihi for support, but they said nothing.

"That's so wrong," I said.

"It's the truth," Vera said, her voice sharply rising. I looked around. She meant everyone to hear. "Binti, now that you're here, I think you need some tough truth."

"Before you have the nerve to disappear in the night again," Omaihi firmly added.

"I . . . I didn't leave at night, I left in the early morning," I muttered. I took a deep breath, slipped my hand into my front pocket, and grasped my *edan*. It was mine, the object that I was studying at the university over a dozen planets away, a place my sisters, my family, had never set foot on.

Vera stepped closer, leaning in as she looked down her nose at me. Her *otjize*-covered locks nearly reached her knees and they made my *okuoko* look like buds to a tree full of blooming flowers. "See Papa! *You* were supposed to take over the shop, so he could sit down and be proud. We're all very happy to see you, Binti. But you should be ashamed of yourself. Your selfishness nearly got you killed!" Now she was pointing her index finger in my face. I could hear my heart beating in my ears. "Then what would Papa do? And . . . and even if you *die,* the world will move on. Who are you? You're not famous."

I was squeezing my *edan,* but somehow, I stayed quiet. The entire room was quiet and listening. Where were my parents? There they were, yards away. My father was sitting now, my mother and uncles beside him. All were just looking at us.

"You'll always be alone if you don't stop this and come home," my oldest sister added. Her voice wasn't as loud as Vera's, but it was much harder. "Jumping back and forth between planets, you have to slow down."

A few people in the room grunted agreement.

"I'm doing what I believe the Seven created me to do!" I said. But my voice was shrill and breathless. I was dizzy from the strain of controlling my outrage, needing to say my piece and feeling that shame that had resided deep within me since I'd left. "Do you even understand what I *did* on that ship? Everyone was *dead,* except the pilot and me! I *saw* them do it! I—"

"Then you befriended the enemy of humanity," my brother Bena said from behind me.

I whirled around and said, "No, the enemy of the Khoush people. You know, the people *you've* been railing against since you learned how to read?" I turned back to Vera, who grandly sucked her teeth, as she looked me up and down with disgust.

"You're so ugly now, Binti," she said. "You don't even sound the same. You're polluted. Almost eighteen years old. What man will marry you? What kind of children will you have now? Your friend Dele doesn't even want to see you!"

That last part was like a snakebite.

"Maybe you shouldn't have come back," Vera growled, her face inches from mine. I could practically feel her keeping herself from punching me in the face. *Do it,* I told her with my eyes. *I dare you.* My cheeks were hot and my body had begun to tremble.

"Some of the girls here now want to do what you did," she said. "You're supposed to be a master harmonizer. Look at you. What harmony do you bring here?"

I tried to grab even the simplest equation, $1 + 1$, $0 + 0$, $5 - 2$, 2×1. I tried to do what I did on that ship, when I held my own life in my hands, when I'd faced a race of people who detested all humans because of a few humans. But every number eluded my mental grasp. All I could see was my sister's *otjize*-covered face with her long silver earrings that clicked to enunciate her words and her elaborate sandstone and gold marriage necklace that meant more to everyone here than my traveling to another planet to be a student at the greatest university in the galaxy.

She stepped even closer. "You bring dissonance! What if . . ."

"Enough!" I screamed at her, shaking with anger. "Who . . . who are you, Vera?" I couldn't find any more words. Instead I inhaled sharply and then did something I'd never thought of doing, even when at my angriest. I spat in her face. It landed on her cheek. Immediately, I regretted my actions. However, instead of shutting up, I continued shouting, "Do you have any clue who I am?" Even as I carried the weight of my regret, it felt wonderful to roar like that at her, at everyone. I was about to say more when Vera shrieked, my saliva still glistening on her face. She scrambled back, falling over a chair. Her elbow knocked over a cup of water on a table, which rolled to the edge and shattered on the floor. I heard my father exclaim. Behind me, I heard Bena gasp and scamper away from me too.

Vera raised her hands, shaking her head, and she whispered, "I'm sorry, I'm sorry, Binti, I'm sorry!"

"Move away from her," I heard one of my uncles say. "Everyone."

"*Kai!*" someone exclaimed. "What is that?"

I saw my four-year-old niece on the other side of the round table drop her drumstick of chicken and bury her face against the leg of my oldest brother, Omeva. He didn't notice her do this because he was staring at me, his mouth agape. People fled the room, covered their eyes, cowered in corners. I met the blank eyes of my mother and held them for a long time and that was when I realized what was happening. My *okuoko*. They were writhing atop my head, again.

"What has happened to my harmonizing daughter?" I heard my father softly ask. "The peacemaker? She spits in her older sister's face." He pressed his right hand to his eyes; the joints were so gnarled.

I let go of the *edan* in my pocket and pressed my hand to my chest. The rage in me retreated. "Papa, I . . ."

"What did that place do to you?" he asked, still covering his face.

I couldn't stop the tears from falling. I didn't *know* what it all had done to me. It was there sometimes, and then sometimes, it wasn't. I was peaceful, then all I could see was war. My siblings had been attacking me. How was peace going to help? I wanted to say these things. I wanted to explain to them all. Instead, I fled the dining room. I left my family to continue talking about me in my absence as they had since I'd left. As I ascended the stairs, I heard them start in. Vera began, then my brothers.

I slammed my bedroom door behind me and just stood there. My entire body was shuddering. I'd traveled so far to come home and rest in the arms of my family and now I'd just cast myself out. "Even a masquerade has its people, only a ghost wanders alone," my father liked to say. *I have to fix this*, I desperately thought. But my mind was too full of adrenaline and fury to think of anything.

The gift on my bed caught my eye. I unwrapped it and unfolded the silky wrapper, matching top and veil inside it, all the deep orange color of *otjize*. "Beautiful," I whispered. Lovely light weather-treated material that would make walking in the desert under the noon sun like standing in the shade. A girl's or woman's pilgrimage clothes were the most expensive and treasured clothes she would have until her wedding day.

I laughed bitterly. These would probably be the most expensive and treasured clothes in my life. "No marriage for me," I muttered. My words made me snicker to myself and then I laughed harder. Soon, I was laughing so hard that my belly muscles were cramping.

When I calmed down, I listened, still hearing my family talking loudly in the meeting room. I shook out my pilgrimage clothes and laid them on my chair. I brought out my astrolabe and *edan* and placed them side by side on my bed. I shut my eyes and was about to do one of the breathing exercises Professor Okpala had taught me when my astrolabe chimed. Someone was trying to reach me. I paused, my eyes closed, going through a list of who it could possibly be.

My sisters? Probably.

My father? No.

My mother? Possibly.

My uncles or aunties? Likely.

I opened my eyes and saw Dele's face filling in the circular screen of my astrolabe. He was looking down at his hands, as he waited for me to accept his call. "Dele," I said and the notification chimes stopped. He looked up, seeing me, and we stared at each other. We hadn't spoken since I left. He wouldn't answer or return my calls and he had never called me. He looked older, now . . . and wiser.

"You have a beard," I blurted. It was light and fuzzy, but a beard it was.

"I've joined the Himba Council." He didn't smile as he conveyed this news. Then he just stared at me. I stared back. The Himba Council? Was he next in line to apprentice for Council Chief? Dele? Council apprentices weren't allowed to leave Himbaland. When had Dele become so . . . rooted? From downstairs, they still talked, voices raised. Now, I heard my mother speaking. Shouting?

"How have you been?" I finally asked.

"Here," he said.

More silence. "What . . . what do you want, Dele?"

"Your sister messaged me to call you immediately," he said. "What's going on?"

"*This* is why you finally reach out to me?"

"You were the one who left, not me."

"So?"

Silence.

"Dele . . . I couldn't tell you," I said. "Everyone . . . *you* just assumed I wasn't going, that I wasn't *supposed* to go. I *wanted* to, Dele. So badly. Haven't you ever wanted something with all your heart, yet . . ."

"Yet, not one person in my family, in my entire *clan*, wanted it for me? No, Binti, never. That would be selfish. I'm not Khoush."

Dele and I had known each other since we were babies and as we grew older, Dele had begun to lean more and more toward embracing the deep Himba way. We used to joke and argue about it, but our friendship always won out over the laws, rules, and mores. Plus, back then, his traditional leanings made him seem so strong and important, despite my dislike of it. Now, he'd grown a beard.

"You're too complex, Binti," he said. "That's why I stayed away. You're my best friend. You are. And I miss you. But, you're too complex. And look at you; you're even stranger now." He pointed into the camera. "You think you can cover those things with *otjize* and I won't see them? I know you."

I sat down hard on my bed, feeling breathless again. Had my sister told him about my *okuoko*? Could he really see them through the camera? They weren't even moving.

"What are you trying to accomplish with all this?" he asked. "I can see it in your face, you're not well. You look tired and sad and . . ."

"Because of what just happened!" I said. "Why don't you ask me about that? Instead of assuming the greatest choice I've ever made for myself is making me sick? *Home* is making me sick! I was fine until I got here." This wasn't all true, of course, but I needed to make my point clearly.

"We all love you," he said. "You don't know how your leaving made your family suffer. Your father's business may have increased because of you, but his health has decreased. That doesn't bode well for our village. He's more our leader than our *chief*! He's master harmonizer! And people here . . . ask your younger sisters, girl cousins how they get treated. You've stained them. Marriage won't be . . ."

"None of that's my fault!"

Dele paused and shook his head, chuckling softly. Then, again, we were staring at each other.

He waved a hand at me. "I can't help you, Binti."

"Can't help you, either," I snapped.

"I hear you're going on pilgrimage tomorrow," he said. "You have strange timing, but good luck."

"Thanks," I said, looking away.

"I trust you will take care of yourself," he said, coolly. Then Dele was gone. And for the first time, it really sunk in. No man wanted a girl who ran away. No man would marry me.

I pushed my astrolabe and *edan* aside, lay on my bed, curled up, and cried myself to sleep.

Night Masquerade

I awoke hours later with a face crusty with tears, dried *otjize*, and snot. I went to the bathroom, blew and wiped my nose, and looked at myself in the mirror. Old *otjize* was flaking from my cheeks and forehead, leaving patches of clear brown bare skin. I needed to remove it all and reapply. I'd feel more myself, I knew. I didn't pause on the knowledge that my current batch of *otjize* was made with clay from another planet. As I stared at my haggard face in the mirror, I glanced at the window facing the back of the house and remembered Okwu was out there.

I tiptoed downstairs and peeked into the main room. There were a few still awake, softly chatting in a corner, my sister Vera one of them. Many were curled up on flat pillows and mats. I snuck out the back door and nearly walked right into Okwu.

"It didn't go well," it said.

"No," I said, stepping around it to go look at its gas-filled tent. The tent's tall puffy girth reminded me of a giant Meduse. Maybe that's what my father was going for when he set it up.

"Your father came out to check on me," Okwu said. "He seemed upset."

I grunted, but said nothing more of it. "Do you want to go see the lake?" I said.

Okwu exhaled out a great amount of gas and I coughed, fanning the air around me. "Yes," it said, its voice so clear that the vibration of it made my head ache.

My home village Osemba was a palette of dusty browns from the dirt roads to stone and sand-brick buildings. The oldest buildings were groupings of several solid stone structures, like the Root with its many traditional conical roofs. The Root sits at the very edge of Osemba. About a mile west, the sand dunes begin threatening to reclaim the clay-rich land. In the opposite direction, straight down the main dirt road, past other homes and a small area reserved for the western morning souq, is the lake. The rest of Osemba spreads along the lake's edges.

Okwu and I walked up the road in the dark of deep night. We, Himba, are a people of the sun. When it sets, we retreat. The night is typically for sleep, family, and reflection. Thus, Okwu and I had the road to ourselves and I was glad. I used my astrolabe to light our way. I glanced at Okwu every so often and noted how as it floated beside me, it turned this way and that, observing Osemba; the first Meduse to ever do this, in peace or war.

"I can smell the water," Okwu said, minutes later.

"It's right in front of us," I said. "Those tables and wooden medians are for the souq that's here every morning; it's similar to the marketplace on Oomza, but with just humans, of course."

"Then that's not like Oomza Blue Market at all," Okwu said.

"No, the setup. People sell things outside. Come, the lake is just past it."

"How can the air smell of water?" Okwu asked in Otjihimba. The awe it felt was clearer when it spoke in my language. I smiled and walked faster, enjoying Okwu's rare excitement.

When I stepped onto the sand, Okwu beside me, I quickly took a deep breath and held it. *Phoom.* Okwu's gas plumed so thickly around me that for a moment all I saw was the line of my astrolabe's light tinted lavender. I took several steps from Okwu, fanning the gas away until I reached breathable space. Still, I coughed, laughing as I did. "Okwu," I gasped. "Calm down—"

But Okwu wasn't there. I quickly flashed my astrolabe's light around me and noticed two things at once. The first was that Okwu was floating to the water, moving swiftly as if blown by a strong wind. The second was that I didn't need my light to see this because the light from the lake was more than enough. *Light from the water,* I slowly thought as another thought competed for my attention. *Can Okwu even swim? Salt is in water, too.*

"Okwu," I shouted, running toward the water.

But Okwu floated into its waters and quickly sunk in. Then it was gone. I splashed in all the way to my knees, the warm buoyancy of the water already feeling as if it wanted to lift me up. "Okwu?" I shouted. Around me was blinking electric green light. It was clusterwink snail season and the water was full of the spawning bioluminescent baby snails, the tiny creatures each flashing their own signals of whatever they were signaling. It was like wading into an overpopulated galaxy.

I waded farther into the water looking for Okwu. I paused, wondering if I should dive in to search for it. I couldn't swim, but because of the high salt content, I couldn't drown; the water would just push me to the surface. Still, if I went after Okwu, the water would wash off my *otjize*. And if anyone saw me, if my people didn't think I was crazy yet, they certainly would after word spread that I'd been outside *otjize*-free.

"Okwu?" I shouted one last time. *What if the water just dissolved its body?* I looked at the glowing water and braced my legs to throw myself farther in and paddle out to find Okwu. Then yards into the water, within the twinkling green stars, I saw a swirling galaxy. Okwu's silhouette surrounded by swirling twinkling baby snails. "What?" I whispered.

Then Okwu's dome emerged; Okwu was adeptly swimming, half-submerged. It came toward me, but stopped when the water got too shallow for it to stay half-submerged. "My ancestors are dancing," Okwu said in Otjihimba, its voice wavering with more emotion than I'd ever heard Okwu convey. Then Okwu swam back into the water. For the next thirty minutes, it danced with the snails.

I sat on the beach, my long skirts covering my *otjize*-free legs, in the twinkling green of my home lake. Traditionally, it's taboo for a Himba woman or girl to bathe with water, let alone openly swim in the lake. I'd developed a love for bathing with water in the dorms on Oomza Uni. Though I'd only do it when I was relatively sure no one was around. As I sat there, watching Okwu dance with its god, I thought about how strange it was that for me to swim in water was taboo and for Okwu such a taboo was itself a taboo.

I remember thinking, *The gods are many things.*

━━━━

I don't know why I was doing it.

Even after seeing Okwu dancing with its god, some of the fury and pain from my dinner with family still coursed through my system. So an hour later, there I sat on my bedroom floor working my fingers over my *edan*'s lines as I hummed to it as Professor Okpala had taught me—mathematical harmonizing plus the soft vibration waves from my voice sometimes reached normally unreachable sensors on some *edans*.

My window was open and outside a cool desert breeze was blowing in from the west, pushing my orange curtains inward. The current of the breeze disturbed the mathematical current I was calling up. The disturbance caused my mind to weave in a tumble of equations that strengthened what I was trying to do instead of weaken it.

As I hummed, I let myself tree, floating on a bed of numbers soft, buoyant, and calm like the lake water. *Just beautiful*, I thought, feeling both vague and distant and close and controlled. My hands worked and soon I slid a finger on one of the triangular sides of the *edan*. It slid open and then slipped off. Inside the pyramid point was another wall of metal decorated with a different set of geometric swirls and loops. Professor Okpala described it as "another language beneath the language." My *edan* was all about communication, one layer on top of another and the way they were arranged was another language. I was learning, but would I ever master it?

"Ah," I sighed. Then I slipped the other triangular side of the pyramid off and the current I called caught both and lifted them into the air before my eyes. "Bring it up," I whispered and the *edan* joined the two metal triangles. They began to slowly rotate in the way they always did, the *edan* like a small planet and the triangles like flat cartwheeling moons. A small yellow moth that had been fluttering about my room attracted to the *edan*'s glow flew to it now and was instantly caught up in the rotating air.

Was it the presence of the moth, tumbling and fluttering between the metal triangles? I do not know. There was always so much I didn't know, but not knowing was part of it all. Whatever the reason, suddenly my *edan* was shedding more triangle sides from its various pyramid points and they joined the rotation. What remained of my *edan* hovered in the center and from the cavernous serenity of meditation, I sighed in awe. It was a gold metal ball etched with deep lines that formed wild loops but did not touch, reminiscent of fingerprint patterns. Was it solid gold? Gold was a wonderful conductor; imagine how precise the current I guided into it would move. If I did that, would the sphere open too? Or even . . . speak?

The moth managed to break out of the cycle and as soon as it did, my grasp slipped. As Professor Okpala would have said, I fell out of the tree. The mathematical current I'd called up evaporated and all the pieces of my *edan* fell to the floor, musically clinking. I gasped and stared. I waited for several moments and nothing happened. Always, the pieces rearranged themselves back into my *edan*, as if magnetized, even when I fell out of the tree.

"No, no, no!" I said, gathering the pieces and putting them in a pile in the center of my bed. I waited, again. Nothing. "Ah!" I shrieked, near panic. I snatched up the gold ball. So heavy. Yes, it had to be solid gold. I brought it to my face, my hands shaking and my heart pounding. I rubbed the pad of my thumb over the deep labyrinthine configurations. It was warm and heavier than the *edan* had ever felt, as if it had its own type of gravity now that it was exposed.

I was about to call up another current to try to put it back together when something outside caught my eye. I went to my window and what I saw made my skin prickle and my ears ring. I stumbled back, ran my finger over the *otjize* on my skin, and rubbed it over my eyelids to ward off evil. My bedroom was at the top floor of the Root and it faced the west where my brother's garden grew, the backyard ended, and the desert began.

"May the Seven protect me," I whispered. "I am not supposed to be seeing this." No girl or woman was. And even though I never had up until this point, I knew exactly who that was standing in my brother's garden in the dark, looking right at me, *pointing* a long sticklike finger at me. I shrieked, ran to my bed, and stared at my disassembled *edan*. "What do I do, what do I do? What's happening? What do I do?"

I slowly stepped back to the window. The Night Masquerade was still there, a tall mass of dried sticks, raffia, and leaves with a wooden face dominated by a large tooth-filled mouth and bulbous black eyes. Long streams of raffia hung from its round chin and the sides of the head, like a wizard's beard. Thick white smoke flowed out from the top of its head and already I could smell the smoke in my room, dry and acrid. Okwu's tent was several yards to the right, but Okwu must have been inside.

"Binti," I heard the Night Masquerade growl. "Girl. Small girl from big space."

I moaned, breathless with terror. My oldest brother, father, and grandfather had seen the Night Masquerade at different times in their lives. My father on the night he became the family master harmonizer over two decades ago. My oldest brother on the night he'd fought three Khoush men in the street outside the market when they'd wrongfully accused him of stealing the fine astrolabes he'd brought to sell. And my grandfather, when he was eight years old on the night after he saved his whole village during a Khoush raid by hacking the astrolabes of the Khoush soldiers to produce an eardrum-rupturing sound. Only men and boys were said to even have the ability to *see* the Night Masquerade and only those who were heroes of Himba families got to see it. No one ever spoke of what happened after seeing it. I'd never considered it. I'd never needed to.

I ran to my travel pod and pulled out a small sealed sack I'd used to store tiny crystal snail shells I'd found in the forest near my dorm on Oomza Uni. I dumped them onto my bed, where they crackled and began to turn from white to yellow as they reacted to the dry desert air. I bristled with annoyance. I'd brought the shells to show my sisters and now they'd be dust in a few minutes.

I pushed them aside and put the pieces of my *edan* into the transparent sack, wincing at their clinking and clattering. The gold sphere with its fingerprint-like ridges was still warm. I paused for a moment, holding it. Would it melt or burn the sack? I put it inside; the sack was made from the stomach lining of a creature whose powerful stomach juices could digest the most complex metals and stones on the planet. If it could withstand that, it certainly could contain my *edan*'s warm core.

I'd just put the sack into my satchel when there came a hard knock at my door. I twitched as the noise sent me back to the ship when the Meduse had knocked so hard on my door. I covered my mouth to hold in the scream that wanted to escape, then I shut my eyes. I took a deep lung-filling breath and let it out. Inhaled again.

Exhaled. *No Meduse at the door, Binti,* I thought. *Okwu is outside and it is your friend.* The knock came again, followed by my father's voice calling my name. I ran to the door and opened it and met his frowning eyes. Behind him stood my older brother Bena, also frowning.

"Did you see it?" my father asked.

I nodded.

"*Kai!*" Bena exclaimed, pressing his hands to his closely shaven head. "How is this possible?"

"I don't know!" I said, tears welling in my eyes.

"What is it?" my mother asked, coming up behind him, rubbing her face. The *otjize* on her skin was barely a film. Normally only my father would see her like this.

My younger sister Peraa peeked from the staircase. She was the eyes of my family, silent and curious about all things. *Had she seen it, too?* I wondered.

Somehow, my father knew she was there, and he whipped around to shout, "Peraa, go back to bed!"

"Papa, there are people outside," she said.

"People?" Bena asked. "Peraa, did you see anything else?"

Before she could respond, my father asked, "What people?"

"Many people," Peraa said. She was out of breath and looked about to cry. "Desert People!"

"Eh?!" my father exclaimed. "What is happening tonight?" Then he was storming down the hall to the stairs, my brother rushing after him.

"Wait," my mother said, holding a hand up to me. "Go in, apply *otjize*. Put on your pilgrimage attire."

"Why? That's not for . . ."

"Do it."

Peraa was still standing at the top of the staircase, staring at me. I motioned for her to come, but she only shook her head and went downstairs.

My mother's eyes migrated to my *otjize*-rolled *okuoko*.

"Do those hurt?" she asked.

"Only if you hurt them."

"Why'd you have to do it?"

"Mama, would you rather I died like everyone else on that ship?"

"Of course not," she said. She seemed about to say more, but instead she just said, "Hurry." Then she turned and quickly headed down the staircase.

———

I applied my *otjize* and put on my pilgrimage clothes. The *otjize* would rub off onto my clothes making tonight the outfit's official event, not my pilgrimage, blessed on this day by my *otjize*. *So be it,* I thought. Before I went out to the front door, I snuck to the back of the house. Okwu was waiting for me. "There are people standing around your home," it said in Meduse.

"I know." I resisted staring at the desert woman yards away watching us. Tall with dark brown skin that looked so strange to my eyes because she wore no *otjize*, she looked a few years older than I, possibly in her early twenties. Her bushy hair was a sweet black and it shivered in the breeze.

"I watched them arrive," Okwu said. "One asked me to come out of my tent. When I did, he spoke to me in Meduse. How do people who live far from water know our language?"

"I don't know," I said. "Did . . . did you see anything near the house? Standing where my window faces?"

"No."

"Okay," I muttered, turning from him. "Hold on. I need to see something." The desert woman watched me as I slowly walked to the spot where the Night Masquerade had been. "I'm just checking something," I said to her.

"Even if you ran, I'd catch you," she said in Otjihimba, with a smirk. "You're why we're here." She motioned to Okwu. "And to see that one."

"Why? What did we do?"

She only chuckled, waving a hand dismissively at me. I stopped at the spot where I was sure the Night Masquerade had been. The sand here was undisturbed, not even a light footprint. It was breezy tonight, but not so much that footprints would disappear in minutes.

"Binti," I heard my mother call.

"Okwu, meet me in the front," I said.

"Okay."

I turned and headed back into the Root.

Blood

The Desert People surrounded the Root the way groups of lake crabs surround their egg-filled holes when the eggs are ready to hatch. There were about seven of them that I could see, probably more on the other side of the house. Some were men, some were women, and all had skin that was "old African" dark, like my father's and mine. They wore the traditional goat-pelt wraps around their waists, blue waist beads, and blue tops. Around their wrists, they wore bracelets made from shards and chunks of pink salt found in dried lakes deep in the desert. None of them wore shoes.

Straight backed, faces stern, they stood silent. Waiting. And though it was very late in the night, a few neighbors had come out to see what was going on. Of course. By sunup, the village's bush radio would carry the word to all of Osemba that Desert People had come to the Root. Khoush communities in Kokure might even hear about it. I felt Okwu's presence not far behind me as it came round the house. I turned and nodded at it.

My father was speaking with a tall old woman. Behind her stood two camels with packs on their backs. I watched for a moment, as the woman's hands worked wildly while she spoke. Sometimes, she'd stop speaking entirely yet her hands would keep going, moving in circles, jabbing, zigzagging, sometimes harshly, other times gently. This was the way of the Desert People, one of the reasons the Himba viewed them as primitive and mentally unstable.

They had no control of their hands; the elders said it was some sort of neurological condition. When the old woman saw me, she smiled and then told my father, "We'll bring her back by tomorrow night."

My mouth fell open and I looked at my father, who did not look at me.

"How will I know?" my father asked.

She looked down her nose at him. "Such a proud son you are."

My father finally looked at me. My mother grabbed my hand. "Not going anywhere," she muttered. I was shocked by so much that I could only stare at her. "We just got her back!" my mother told my father.

"You people are so brilliant, but your world is too small," the old woman who was my father's mother, my _grandmother_, said. "One of you finally somehow grows beyond your cultural cage and you try to chop her stem. Fascinating." She looked at my father. "Don't you remember what happened with your father?" She straightened up. "Your daughter, _my_ granddaughter, has seen the Night Masquerade."

My sister Peraa, who was standing beside me now, gasped and looked at me. "You did?" she whispered.

I nodded at her, still unable to speak.

She grabbed my other hand. "Is that why you—"

"No, she hasn't!" my mother snapped.

The old woman chuckled and her hands twitched and began to move again, zigzagging, punching, waving. The astrolabe around her neck bumped against her chest, not once touched by the woman. "Why do you think we came out here? There are rituals to be performed."

Even from where I stood, I could see that her astrolabe was one that had been made by my father. The unique slightly oval shape, the rose-tinted sandstone, this was an astrolabe he'd made some time ago. My mother must have noticed this too, because she turned and gave him a dirty look.

The other Desert People standing close by all laughed, some of them making the strange hand motions. I looked back at Okwu and frowned. Several of my relatives had now gathered, none of whom wanted to stand near Okwu. It stood behind them all, but beside it stood one of the Desert People, a bushy-haired boy of about my age.

"We'll take your daughter, *our* daughter, into the desert," my grandmother said. She turned to Okwu. "Your daughter, too. She will speak with our clan priestess, the Ariya. We bring her back the night after this one."

═══

My mother wept and my father had to pry my hand from hers. Seeing her weep made me start to weep. Then Peraa started weeping. My brothers just stood there and I saw my sister Vera angrily walk away. More neighbors came out and there was self-righteous nodding and some mumbling about me bringing the outside to the inside. I heard a gravelly voiced friend of my mother's loudly say, "She should have stayed there."

Okwu said nothing. Nothing at all.

Hinterland

I was walking into the desert with the Desert People.

I turned back to the Root, my legs still moving me up the sand dune. I could still see my brother's garden, my bedroom window, and even the spot below where the Night Masquerade had stood. Then we were moving down the sand dune and I looked back until I couldn't see the Root any longer. "What am I doing?" I whispered.

My grandmother was walking beside me, tall and lean as a tree. "Did you bring *otjize* in your satchel?" she asked.

"Yes," I quietly said, patting my satchel.

She laughed loudly. "Of course you did." She moved her hands in front of her face, a smile still on her face, and I frowned, watching her. She said nothing when we were walking up the second sand dune and I took out the jar and began to reapply it to my arms and face, the places my mother had held me and tears had run.

Contrary to what my family thought, I knew exactly who I was going to see and I needed to look my best when I saw her. I had been eight years old and terrified when I met the Ariya completely by chance. She was the first person to whom I'd shown my *edan*, even before my father. She hadn't called it an *edan*, she'd called it a "god stone" and said I was lucky to have it. And now I was being brought to her with the thing in pieces.

========

There were dangerous creatures in the hinterland, and at night many didn't sleep.

A lean boy about my age and height named Mwinyi was charged with protecting the group. He was the one whom I'd glimpsed standing beside Okwu. Unlike the others who had dark-brown hair like me, Mwinyi had a head of bushy red-brown hair and I couldn't tell if the color was due to his hair being full of the desert's red dust or if this was its natural color. And he had a thick matted braid growing in the middle that was so long it reached his knees. It swung about his back like a snake when he walked. I couldn't understand how this boy was going to protect a group of nineteen adults until I saw what he could do.

Three hours after we'd scaled that first sand dune, the pack of wild dogs came. There were at least thirty and you could hear them coming from far away. They yipped and barked with the confidence of a pack that didn't need stealth to catch food or stay safe. They spotted and came at us without hesitation. Only I was terrified. Everyone else simply stopped and sat down on the sand, including the two camels. My grandmother put her hand on my shoulder to keep me calm. "Shhh," she said.

Mwinyi was the only one standing. Then he walked right to the dog pack, his hands moving in the Desert People way. Not slowly. Not quickly. In the soft moonlight, the sight was mystical, like watching something right out of the stories my father liked to tell during the Moon Fest. I couldn't hear him clearly, but I heard him speaking the language of the Desert People. He laughed as the dogs crowded him, sniffing and circling. Then Mwinyi said something and every single one of them stopped moving. And they were looking at him, at his face, as he spoke softly to them.

Then, just as suddenly, every single dog looked at *us*. I gasped and pressed my hands to my gaping mouth. I softly spoke a few choice equations and dropped a degree into meditation, just enough to stop shaking. I wanted to *see* this with all my senses and emotions sharp. Mwinyi was speaking to the dogs who would have harmed us. Several of the dogs near the back yipped agreeably, took one more look at us, and then went on their way. The others followed after a moment.

"He's a harmonizer?" I asked.

My grandmother looked at me. "We don't call them that."

"Then what do you call him?"

"Our son," she said, standing up. Mwinyi waved at us and we continued on our way. As we walked, I reached my hand into my pocket and touched the pouch full of my dissembled *edan*. Even in pieces, it was as much of a mystery to me now as it was when I'd found it . . .

Destiny Is a Delicate Dance

. . . **nine years ago. I was** out there that morning because I'd grown profoundly angry and run away from home. No one knew that I was angry and no one realized I'd run away. What had upset me was so trivial to my parents and older siblings that they didn't even realize I was upset. There was to be a dance at the Annual Wind Fest and though all of my age mates were participating, my parents and older siblings had decided it was best for me not to take part in it.

The Diviner had officially tapped me as the next family master harmonizer the week before and so much had already changed about how I was treated and what I was allowed and not allowed to do. Now this, all because I had to "sharpen my meditating skills and equation control" when I was already able to tree faster than my father.

Nevertheless, one does not argue with elders. Thus, I had accepted the restriction quietly as I had accepted being tapped as the next master harmonizer, despite the fact that I could never own the shop because I was a female. Shop ownership was my brother's honor. For our family to prove that it could produce a next generation of harmony brought fortune and great respect to us, so I was proud.

But I wanted to dance. I loved dancing. Dancing was like moving my body in the way that I saw numbers and equations move when I treed. When I danced, I could manifest mathematical current within me, harmonizing it with my muscles, skin, sinew, and bones. And now the opportunity had been snatched from me for no other reason besides, "It's just not for you." So I woke up that next morning, dressed in my weather-treated wrapper and top, wrapped my *otjize*-rolled locks in my red veil, quietly packed a satchel, and walked out of the house into the desert before anyone got up.

The desert wasn't a mystery to me. I wasn't supposed to, but I went into it quite often. Sometimes, I went to play, other times I went to find peace and quiet so I could practice treeing. The desert was largely responsible for why I'd gotten so good at treeing so young.

If my family had known that I went out there regularly, instead of going to the lake like all the other children, I'd have been punished with more than a beating. I was smart and stealth even back then. That early morning, I tiptoed into my parents' room and told them I was going to sit by the lake and watch the early crabs run about. Then I went outside and instead of going toward the lake, I went the other way, into the desert.

I liked the desert in the morning because it was still cool and it was still. I could go out there and my mind would clear like the sky after a violent power-outing thunderstorm. I would rub an extra-thick layer of *otjize* on my skin and go out sometimes as far as five miles. My astrolabe would start beeping and threatening to alert my parents about my whereabouts if I went any further. I'd see nothing around me but sand, not even the tops of the tallest Osemba buildings, which weren't very tall anyway.

In my childish anger, I was never going to return home. In my mind, I was becoming a nomad, wandering in the desert and letting the sand and wind take me where it would. And as I walked, sometimes, I would dance as I hummed to myself. My feet took me on a two-hour walk north, past the dried cluster of palm trees visible from my bedroom, the patch of hardpan where I'd once found an old seashell, to a place I'd discovered months ago, where a group of gray stones jutted out of the ground like flattened old teeth.

The stones were large enough to sit on and arranged in a wide semicircle that opened west. I'd never asked my parents or school-teachers about them because then I'd have to tell them where I saw such a thing. I came here often. Sometimes, I brought my small tent, set it up in the middle of the semicircle, and sat inside it while gazing out at the desert as I practiced equations, algorithms, and formulas for mathematical currents that I'd use in astrolabes I was making.

I'd needed the hard silence of the desert because I was still learning back then. This place was perfect. When I practiced, I liked to dig my fingers in the sand and scratch circles, squares, trape-zoids, fractals, whatever shapes I needed to visualize the equation. This day when I was eight years old and had run away, I'd set up my tent beside the furthest stone and my fingers drew circles upon circles.

My eyes were half-closed as I watched swirls of sand tumble down a nearby dune. I was whispering a current into being as di-viding numbers tumbled through my head. I worked hard not to think about the self-righteous look on my oldest sister's face as she said, "It's just dancing. You have to start sacrificing things like that now."

I was angrily digging my left index finger hard in the sand when I felt it. My nail grazed over it first and I noticed, but unconsciously. I was seeing a short hazy blue line dance before me. Tears fell from my eyes. My family was right. For three years they'd been pushing and pushing me, my mother, father, sisters, brothers, aunts, and uncles. They were all so sure of what I was, that I had the gift. I did have it and now everything was changing because of it. But I just wanted to dance.

The current whirled itself into a perfect circle. Now it was a connection. This would have powered an astrolabe if I had it assembled and positioned for "turn on." I felt a sting and hissed with pain. My hand. My finger. The blue disappeared as I brought my finger to my face for a closer look, my heart slamming in my chest. A scorpion bite all the way out here in the desert, while alone, was very bad news.

My thumb dripped blood and sand was ground into the wound. A tiny gray point poked from the spot where I'd been making circles with my fingers and thumb. Beside it was a small yellow flower. *How'd I miss that?* I wondered. I tried to pick the flower and realized that it was attached to a thin dry but strong white root that clung to whatever was poking from the sand. I put the flower down and grasped the point. It wouldn't budge. I shifted to my knees and leaned closer for a better look.

"Oh," I whispered. "It's not just . . ." I sucked on my finger as I looked at it. Then I started digging around it with my other hand. Soon I was using both hands, disregarding the stinging and light bleeding. Whenever my father allowed me to buy a new book, I spent hours in my room with my eyes closed as I listened to it on my astrolabe. In many of those stories, a curious person would find a secret or magical object that would change her or his life. I'd always wanted that to happen to me. And now I was sure this was it.

This was the Book of Shadows that appeared on the boy's astrolabe when he passed too close to a tree that had just been struck by lightning. This was the jeweled eagle figurine that the girl bought in the market that caused all the birds to come. This was the plant that began to grow in the old man's bedroom after a strange dust storm.

The thing I dug up was a stellated cube. It fit into the palm of my hand and was made of a tarnished metal. There were intricate designs all over it, adept loops and swirls and spirals whose lines never touched each other. I turned it over this way and that, marveling at its complex pointy shape.

"What *is* this thing?" I whispered, awed.

I knocked off the remaining sand and used some of my *otjize* to polish it. This worked better than I expected, for soon its tarnished appearance changed to one of amazing shine. And each time I moved it, it produced a . . . a soft sound. Like the low husky voice of a woman. It was a little scary . . . and fascinating. There was somehow old *current* in this thing. Nevertheless, the more I moved it, the softer the sound until it stopped all together.

Father's eyes will bug out when I show this thing to him, I excitedly thought. And that was how I decided that I was not running away after all. I couldn't wait to hear what he had to say about the mystery device I'd found. Or if he could tell me the best way to study it. *Maybe I can get it to do whatever it was made to do,* I thought. I giggled to myself, sitting on one of the stones and holding the strange thing to my face.

When someone tapped my shoulder, I nearly screamed. And when I whipped around and saw the tall dark-skinned woman with a corona of black hair so huge that it blocked out the sun shining behind her, I did scream. I jumped to my feet and nearly fell over my satchel.

She was one of the Desert People. She looked ten feet tall and everything about her, from her hair to the light sheer blue cloth wrapped around her head to her flowing pants and top made of the same blue material, was blowing in the soft breeze. Slung over her shoulder was a small capture station, its catch bag, and a blue old-looking backpack. I squinted up at her in the sunshine. She was so very tall and so . . . blue. The tallest person I'd ever seen. And somewhat old like my mother's mother. She grasped a thick gnarled walking staff with her long-fingered hands, but she wasn't leaning on it.

"What are you doing out here?" she asked. Her voice was dry and commanding, also like my grandmother, and I immediately stood up straighter.

"I . . . this . . . this is where I . . . please . . . my . . ."

"Oh, shut up, child," she sighed. "Forget I asked." She rested her staff on her side and began doing that which I'd heard the Desert People did; she moved her hands this way and that, like a child swatting at a fly. I took the moment to quickly look around. There were no others. Could I outrun her? The woman wore no shoes. *How can she stand the hot sand?*

"Binti," she said. "Daughter of Moaoogo Dambu Kaipka Okechukwu Enyi Zinariya."

"That's my name, my father . . . how do you know?" I whispered. I'd decided that there was no way I could outrun the woman. She was old and carried a staff, but something told me she was strong like a man and she didn't use that staff for walking.

"Do you know who I am?" she asked.

"A desert person?"

She nodded, working her hands before her. It was as if they weren't even part of her body. In my pocket, my astrolabe buzzed. The sun had just reached its highest peak and it was best to sit in the shade for the next hour. I reached into my pocket to stop it from buzzing.

"I journeyed all the way to this place so I can think," the woman said.

"I . . . I did, too," I said.

And for a moment, we stared at each other.

"I've been coming here since before your mother was a thought in your grandmother's womb," she said, with a chuckle. "What is that you've found?"

I grasped it more tightly and took a step back. "Nothing. A pretty chunk of . . . metal." I felt sweat prickle in my armpits. To lie to an elder is a sin.

"Don't worry," she said. "I'm not going to take it from you."

"I . . . I never said that," I said.

"I know your grandmother, Binti."

I nearly dropped the *edan* when I looked at her with surprise . . . and understanding. My father's mother was a desert woman and he never spoke of her. Himba men did not wear *otjize*, but sometimes they used it to palm roll or flatten their hair. My father used it to flatten his coarse bushy hair, to mask it. And like me, he was the shade of brown like the Desert People and he'd never liked this fact. My mother was a medium brown, like most Himba, and I knew for a fact that he was proud that all their other children were too . . . and that the one who got the desert complexion and hair made up for it by being a master harmonizer.

I'd once asked my father about the Desert People when I was about five years old and he'd snapped at me to never speak of it again. As I looked at this tall woman now, I wanted to go home. I *needed* to go home. My father would kill me for speaking to this woman. I wasn't supposed to be out here in the first place, so meeting her was entirely my fault.

"Do you know what that is you've found?"

I shook my head.

"It's a piece of time from before our time. An ancient work of art and use. It's old, but old doesn't always mean less advanced."

I opened my hand and looked at it. It rested in my palm, comfortable there, but so strange.

"Want to know how to use it?"

I shook my head. "I have to get home," I said. "My father has work for me to finish later today."

"Yes, your gifted father who is so proud of himself." She paused looking me over and then said, "The thing you have, the Himba will call it an *edan*, but we call it a god stone. You're blessed it's found you." She did a few hand motions and laughed. "When you are ready to know how to really use it, find us."

"Okay," I said, smiling the most false smile I had ever smiled. My legs were shaking so vigorously that I felt I would fall to my knees.

"Safe journey home," she said. Then she knelt, touched the sand, and said, "Praise the Seven."

I stood there for a moment surprised, thinking, *Desert People believed in the presence of the Seven too?* I wondered what my mother would say to this fact, since she thought Desert People were so uncivilized. Not that I'd ever tell her about meeting this woman.

I swiped *otjize* from my face and did the same. Then I turned and ran off. I didn't look back until I was about to crest the first sand dune. She still stood there, beside the gray stones where I'd found the *edan*. I wondered what she'd make of the plant growing there.

━━━━━

Early crabs were sneaky and quick, so my parents weren't surprised when I returned empty-handed. I was no longer that angry with my parents, so when I took the *edan* to my father two days later, I didn't have to stifle my emotions. I didn't tell him about the plant growing on it or where I found it. It's the only time I'd lied to my father. I told him I'd bought the thing at the market from a junk seller.

"Who was selling it? Which junk man?" my father anxiously asked. "I need to talk to him! Look at this thing it's—"

"I don't know, Papa," I quickly said. "I wasn't really paying attention. I was so focused on it."

"I'll go to the market tomorrow," my father said, pulling at his scruffy beard. "Maybe someone will have another." He took it from me, his eyes wide. "Beautiful work."

"I think it does something that—"

"The metal," he whispered, staring at the object. He looked at me, smiled and apologetically patted my head. "Sorry, Binti. You were saying?"

"It's okay. What about the metal?"

My father brought it to his teeth and bit the tip of one of the points. Then he touched it with the tip of his tongue and brought it so close to his left eye that he nearly touched his eyeball. He held it to his nose and sniffed. "I don't know this type of metal," he said. He smacked his lips. "It leaves a taste on the tongue, like when you taste the salts that gather on the Undying Trees during dry season."

The Undying Trees grew all over Osemba. They had thick rubbery wide leaves and trunks spiked with hard thorns that had lived longer than any generation could recall. Their ancient roots were so strong and they snaked so deeply beneath Osemba that the town's waterworks were not only built around them, they were built *along* them. The Undying Trees led the founders of Osemba to the only drinkable source of water for a hundred miles.

Nevertheless, the trees were strange. They vibrated so fast during thunderstorms that they made a howling sound, which permeated the city. During dry season, they produced salt on their leaves, which was used by healers to cure and treat all sorts of ailments. Life salt, it was called. The device I'd found tasted like life salt.

"It's an *edan*," my father said and I'd nodded like I'd never heard the word before. He explained to me that "edan" was a general name for devices too old for anyone to know their functions, so old that they were now more art than anything else. That's what my father wanted it for, as a piece of art to brag about to his friends. But I insisted on keeping it for myself and because he loved me, he let me.

Now here I was walking into the desert with the Desert People. How different my life would have been if my parents had just let me dance.

Lies

===

By sunup, I knew the Desert People had lied.

"Can you reach your Meduse?" my grandmother asked me. We'd walked through the remainder of the night and morning. Now, it was approaching midday and we stopped until night. We stood in the shade of one of the camels, some of the others bringing out dried dates and switching on noisy capture stations to collect water. I was nearly asleep on my feet, barely able to keep my eyes open. My grandmother's question woke me right up.

"Reach?" I asked. My eyes met Mwinyi's, who sat a few yards away crunching on what looked like dried leaves.

"Yes, speak to it," my grandmother said.

"I don't know," I muttered, looking out into the desert. "Maybe? Do I really—"

"Tell it that we will bring you back when we bring you back," my grandmother said. "Our village is three days' walk away."

"What? Why didn't you tell them this before? Why didn't you tell *me*?" I'd wondered why we were still walking when they'd promised to have me back by nightfall. It had been easier to stay in denial. I groaned. I'd gone from one extreme to another, days confined on a ship, then not even twenty-four hours later, days walking through open desert.

"Sometimes it's best to tell people only what they need to hear," my grandmother said.

"Can't someone go back and tell them? I don't know if I can tell Okwu anything detailed," I breathed, my heart starting to beat the talking drum. "What if I can't do—"

"It's up to you, Binti," she said, dismissively. She spoke over her shoulder as she walked to two women who'd just set out a large bowl of dried dates. "You do it or you don't."

My grandmother wasn't offering me any real choice. If I didn't come home tonight, my family would fly into panic. Again. For the second time, they would be forced to deal with my disappearance and the fact that they couldn't do a thing about it. My mother would get terribly quiet and stop laughing, my father would work too hard in his shop, my siblings would feel an ache akin to one caused by the death of a loved one. Family. I had to reach Okwu.

However, I still didn't know much about my *okuoko*. I didn't understand how they affected me. How they connected me to the Meduse, especially Okwu. Why I could feel sensation through them. Why they writhed when I was furious. What I knew was that I could sense Okwu when I was on Math City and he was in Weapons City, which were hundreds of miles away and that I had once had a very weak but definite sense that the Meduse Chief who was planets away was checking up on me.

I could wiggle my *okuoko* on purpose, but I couldn't explain to anyone how I did it. It was like moving my nostrils, I just could. In this way, while petting the shaggy fur of the camel beside me, I reached out to Okwu. I thought about it, *willed* it. Seconds passed. Nothing. I sighed and glanced at my grandmother, who was watching me. I looked up into the blue sky and spotted a ship from afar that was leaving the atmosphere. A mere speck. The launch port was maybe a hundred miles away. I wondered if it was Third Fish. *No*, I thought. *Third Fish is giving birth soon.*

I shook my head. *Focus*, I thought. *Okwu.* I imagined the tent my father had set up outside the Root. How it was full of the gas the

Meduse breathed. Okwu was the first of its kind on Earth since the Khoush-Meduse Wars. Okwu doing whatever Okwu did in its tent when it avoided interaction with any of my family or other curious Himba. And I softly slipped my mind into a set of equations that reminded me of space and movement across small lengths of it.

Now I reached out again, my hand flat on the camel's rump, slowly moving up and down with its steady breathing. I strained to reach Okwu and it realized this and reached for me. I felt it grasp and suddenly I felt Okwu's mind. Sweat poured down my face and I felt all things around me tint Okwu's light blue.

Binti, I felt Okwu say through one of my *okuoko*. It vibrated against my left ear. *Where are you? You are far.*

In the hinterland, I responded. *I won't be back tonight.*

Do I need to come get you?

No.

Are you well?

Yes. The village is just far. Days away.

Okay. I will wait here.

Then just like that, Okwu let go and was gone. I came back to myself and my eyes focused on the desert before me.

"Done?" my grandmother asked. She stood behind me and I turned to her.

"Yes. It knows."

She nodded. "Well done," she said, holding her hands up and moving them around. She walked away.

━━━━

They pitched their elaborate goatskin tents facing the desert to give everyone the semblance of privacy. Two men built a fire in the center of the tents and some of the women began to use it to cook. The soft whoosh of capture stations from behind two of the tents and their cool breath further cooled the entire camp. Soon, the large empty jug one of the camels had been carrying was rolled to the center of the tents and filled with water.

"You'll stay with me," my grandmother said, pointing to the tent two men had just set up for her. She handed me a cup. "Drink heavily, your body needs hydration." Inside, the tent was spacious and there were two bedrolls on opposite sides. For "dinner" there was flat bread with honey, a delicious strong-smelling hearty soup with dried fish, more dates, and mint tea. As the sun rose, everyone quickly disappeared into his or her tents to sleep.

I was pleasantly full and tired, but too restless to sleep just yet. So I sat on my mat, staring out at the desert, my grandmother snoring across from me. Since we'd walked into the desert, the flashbacks and day terrors I was used to having had disappeared. I inhaled the dry baking air and smiled. The healing properties of the desert had always been good for me. My eye fell on Mwinyi, who'd been watering the camels and now sat out on a sand dune facing the desert. His hands were working before him. I got up and walked over to him.

He looked at me as I approached, turned back to the desert, and continued working his hands. I paused, wondering if I was interrupting. I pushed on; I had to know. Plus, I'd seen several of them talking and laughing as they moved their hands like this, so I doubted it was like prayer or meditation.

"Hi," I said, hoping he'd stop moving his hands. He didn't.

"You should get some sleep," he said.

I cocked my head as I watched him. He was frowning as he pushed his blue sleeves back, held up his arms, and moved his hands in graceful swooping jabbing motions.

"I will," I said. I paused and took a breath. I wondered what would happen if I called up a current and connected it to his moving hands. Would the zap of it make him stop? "What is this that you're doing?" I blurted. "With your hands? Can you control it?" I waited, cringing as I bit my lip. For a moment, he only worked his hands, his eyes staring into the desert.

Then he looked up at me. "I'm communicating."

"But you do it when you . . . like now," I said as he did a flourish with his hands. "You're not talking to me right there. I don't understand it, if you are. And I see people doing it while talking to other people, too."

He looked at me for a long time and then glanced at the camp and then back at me.

"This is something your grandmother should tell you. Go ask her."

"I'm asking you," I said. "You all do it, so why can't I ask anyone?"

He sighed and muttered, "Okay, sit down."

I sat beside him, pulling my legs to my chest.

"Auntie Titi, your grandmother, is my grandfather's best friend," he said. "So I know all about your father and his shame. You have the same shame."

I blinked for a moment as two separate worlds tangled in my mind. Back when I was on the ship with the Meduse, they had referred to my *edan* as "shame" and now here was that word again, but in a completely different context. "I don't underst—"

"I saw how you looked at us," he said. "Just like every Himba I have ever encountered, like we're savages. You call us the 'Desert People,' mysterious uncivilized dark people of the sand."

I wanted to deny my prejudice, but he was right.

"Despite the fact that you're darker like us, have the crown like us, have our blood," he said. "I wonder how surprised you were when you saw that we could speak your language as well as our three languages. 'Desert People.' Do you even know the actual name of our tribe?"

I shook my head, slowly.

"We're the Enyi Zinariya," he said. "No, I won't translate that for you." He looked directly at me, into my eyes, and I didn't turn away. I wanted an answer to my initial question and I knew when I was being tested. There is nothing like being a harmonizer and looking directly into another harmonizer's eyes. Nothing.

Everything around us dropped away and there was a sonorous melody that vibrated between my ears that was so perfectly aligned that I felt as if I were beginning to float.

"I only know what I am taught," I whispered.

"That's not true," he said.

"I . . . I met one of you once," I said.

"We know," he said. "And was she a savage?"

"No."

"So you knew that back then."

"Okay," I said, shutting my eyes and rubbing my forehead. "Okay."

He chuckled. "When we heard about what you did, we all cheered."

"Really?"

He turned away from me, finished talking. "You should go. Get some sleep."

"Answer my question first," I said. "Please."

"I did. I said we are communicating."

"With who?"

"Everyone."

"As you speak to me, you're speaking to others?"

"It's the same with your astrolabe," he said. "Can't you use it while you talk to other people?"

"But no one is here."

"I was talking to my mother back in the village," he said. "She was asking about you."

"Oh," I said, frowning deeply. "So you can speak like how I speak to Okwu?"

He paused and moved his hands. Then he turned to me and flatly said, "Ask your grandmother."

I was about to get up, but then I stopped and asked, "Crown? You said I have the crown like you?"

He grasped a handful of his bushy red-brown hair, "This is the crown." Then he laughed. "Well, you used to have it. Before the Meduse took it and replaced it with tentacles."

I wanted to be offended but the way he said it, in such a literal way, instead pulled a hard laugh out of me and suddenly we were both giggling. When I calmed down, the fatigue of the journey hit me and I slowly got up. "What was the name of your clan again?" I asked.

"You're Himba, I'm Enyi Zinariya," he said.

"Enyi Zinariya," I repeated.

He nodded, smiling. "You pronounce it well."

"Okay," I said and went back to my grandmother's tent, lay down, and was asleep within seconds.

—

"Get up, girl."

I opened my eyes to my grandmother's face and the sound of the tent walls flapping from the wind. I stared into her eyes, blinking away the last remnants of sleep. When I sat up, I felt amazingly well rested. The cooling breeze of evening smelled so fresh that I flared my nostrils and inhaled deeply. I'd slept for nearly six hours.

My grandmother smiled, the strong breeze blowing her bushy hair about. "Yes, it's a good time to move across the desert."

The desert looked absolutely stunning, bright moonlight and the soft travel of the sand blending to make the ground look otherworldly. I could hear the others talking, laughing and moving about, and the two camels roaring as they were made to stand up. The smell of flat bread made my stomach grumble.

"Grandma," I said. "Please, tell me why the Enyi Zinariya speak with their hands."

Her eyes grew wide for a moment and I quickly said, "I've been planets away and learned about and met people from other worlds. It's wrong that I don't even know of my own . . . my own people." I let out a breath as my words sunk into me. They were the truth now, a truth that had been different a day ago when I had been ashamed and quiet about my blood. Seeing the Night Masquerade had lived up to its mythology. To see it *did* signify immediate drastic change.

"Walk with me," my grandmother said, then she left the tent. I followed, grabbing my satchel. As we walked away from the camp, I saw two of the men go to our tent and start breaking it down. She led me up the nearest high sand dune. When we reached the top, she turned toward the camp and sat down. I sat beside her. Below, the camp was aflutter with activity, all the tents packed up except ours. I was clearly the last to wake up.

"You've somehow learned the name of our clan."

"I asked Mwinyi."

"Having curiosity is the only way to learn," she said. She worked her hands before her for a moment and then looked at me. "That was me communicating with your father."

I raised my eyebrows.

"You Himba are so inward-looking," she said. "Cocooned around that pink lake, growing your technology from knowledge harvested from deep within your genius, you girls and women dig up your red clay and hide beneath it. You're an interesting people who have been on those lands for generations. But you're a young people. The Enyi Zinariya are old old Africans.

"And contrary to what you all believe, we have technology that puts yours to shame and we've had it for centuries." She paused, letting this news sink in. It wasn't sinking in to me easily. All that she'd said was so contrary to all that I had been taught that I'd begun to feel a little dizzy.

"We didn't create it, though," she continued. "It was brought to us by the Zinariya. Those who were there documented the Zinariya times, but the files were kept on paper and paper does not last. So all we really know is what elders read and then what the elders after those elders remembered and then what the next elders remembered and so on.

"The Zinariya came to us in the desert. They were a golden people, who glinted in the sun. They were solar and had landed in Earth's desert to rest and refuel on their way to Oomza Uni."

I couldn't control myself. "What?" I shrieked.

She chuckled. "Yes. We 'Desert People' knew of Oomza Uni before other people on Earth even had mobile phones!"

"Oh my goodness," I whispered. I couldn't imagine anyone on Earth back then being able to comprehend the very idea of Oomza Uni. Human beings on Earth hadn't even had real contact with people from outside yet, and the nonhumans who had had contact with extraterrestrials never bothered to convey anything to human beings. It was centuries later and I, who had been there, was still trying to wrap my brain around the sheer greatness of Oomza Uni.

"Our clan was even smaller and nomadic back then, and we became fast friends with the Zinariya. Though many of them left for Oomza within a few months, a few stayed with us for many years before going on to Oomza. Before leaving, they gave us something to help us communicate with them wherever they were and with each other wherever we were. They also called this 'zinariya.' It was a living organism tailored for our blood that every member of the clan drank into his or her system with water. Biological nanoids so tiny that they could comfortably embed themselves into our brains. Once you had them in you, it was like having an astrolabe in your nervous system. You could eat, hear, smell, see, feel, even *sense* it."

How had I not been able to guess this? Not that it was due to alien technology, but that they were working with a platform. They were manipulating a virtual platform like the ones astrolabes could project! One that only the Enyi Zinariya could see and access. I felt a sting of shame as I realized why I hadn't understood something so obvious. My own prejudice. I had been raised to view the Desert People, the Enyi Zinariya, as a primitive, savage people plagued by a genetic neurological disorder. So that's what I saw.

My grandmother nodded, a knowing smirk on her face. "And once the zinariya was in those who drank it, the nanoids were passed on to offspring through their DNA." She stopped talking and looked at me, waiting. Seconds passed and I frowned, anxious. I was about to ask if she'd told me all she was going to tell me when it exploded in my mind. My world went fuzzy for a moment and I was glad that I was sitting down. I shut my eyes and grasped at the first mathematical equation I could. Equations were always rotating around me like moons and this thought was soothing. Gently, I let myself tree. Then I opened my eyes, calm and balanced, and faced a very jarring bit of information.

"My father has the zinariya in him," I said.

My grandmother was looking at me, smirking. "Yes."

"And so do I and all my siblings."

"Yes."

"We carry alien technology."

"Yes."

The information tried to knock me down and I sunk deeper into meditation. If I wanted to, I could call up a current and send it streaming across the sand. *I am Himba*, I said to myself between the splitting and splitting fractals of equations, my most soothing pattern. *I am Himba, even if my hair has become* okuoko *because of my actions and even if I have Enyi Zinariya blood. Even if my DNA is alien.*

"Binti," my grandmother softly said.

"Why can't I see it? Why can't any of my siblings or my father? None of us goes about waving our hands, manipulating objects that no one else can see."

"Your father can and does," she said. "When he so chooses. Didn't I tell you I'd just communicated with him? You think a son would abandon his mother? Just because he marries a Himba woman and decides to use his harmonizing skill in 'civilization' instead of the hinterland?"

I sighed and pressed my hands to my forehead. I felt so strange. This was all so strange.

"If you could reach my father, why'd you need me to reach out to Okwu?"

"To see if you could," she said, smiling.

I frowned.

"Now listen," she said. "The zinariya cannot just be used. It has to be switched on; it has to be activated. If it is not, you can live your whole life without even knowing it's in you. As you have."

"How does one switch it on?"

"The clan priestess does it. The Ariya. You will meet her to-morrow."

━━━━━

I wanted to turn back.

Oh, I wanted to turn back so badly. Enough was enough was enough was enough. I could have made it home. Then I could have still made the trek out onto the salt trails on my own and caught up with the women and completed my pilgrimage. I could have become a whole woman in my clan, a complete Himba woman. All I had to do was walk into the darkness and use my astrolabe to tell me which way to go. However, we were days into the hinterland and if something did not kill me in the night, my lack of food or a proper water-gathering capture station would.

Plus, I didn't want to turn back. Why don't I ever want to do what I'm supposed to do?

━━━━━

So I went with Grandmother. I went with the Desert People.

It was another forty-eight hours of walking during the night, sleeping during the day, eating dates, flat bread, and palm-oil-rich Enyi Zinariya stews. Three more times, I saw Mwinyi protect us from packs of predatory animals—once from another pack of wild dogs and twice from hyenas. And I watched the Enyi Zinariya with new eyes; I especially watched their hands.

In the meantime, I barely touched my astrolabe. There was so much around me to take in; I just didn't need it. Nor did I touch the pieces of my *edan*; I didn't want to think about it. Okwu checked on me once that second day and was even curter than it was the first time.

You okay, Binti?

Yes.

Good.

That was all. On the third, it didn't check in at all. I tried reaching it later that day as I had the first time, but it didn't respond. I wondered what it was doing back at the Root, but I wasn't worried. My grandmother was in touch with my father, so everyone knew everything anyway.

━━━━━

On the fourth night, the land changed. We simply came to the end of the sand dunes and the beginning of smooth white limestone. And soon after that, we reached a sudden drop and before I could understand what was happening and what I was seeing, I heard joyous ululating.

Gold People

The Enyi Zinariya lived in a vast network of caves in a huge limestone cliff. Within the bowels of these caves were winding staircases that led from cave to cave, family to family. Some caves were tiny, no larger than a closet, others were as vast as the Root. Upon arrival, I was taken for a quick tour of my grandmother's family's caves. I met so many of her people, young to old, all enthusiastically waving their hands about, that I could not understand the logic of where people lived.

It seemed everyone could stay wherever he or she was most comfortable, from child to elder. I saw a cave where an old man and his teenage granddaughter lived, the girl's parents (one of whom was the old man's daughter) living in a cave connected by a narrow tunnel. The old man and granddaughter were both obsessed with studying, collecting, and documenting stones, so their cave was full of stone piles and stacks of yellowing paper with scribbled research.

"Best to just have only one cave full of rocks," her mother told me with a laugh. "Those two are happy together." My grandmother's cave was tiny, but sparse and tidy with colorful shaggy blue rugs, delicate mobiles hanging from the ceiling made of crystals one of her daughters had collected, and bottles of scented oils they specialized in making. The room also smelled immaculate.

It was brightly lit by a large circular solar lamp in the room's center. What was most striking was that my grandmother's cave was full of plants. It reminded me of one of the Third Fish's breathing rooms. There were pots with leafy green vines tumbling out of them hung near the high ceiling beside her bed. There were several large woven baskets full of sand with complex light green treelike succulents growing from them and dry bioluminescent vines that grew directly on the cave's walls. Right there in the cave, my grandmother was growing five different types of tomatoes, three types of peppers, and some type of fruiting plant that I could not name.

"I'm a botanist," she said, putting her satchel down. "Your grandfather was, too."

"Was?"

She nodded. "He was Himba." And that was all she would say, though there was clearly so much more. I wanted to ask why he left the Himba and if he stayed in touch at all. I wanted to ask how he felt when my father decided to leave and return to the Himba. I wanted to ask if this was where my father had stayed when he was a child. I wanted to ask why she loved plants. I wanted to ask why she lived alone when everyone else in the village lived happily with many, even in the smaller caves. Instead, I looked at my grandmother's many thriving plants and breathed the lush air that smelled so different from the other caves and the dry desert outside.

I stopped at a small yellow flower growing from a dry root in a pot bigger than my hand. This was the same type of flower that had been growing on the *edan* years ago when I'd found it.

"What's this one?" I asked.

"I call it ola edo," she said. "Means 'hard to find, hard to grow'." She laughed, "And not very pretty. Okay, time for you to rest, Binti. Tomorrow is your day."

As I had in the Third Fish's breathing chamber, I slept well here.

The Ariya

The Ariya's cave was a mile from the cave village in the center of a dried lake.

"Something used to live in it, back when this was a lake," Mwinyi said as we walked. "Maybe even dug the hole in the rock, itself."

"How do you know?" I said, looking at the ground as we walked. At some point, the smooth limestone had become craggy, making it hard to walk. I had to concentrate on not tripping over jutting rock.

"It's in the Collective," he said, glancing at me. "That's the Enyi Zinariya's memory that we all can touch."

I nodded.

"But no one knows exactly what kind of creature it was," he said. He waved his hands before him.

"Did you just tell her we're close?" I asked.

He looked sharply at me, frowning. "How'd you—"

"I'm not a fool," I said.

He grunted.

I laughed and pointed up ahead. "Plus, I see something just up there. A hole or something."

To call it a hole was to put it lightly. The opening in the hard ground was the size of a house. When we stepped up to it, I noticed two things. The first was that there was a large bird circling directly above the opening. The second was that rough stone steps were carved into the stone walls of the hole wound all the way to the bottom.

We descended the steps, Mwinyi going first. I ran my hand along the abrasive wall as I recited soft equations in my head. I called up a soft current and the mild friction from the current and my hand running over the coarse stone was pleasant beneath my fingertips. The deep cavern's walls were lined with books, so many books. The location of the sun must have been directly above, for the strong light of midday pleasantly flooded into the space. However, along with the light, bioluminescent vines grew in and lit the darker corners.

She stood in the shadows, beside a shelf of books, her arms crossed over her chest. "You haven't changed a bit," she said. Nearly a decade later, her bushy crown of hair a little grayer, her face a little wiser, and I still would know this woman anywhere. Could old women grow taller over the years?

"Hello, Mma," I said, looking up at her. I used the Himba term of respect because I didn't know what else to use.

"Binti," she said, pulling me into a tight hug. "Welcome to my home."

"Thank you for inviting me," I said.

She gave Mwinyi a tight hug, as well. "Thanks for bringing her. How was the walk?"

"As expected," he said.

"Come back for her at sundown."

"Ugh," I blurted, slumping. It was morning and I hadn't expected this to be an all-day thing. Though maybe I should have; springing things like this on me seemed to be the Enyi Zinariya way.

Mwinyi nodded, winked at me, and left.

She turned back to me. "Don't you know how to go with the flow yet?" she asked. "Adjust."

"I just didn't think that . . ."

"You saw the Night Masquerade," she said. "That's no small thing. Why expect what you expect?" Before I could answer, she said, "Come and sit down."

I took one more glance at Mwinyi, who was now near the top of the stairs, and followed the old woman.

We moved deeper into the cave and sat on a large round blue rug. It was cool and dark here, the air smelling sweet with incense. The place reminded me of a Seventh Temple, mostly empty and quiet. But *she* didn't remind me of a Seven priestess at all. She wasn't demure, she didn't cover her head with an orange scarf, she wore no *otjize,* and she got straight to the point. "Why do you think you saw the Night Masquerade?" she asked. "You're not a man."

"Is it even real?" I asked.

"Don't answer a question with a question. Why do you think you saw it?"

"I don't know."

"Remember when we first met?"

"Yes."

"Why were you out there?"

"I found that place, I liked it," I said. "I wasn't supposed to be out there, I know."

"And look where it got you."

"What do you mean?"

"If you hadn't found the *edan,* would you have questioned and grown? Would you have gone? And even if you would have, would you be alive now?"

It came suddenly in that way that it had been for so many months. The rage. I felt it prick me like a needle in my back and my *okuoko* twitched. I took a deep breath, trying to calm it. "It doesn't matter," I muttered, my nostrils flaring.

"Why?"

Another wave of rage washed through my body and I angrily reached into my pocket, glad to have a reason to move. I felt my *okuoko* wildly writhing on my head and Ariya's eyes went to them, calmly watching their motion. *No matter,* I thought, bringing out the small pouch. I leaned forward, breathing heavily through my flared nostrils, and wildly dumped it all out before her onto the carpet. The sound of tumbling metal pieces echoed and then came a *thunk* as the golden grooved center fell out. I motioned to it with my hands to emphasize it all. "Because I *broke* it!" I shouted, my voice cracking. "I broke it! I'm a harmonizer and I de-harmonized an *edan*!" My voice echoed around and up the cavern. Then silence.

I should have treed to calm myself. This was Ariya, priestess of the Enyi Zinariya, I'd just met her, and here I was behaving like a barbarian. "I know," I added. "I'm unclean. This was why I came home. For cleansing through my pilgrimage. But I didn't go . . . I'm here instead . . ." I trailed off and just watched her stare at the pieces and the golden center. What felt like minutes passed, giving me time to calm down. My *okuoko* grew still. The rest of my body relaxed. And my *edan* was still broken. *I broke it,* I thought.

"Unclean? No," Ariya finally said, shaking her head. "That part of you that is Meduse now, you just need to get *that* under control."

In one sentence, she explained something that had been bothering me for a year. That's all it was. The random anger and wanting to be violent, that was just Meduse genetics in me. *Nothing is wrong with me?* I thought. *Not unclean? It's just . . . a new part of me I need to learn to control?* I'd come all this way to go on my pilgrimage because I'd thought my body was trying to tell me something was wrong with it. I hadn't wanted to admit it to myself, but I'd thought I'd broken myself because of the choices I'd made, because of my actions, because I'd left my home to go to Oomza Uni. Because of guilt. The relief I felt was so all encompassing that I wanted to lie down on the rug and just sleep.

Ariya slowly got up, her knees creaking. She dusted off her long blue dress. "Sometimes, the obvious is too obvious," she muttered, walking away. Then over her shoulder, she said, "Stay there."

I watched her ascend the stairs and when she reached the top, she walked off.

I lay on my back and sighed. "Just Meduse DNA," I muttered. "Or whatever it is they have for genetic code. That's all." I laughed, sitting up on my elbows. My eyes fell on the disassembled *edan* still lying on the rug. I stopped laughing.

═══════

She was gone for what might have been an hour. I'd dozed off right on that round blue rug, lulled by the cool darkness and incense. The sound of her sandals at the top of the stairs woke me. She stepped onto the first stair, paused, and then quickly descended. The moment her upper body came into sight, I saw the creature. Was I seeing what I was seeing? When she reached the bottom of the stairs, I stood up. It was an almost involuntary action. But what else was one to do when a great woman came down the stairs with a great owl perched on her arm?

The owl was about two feet tall with white and tan feathers, a black bill, a rounded frowning bushy eyebrowed face, and wide yellow eyes. At the top of its head were brown and black feathers that looked like horns. Ariya's arm was protected by a brown leather armband, but that was all the protection she had. The owl could pluck out her eyes, slash her with its long white talons, slap her with its massive powerful wings if it wanted to. Instead, it stared at me with such intensity that I wondered if I should sit back down.

"If it's waiting outside, then it is right," she said. "It was right there when I came out. Help me."

I assisted as she slowly sat down with the owl perched on her arm. I sat across from them and gazed at the enormous bird.

"Is it heavy?" I asked

"Birds who spend most of their lives in the sky can't be heavy," she said. "No, this one is light as . . . a feather."

"Oh," I said.

"In my forty-five years as priestess, I have not done this," she said. "Not even once."

Suddenly, I felt cold. Very very cold. With dismay. Deep down, I knew. From the moment my grandmother told me about the Zinariya, I'd known, really. Change was constant. Change was my destiny. Growth.

"Why?" I still asked.

"Because it's the only way you can fix it and you have to fix it, so you can use it to do what it needs to do." The owl hadn't taken its eyes off of me. "Do you know what zinariya means in the old language?"

I shook my head.

"It means 'gold.' That's the name we gave them because we couldn't speak their true name with our mouths and because that is what they were made of. Gold. Golden people. Their bodies, their ship, everything about them was gold. They came to the desert because they needed to rest and refuel and they loved the color of the sand . . . gold. Your *edan* is Zinariya technology; I knew this when I met you. I just thought, since it allowed you to find it, you could solve it without . . . without—"

"Needing to be activated."

She nodded. "No one who was not one of us has ever known about the zinariya and those who marry out or leave, they're so ashamed of being Enyi Zinariya that they don't tell their families."

"Like my father," I said. "It's like having some genetic disease, in a way. If Himba or Khoush knew of it, they'd . . ."

Ariya smiled. "Oh, they know, someone in those clans knows enough to build toxic ideas against us right into their cultures. That's really why we are so outcast, untouchable to them. To Himba and Khoush we are the savage 'Desert People,' not the Enyi Zinariya. No one wants our blood in their line. Anyway, the Collective knows the names and faces of all your siblings and their children."

"Oh," I said, feeling a little better. "Well, that is good."

"But that's all."

We stared at each other for a moment.

"Do you want to do this?" she asked.

"Do I need to?"

"Hmm. You're still ashamed of what you are."

"No," I said. "I'm Himba and proud of that."

She raised her eyebrows. "Not your grandmother. She is Enyi Zinariya. And we are a matriarchal clan, so your father is, too."

"No," I snapped. "Papa is Himba." I could feel the sting of my own nearsightedness. It was irritating and pushing me off-balance in a way that made it hard for me to think. My confusion evoked a flash of Meduse anger.

"Do you want it?" she asked.

I opened my mouth to answer, but I didn't speak it because what I'd have spoken was stupid. It was wrong. But it was the truth, too. If I went through with this, I was taking another step outside what it was to be Himba, away from myself, away from my family. I wanted to hide from the owl's unwavering gaze.

"Do you want it?" she asked again.

I sighed loudly and shook my head. "Priestess Ariya, I don't understand any of this. If the *edan* is Zinariya technology, why does the outer metal kill Meduse? I'm part Meduse now, so why doesn't my *edan* kill me? I don't understand what is happening to me, why my *edan* fell apart, what that ball is, why it matters, why I'm here! I came here to go on pilgrimage; I'm not even there. I'm here. I don't know what I'm doing or where I'm going!" I stared at her with wide eyes, breathing heavily. I couldn't breathe. I couldn't think. I couldn't tree.

I was seeing all the Khoush in the dining room on the Third Fish. Dead. Chests burst open by the stingers of Meduse. *Moojh-ha ki-bira*, the "great wave." The flow of death like water I'd fallen into that in some twisted way gave me a new life. I leaned to the side, pressing my hand to my chest. Angry tears stung my eyes. How could Okwu have been a part of this slaughter? Why did the Seven allow this to happen? Yet, drowning in the waters of death gave me new life. Not drowning in it, carried by it.

"Shallow breaths, increased heart rate, you're having a panic attack," my astrolabe in my pocket announced in its stiff female voice. "I suggest you drop into mathematical meditation." I wanted to smash it to bits.

The priestess did nothing but watch me. The owl puffed out its throat and hooted three times. Soft and peaceful. My eyes wide as I stared into the owl's, I inhaled a deep breath, filling my lungs to full capacity. When I exhaled, the owl hooted softly again and the sound calmed me more. Then it hooted again, leaning down and bringing its neck low near its feathery legs, as it held my eyes. Soon the panic attack passed.

"Do you want it?" Ariya asked a fourth time.

The voice came from deep in me, but it was familiar. I'd been hearing it since I left home, ignoring its steady matter-of-fact low voice: "You did not succeed your father. No man will marry you. Selfish girl. Failed girl." I was supposed to be these things in order to be. I had not taken my place within the collective. This had left me feeling exposed and foundationless, even as I pursued my dreams. Now here I was about to make another choice that would further ensure I could never go back.

I shut my eyes and thought of Dele, who'd been my friend but had looked at me like a pariah when we'd last spoken. His judgment and rejection had stung me in a way I'd not been prepared for and reminded me that I'd made my choice. And my choice had been to come home. *Dele has always seen things so simply,* I thought. *Even when they're infinitely complex. He's not a harmonizer.* I opened my eyes and looked at Ariya.

"What will it . . . do?" I breathed.

"Connect you to an entire people and a memory. And allow you to solve your *edan*."

"I'll be a desert person," I moaned. I blinked, wanting to kick myself. "I'm sorry. I meant to say Enyi Zinariya. Himba people see you as savages. I've already been changed by the Meduse. Now I'll never . . ."

"What will you be?" she asked. "Maybe it is not up to you."

I looked at my hands, wanting to bring them to my face and inhale the scent of the *otjize* covering them. I wanted to go home. I wanted to chase crabs near the lake until the sun set and then turn around to look at the Root and admire the glow of the bioluminescent plants that grew near the roof. I wanted to argue with my sisters in the living room. I wanted to walk into the village square with my best friend Dele to buy olives. I wanted to sit in my father's shop and construct an astrolabe so sophisticated, my father would clap arthritis-free hands with delight. I wanted to play math games with my mother where sometimes she'd win and sometimes I'd win. I wanted to go home.

More tears rolled down my face as I realized I'd left my jar of *otjize* in my grandmother's cave with my other things. I flared my nostrils and squinted in an attempt to prevent any more tears from falling. It worked. I steadied. I was clear now. I wanted to go home, but I wanted to solve the *edan* more. Everything comes with a sacrifice. I wiped my face with my hand and looked at my *otjize*-stained palm. "Okay," I whispered. I straightened my back. "What's the owl for?" I asked in a strained voice.

"I'm no mathematical harmonizer, but Mwinyi told me what treeing feels like, what it does." She paused. "I suggest you do that when I start. From the start. Do it while you are calm."

"Okay," I said. "But what of the owl?"

"She's not an owl," Ariya said.

Initiative

"Drink this," she said, handing me the clay cup.

It tasted both sweet and smoky, and as I swallowed the liquid it coated my throat and warmed my belly. She took the cup from me and set it on the ground beside her. We were sitting outside in the hot sun, not far from the lip of the underground cave. Here, I really noticed the soft whoosh of the air moving up and out of the cave. Above, the owl flew in wide circles.

Ariya handed me the long feather the owl had allowed her to pluck from its wing. When she'd taken it from the owl, it had flapped its wing right after she'd plucked it, as if it were in pain and trying to beat the pain away. When she handed it to me, I noticed that the end of the feather was needle sharp.

"She has no name," Ariya now said. "But she's the only animal alive from back when the Zinariya were among us. She used to live with the one that gave the zinariya to the first group of us. They had no clear leader and were all so connected that you couldn't tell them apart, except for that particular one who was always with this creature. Today, she looks like a horned owl, but there are other days . . . when she does not. Anyway, when they left, she was given many things, including a task."

I looked at the feather tip. In the sunlight, it glinted the tiniest bit; it was wet with something.

"Prick your fingertip with it," she said. "Hard. Then hold it there."

I bit my lip. I didn't like doing harm to myself on purpose or accidentally.

"It has to be you who does it. Your choice. There are catalysts in the feather and they need to enter your bloodstream."

"Okay," I whispered. But before I did, I said, "$Z = z^2 + c$." It split and split and split in its lovely complex and convoluted way. Faster and faster, until I saw the coiling design in my mind and before me. Soon that became a current. A soft blue current that I harmonized with a second current I called up from the same equation. With my mind, I asked them to wrap around me, to protect me. And in the sunshine in the middle of the hinterland, as the priestess of the Desert People who were the Enyi Zinariya watched, I plunged the sharp tip of the feather into the flesh of my left thumb.

In the stories of the Seven, life originated from the rich red clay that had soaked up rains. Microorganisms were called into active being when one of the Seven willed it and the others became interested in what would happen. That clay was Mother, *otjize*. I was clay now. I was watching from afar, feeling nothing, but able to control. I held the feather to my finger. And then, from that place waving with equations, the blue currents braiding around each other connecting around me, my body acted without my command.

When I was five, I had asked my mother what it was like to give birth. She smiled and said that giving birth was the act of stepping back and letting your body take over. That childbirth was only one of thousands of things the body could do without the spirit. I remember asking, "If you step away from your body to give birth, then who is there doing the birthing?" I wondered this now, as my body acted.

I couldn't see it happening, but I could distantly sense it—my body was pulling something, energy from the ground. From the earth, from deep. My body was touching the Mother, nudging her awake, and then telling her to come. *The Seven are great*, I thought. This was not my pilgrimage where I would have honored the Seven and entered the space only those who have earned the right could enter. I would probably never have that now. This was something else.

The Mother came.

I was treeing, but now I felt her fully. My entire body was alight. If I had not been treeing, what would have been left of my sanity? How could those who could not tree ever go through this? The glow within me became a shine that engulfed me, one that took on the color of the currents I still circulated. For a moment, I glimpsed up at Ariya and met her wide surprised eyes. I was reminded of my teacher Professor Okpala back on Oomza Uni that day I saw . . .

Iridescent white lights drowned it all out, through a jellylike substance.

Then darkness.

Then I was there again . . .

. . . *I was in space. Infinite blackness. Weightless. Flying, falling, ascending, traveling, through a planet's ring of brittle metallic dust. It pelted my flesh like chips of glittery ice. I opened my mouth a bit to breathe, the dust hitting my lips. Could I breathe? Living breath bloomed in my chest from within me and I felt my lungs expand, filling with it. I relaxed.*

"Who are you?" a voice asked. It spoke in the dialect of my family and it came from everywhere . . .

I fell out of the tree.

My *okuoko* were writhing. Then . . . rain? Wetness? Something was tearing. I was coughing, as I inhaled what my lungs could not tolerate. The gas was all around me, then it was not. I inhaled deeply, again, filling my lungs with air this time.

I opened my eyes wide. To the desert. And the smell of smoke. Ariya was feet away, her mouth open with shock, as she smacked at her garments. Smoke was rising all around her. She was putting out fire. Her clothes were burning. *From my current?* I wildly wondered. *Did I lose control of it?* Never in my life had I done such a thing.

I put a hand out to hold myself up. As a harmonizer, you saw numbers and equations in everything, circulating around you like the eye floaters you see on the surface of your eye if you pay too close attention. I was used to that. However, what I was seeing now was alien. Circles of various proportions from the size of a pea to that of a large tomato, and various colors all arranged in an order, all around me. They pulsed, becoming transparent and then solid, with each breath, with each movement, with each of my thoughts. Nevertheless, there was something far more urgent that I had to deal with.

"Okwu," I said, staring at Ariya. My heart felt as if it were slashing up the inside of my chest. "My Meduse. Have they killed it? I have to go back."

Ariya said nothing. I got up on shaky legs. "I have to go," I said, tears filling my eyes. I turned and looked in the direction Mwinyi had brought me. From afar, I could see a glimpse of the village caves. I took a step when I noticed something falling out of the sky. It was red orange, like my *otjize*, and it was on fire. It came right at me and I would never be able to outrun it.

I turned to it. *Let it slam into me and burn me to cinders*, I thought. *Let it.* I watched the fireball hurl toward me. I submitted to my death, as I had submitted to it on the ship when the Meduse had killed everyone. I felt its heat bear down on me and a blast of wind blew past me that was so strong I stumbled and sat down hard on the ground. The pain of it shook me from my hysteria. I blinked away the sandy tears in my eyes. They'd mixed with my *otjize*, sweat and sand on my skin.

Ariya slowly came to me. "Calm yourself," she harshly said. She was carrying her walking stick. *When had she gotten that?* And now, she was leaning on it. "Binti, you have to calm yourself." The old woman looked toward the village then at me. "You have just been initiated," she said. "*I* threw that fireball at you to snap you out of it."

"You?"

"Hold your hands up," she said. She held both her hands before her. "Like this. See them. Your will controls the controls. You make them come and go."

I held my hands up and there were the colored circles again. This time right before my face and solid like hard honey candies. I slowly reached out to it, expecting my hand to pass right through. I tapped on it and I heard the light *tick tick* of my nail against thin hard material. I pressed it and the words *Like this. See them. Your will controls the controls. You make them come and go* scrolled out about a foot from my face in *otjize* red-orange loopy Otjihimba writing.

I touched the words and they faded away like incense smoke and I could softly hear Ariya speak those same words again.

"What is—"

"It's zinariya," Ariya said. "You're now one of us."

I pressed my hands to the sides of my head, as if I could stop that which I couldn't stop. Just like the strange sensation of my *okuoko* when I first felt them, this was . . . this was beautiful. I felt the pain and glory of growth, was straining and shuddering with it. The stress of it caused a ringing in my eyes as I looked around, thinking hard. Then I was seeing the words. *Binti? Why are you . . . is that you? Why are you . . . have they . . . Oh no, no, no, what have you done?*

I sat there, a sob caught in my throat. Even in that moment of strangeness, the utter dismay so clear in his words made my heart sink. I felt a powerful regret and wished I had not had the zinariya activated. Anything to not inspire such disappointment in my father, after all I'd already done to him, to everyone, to myself. I fought for focus. "Papa!" I shouted. "What is happening? What happened?"

"He won't hear you," Ariya said. "You have to *send*."

Astrolabe, I thought frantically. *Like astrolabe. But more primitive.* I couldn't see him but I could "send" to him. I did it intuitively, imagining I was using the holographic mode of my astrolabe where it would project a page in the air, type onto it, and move things around. As I did so, I was vaguely aware of the fact that I was doing those hand movements the Enyi Zinariya were known for, like a madwoman. And at the moment, I was.

Papa, I sent. *What has happened? What happened to Okwu? Where are you? I am in the hinterland.*

His answer came immediately. *Why did you allow this? You used to be such a beautiful girl.* His words hit me like a slap and I felt it slip through my body and for a moment, I forgot everything. I rubbed my forehead then ran a finger over my *okuoko. Mine,* I thought. *These are mine.* I raised my hands and wrote, *Papa, I'm fine. Please, what is happening?*

There was a long pause before the words came. And when they came, I sat back down on the ground and the words moved down with me. *The Khoush came and there was a fight with Okwu. It took many, but they may have killed it. Now the Meduse are coming. We can't get out. The Khoush have set fire to the Root. We cannot get out. But the walls will protect us. The Root is the root. We will be okay. Stay where you are.*

Papa! I sent. I sent again and again, but he did not respond. My words wouldn't even melt away. They wouldn't go! I shuddered with rage and then grabbed some sand and threw it, screaming, tears flying from my eyes. I stared out into the desert for a long moment. I stared and stared. Sand and sky, sky and sand. I tried to reach Okwu. Again, nothing.

I dropped into meditation, the numbers flew like water, the controls faded but did not disappear, the *okuoko* on my head writhed. I stood up. "I'm going home," I told Ariya. She only nodded, her attention on the figure coming up the desert. It was Mwinyi and he was leading a camel. "You'll go with him," Ariya said.

"The Enyi Zinariya won't come with us?" I asked.

She only looked at me. Then she said, "We'd come if there was a fight to fight."

I didn't ask her what she meant. Above, the owl circled.

━━━━━━

When Mwinyi and I climbed onto the camel and got moving, the owl followed us overhead for several miles. Then it turned back. It returned to Ariya, I assumed. Its job was complete. I was Himba, a master harmonizer. Then I was also Meduse, anger vibrating in my *okuoko*. Now I was also Enyi Zinariya, of the Desert People gifted with alien technology. I was worlds. What was home? Where was home? Was home on fire? I considered these things as Mwinyi and I rode. But not for very long. Mwinyi had brought my satchel and now I reached into it. I worked my fingers into the pouch to touch the metal pieces of my still broken *edan*. I grasped the grooved golden ball. It was warm.

There was no fight to fight, Ariya had said. *We'll see*, I thought, grasping the huge camel's thick coarse fur. *We will see.*

BINTI

THE NIGHT MASQUERADE

Dedicated to those who aren't supposed to see the Night Masquerade, but see it anyway. May you have the courage to answer the Call to Adventure.

CHAPTER 1

Aliens

It started with a nightmare . . .

═══

"We still cannot get out," my terrified father told me. His eyes were stunned and twitchy. He was underground. We were in the cellar of the Root, the family home. Everyone was. Covered in dust, coughing from the smoke. But only my father was looking at me. I could hear my little sister Peraa nearby asking in a terrified voice between coughs, "What's wrong with Papa? Why's he doing that with his hands?"

My perspective pulled back and now I was just looking at it happening. My family was trapped in there. My father, two of my uncles, one of my aunts, three of my sisters, two of my brothers. I saw several of my neighbors in there too. Why was everyone in there in the first place? All huddled in the center of the room, grasping each other, wrapping themselves with their veils trying to hide, crying, tears running through otjize, praying, trying to call for help with their astrolabes. Bunches of water grass, piles of yams, sacks of pumpkin seeds, dried dates, containers of spices sat in corners. Smoke was coming through the fibrous ceiling and walls of the cellar. The old security drone that had stopped working before I was born still sat in the corner covered with its woven mat.

"Where is Mama?" I asked. Then more demandingly, I said, "Where is MAMA?! I don't see her, Papa."

"But the walls will protect us," my father said.

I felt the pressure of his strong hands as he grasped me. They didn't *feel arthritic at all.* "The Root is the root," *he said.* "We will be okay. Stay where you are." *He brought his face close to mine, then the words appeared before my eyes. Red as blood.* "Because they are looking for you."

"Where is Mama?" *I asked again, this time waving my hands in my nightmare, as I clumsily used the zinariya, the activated alien technology in my DNA.*

But I was suddenly in the dark, alone with my words, as they floated before me like red desert spirits. Where is Mama? *Instead, the sound of hundreds of Meduse thrumming filled my head and the vibration traveled deep into my flesh. Laughter. Angry laughter. I sensed anticipation, too.* "Binti, we will make them pay," *a voice rumbled in Meduse. But it wasn't Okwu. Where was Okwu . . . ?*

———

I awoke to the universe. Out here in the desert, the night sky was so bright with stars. It was almost as clear as the sky when I'd been on the Third Fish traveling to and from Earth. I stared up, hearing, seeing, and balanced equations whispered around me like smoke. I'd been treeing in my sleep. It was that bad. I hadn't even done this while in the Third Fish after the Meduse killed everyone but me. I was having so much trouble adjusting to the zinariya. But that wasn't just a dream about my family, it was also a message sent using the zinariya from my father. I couldn't awaken fully before receiving it and so my mind protected me from the stress of it by treeing.

Mwinyi and I had left the village on camelback hours ago and then we'd stopped to rest. I'd lain in the tent Mwinyi set up, while he'd gone off for a walk. I was so exhausted, scared for my family, and overwhelmed. Everything around me felt off. Trying to get some sleep had not been a good idea.

"Home," I whispered, rubbing my face. "Need to get . . ." I stared at the sky. "What is that?"

One of the stars was falling toward me. The zinariya, again. "Please stop," I said. "Enough." But it didn't stop. No. It kept coming. It had more to tell me, whether I was ready or not. Its golden light expanded as it descended and I was so mesmerized by its smooth approach that I didn't tree. When it was mere yards above, it exploded into showers of brilliance. It fell on me like the golden legs of a giant spider and then the zinariya made me remember things that had never happened to me.

════

I remembered when . . .

Kande was washing the dishes. She was exhausted and she had more studying to do, but her younger twin brothers had wanted a late night snack of roasted corn and groundnuts and they'd left their stupid dishes. How they'd managed to eat something so heavy this late at night was beyond her, but she knew her parents wouldn't complain. This was why at the age of six they were so plump. Her parents never complained about her brothers. Still, if Kande left the dishes for the morning, the ants would come. It was a humid night, so she knew other things would come too. She shuddered; Kande detested any type of beetle.

She finished the dishes and looked at the empty sink for a moment. She dried her hands and picked up her mobile phone. It was already eleven o'clock. If she focused, she could get a good hour of studying in and still manage five hours of sleep. In her final year in high school, she was ranked number six in her class. She wasn't sure if this was good enough to be accepted into the University of Ibadan, but she certainly planned to find out.

She put her phone in her skirt pocket and switched off the light. Then she stepped into the hallway and listened for a moment. Her parents were watching TV in their room and the light in her brothers' room was off. Good. She turned and tiptoed to the front of the house, quietly unlocked the door, and sneaked outside. It was a cool night and she could see the open desert just beyond the last few homes in the village.

Kande leaned against the side of the house as she brought out a pack of cigarettes from her skirt pocket. She shook one out, placed it between her lips, and brought out a match. Striking the match with her thumbnail, she used it to light her cigarette. She inhaled the smoke and when she exhaled it, she felt as if all her problems floated away with it—the ugly face of the man her parents said she was now betrothed to, the money she needed to buy her uniform for her school dance group, whether Tanko still loved her now that he knew she was betrothed.

She took another pull from her cigarette and smiled as she exhaled. Her father would be furious and beat her if he knew she had such a filthy habit. Her mother would wail and say no man would want her if she didn't start behaving, that she was too old for rebellion. Kande was looking toward the desert as she thought about all this and when she first saw them, she was sure that her brain was trying to distract her from her own dark thoughts.

They were a house away before she even moved. And by then, she was sure they'd seen her. Tall, like human palm trees and not human at all. And even in the moonlight, she saw that they were gold. Pure shiny gold. Not human at all. But with legs. Arms. Bodies. Long and thin. Walking slowly toward her in the night. There wasn't another soul silly enough to be outside at this time of night. Just her.

Kande didn't know it, but everything depended on those moments after she saw them. What she did. The destiny of her people was in her hands. She stared up at the aliens who saw themselves as one thing but accepted the name of "Zinariya" (which meant "gold") that human beings gave them and . . .

======

. . . I fell out of the tree. Mwinyi was shaking me. Gusts of sand and dust slapped at my skin when I turned to him and I coughed hard.

"Binti! Come on! Pull yourself out of it!"

At first, I saw all things around me as the sums of equations, numbers splitting and unfurling, falling away, rotating, all in harmony. My eyes focused on his tall lanky frame; his caftan and pants that were blue like Okwu flapped in the sandy wind. Grains of sand blew about pretending chaos, but each arced a trajectory that coincided with those around it. I shook my head, trying to come back to myself. My mouth had been hanging open and I spit out sand.

I twitched as a rage flew into me like an explosion. *My family!* I thought, frantic. *My family!* Before I could shout this at Mwinyi . . . I saw Okwu hovering behind him. My eyes widened and my mouth hung open again. Then Okwu was gone. Instead, behind Mwinyi were small skinny red-furred dogs; they ran about flinging their heads this way and that way. I felt one touch my face with its cool black nose, sniffing. It yipped, the sound close to my ear. The dogs were running all around us, at least as far as I could see, which was only a few feet. Our camel Rakumi was roaring with distress. I was seeing words now as Mwinyi desperately tried to reach me using the zinariya.

The floating green words said, "Sandstorm. Dog pack. Relax. Grab Rakumi's saddle, Binti."

I am not a follower, but there are times when all you can do is follow. And so yet again, I submitted. This time it was to Mwinyi, a boy I had only known for a few days, of a people I'd viewed as barbarians all my life and now knew were not, my father's people, my people.

I was breaking and breaking and into that moment I followed Mwinyi. He led us out of that sandstorm.

The sun broke through.

The air cleared of dust.

The storm was behind us.

I sighed, relieved. Then the weight of the sudden quiet made my legs buckle and I sank to the ground at the hooves of our camel Rakumi. I pressed my cheek to the sand and was surprised by its warmth. There I lay, staring at the retreating sandstorm. It looked like a large brown beast who'd decided to leave, when really it just happened to travel the other way. Churning, roiling, and swirling back the way we'd come. Toward the Enyi Zinariya village. Away from my dying, maybe even dead, family.

I weakly raised my hands and moved them slowly, typing in the air. The various names of my father. Moaoogo Dambu Kaipka Oke-chukwu. I tried to send it. But they wouldn't go. I rolled my head to the side in the sand, feeling the grains ground into my *otjize*-rolled *okuoko*, blue tentacles layered with sweet-smelling red clay and now sand. I tried to call Okwu. I tried to reach it. To touch it with my mind as I had days ago, now. Again, nothing.

Then I started weeping, as the world around me began to do that expanding thing that it had been doing since we'd left the Ari-ya's cavern over a day ago. As if everything were growing bigger and bigger and bigger, though it was still the same. Mwinyi said it was just my body settling with the zinariya technology that Ariya had unlocked within me, but what did that matter? It didn't make it any better. The sensation was so jarring that I constantly felt the Earth would decide to fling me into space at any moment.

I shut my eyes and it was as if I'd fallen again. Into my other nightmare. The nightmare from a year ago. Now I was back on the Third Fish, sitting at the dining hall table. I could taste the sweet milky dessert in my mouth. My *edan* was in my hand, the strange gold ball back inside the stellated cube–shaped metal shell; it was whole again. And I was gazing at Heru, the beautiful boy who'd noticed that I'd braided my *otjize*-rolled locks into a tessellating triangle pattern that reflected my heritage. His granite black hair was falling over one of his eyes as he laughed. He glanced at me, and I smiled. And then his chest burst open and his warm blood spattered on my face and I fled within myself, quivering, silently screaming, breaking. Everyone was dead.

The dining hall grew red, even the air took on a red tint. There was Okwu, behind Heru. I could smell blood, as I tasted the sweet milky dessert in my mouth. Everyone was dead. I had to survive. I slowly got up, clutching the *edan* in my hand, and when I turned, it wasn't a Meduse I faced but my cowering family inside the bowels of the Root. In the large room, below, where all the foodstuffs and supplies were stored.

The smell of blood turned to one of smoke. I'd moved from one nightmare to another. My eye first fell on my oldest sister shrieking in a corner as her long, long hair went up in flames. I was coughing and then looking frantically around as I waited to smell the burning of my own flesh because flames were consuming the entire room. Now my family was all around me, my father, siblings, several of my cousins, aunts, uncles, nieces, nephews, shrieking, stumbling, thrashing, lying still as they burned. Everyone was burning, alive or already dead.

I whimpered, my flesh feeling too hot. *Let me die too*, I thought, waiting, hoping, for the burning to intensify. *My family.* Instead, the fire consuming my family stopped biting me and shrank away. It calmed. It didn't stink of burning flesh now. The fire smelled woodsy and the center of it looked like a pile of glowing rubies. Everything undulated and when it resettled, things looked more real, no red tint, so solid and clear that I could touch the dry ground beneath me, warm my hand at the fire before me.

I distantly felt my *okuoko* writhing with anger. I reached up, grasping them, trying to calm their wriggling. All this was confusing me. I was just coming out of flashbacks of the deaths of my friends and family and now the zinariya was forcing history on me again . . .

═══════

The old man was named Takeagoodposition. He stood before five other old people, holding a slender pipe to his lips. The smoke smelled sweet and thick and when it blended with the smoke from the fire, it smelled awful.

"The child is a dolt," Takeagoodposition said. "Kande is one of those girls who would follow a lion to her death if the lion flashed a pretty grin."

The men in the group all laughed and nodded.

"No, we won't put the community in the hands of a girl; how would we look?"

"But they came to her first," a tall man said, his long legs crossed before him. "And let's be honest, if those things had come to any of us, what would we have done? Fled? Fainted? Tried to shoot them? But she somehow learned to speak with them, gain their trust."

"Look what it cost her," the only woman in the group said. "She is like a girl possessed, seeing things that are not there."

"My grandson said it was like they put alien Internet in her brain," another elder said.

There was more soft laughter.

Takeagoodposition frowned deeply. "None of that matters now," he snapped. "The Koran says to be kind and open to strangers. Let us welcome them. The girl will introduce us and we will take over."

"Have you seen them?" another of the men asked. "They're beautiful, especially in the sun."

"And probably worth millions if we divide them into coinage," someone remarked.

Laughter.

"These Zinariya, they are aliens," Takeagoodposition said. "We'll be cautious."

It was as if I were sitting with the men and woman. Listening to them talk about the Zinariya. Some movement behind a cluster of dry bushes caught my eye and I was sure I saw someone slowly back away and then run off.

"Kande," a woman's voice said. It seemed to come from all around me. "She did well, for a child who liked to smoke."

I frowned, wanting to stop all this nonsense and scream, "What does smoking have to do with aliens?!" But then I saw something bouncing around within the circle of people. A giant red ball. It disappeared in the swirls of dust and then bounced back on the ground. It rolled up to me and flattened, shaped like a red candy-like button embedded in the sand.

I stared at it.

"Press it." The words appeared in front of me in neat and careful green and then faded like smoke. Mwinyi was speaking to me through the zinariya.

I smashed the button with my fist, vaguely feeling the button's hardness. I heard a soft satisfying click. Everything went quiet. Nothing but the sound of the soft wind rolling across the desert. I rested my forehead on the sand, weeping again.

"Can you get up?" Mwinyi asked, kneeling beside me. "Has it stopped?"

I raised my head and looked up at him. His bushy red-brown hair was coated with sand and the long lock that grew in the back of his head was dragging on the ground beside my knee, collecting more sand. The world behind him, the blue sky, the sun, started expanding again. But not as badly as before, nor was I seeing the death of everything I loved. But I knew of it.

I opened my mouth and screamed, "Everyone's dead!" I rolled to the side, grinding the other side of my head into the sand. My face to the sand, feeling its heat on my skin and blowing out sand,

I wailed, "MY FAMILY!!!! I DIE! EVERYTHING IS DEAD! WHY AM I ALIVE?! OOOOOOH!" I sobbed and sobbed, curling in on myself, shutting my eyes. I felt him press a hand to my shoulder.

"Binti," he said. "Your family—"

"DON'T! LEAVE ME ALONE!"

I heard him angrily suck his teeth. Then he must have walked away.

I don't know how long he left me there, but when he pulled me to a sitting position, I was too defeated to fight him. I slumped there, the hot sun beating down on my shoulders.

He sat across from me, looking annoyed.

"I don't have a home anymore," I said. I felt my *okuoko* writhe on my head.

"Ah, there's the Meduse in you," he said.

"I am *Himba*," I snapped.

"Binti, they might be alive," Mwinyi said. "Your grandmother back in my village communicated with your father in Osemba."

I stared at him, shuddering as I tried to hold back the flash of rage that flew through me. I couldn't and it burst forth like Meduse gas. "I saw them trapped . . . I SAW THEM!" I shouted. "I smelled them b-b-burning!"

"Binti," he said. "Remember, you've just been unlocked! And you have that Meduse blood. I've heard you whimpering in your sleep about what happened last year on that ship. And we're out here in this desert, exhausted and far from your home. You're all mixed up. Some of what you see is communication, some is probably the zinariya showing you stuff it wants you to know, but some is delusion, nightmare."

I raised a hand for him to be quiet and rested my chin to my chest; I was so exhausted now. Tears spilled from my eyes. Everything I'd seen was so real. "I don't know anything," I softly said.

I felt Mwinyi looking at me. "Your father said the Khoush came after Okwu," he said. "They don't know what happened."

"Who is 'they'?" I asked.

"Your grandmother and father. As I'm sure you know, your Okwu is a small army in itself. Your family took shelter in the Root when the fighting began."

"So they *are* in the cellar," I muttered. "That part is true."

"Yes."

I had to process the idea that my father had spoken with my grandmother through the zinariya. "When?" I asked. "When did he talk to her?"

"Just after you were unlocked."

"Just after I sensed Okwu was in trouble," I said. "So he could be—"

"I don't know, Binti. We don't know. Sometimes when the zinariya communicates, it disregards time. We're going to find out."

"You could have told me hours ago."

Mwinyi paused, his lips pursed. "They told me not to. They didn't think the news would help you."

When I said nothing to this, he said, "If you want to get home to help, we can't waste time like this."

I glared at him.

"Don't give me that look," he said. "Aim your Meduse rage that way." He pointed ahead of us. "Last night, I thought I was free to do whatever I wanted. Instead, I'm here, taking you to what can't be a place of peace. And I do care about your family; I'm doing my best."

I ran my hand down my face, wiping away tears, sweat, snot. I paused, realizing I'd probably also just wiped a lot of my *otjize* from my face too. I sighed, flaring my nostrils. Everything was so wrong. "You don't have to take me anyw—"

"I *do* and I will," he said. "You want to know what I think?" He looked at me for a moment, clearly trying to decide if it was better to keep his words to himself.

"Go on," I urged him. "I want to hear this."

"You try too hard to be everything, please everyone. Himba,

Meduse, Enyi Zinariya, Khoush ambassador. You can't. You're a harmonizer. We bring peace because we are stable, simple, clear. What have you brought since you came back to Earth, Binti?"

I stared nakedly at him; the hot breeze blowing on my wet face felt cool. My *okuoko* had stopped writhing. I felt deflated. "I need my family," I said hoarsely.

He nodded. "I know."

I grabbed the sides of my orange-red wrapper as I looked straight ahead, toward where we were to go. Right before my eyes, the world seemed to expand, while staying the same, as if reality were breathing. It was a most disconcerting sight. I let myself lightly tree, as I took in several deep breaths. "Everything is . . . still looks as if it's growing," I said. I looked directly at him for the first time. "I . . . I know that sounds crazy, but that's really what I'm *seeing*."

Mwinyi frowned at me, twirling his long matted lock with his left hand, two of the small brown wild dogs sitting on either side of him like soldiers. Then he said, "I can get you home, but I don't . . . I don't know how to help you, Binti. I never needed to be 'activated'; I don't even know what you're going through."

I clutched the front of my orange-red top and whimpered, thinking of my family back in Osemba. After traveling all day, then through the night, we'd traveled much of the next day. When the sun was at its highest, we'd settled down in our tent for some rest. We'd finally fallen asleep when the sandstorm hit. "I know you think I'm too much but—"

"That's not what I said."

I cut my eyes at him. "You did. Don't worry, it's not the first time something like this has happened to me," I said, shutting my eyes for a moment. When I opened them, I felt a little better. "Let's keep going. We can travel through the night again."

When I tried to get up, he quickly stood and said, "No. Rest."

"I'm okay," I said. "Just give me a minute and we can go as soon as—"

"Binti, we stop. You have to rest. The zinariya is—"

"But if they're in the cellar . . ." I started shaking again. I wrung my hands, my heart beating fast.

"Whatever is happening there, we can't stop it," he said.

I tried to get up and he put a hand firmly on my shoulder. I wanted to fight him, but the feeling of vertigo was back and I could only roll to my side in the dirt, shuddering with misplaced outrage, my *okuoko* writhing again.

"We're making fast time, but we're still a day away," he said. "Binti . . . calm down. Breathe."

"Even with the wild animals out here? The slower we go, the more we risk—"

"Wild animals don't scare me," Mwinyi flatly said, looking me so deeply in the eyes that everything around me dropped away. My *okuoko* slowly settled on my shoulders and down my back. The Meduse rage, which I was still learning to control, left me like cool air flees the morning sun. There is nothing like gazing into the eyes of a harmonizer when you are also a harmonizer.

We stayed and without further exchanging words, we set up camp. I was glad when he walked off into the desert for an hour to see if he could find anything fresh to eat, the small pack of dogs following him like curious children. I needed the quiet. I needed to be alone with . . . it.

"It's not something to learn," he said, over his shoulder. "It's *part* of you now. Intuit it."

And that I understood. I sat on the woven raffia mat in the open tent. I had been studying my *edan* for over a year—a mysterious object I'd found in a mysterious place in the desert, whose purpose I did not know, and whose functions I had first learned of by accident. An object that had saved my life, been the focus of my major at Oomza Uni, and was now in about thirty tiny triangular metal pieces and a gold ball in my pocket. Yes, I understood intuiting things.

I brought up my hands and used the vague virtual device that rose before me to type out Mwinyi's name and the word "Hello" in Otjihimba. Then I envisioned Mwinyi, who was most likely on the other side of the sand dune he'd disappeared over. Before I saw him in my mind, I felt his nearness, his alertness. He was monitoring me, even from where he was; I wasn't just guessing this, I knew it for a fact. His response appeared before me in green letters that were a different style from mine, neat but relaxed and in Otjihimba, "Are you alright?"

"Yes," I responded.

Then, yet again, I tried to reach my father. "Papa," I wrote. I tried to push the red letters as I held my father's image in my mind. It was as if the words were fixed onto a wall, I couldn't send or even move them. I waved my hands and the words disappeared. I tried another five times before giving up, growing increasingly more agitated, the letters looking sloppier and sloppier. I wiped tears from my cheeks and then before my mind started going dark again, I tried reaching out to Okwu. Five times. Again, nothing.

I rubbed my eyes and when I looked at the backs of my hands, for the first time in hours, I realized that they were nearly free of *otjize*. I gasped, touching my face, looking at my arms, my legs. The sand from the storm had stripped most of it away. Mwinyi had said nothing about this, or maybe he hadn't noticed. I felt like shrieking as I fumbled with my satchel. I had about half a jar left. When I'd arrived on Earth, I'd assumed I would have time to make more.

I gazed at the jar. The red paste wasn't as rich as the one I could make from the clay I dug up around the Root. It was *otjize* different from any *otjize* made by a Himba girl or woman. Mine was from a different planet. I held it to my nose and sniffed its rich scent and saw the tall trees of the forest where I collected the clay, the piglike creature who foraged in the bushes. I saw the face of Professor Okpala, the large pitcher plants that grew beside the station, my classmates, like Haifa and Wan. However, I also saw the Root. And the faces of my family, the dusty roads of Osemba and its tranquil lake.

Rubbing it onto my face, I looked out at the desert. Dry, expansive, free. I inhaled deeply, to control my breathing. No more tears that would wash away the *otjize* I'd just put on my face. And I did what I'd unconsciously done with my *edan* on the Third Fish, but this time instead of speaking to my *edan*, I spoke to the zinariya. And it answered. It was gentle and kind, but I didn't have the unaffected fresh mind of a baby. I was seventeen years old, the second youngest girl in my family, who'd been tapped to be my community's next harmonizer. I'd instead chosen to leave Earth and go to Oomza Uni and nearly died for my choice. I'd lived and then learned, so much. To engage with the zinariya was to overwhelm all my senses. In the distance, I saw a yawning black tunnel swallowing the soft light of the setting sun.

I don't know what happened.

Mwinyi returned an hour later carrying two dead rabbits. He found me lying on the mat, saliva dribbling from the side of my mouth. I'd watched him approach through dry gummy eyes. As I gasped his name and weakly typed it on the virtual device now hovering on my lap, I saw the red word appear before me. His name floated above him, slowly descending onto his head, where it settled and oozed onto him like melted candle wax. I groaned and when I did, I saw the phonetic spelling of the sound creep from my mouth onto the sand like a caterpillar. It was as if the zinariya itself was mocking me.

It was all too much and when I tried treeing to make it better, my world filled with so many numbers that I felt as if I'd kicked a hornet's nest. I couldn't see around me and some of the numbers grew more aggressive the angrier I got, zooming around and darting at me.

"How am I supposed to get up tomorrow?" I whispered. "So I can . . . my family." I started weeping, though I knew it would wash off even more of my *otjize*. I turned away from Mwinyi, repulsed by the thought of him seeing me so naked. One of the wild dogs trotted up to me and sniffed my *okuoko*. I heard Mwinyi put the two large rabbits he'd caught down and I assumed the soft yipping I heard was him telling the dogs not to touch the rabbits.

"Can you see?" he asked.

"No," I said.

He clucked his tongue with annoyance. "Get up, Binti."

"I can't." I started crying harder. Then I thought about my *otjize* and my crying turned to sobs. I felt another of the dogs sit on me and I heard Mwinyi walk away. Then I must have fallen asleep because when I woke, I smelled cooking meat. My stomach rumbled and slowly I sat up. The dog who'd sat on me had also apparently fallen asleep and now it lazily stepped off my legs.

I looked around. My world was stable. No expanding, no numbers, no words bouncing, crawling, oozing about with every sound I made. No tunnel in the distance. No feeling like the Earth would hurl me from its flesh into space. I sat back with relief. It was a dark night, the sky overcast with thick clouds. Our camel Rakumi was resting nearby, her saddle on the ground beside her. Mwinyi sat before the fire he'd built, eating. In the darkness, the fire was a welcome beacon. I stood up and then hesitated.

"I'm not Himba," he said, without looking away from the fire. "Your *otjize* looks like adornment to me. You don't look naked. Come and eat. We're not staying here long."

Regardless, as I crept up to him, I burned so hot with embarrassment that I could only approach walking sideways. I sat right beside him. This way, he'd have to make more of an effort to look at me. When I looked up, I noticed the dogs lying on top of one another on the other side of the fire, a pile of small bones beside them.

"Aren't they wild dogs?" I asked.

"Yes," he said.

"So why are they still here?"

He shrugged. "The fire's warm and they like me." He turned to me. Surprised by his sudden look, my eyes grew wide and I crossed my arms over my chest and instinctively tried to pull my head into my top. It was such a silly thing to do that he grinned and laughed. I found myself smiling back at him. He had a nice smile.

He turned back to the fire and said, "And I gave them one of the rabbits I caught."

I laughed, again.

"We made an arrangement," he continued. "I feed them and they stay and stand guard for a few hours while you and I get more sleep."

"They told you this?"

He nodded. "Wild dogs are free and playful, once you convince them not to attack you," Mwinyi said. "I suspect we have until their bellies have settled and our fire dies down. I don't think there are many other dangerous animals out tonight. But Binti, something's clearly happening in your homeland . . . and maybe not just in your homeland."

And what if it's because of me? I thought. Maybe he was thinking it too because he was quiet and pensive and for several minutes neither of us spoke.

I changed the subject. "My best friend Dele . . . well, he used to be my best friend," I said, gazing into the fire. "Now, I don't think he's a friend at all."

"Sorry to hear that," Mwinyi said.

"It's okay," I said. "I think I lost all my friends when I left, really." We were silent for a moment. I continued, "Dele was always interested in the old Himba ways. He knew everything. He was always talking about how we Himba see fire as holy. A medium to communicate with the Seven. *Okuruwo*, sacred fire." I sighed, the warmth of the fire toasting my legs and face. "During Moon Fest, I'd sit beside Dele with the other girls and boys. While everyone else sang, I wanted to dance in front of the fire because I always thought the Seven preferred dance and numbers to singing. After I was tapped to be master harmonizer, Dele said I would be disgracing myself if I danced." I frowned. When I'd last spoken to him, he'd been apprenticed to train as the next Himba chief; he'd looked and spoken to me as if I were a lost child.

"To us Enyi Zinariya, fire is sacred too," Mwinyi said.

Something large and green zipped past my ear, zoomed a circle over the fire, and then plunged into it. There was a small burst of sparks and a soft *paff!*

"What was that?" I said, jumping up.

"Sit," Mwinyi said. "And watch."

I didn't sit. But I watched.

A second later what looked like an orange, yellow, red spark the size of a tomato flew from the flames, shooting straight up into the black night sky. Then it silently went out.

"I thought you'd spent time in the desert before," he said.

"Only during the day."

"Ah, that explains why you've never seen an Icarus," he said. "They're large green grasshoppers who like to fly into fires. Then they fly out of the flames and dance with their new wings of fire and fall to the ground wingless. The wings grow back in a few days. Then they do it again. The zinariya says that some woman genetically engineered them as pets long ago."

I looked around for the wingless grasshopper. When I saw the creature, I ran to it. I picked it up and held it to my face. It smelled like smoke. "Ridiculous," I whispered as it jumped from my hand to the sand and hopped wingless into the darkness.

"Can . . . can you harmonize with them? Ask them why they do it?" I asked, coming back to the fire.

"Never bothered. I doubt they know why they do it, really. It's how they were programmed by science, I guess."

"Well, maybe," I said. "But I'm sure they rationalize it somehow."

"True. I'll ask one someday."

I sat down at my spot and as I did, he moved his hands before him and then asked, "How are you feeling?"

"Who wants to know?" I asked.

"Your grandmother."

"Why doesn't she ask me?"

He cocked his head and laughed. Then moved his hands again. Moments later, my world began to expand and I shrieked. The words came at me like a cluster of beasts zooming from the depths of the desert. I thought they were going to smash into me, so I raised my hands to protect myself. Bright like sunshine the words read, "ARE YOU ALRIGHT?"

"Okay," I whispered, still hiding behind my raised hands. "Tell her I am okay."

The words receded, but my world did not stop expanding. I touched the ground, grasping cool sand with my fists and digging my feet into it. I felt better.

"Ariya says don't try to use the zinariya except with me," Mwinyi said. "Give it about a week. You have to ease into it or it'll make you really ill. Focus on what's ahead more than what's behind, for now."

I nodded, rubbing my temples.

"Do you want to hear how I learned I was a harmonizer?" he asked, after a moment.

I nodded, digging my fingers and toes deeper into the sand. Anything to take my mind from the terrible feeling of leaving the Earth.

"When I was about eight years old—"

I gasped. "I was eight when I found my *edan*!" I said. "Is that when you—"

"Binti, I'm telling you the story of it. Just listen."

"Sorry," I said, wishing everything would stop undulating.

"So, when I was eight, I walked out into the desert," he said. "My family was used to me doing this. I never went far and I only went during the day, in the mornings. I would walk until I could not see or hear the village."

I smiled and nodded, the thought taking my mind off my rippling world a bit. I, too, had loved to walk into the desert when I was growing up. Even though I was never supposed to. And doing so changed my life.

"This day, I was out there, listening to the breeze, watching a bird in the sky. I unrolled my mat and sat down on a patch of hardpan. It was a cloudy day, so the sun wasn't harsh. They came from the other side of a sand dune behind me, or maybe I'd have seen them. I hadn't heard them at all! They were that quiet. Or maybe it was something else."

"What? What were 'they'?" I asked. "Another tribe?"

He nodded. "But not of humans, of elephants."

My mouth fell open. "I've never seen one, but I hear they hate human beings! The Khoush say they kill herdsmen and maul small villages on the outskirts of—"

"And they always kill every human being they come across, right?" he asked, laughing.

I pressed my lips together, frowning, and unsurely said, "Yes?"

"Because I'm actually a spirit," he said.

I shivered at his words, thinking, *Is he?*

Mwinyi groaned. "Haven't you learned *anything* from all this? What'd you think I was a few days ago? What did you think of all Enyi Zinariya?" I didn't respond, so he did. "You thought we were savages. You were raised to believe that, even though your own father was one of us. You know why. And now I'm sitting here telling you how I learned I was a harmonizer and you're so stuck on lies that you'd rather sit here wondering if I'm a *spirit* than question what you've been taught."

I sighed, tiredly, rubbing my temples.

Mwinyi turned to me, looked me up and down, sucked his teeth, and continued, keeping his eyes on me as he spoke. Probably enjoying my discomfort with his gaze. "They rushed up to me," he said. "The biggest one, a female who was leading the pack. She charged at me. When you see elephants coming at you as you sit in the middle of the desert . . . you submit. I was only eight years old and even I knew that. But as she came, I heard her charge, 'Kill it! Kill it!' I looked up and I answered her. 'Why?!' I shouted. She stopped so abruptly that the others ran into her. It was an incredible sight. Elephants were tumbling before me like boulders rolling down a sand dune. I will never forget the sight of it.

"When they all recovered, she spoke to me, again, 'Who are you? How are you able to speak to us?' And I told her. And I told her that I was alone and I was a child and I would never harm an elephant. The others quickly lost interest in me, but that one stayed. She and I spoke that day about tribe and communication. And for many years, we met there when the moon was full, as we agreed. A few times we met when I needed her advice, like when my mother was ill and when I quarreled with my brothers who were bigger and older than me."

"What of your sisters?"

"I don't have any," he said. "I'm the youngest of six, all boys."

"Oh," I said. "That's strange."

"What's stranger is that I'm the only one who doesn't look like he could crush stone with his bare hands," he said, smiling ruefully. "Even Kam, who's a year older than me, just won the village wrestling championship."

I laughed at Mwinyi's outrage.

"Anyway, during these times, when it wasn't a full moon, I was able to call Arewhana, that was her name, from far away. She taught me how to do it. It was something she said I could do with larger, more aware animals like elephants, rhinos, and even whales if I ever ventured to the ocean.

"Arewhana taught me so much. *She* was the one who told me I was a harmonizer. And she was the one who taught me how to *be* a harmonizer. Elephants are great violent beasts, but only because human beings have treated them in a way that made using violence the only way for elephants to survive. There are many elephant tribes in these lands and beyond."

An elephant had taught him to harmonize and instead of using it to guide current and mathematics, she'd taught him to speak to all people. The type of harmonizer one was depended on one's teacher's worldview; I rolled this realization around in my mind as I just stared at him.

Mwinyi's bushy red hair was still full of dust and sand and he didn't seem to mind this, but his dark brown skin was clean and oiled. I'd actually seen him rubbing oil into his skin earlier. I knew the scent. It was from a plant that grew wild in the shade of palm trees and some women used it to flavor desserts because it tasted and smelled so flowery. He carried some in a tiny glass vial he kept in his pocket. A few drops of it went a long way. The oil protected his skin from the desert sun in a way quite similar to *otjize*, and it brought out its natural glow. I wondered if this plant smell had also set the elephants at ease.

I chewed on this thought, while gazing at Mwinyi. My world had stabilized again.

———

As I settled on the mat in the tent, I could hear Mwinyi moving about outside while he softly yipped and panted. I watched as the wild dogs got up; soon our tent was surrounded by the group of about eight dogs. None of them slept now; instead they sat up and watched out into the night like sentries.

Mwinyi came into the tent and lay beside me. "Better sleep now," he said. "I think we have about three hours of safety at most. Then they'll leave and if there are hyenas or bigger angrier dogs out there, *those* can sneak up on us."

He didn't have to tell me twice. Sleep stole me away less than a minute later.

CHAPTER 2

Orange

Every week, the village market opened in the desert. *Always at noon, when the sun was highest in the sky. The village was small, but it wasn't isolated. People came from different villages, towns, communities. But these connected communities were small and all of them were insular, secretive, and happy. And that's why it worked.*

The children loved their mobile phones and social networks; some of them ventured out into the rest of the country or even the world. A few never came back. But most stayed and all kept the area's secret. There were never any uploaded photos, drawings, paintings, or videos. No blog posts, no interviews, no news stories. No need to share. The people in this part of the country took from the rest of the world, but kept to themselves and explored from within. The people here preferred to venture inward rather than out. Because what was within was already a million times more advanced, more modern, than anything on the planet. And what was inside had come from outer space. Thus, the rest of the country never learned of the friendly "alien invasion," the friendship that took root and was on full display in the market every week.

Women squatted before pyramids of tomatoes, onions, dried leaves, spices. Men brought in bunches of plantain on their heads, reams of Ankara cloth. The local imam was holding a meeting. Children ran errands and into mischief. And among them all walked twenty-foot-tall, slender beings who seemed to be made of molten gold. They glinted in the sunshine and people sometimes shaded their eyes against the glare, but other than that, these extraterrestrial people mingled easily and naturally.

One girl ran around one of them, stopped, and brought up her hands.

She motioned wildly and then kept running. She wove around two women haggling over a yam, squeezed between the group of men listening to the local imam preach, and ran right up to the tall golden figure waiting for her. She smiled and held up an orange whose peel had been cut away. "You bite into it," she said. "Like this."

━━━━━

I awoke with the taste of oranges in my mouth. When I opened my eyes, I was facing the desert and I could see the dream that wasn't a dream retreating from me into the distance, like something sneaking away.

"Why bother hiding?" I muttered. "Why don't you just ask if you want to tell me stories? I am a student. I will listen."

I sat up and looked around. The dogs were gone. The sun was about an hour from rising and Mwinyi was already preparing Rakumi for the journey. I sat up and watched him for a moment as he grunted and patted the camel's back before strapping the saddle onto her. There was a strange moment when Rakumi turned and looked right at Mwinyi and he gazed right into her eyes. Then the camel touched her soft lips to his forehead and turned forward and Mwinyi finished putting the saddle on.

I reached for my jar of *otjize* and held it before my eyes. So little left. I applied some to my face and a thin layer to my arms and lower parts of my legs, rubbing some into my anklets. If my family saw me like this, they'd be mortified. At least during more normal times. I climbed out of the tent and stretched my back. I was stiff, but okay, having slept about four solid hours.

"Good morning," I said.

He turned around and nodded. "Not yet, but soon."

"Can we make it there by the end of the day?" I asked.

"Maybe. If we move quickly."

But what will we find? I thought. I shivered and went to relieve myself a distance away from our camp. As I walked back, I called up a current and let myself tree while I looked up at the night sky. There were stars now. The clouds had dissipated. I would see things clearly when I returned home.

I reached into my pocket and brought out the golden ball with the fingerprint-like designs on it. Running a current around its surface, I watched as the ball lifted from my palm and rotated before me like a tiny planet. Then I retracted the current and let the ball drop into my hand. When I put it back in my pocket, I ran my fingertips over the triangular metal pieces sitting at the bottom.

I reached into my other pocket and brought out my astrolabe. Holding it to my face, I stopped walking. I stared at the elegant device. What I realized made me sick to my stomach and my legs grow weak. After all the changes I'd been through in the last year, becoming part Meduse, making *otjize* on a different planet, but especially with the activation of the zinariya, my astrolabe didn't seem like the most advanced technology anymore. Astrolabes were the only object that also carried the full record of your entire life on it—you, your family, and all forecasts of your future. The chip in it had to be transferred if the astrolabe broke, which they rarely ever did if they were made by my father or me. My family's fortune and identity were based on the importance of astrolabes to the world and beyond and the superiority of the ones we made. Even peoples at Oomza Uni used astrolabes. However, I'd barely even glanced at mine since I'd been taken into the desert.

Now I touched it to turn it on and my heart sank even lower. It wouldn't turn on. I called up a current and used it to "inspire" my astrolabe. I'd built this astrolabe myself, special specific part by special specific part. I'd made it to last. But because I knew every inch of it, I knew that now it was pointless trying to turn it on, reset it, shake it, smash it against my leg. My astrolabe was dead. I whimpered as it crossed my mind that maybe even the chip inside it was now unreadable. This would mean that I'd just lost my entire identity. I put the astrolabe in my pocket and took five deep breaths, the tears in my eyes drying more with each breath. Mwinyi finished packing the tent on Rakumi's back.

"I'm ready when you are," I told Mwinyi.

━━━━━

Rakumi walked at a steady strong pace, her onward wavelike movement seeming to say, "Forward, forward, forward." The motion was uncomfortable at first, but I grew used to it. Mwinyi sat right behind me and I leaned against him and this is how we stayed for several hours.

"Binti?" Mwinyi asked, breaking the silence.

"Yes?"

"We're close."

"I know. The land looks the same but it's somehow familiar."

"I have something to tell you," he said. "From your grandmother."

My astrolabe was broken and in order for my world to stay as it was, I had taken Mwinyi's advice and not tried to use the zinariya at all since going to sleep. I hadn't bothered trying to reach Okwu through my *okuoko,* either. In this way, the last several hours of disconnection had been the most peaceful hours I'd experienced in quite some time. My heart began to pound and suddenly it felt difficult to breathe, and an image of Heru's chest bursting flashed through my mind.

Mwinyi climbed off Rakumi and I did the same. We stood there facing each other.

"What . . . did she say?" I whispered.

He hesitated for several moments and I wanted to hug him for those moments. "Three days after we left your home, you stopped hearing from your partner Okwu."

I frowned at the word "partner." "Yes. I'd just learned I could reach it through a sort of . . . connection we had. I said I was okay,

Okwu said it was okay, then that third day, nothing." I turned to Mwinyi and he looked at me as if he wanted to put some distance between us. "Why?" I asked.

"I know more of what happened now," he said. He looked at his feet. "The Ariya told me everything a day ago."

I frowned deeply at him.

Mwinyi looked me in the eye now. "I thought it better to tell you now than a few hours ago."

We stared at each other. Rakumi's reins clicked and dragged on the sand as she looked curiously at us.

"That wasn't your choice to make," I finally said, but the words didn't come out in an angry growl, they came out choked. I pressed the tips of my right fingers to my forehead. "I'd rather know ev—"

"They came for Okwu."

I sighed. "Khoush soldiers," I said. "We know that. They fought and my family fled into the Root, into the cellar. Right?"

"Yes."

It felt as if there were hot embers in my chest. "Okwu . . . Did they . . ." I didn't want to say it. "Tell me, Mwinyi!"

A pained look crossed his eyes and that made everything he said next more devastating. "Things . . . things didn't happen exactly as I thought." He took a deep breath and surprised me by stepping closer. "The Khoush did come for Okwu. They'd always planned to come for it. The Meduse-Khoush War . . ."

"I understand," I snapped. "Go on."

Mwinyi nodded and continued. "Your father said they blew up its tent, but Okwu wasn't in it. Okwu wasn't there. The Khoush soldiers demanded that your family tell them where it was. Your family refused. They threatened to kill your father."

I pressed my hands to my mouth. "They killed my—"

"No, no," he said, taking my wrists. "But your family would not give up Okwu."

I looked into Mwinyi's eyes and said, "If they burned Okwu's tent, that's deep, deep disrespect to Himba land . . . Land is sacred to us. We would never, *ever* cooperate after something like that."

Mwinyi nodded. "This angered the soldiers and they used their weapons to set the Root on fire," Mwinyi said. "And . . ."

I was suddenly faint. "The Himba don't go out, we go in," I said, breathlessly. "My family ran into the Root . . . and the Khoush set it on fire, didn't they? What I saw *was* true!"

Mwinyi kept talking as I paced in circles, my hands grasping my *okuoko*. "Your father believes Okwu killed many of them," Mwinyi said. "Even as the Root was burning with all of them inside, he could hear it. Khoush screaming, over and over. The only Meduse there was Okwu, so it had to be Okwu doing it. And it most likely sent a distress call to other Meduse. But eventually, the noise stopped. All this, your father communicated to your grandmother."

"As the Root was burning around him, around everyone?" I shouted at him.

Mwinyi paused, seeming to question whether or not to say more. "At some point," he continued, "he stopped communicating with her through the zinariya. So Binti, I . . . I don't know what we're going to find when we get there."

"The Ariya knew all this before we left?"

"Yes."

"Yet she told us half-truths and didn't try to stop me from leaving."

"No."

"She would not have succeeded," I muttered. I felt numb. Dead. Mwinyi may not have known what we'd find there, but I did. Charred bones. My family was dead. My family was dead. My family was dead . . . five five five five five five five five five five five. I climbed high into the tree and when I turned to Mwinyi, the motion felt slow, and I could have been looking at him from outer space. "If you think I'm such a mess, why did you come with me?"

His eyebrows rose. "I'm the only one who could get you here safely on my own."

We stared into each other's eyes and I knew he wasn't telling me all of it. I waited. And waited. When it was clear he wasn't going to speak, I blurted, "If Okwu called on its people, it's the Khoush-Meduse War all over again."

He looked away. "Maybe."

"What if no one is left?"

"I don't—"

"You know you don't have to *say* it to say it to me," I said. "And, Mwinyi, I came back with a Meduse, the Khoush nearly killed both of us the minute we stepped off the ship, why would they leave it at that?" I stepped over to Rakumi, my legs feeling like someone else's legs. The number five was in everything and I was glad. I patted Rakumi's neck. "And why would Okwu *not* fight back? It wanted a reason to use the weapons it made at Oomza Uni, the same place the Khoush brought the chief's stinger. Okwu hadn't forgotten anything. And the Khoush have always been jealous of the Himba; why not find a reason to burn down Osemba's oldest home?" I shut my eyes, whispering, "Z = z^2 + c." When my heart rate had decreased, I said, "All because I came home."

"Binti," Mwinyi said. "It wasn't your homecoming, it was a matter of *time*."

I was listening to his every word, from deep in the tree, but in my heart, I burned.

"Ouch!" Mwinyi hissed. I felt the electric shock all over my body, but mainly in one of my *okuoko*. Rakumi bucked and groaned loudly, turning an eye toward us to see what was going on. "Why does your hair do that?"

I frowned, staring ahead. "It's not hair."

"What?"

"When I was on the ship, the Meduse, they did this to me."

"Sorry," he said. "I'm sorry . . . I didn't . . . can I ask you . . . why . . . why did you let them—"

"I didn't *let* them!" I shouted. My eyes were hot with tears. I needed to get home. "But it was done. I couldn't turn back." The world had started exploding again. If I looked behind me, I knew I'd see the tunnel that was often there, the one that led to the alien mind of my other people. I wanted to scream. I was too many things and my family was charred bones in the ruins of my home . . . five five five five five five five. I sat down right there in the sand beside Rakumi's front leg. I climbed higher up the tree and stayed there.

Mwinyi climbed back on Rakumi. Minutes later, I got up and did the same. And for the next hour, we were quiet again. Tears fell from my eyes as I stared at the open desert ahead. I had to drink more water than usual because of it. The number five flew around me like a swarm of gnats at sunset. And behind me loomed the tunnel, I knew. Every so often, I felt Mwinyi shift about as he moved his hands this way and that, speaking to whomever he was speaking to. I didn't care; I wasn't interested in talking to those who were behind us.

———

"What's that?" we both said at the same time. Mwinyi was looking at the stones, I was looking at the smoke.

"Stop!" I screamed. "Oh stop! Rakumi, stop!" When the camel kept walking, I started climbing down. Mwinyi grunted deep in his throat and Rakumi stopped just as my sandaled feet reached the sand. I landed hard and bent low, then I started running. We were still miles away. As I ran, I heard my anklets clicking and I was reminded of the sound of my sisters and mother moving about the Root and of Himba women dancing during Moon Fest.

I stopped among the stones and fell to my knees as I stared. The

Root. No, not just the Root, the part of Osemba closest to it too. Burning, crumbling, attacked. Even from here, I could smell the smoke. Billowing up from burning or burned homes and buildings. I could not see exactly what, but I knew Osemba enough to know where things were.

"As we were coming, I was dying," I whispered, my hands pressed to my mouth, my eyes wide and dry as the hot breeze blew. They hadn't just destroyed the Root. They'd taken much of Osemba, too?

I felt Mwinyi's hand on my shoulder as he knelt beside me. I inhaled and exhaled, focusing on each breath, just as my therapist had taught me. I calmed some. "When I first left here," I said quietly, wringing my hands, "I left on a ship called Third Fish. It was . . . *she* was alive."

"Bigger than a whale?" he asked.

"What?"

Mwinyi only shook his head. "Not important. Tell me about your Third Fish."

"Miri 12s," I said, trying to focus on the image of the Third Fish in my mind, instead of what I saw ahead. "They are probably the finest technology, finest *creature*, this planet has ever produced. What else can leave Earth with nothing but itself and travel through space? But *it* all happened in Third Fish. Everyone was killed by the Meduse. I nearly died in there. When I came back here, I happened to get Third Fish again for the journey. I stepped onboard Third Fish and I felt such a . . . comfort. I wish I were on her now, her peacefulness swallows everything bad."

We were at the place where I'd found my *edan*; the group of gray stones jutting out from the ground like flattened old teeth. This was where I had practiced treeing and prepared for my Oomza Uni interviews. The stones were large enough to sit on and arranged in a wide semicircle that opened west, facing my hometown. Mere feet away, beside one of the stones, was the spot where I'd dug up my *edan*.

I looked at this place and suddenly I saw that the ground around it shimmered as if sprinkled with flecks of gold. Mwinyi seemed to see it too. I wasn't ready to stand up, so I crawled there, grinding sand into my red skirt, feeling it enter the bottoms of my sandals as it stripped away the *otjize* on my knuckles. I didn't care about any of it. I sat down at the spot where I'd been, where I'd dug up the *edan*, back when my life had been simple, and looked at the speckled ground. Mwinyi came and stood over me.

"The shimmer isn't physically there," he said. "The zinariya is showing it to us."

I touched the sand where the sparkles were, rubbing it between my fingers. No matter how hard I tried, and no matter how real the gold flecks in the sand looked, I could not touch them.

"It *was* there," he added, kneeling down beside me. "A long time ago." And as if his words cued it to happen, the world expanded again, but this time, I didn't feel as if it would repel me into space. Instead, it was as if the sand around us was disappearing, all of it shifting away, and as it shifted, I . . . we, both Mwinyi and I, lowered. Mwinyi grabbed my arm and I knew that he too was seeing it happen. We both looked around as the stones seemed to grow taller and wider and then their bases became shiny thick very solid gold, as did the ground beneath us. A large imperfect circle about the size of the Root emerged, the semicircle of gold-based stones in the center. I ran a hand over the smooth surface that shined so brightly in the sun we both had to squint and shade our eyes. It was warm.

Mwinyi grasped my arm more tightly and said, "Don't move. It's alright." If he had not done this, I'd have fled for my life, and my confused perspective of what was now and what was decades ago was so skewed, I probably would have run right into one of the stones.

These People had limbs, two arms and two legs, each over twenty feet long and thin like the trunks of palm trees. Their bodies were smooth and long. And they looked made of solid gold.

They walked with a slow grace that suggested fluidity. Gold was malleable when it was warm, and they were solar, their form of life might have been energy akin to the currents I could call using mathematics.

They were coming toward the gold plane. They were not slow, but their motions were watery. Had they always been shaped like this, I did not know, for this clearly had been after they'd been around human beings for those few years. The first stepped in the center while the others waited on the sand. It stood up straight and raised its hands above its head. Then its arms then legs fused. I could hear it, soft slurping, ripples running over its flesh as it flattened and smoothed itself out into what looked like a five-foot-high, ten-foot-wide wedge.

The rocks around us began to vibrate and *phoom*, off the golden wedge shot into the sky, so fast that it was gone in seconds. There was no sonic boom, no smoke, not even a gust of air, like with the Third Fish. But high in the sky, I could see a wink of gold, then nothing. The next one stepped onto the platform and did the same.

"These are the Zinariya, the aliens who gave us the zinariya technology," Mwinyi said, awed. "We loved them so much we named our tribe after them. I've never seen them before. Not like this! I've never thought to ask."

"And this was the launch port," I said, as we watched the second one shoot into the sky. When the third one stepped onto the platform, it stopped and turned to us. Mwinyi's hand clenched my arm tighter and we pressed closer to each other. It leaned down and brought forth an arm whose end became a hand with long, long fingers. In its hand was what might have been the golden center of my *edan*, except its surface was smooth, not fingerprint ridged. As Mwinyi and I watched, silver slivers rose from the golden ground, flipped up, and fitted around it, clicking and clacking, until it became the object that I had known until recently. It dumped the *edan* to the ground but instead of falling, it hovered before us. Then the world around us shifted, the sand rose, and the Zinariya people disappeared and we were back where we had been.

"Do you know what that meant?" Mwinyi asked.

I shook my head and was about to say more when a ship zoomed in from the north toward my village. I could see its sleek yellow design. It seemed to land nearby. A Khoush ship in Osemba. Unheard of. I started walking home.

CHAPTER 3

When Elephants Fight

The Root was still burning.

It was made of stone and concrete; *how* was it on fire? The bio-luminescent plants that covered it had burned to ash. The solar panels on the roof had wilted like plants, some of them were probably puddles of synthetic steel in the debris. Six generations of my family had lived here. The Root was the oldest house in my village, maybe the oldest in the city. This was where we had family and community gatherings because the living room was so spacious that it could fit a hundred people.

Powerful Khoush weapons had been shot into it, exploding and then burning so hot that they could even combust and melt stone. All the floors of the Root had collapsed, burned, and smoldered into a heap. Chunks of concrete and rubble blown out when the house exploded were littered around the heap. What remained looked like a giant mound of still smoking blackened char.

"Mama!" I called, walking toward it as I looked around wildly. I coughed as smoke wafted in my direction. "Papa!" I stopped yards away, everything around me was silent but the sound of embers crackling and softly popping. I looked away. Then, slowly, I turned to face what was left of my home. *Because of me,* I thought. And I could feel my *okuoko* begin to writhe on my head and against my back. My Meduse anger sharpened everything. The Khoush had always seen my people as expendable, tools to use, toy with, and discard, useful animals until we weren't useful anymore. During war, we were just in the way.

"When elephants fight, the grass suffers." The green words appearing before me seemed so out of place and the words so profound that I was snapped from my dark thoughts. Mwinyi had sent them to me through the zinariya.

My eye went to the base of the house where the embers were glowing.

"It wasn't just called the Root because it was a family place," I said. "Most of the house's foundation was actually built on the old root of an Undying tree." My mother had told me this when I was about five years old. I'd been sure she was just joking until the next thunderstorm when I realized the house wasn't groaning because of the wind. "The cellar was—" I couldn't say it. I knew what we'd find in the cellar.

Mwinyi left me and walked around the house.

As I stood there, I felt it more than I heard it and every part of me reacted. My *okuoko* writhed, one of them actually slapping the side of my face as if to say, "Look!" The zinariya contracted and expanded my world and I heard distant voices commenting from a distant place, just softly enough for me not to understand. I automatically called the simple equation that always focused my mind, $a^2 + b^2 = c^2$. Then over and over, I spoke the number that relaxed me, "Five, five, five, five, five, five, five." I let my mind follow the zipping dancing fives and with each triangular motion, I steadied. When I looked toward the road leading to the Root, I was thankfully calm enough to simply observe what stood there like the spirit it was.

The Night Masquerade. Again. This time during the *day*! And now I was seeing it from much closer than I had the first time when I stood in my bedroom a few days ago, before my bedroom had been burned to ash. It looked taller, standing about my father's height. Its raffia body cracked and snapped as it stretched an arm to point its long finger at me, fingers of gnarled sticks. The wooden mask's mouth was full of yellow teeth.

Only men were supposed to see the Night Masquerade and it was believed its appearance signified the approach of a big change; whether it brought change with its presence or change came afterward was never clear. The Night Masquerade was the personification of revolution. Its presence marked heroism. To also see it during the day was doubly unheard of. My family was dead; what more change could I endure? What was heroic about this happening? If this was a revolution, it was an awful one.

It spoke in Otjihimba and its voice was like the sound of a vibrating Undying tree during a thunderstorm. "Death is always news," it said, the acrid smoke billowing from its head thickening.

I felt the world swim around me as the weight of my family's death and my own terror tried to pull me down. Around it, everything seemed to vibrate. My eyes watered, and I kept blinking and blinking away the blurriness. The Night Masquerade slowly stepped toward me and I nearly screamed. Instead, I coughed as I inhaled a great whiff of its smoke.

"A bird who has flown off the earth and then returns to land is still on the land," it said. "Remove your shoes and listen."

Phoom! The smoke from its head was copious now and when it finally cleared, the Night Masquerade was gone.

"Oh, thank the Seven," I whispered. But its presence stayed with me and its words echoed in my mind. I looked down at my dusty sandals. I'd bought them on Oomza Uni in the local market. They were made from the secretions of a friendly spider that lived in swamps. When fresh, the webbing could be molded into anything. When it dried, it kept that shape for a thousand years, the seller told me.

I was considering taking them off when Mwinyi called, "Binti. Come here."

He and Rakumi were on the other side of the house and as I jogged there, I felt faint. My family was in the cellar. Dead. Had they burned? Suffocated first? "We cannot get out," my father had said. I stopped and realized that beside me were the charred remains of the sandstorm analyzer my brother had built and placed on the roof. The steel box with its optical particle counters looked like the discarded head of a primitive robot. He'd been so proud of that instrument and so had my mother.

As I ran around the side of the house, I stopped again. My mouth fell open. Then I shut it because I could taste the stench through my mouth just as much as I could smell it through my nose. There were bodies all over and vultures stood and were pecking at some of them. Khoush soldiers. Men and women. With their chests burst open. I twitched and I was back on the ship in the middle of space. The smell of blood and now decay. *How is that possible?* I thought, because my stunned senses were telling me I was alone on the Third Fish again and the Meduse had just performed *moojh-ha ki-bira*. It had just happened.

Happened.

No warning.

So many.

I saw stars. Red and blue and silver. Bursting before my eyes. My mouth was full of decay, as it hung open, trying to pull in air. Now I couldn't breathe. None around me were breathing. I stumbled, gasping, and one of the vultures lazily spread its wings and hopped away.

I blinked and I was back at the remains of the home where I'd been born. The violence was here now. I'd brought it by leaving home and coming back home. I was hyperventilating now. *What did my therapist Saidia Nwanyi say I should do when I can't breathe?* I thought. I put my hands behind my head, though doing so made me feel more exposed to the gruesome sight before me. There had to be fifteen, maybe even twenty bodies strewn about like fallen trees. "Five, five, five, five, five," I chanted as I let myself tree. Each time the number left my lips, I was able to take in more breath. And with each breath, I came back to myself. The moment I could move, I fled.

When I reached the back of the house, I stepped onto a sheet of solid yellow glass. It cracked and shattered beneath my foot. I took another step and stopped, realizing this was the spot where Okwu's tent had been. Mwinyi stood in the blackened center. Not far to the left was what remained of my brother's garden, a charred skeleton of tomato bushes and ash. Rakumi sniffed the greener parts and began munching on a tomato bush.

"Did you see—"

"Yes," he said, still looking at the cracking glass beneath him.

"I think Okwu did that," I said.

"Maybe because the Khoush did this," he stamped on the glass and his sandal went right through it, shards flying this way and that.

I shut my eyes and took deep breaths, holding myself shallowly in the tree, numbers and equations cartwheeling and floating around me. "This explosion would have killed anything it hit," I said. "Unless Okwu wasn't in the tent."

"I don't think they killed it," Mwinyi said.

"Why?"

"Your family was hiding inside the Root when they set it on fire." He paused to inspect my face. "They burned the Root because they couldn't find you or . . . or Okwu."

The idea hit me so hard that when I turned and ran off, I didn't care about the possibility of glass cutting my feet through my sandals.

The road into town was dusty and my sandals kicked it up with every step. Even as I ran further and further from home, the air continued to smell of smoke. The Yennes' house was still burning. The Mahangu building was blown to bits. The Omuzumbas' house was still intact and I glimpsed someone on the balcony watching me run by. How many others were watching me run down the road? How many had fled the destruction?

A Khoush ship had just flown by, which meant they were still in the area. I didn't care. I passed the remains of the souq, where it looked as if the market's women and men had left everything behind in a rush. There were overturned tables and booth dividers and in some places crushed and rotten meat, vegetables, piles of grains, and crushed baskets. The smell of spices, snuff, and incense mixed with the stench of smoke here. I leapt over an overturned bench. Sweat was pouring down my face now, and my heart felt like it would smash through my chest.

I stopped at the lake and stood there. Its water was so serene that it looked like the glass burned into the sand where Okwu's tent used to be. "So calm in all this chaos," I said, breathing hard. The sweat was getting into my eyes, so I wiped my hand down my face. My hand came away red orange with *otjize*. I heard someone behind me.

"What . . . are . . . you doing?" Mwinyi asked, jogging up. He bent forward to catch his breath, putting his hands on his knees. "We don't know if the Khoush are around here!"

"I . . . saw the Night Masquerade again," I said. "In broad daylight. We don't know *anything* anymore."

"Back at the Root?" he asked. Even Enyi Zinariya people believed in the Night Masquerade.

I nodded. There was movement to my right and I turned my head. Two men. Himba. I knew them. I knew most everyone in my village. The Council Elder Kapika and his second wife Neeka.

"Binti?" Chief Kapika said, coming closer. Neeka followed. And as they came closer, I noticed more people peeking from behind market dividers and from within homes across the street.

I hesitated, then turned to the water and walked into it. I felt all eyes on me as the lake water washed off the thin layer of *otjize* on my legs and sweat washed it from my face, neck, and arms. In front of all these people, Himba people. I went in up to my waist, then I opened my mouth and shouted, *"Okwuuuuuuuuu!"*

My voice echoed across the water and then there was silence. I could hear people behind me whispering. Still, I waited.

And then the water began to ripple as Okwu swam up and rose before me. I smiled, tears stinging my eyes. Its dome was a deep blue in the sunshine. And it was covered with clusterwink snails. I stepped back as more domes emerged around it. More Meduse. A woman screamed from the group of people and there was the sound of scuffling feet as people fled.

I waded back to the land, joining Mwinyi. "How did you know?" he asked. He sounded more than nervous, but he didn't step away as the Meduse emerged from the water.

"Because I know Okwu," I said, turning to Okwu. In Meduse, I asked it, "Are you alright?"

"Yes."

"Why didn't you answer me?"

"I didn't want you to come."

"I thought you were dead!" I said.

"It's better than you being dead, Binti."

"W—. . . what happened? Why is . . . The Root! They burned it! And there were dead soldiers. Many! What happened?" I was shaking and crying now.

Okwu blew out gas and both Mwinyi and I started coughing.

"When you left, I stayed in my tent," he said in Otjihimba. "Your family was kind to me, except for your sisters, who like to yell. Your family had a meeting that evening, so many were there. The Khoush came in the night when your father took me out in the desert to meet with your elders in private. The elders wanted to speak with me. And as we talked, from where we were we saw the Khoush ship fly in and blow up my tent."

"What?" I whispered.

"The elders told me to stay with them in the dark, as your father ran back, shouting at the Khoush to stop. He told all your people to run inside for safety. There were Khoush on the ground at this point. One of the Khoush argued with your father. I could hear it; the man called himself General Staff Kuw and he had no hair or *okuoko* on his head. He didn't think I was in the tent and he wanted to know where I was. Your father refused to tell him and the general accused him of sympathizing with the enemy and having a daughter who'd even mated with a Meduse—"

"Mated?" I exclaimed. The Meduse hovering around Okwu all thrummed their domes.

"Yes, the Khoush are a stupid people," Okwu said. "Your father said they were the enemy because they'd just blown up part of his property. This angered General Kuw. That's when he ordered his soldiers to firebomb the Root. I think they expected everyone to run out. They didn't expect your father to run inside as it was burning. But that's what he did and no one came out."

"The Himba do not run away, we run within," I said, quietly. "They went inside, even as it was burning." I clucked my tongue, as my hands began to shake and my mind tried to cloud. "The Khoush like to joke that we are a suicidal people."

"As the elders watched the Root burn in the night, I left them . . . who just stood there staring at the fire that was so huge, it showed light far into the desert," Okwu continued. "As the Khoush, in a stupid rage, went on to firebomb more homes in Osemba. They weren't even looking for me. I activated my armor, crept up to those standing near the house, and killed as many of them as I could. I wanted to kill that General Kuw, but he had already fled onto a ship. Coward.

"For you, for your family, they all deserved to die. When I could kill no more, I covered the air and escaped as they coughed. There were too many who were coming from their ship. One does not fight a war it cannot win. I hid in the lake and waited for the others. Now when the time comes, we will fight the war we will win."

"They burned everything!" I heard Kapika yell from behind me. He pushed his wife away as she tried to hold him back. Several of the people had come back to listen too. "The Khoush came and burned everything! Out of spite! Because of you people!"

There were about ten Meduse and the only one who was not blue floated up so quickly that I thought it would barrel over me. It was so clear that I could see the white of its stinger as the sun shined right through it. The Meduse chief.

"See what they did to Okwu? You see why we kill them?" the chief rumbled. "We have come. They don't know we are here. We will meet them when they are not ready."

I stepped back and looked at them all. "You need to make peace," I said.

"No," the chief said. "We are here. We will make war. You should *want* war."

I felt my *okuoko* twitch as it dawned on me. I looked beyond the Meduse, at the lake. I moaned. I turned to Mwinyi, then to the Himba standing around us. "Chief Kapika," I said, stepping over to him. I put my chin to my chest as I took his hands. I felt him twitch, wanting to pull away from me. My *otjize* had washed off. I stood before him, before *everyone*, naked, so I was not offended by his discomfort. "Please," I said. "I know I come to you as a barbarian. Please, put that aside for now, and focus on the fact that I am a Himba daughter, regardless of how I look and where I have been . . ."

"And what pollutes you," he added.

I paused, restraining my Meduse prideful anger. I let myself tree and called up a current. As the numbers flew around me, through me, I felt calmer, clearer, and more confident, though the anger still boiled beneath, trying to push thoughts of my dead family to the forefront of my mind. I continued to hold his hands, my head respectfully bowed. "Yes, what pollutes me. But I am still a master harmonizer," I said in a steady voice, loudly enough for the others to hear. "I am more than and better than what I was when I left here. I want to call an urgent meeting of the Council Elders." I looked up into his eyes. "It is urgent and a matter of peace in these lands. Please. We can't have more die." I hesitated and then pushed on. "C—. . . call an *Okuruwo*."

An *Okuruwo* was only called when the lifeblood of the Himba people was in grave danger. It was only called by elders, because it was to call on the soul of the Himba to heal itself and that took a power only the old could wield. Usually. The healing power of the Himba is carried within the elders, even the word *Okuruwo* is usually only spoken by older Himba. Thus, the word felt hot coming out of my mouth. I cleared my throat as we stared at each other. His irises were a deep brown, the whites of his eyes yellowed by the sun. "Have you not looked around?" he asked in his soft voice. "Your childish *selfish* actions led to all this strife. We don't leave our lands for a reason, Binti. Now you speak beyond your years. What makes you think *you* can call an *Okuruwo*?"

I didn't miss a beat. "Because there are Meduse ships in the lake and if we don't do something immediately, we'll be the grass crushed beneath the feet of two fighting elephants."

———

The Council Elders use the same method of communication that Himba women use to spread the word about the date of the pilgrimage: a large leaf is cut from a palm tree and passed from member to member. The Himba people are the creators and makers of astrolabes, devices of communication. However, the Himba people have been communicating important meeting announcements in this old, old way for centuries and we will continue to do so.

So I watched a young girl climb a palm tree, use a large machete to cut a large leaf, climb down, and hand it to Chief Kapika. Okwu, Mwinyi, and I stood there silent as he took it and went into his home and came out with a jar of his wife's *otjize*. He held the jar out to me.

"You're calling the *Okuruwo*, so you draw the circle."

"Why don't Himba males put *otjize* on their skins?" Okwu asked, floating up beside me.

From behind me, Mwinyi chuckled. I took the leaf and the jar, ignoring Okwu's question.

"What reason does a man have to be beautiful?" Chief Kapika asked as he watched me spread the leaf on the dry dirt.

"Beauty does not need a reason," Okwu responded.

I opened the jar. The *otjize* was so fragrant that for a moment, I swooned. It had been so long since I'd smelled Earth-made *otjize*. The zinariya squeezed and expanded my world as images of home tried to flood my brain—town's square, the lake, the schoolhouse . . . his wife must have collected the clay from near there. *My* otjize *no longer even smells like this*, I thought.

"You will never understand us," Chief Kapika said dismissively to Okwu.

I drew the circle with *otjize* and handed him the leaf. He looked at the circle and then at me. "Make sure the Meduse stay in the water," he said. "We will meet and try to make this better." He looked at Okwu, but spoke to me. "*Their* tribesman is alive, there is no reason for war. They have destroyed enough."

"That is not for you to decide," Okwu said. "Unprovoked aggressive action is reason for war."

"The Khoush killed my family," I added flatly. "For we, Himba, that should be an act of war, shouldn't it?"

"I'm sorry, Binti," Chief Kapika said, touching my shoulder. "But if you chose to mingle with the Meduse and if your family chose to welcome one into its home, even built a home for it, why should the rest of us—"

"Because we are Himba!" I shouted, clenching my fists. "Osemba is my home!"

He waved his hand. "Save it for the *Okuruwo*," he said. "I won't speak for the council." He rolled the palm leaf up and began to walk away. He stopped and turned back to me. "When you come, please apply *otjize*. Use what I gave you, if you have none. You look like a savage." He gave Mwinyi a foul look.

I shot a glance at Mwinyi, who glared at Chief Kapika but held his tongue. When Chief Kapika was out of hearing range, Mwinyi said, "And that's why we will not come to fight for the Himba."

I bit my lip. "He only knows the little we know here," I said. "Forgive him for that."

Mwinyi only looked away, moving his hands smoothly as he turned his back to me. I didn't ask who he was speaking to.

"Are all your people so afraid?" Okwu asked.

I glared at it.

"I think we should leave here," Mwinyi said, turning back to me. "The conflict between the Meduse and the Khoush is old. It's a large part of why the Enyi Zinariya have stayed away from these lands. Binti, it's not your fault. This was all going to start again, sooner or later. You did what you could on that ship, but even you had to have known it was temporary."

But was it, I wondered. Things had been peaceful all my life and well before that. The pact had held. And in that time, the Himba had flourished. My father was able to build up his shop. Many of us traveled regularly to Khoush cities to sell our astrolabes. Even all that had happened on the Third Fish and with the stinger on Oomza Uni would have remained planets away if I had not been there. No, I had disturbed all of that when I decided to do what we Himba never do.

"I have to try and make it better," I said. "I can't just leave here." *My family*, I thought. Almost all of my loved ones had burned alive and were now charred remains in the Root, the home in which we'd all grown up—my mother, father, siblings, cousins, nieces, nephews, family friends. I shuddered, reaching into my pocket and touching the golden ball of my *edan*. It felt warm and I grasped it.

The feeling of its grooved surface was instantly soothing, the feel of the numbers running through my mind as I lightly treed such a relief that my legs felt weak.

I sighed and walked over to a market bench and sat down. "Where is Rakumi?" I flatly asked.

Mwinyi pointed up the road toward the Root. I nodded. "Are you alright?" He sat beside me.

"No," I said. "I will never be alright again."

Okwu glided over to us. "Shall I go with you?" it asked.

I thought about it for a moment. I nodded. "Yes," I said. "For now, though, go back to the chief and the other Meduse and keep them from showing themselves."

"Have the Khoush returned here?" Mwinyi asked.

"They will, "Okwu said and it sounded almost hungry at the prospect. "They are still searching for me. Soon they will realize that I have been hiding in plain sight." Its dome vibrated. Laughter. "You should hope this meeting is successful. Otherwise, tomorrow, there will be war."

Mwinyi looked at me. "When will . . ."

"O . . . O . . ." I paused. The word was still hard for me to speak. "*Okuruwo* are always held at sunset," I said. "'When the fire and the sky are in agreement.'"

———

Mwinyi and I stayed in the empty souq for much of the day, then Mwinyi went back to the Root to get Rakumi; I didn't want to go with. Okwu had returned to the lake, where it quickly disappeared into the water. Once, while in there, it had reached out to me through my *okuoko* and asked, *Are you alright?*

"I am here," I responded.

Mwinyi returned with Rakumi, who must have eaten her fill of what was left of my brother's garden. The camel sat down beside my unrolled mat and went to sleep. The remaining Himba in the area who hid in their homes kept their distance. Once in a while, I could see people walking in small groups up or down the road. People looked our way but quickly moved on.

I spent those few hours resting on my mat, my golden ball levitating before me as I treed. I left the other pieces in my pocket. Somehow, they no longer felt like part of the *edan* anymore. They were like bits of shed skin. I wondered if the golden ball was still poison to Okwu, or if it was just the outer silver-looking pieces. The golden ball had the same tang of the pieces when I touched it to my tongue. "It's not really a good time to ask Okwu," I whispered to myself, and I watched the golden ball rotate before me. The current I sent around it was like an electrical atmosphere around a small planet.

Mwinyi sat beside me, watching for a bit, and other times getting up and walking along the edge of the lake. At one point, he stopped and stood with his back to the lake and looked toward the sky. He stayed like this for nearly an hour. I watched him, while deep inside a flow of mathematics, the golden grooved ball slowly rotating before me, my mind clear, sharp, calm, and distant. Mwinyi's face was peaceful, his lips seemed to be saying something, his hands to his sides, his light blue garments fluttered in the wind, and he stood on the discarded shells of the clusterwink snails who lived in the lake.

I wondered what he was doing. A harmonizer knows when a fellow harmonizer is harmonizing. Who was he speaking to? Maybe the Seven. Eventually, he roused himself, then moved his hands for several minutes. He came back to me and sat on his mat. "Was it a good conversation?" I asked him.

He chuckled, rolled his eyes, and said, "You wouldn't believe it."

I went back to working with the golden ball. If he didn't want to tell me, I was fine with that. Maybe he'd been speaking with my grandmother, or the Ariya, or maybe his parents or brothers. It wasn't always my business.

———

At sunset, I breathed a sigh of relief. The Khoush military hadn't returned. This meant there was still a chance that an *Okuruwo* would help the Himba organize, and maybe I could get us to serve as mediator between the Khoush and Meduse and prevent all-out war. If war intensified between the Khoush and Meduse, if more Meduse came and more Khoush from farther lands came, the fighting would spread and even bleed into other peoples' business. All because of me. On the Third Fish, I had accidently found myself in the middle of something. This time I *was* that middle.

We packed up and Mwinyi and I ate a large meal of leftover roasted desert hare, dried dates, and ground roots. I stepped behind one of the booths and used most of the remaining *otjize* I had to cover myself with a thick layer, rolling my *okuoko* with so much of it that one would not be able to tell that they weren't hair but *okuoko*, tentacles.

I sent a message to Okwu that it was time to go and it emerged from the water less than a minute later. There was an odd moment when Okwu glided up to Mwinyi and they both stayed like that for about thirty seconds. Something passed between them, I was sure. Though Mwinyi had no *edan* or *okuoko*, he was still a harmonizer; where I used mathematics, he used some other form of access to speak with various peoples.

As we left, heading further down the dirt road, I couldn't shake the feeling that from all the sand brick homes and buildings that still stood (once we were a few minutes' walk further from the Root, there was no further Khoush damage), people were watching us. They all must have known about the *Okuruwo* by this time, the news traveling rapidly by astrolabe and word of mouth as the palm leaf was passed from council member home to council member home. And if I knew my people as well as I knew I did, they were hopeful for my success even as they raged at me.

═══

The stone building where the council regularly met was on the other side of Osemba, about a two-mile walk. We went around the lake and then set onto the main dirt road. Here, people stared from doorways, windows, and even came out of their homes to look at me, the "one who'd abandoned her people," or Okwu, a "violent Meduse," or Mwinyi, a "savage desert person."

"Why let so many of those grow here?" Mwinyi asked as we passed a large group of trees with thick rubbery leaves and wide trunks covered in hard sharp thorns. He held up his hands and made several motions. A woman standing in the doorway of a large stone house we were passing gasped when she saw this, grabbed her staring toddler, pulled him inside, and slammed her door.

"The Undying trees?" I said, glancing at the closed door. Mwinyi didn't pay the woman any mind. "We couldn't dig them up even if we wanted to, their roots go too deep. Plus, because of them, we found drinkable underground water sources for Osemba; because of them, we can live here. We built our water systems around them."

"I can see children accidentally impaling themselves on them while playing games in your street," Mwinyi said. "Why are they called 'undying'? Do spirits live in them?"

"Spirits live in everything," Okwu said.

"Because they're older than the Himba," I said. "We respect them. When there are thunderstorms, it's like they come to life. They vibrate. Fast enough to make a howling sound. You have to see it happen to know how incredible it is. And they make this salt that you can scrape from the leaves that'll cure all kinds of sicknesses."

Mwinyi was moving his hands fast now and when he finished by making a pushing motion forward, I saw the air before him warp for a moment. My head ached and I turned to look ahead of us until it stopped.

"Who are you talking to?" I asked.

"Your grandmother," he said. "You know how she loves plants. These will blow her mind." He paused. Then he chuckled. "She knows of them already."

I smiled then I coughed, Okwu's gasp billowing all around me. I heard footsteps scrambling away. When I looked back, I saw a group of children hiding behind the Undying trees, several of them giggling.

"They're just curious," I told Okwu in Meduse, hoping the low rumbly vibration of the language would scare the young girls off. It didn't.

"One of them touched my *okuoko*," Okwu rumbled back. The children fled at the sound of its Meduse voice. "If they want death by stinger, I will give it to them."

"Remember," I said, switching back to Otjihimba. I smiled. "My *otjize* healed your *okuoko*. The little girl who touched you was covered with *otjize*. She can't be bad for you."

"Her *otjize* would burn my flesh," Okwu rumbled in Meduse, irritably.

"If she touched you, then her *otjize* is on your *okuoko*," I said, laughing. "I smell nothing burning."

"Your people are rude," Mwinyi suddenly snapped. He was glaring at three men standing at the front of a building laughing. One of them pointed at Mwinyi and opened and closed his hand. "Crude, rude people."

I grasped his arm and pulled him along. "I apologize on their behalf," I said.

"Small-minded insular people," he muttered. "I can speak their language, they can't even greet me in mine." Thankfully, he let me pull him along. I didn't allow myself to think about what they must have been saying about me all this time. And now that there was Khoush-Meduse violence again that had led to the destruction of part of Osemba, and here I was bringing a Meduse to the town's most sacred space, those sentiments would surely worsen. But in our walk across Osemba, though more kids and a few adults taunted Okwu and several spat and shouted at Mwinyi, not one person spoke to me.

———

The Osemba House was a giant smooth dome made of sandstone that sat on the eastern edge of town. The Root was on the western-most edge, so the two buildings were as far from each other as one could get and still be in Osemba. The Osemba House was built between three Undying trees and inside was a stone platform built around the Sacred Well.

Daily, women from this side of Osemba came to collect water to drink, for the water here had a refreshing taste and settled upset stomachs in a way that the water pumped around town from the underground river did not. My mother would venture to this side of town once in a while and when she brought home the strange wa-ter, we'd all fight each other for our tiny cup of it that we'd sip after dinner. In the back, the outdoor meeting grounds faced the open desert.

"Let's go around," I said. "That's where they'll be." I wasn't sure how anyone would tolerate the three of us, tainted individuals by Himba standards, walking so close to the Sacred Well.

Okwu stopped for a moment and seemed to contemplate the building. When I turned to look at it, I laughed despite everything. "The Himba are a passive-aggressive people," it said in Meduse.

I nodded. "We have ways of making our point strongly without saying a word." It was only now, after being so close to a Meduse, that I gazed upon the Osemba House and realized it looked very much like a Meduse, the enemy of a people who treated the Himba like intelligent slaves. *Everything is so complicated and connected*, I thought. *Everything. And nothing is coincidence, or so my mother used to always say.* The space between my eyes stung. *"Used to."* No longer. I walked faster.

Before I came around the side of the building, I heard the fire. The Sacred Fire was always burning, but only when an *Okuruwo* was called was it grown to this size. They all turned. They had all been waiting for us. Five old men, including Chief Kapika, two old women, including Titi—the woman who led the pilgrimage into the desert—and one young man.

I sighed, my eyes meeting the young man's eyes. It was Dele, my best friend who'd stopped being my best friend when I snuck away to attend Oomza Uni. Who over the last year had decided to grow a beard and was tapped to become an apprentice to Chief Kapika. I had spoken to him just before the Enyi Zinariya came for me. He'd contacted my astrolabe. We'd spoken briefly and he'd looked at me with a pity so painful I'd been glad when the conversation was over. The last thing he'd said to me was, "I can't help you, Binti."

They all sat around the fire, the men wearing deep red kaftans and pants and the women wearing clothes similar to mine, a red wraparound skirt and a stiff red top. Both Titi and the other women had *otjize* rolled locks, braided into tessellating triangle patterns and extending down their backs. Dele's head was shaven on both sides, the dense hair on top twisted into a thick braid that extended behind his head like a horn, stiff with a thin layer of *otjize*.

"Come," Chief Kapika said.

Okwu's voice came to me as if it were thrown. *I don't like fire,* it said.

I approached the Himba Council. *It won't hurt you if you don't get too close,* I responded. *Stay behind me.* I glanced at Mwinyi and he gave me a brief nod. I led the way, Mwinyi behind me and Okwu behind him. I still wore my pilgrimage outfit that my mother had bought me. Fine, fine clothes for one of the finest moments in my life. But now the red skirt was caked with sand and my stiff top was dirty with my own sweat and old *otjize*. And my family was dead.

They sat around the Sacred Fire, Dele on the other side, beside Chief Kapika and another man, the two women on both sides of me, Titi to my right. I took a seat in the space made for me, completing the circle, and Mwinyi and Okwu settled behind me.

I lowered my head. "I'm honored that the Himba Council has answered my call for this . . . *Okuruwo*," I said, speaking the word a bit too loudly as I pushed it from my lips. "Thank you."

"The council recognizes its daughter," all of them responded. Except Dele, who said nothing. But he was not here as an elder, so he could not speak as one.

"Binti," Chief Kapika began. "You left us like a thief in the night, abandoning your family—"

"I didn't 'abandon' my family," I insisted.

"You gathered us here tonight, small woman," Titi snapped at me. "Don't interrupt an elder."

I fought my indignation and the others waited to see if I could control myself. I exhaled a long breath and lowered my eyes.

"You abandoned your family," Chief Kapika repeated. "Like a thief in the night. For your own needs. Nearly died for your decision and were forced to accept a partnering with the Meduse in order to survive." He paused, looking at the others. "But blood is thicker than . . . water. Like a good Himba, you came home. But you brought the enemy of a people who sees us as less than they are. And when the Khoush came for it, they came for us, too. Now there is war in our homes and around our lands again. Instigated by the actions of one of our own, you. Your lineage here is dead and you've bonded with the savage other part of your bloodline . . . why shouldn't we simply run you out of Osemba?"

I looked up sharply. Angry. "Because the Himba do not turn their own out. We go inward. We protect what is ours by embracing it," I said. "Even when one's bloodline is . . . dead." I paused, the rage and the sight of the roaring fire making me feel more powerful. I stood up before the Sacred Fire. "I left because I wanted more,"

I said. "I was not leaving my family, my people, or my culture. I wanted to *add* to it all. I was born to go to that school and when I got there, even after everything that happened, that became even clearer. I fit right into Oomza Uni.

"But I had to come home, too. I need it all, you, school, space. I wanted to go on my pilgrimage in order to align myself . . . but it wasn't my path." I paused, to gather my thoughts. "Okwu is my friend . . . yes, fine, my partner. So I also wanted to show it my home. I guess I wanted to open things up here, too. Harmonize the Khoush, Meduse, and Himba"—I motioned to Mwinyi—"and now the Enyi Zinariya, too." I turned back to the fire. "This is why I called this gathering. There's been terror and death and destruction, but I want to pull harmony out of that now. We can." I looked at each of their frowning faces. "Dele," I said, looking straight at him. He jumped a little, surprised. "You know me better than everyone here. You know my heart. You know how much I love everyone and how much I will give to protect and make everyone happy. Hear what I am about to ask."

I pointed in the direction of the lake and said, "Right now as we speak, the Meduse wait in the lake."

Every single council member gasped.

"Binti, no!" Dele exclaimed. "That can't be true!"

"Eh!" one of the elders I didn't know exclaimed. "At this moment?"

"Yes," I said. "There's a ship hiding in the water. Maybe more than one." I let my words sink in. Dele continued staring at me with wide eyes as the others whispered among themselves.

"Your people are not the type to survive war," Okwu said from behind me in Otjihimba.

I heard Mwinyi chuckle.

"The Khoush tried to kill a Meduse, despite the pact, despite Okwu being a *peaceful* ambassador who'd come to Khoushland in peace," I said. "Oomza Uni gained permission from both the

Khoush government and Meduse chief for Okwu to come here. And the Khoush burned my home, k-killing my family when they could not find and kill *me*, an honorary Meduse. The Meduse have reason to start war. And the Khoush want it, too. And they will fight over Osemba and Khoushland will burn and broil again. Unless we Himba meet with both sides and stop them." Then I asked what I hadn't even told Mwinyi or Okwu about because they weren't Himba and thus could never understand. "Please, call on the Himba deep culture."

"No!" Titi suddenly shouted.

"Please," I said, barely able to believe what I was doing, what I was saying. A year and half ago, I could never have imagined I'd be right here in this moment. Deep culture goes deeper than what it is, it goes deeper than culture, it crosses over. It communes with the mathematics that dwell within all things and only the collective of Himba Councils could evoke it.

"We will *not*! Who are you to ask that?" Titi snarled, disgusted. She took a deep breath, composing herself. When she spoke again, she was much calmer. "This isn't our fight, Binti. We pack up and go to the pilgrimage grounds and wait there until the Khoush and Meduse exhaust or kill themselves. We bring all our astrolabe supplies, all of our valuables, we go nomad as we were so long ago and we stay together, until this is over!"

"I've . . . I've seen the Night Masquerade," I admitted. "Again. In the day. Don't you have to listen to me?"

Silence, as everyone turned to look at Chief Kapika, as if waiting for him to say something. Chief Kapika only shook his head, refusing to speak on this subject. Again, I heard Mwinyi chuckling behind me. He seemed to be enjoying this more than everyone else here. "These people don't understand anything," he muttered.

In the silence, Dele suddenly got up and came to me. He stood over me and looked down. "Get up, Binti." When I did, he roughly grabbed my shoulder. "Come on."

Mwinyi was already up. "Where are you taking her?" he demanded. "I'm coming too." Okwu also floated to us.

"Stay here," Dele said, holding up a hand. "Talk to them. Say what you can. She's safe. I just need to speak with her."

"Binti?" Mwinyi asked, looking at me. "Alright?"

"I'll be fine," I said. *And I can call Okwu if I need help,* I said with my eyes. As if he understood, he nodded and stepped back.

Then Dele was pushing me toward the Osemba House back entrance. I glanced behind me at Okwu and Mwinyi, but Mwinyi was facing the still shocked and confused-looking council and saying, "My name is Mwinyi and I'm from the desert and I guess I'm representing the Enyi Zinariya. From what I know . . ."

Then we were inside and Dele was leading me to the Sacred Well in the center of the dome. "What is wrong with you?" he asked. He looked down at me. When had he gotten so much taller?

"What's . . ." I froze when I looked into his dark eyes. They were glistening with tears. I'd known Dele practically all my life. Even when we were small children, I'd never seen Dele cry. Never.

"You saved yourself before," he said. "Do you want to die now?"

"If we don't do something, we'll all die," I said. "The Khoush had to have detected when the Meduse came. They let them so they can attack from the ground. They're flying about looking for the Meduse now. There's not time for us to get out of here before it starts. Not with our things. We'll die in that desert if we leave now."

"The Night Masquerade has shown itself to you, a *girl*, twice! And the second time, it couldn't even wait for the night! You need to stop! You bring chaos," he said. "I shouldn't . . . s—" He looked away.

I stepped back from him. Staring. I knew what he'd meant to say, "I shouldn't even be speaking to you." I should have been dead to him already, for traditionally a woman who ran away from home was useless. And one who saw the Night Masquerade no longer existed. I was a ghost to him, a spirit.

"They have taught you well," I said. "Rigid. Have you dug a shelter beside an Undying tree where you will take all your wives and children and hide deep inside until the war passes? Will they use the red clay of the shelter's wall to make themselves beautiful for you while you pass the time speaking natural mathematics to the Seven? Big man you are now with your beard and apprentice status."

"You mock your own people now," he said.

"I'm trying to *save* it!"

"If you hadn't left in the first place, this wouldn't be happening," he snapped.

"I *had* to leave," I said. "Dele, I'm not . . . I'm not meant to stay here. You know it. You've always known it. I was always going out into the desert. You know? Because it's huge, it's vast. When I look back, the desert and space, they feel similar."

"Well, *I* was always meant to go inward, into what makes us *us*," he said. "And that's just as vast. And doing that will make me the next chief, not get us destroyed."

His words were like a punch in the chest and suddenly I felt breathless. War was coming as we stood here arguing. Who knew what Mwinyi and Okwu were saying to the elders. And the one who knew me even before I was fully me harbored such a dislike of me that it seemed he would have been happier if I'd died on the Third Fish last year.

"Let me do my part to fix this, Dele," I begged him. "The elders can convince the Khoush to come. I know how to call the Meduse to come. Then, the Himba Council can use Himba deep culture to get them to make peace with the Meduse."

Dele seemed to think about this, walking away from me toward the Sacred Well. He leaned against the stone wellhead and looked down into it. He turned to me. "You can call them? How?"

I didn't look away. I was what I was and I was many things now. I touched my *okuoko*. "With these."

"Your hair?"

"They're not hair anymore."

"So it's true," he said. "You've become the wife of a Meduse."

I frowned. "I'm no one's wife."

"You came home and you came with it," he said. "It stayed at the home of your family. It's been intimate with you enough that your body has changed."

"Okwu didn't do this," I said. "I don't even know which of—"

"The Meduse are a hive-minded people," he said. "What one does, they all do. If you use those to communicate with Okwu, you're communicating with the others, too."

"No," I said. "Only Okwu. And in a distant way, the Meduse chief. You don't understand."

"I've heard some of the story of what you went through from your father. Okwu would have killed you on that ship, but on Oomza University, it's your closest companion. You've become Okwu's wife."

I dismissively waved a hand at him. "Just help me, Dele. Just go talk to them. They'll hear you."

"Did you really see the Night Masquerade?"

I nodded.

"Twice?"

I nodded again. "Second time was on the road outside the Root."

"Earlier today?"

"Yes."

"During the day?"

"Yes."

"Unbelievable. *Kai!*" he exclaimed, striding away from me. Then he stopped and came back.

"What?" I softly asked as he walked up to me. I flinched as he reached forward and took one of my *okuoko* and lightly pressed it. My hand shot out before I realized I was going to do it and slapped his hand away. "Stop!" I said.

He looked at the *otjize* on his hand and then at my *okuoko*, whose transparent blue now showed a bit. He sniffed my *otjize* and then gazed at me for several moments. He eyed me as he rubbed his short beard with the *otjize* on his fingers, then he turned and walked away.

I stepped over to the wellhead and looked down into the water. Down into the darkness that was nothing like the darkness of space. Not as complete. Not as foreign. When I heard shouting and then rumbling loud enough to shake the building, I turned and strode outside. "No, no, no, no!" I muttered. We'd run out of time.

The Khoush sky whales, each the size of two houses, landed in the desert, close enough to whip dust into the air that nearly put out the Sacred Fire. The Khoush knew exactly where they were landing. The Khoush had no respect for my people. Each ship was covered with blue and white solar tiles with giant wind turbines under each wing. They'd always reminded me of beetles with the skin of lizards. And though they moved smoothly through the sky like water beetles in water, they landed in such a way that everyone in the area would know it.

As two of the elders scrambled to stand before the fire and hold open their garments to protect it, Dele, Chief Kapika, and Titi gathered together to meet whoever alighted from the sky whales. I ran to Okwu and Mwinyi.

Okwu, hide! I shouted through my *okuoko*. It turned to me. *You should—*

Okwu flew at me just as I heard a sharp *zip!* Then Okwu's *okuoko* and then its dome was covering me. I felt every part of my body tense up. There was weight but not much, but also a sense of being enveloped and gently held, hugged. Protected. Okwu's flesh smelled like pepper seed, spicy and hot. I could see everything right through it, tinted a blue. Chief Kapika and Dele were running at the sky whales, waving their hands, shouting, putting themselves in the space between Okwu, Mwinyi, and me and the sky whales. Then

Okwu was releasing its gas all around us and the shocked look of Mwinyi, the laboring smoky fire, and a few of the elders who'd turned our way disappeared. I instinctively held my breath.

Seconds passed and I leaned back, my own *okuoko* writhing on my head. I could feel the vibration of Okwu's body and then a hardness against my arm. Its stinger. White and sharp. And a thought came to me heavy with relief. If Okwu was protecting me, then it was not killing Khoush. I felt Okwu shudder and I was ex-pelled. I tumbled onto the sand and without looking at myself, I knew most of my *otjize* had been sucked off. The night air felt cool on my bare flesh.

I looked back at Okwu and saw that several of its *okuoko* were hanging by a thread or shot off, its blue color looking lighter in the firelight. Maybe pink. *Red?* I wondered. Then I was sure. Okwu was spattered with blood. *My blood?* I thought, but I didn't look at my-self because Okwu lowered to the ground. I'd never seen a Meduse touch the ground. "Okwu!" I exclaimed, scrambling to it on my knees. Okwu now lay to the side, like a deflated balloon. I gently touched its dome, tears squeezing from my eyes, barely able to breathe. Okwu's dome felt tough like the bladders of water that women carried to and from the lake. Cool beneath my touch. "What's the matter?" I shouted. "*What's the matter?*"

"They shot it," Mwinyi was saying as he came and knelt be-side me.

"Why didn't you use your shield?" I asked.

"You'd . . . have . . . died if I did," it said, its voice deeper and rougher than ever. It made my head hurt.

Mwinyi placed a hand on Okwu's dome as he stared intensely at it. Okwu's flesh twitched at his touch, but then calmed. I looked behind us and gasped. There had to be at least a hundred Khoush soldiers; men and women standing stiffly in tight desert pants and tops, the women in black and the men in white. Two Khoush men and one Khoush woman, all also in army gear, stood speaking with

Chief Kapika, Titi, and Dele, the others standing eagerly behind them.

"It is in pain," Mwinyi said. "It won't speak to me."

I couldn't think. Mama, Papa, my siblings, family dead. Zinariya crippling me. The Night Masquerade's ominous appearance. War was here. I could barely take in enough breath to keep from passing out. My heart felt as if it would burst through my chest. *Heru's chest burst open and his blood on my face was warm.* I wanted to throw myself over Okwu and scream and wail. Submit. I looked at Okwu, then back at the Khoush and the elders, then back at Okwu. I frowned, reaching into my pocket and touching the gold ball. My hand brushed against my jar of *otjize.* I was about to let myself tree for clarity. Then to myself, I said, "No."

Mwinyi looked at me questioningly.

I grabbed the jar of *otjize* in my pocket. Okwu's insides were slathered with a lot of it already. "Mwinyi, put this where Okwu's been injured," I said. I paused and then added, "Use all of it."

I stood up.

As I walked toward them all, they could have shot me. They'd just tried. I was too angry to care. The Khoush soldiers stood like statues as I approached. In rows, before their sky whales, the darkness of the desert extending behind them, the stars above. My sandals dug into the sand. My red skirt lapped at my legs and my red top was wet with sweat. No *otjize.* I was naked.

"Binti," one of the Khoush men said.

"I don't know who you are," I said, standing beside Dele. He was staring at me like I was a creature from outer space. All of them were.

"Qalb Leader Iyad," he said. "And these are my co-leaders, Qalb Leader Durrah." The tall woman with the thin braid hanging to her knees nodded at me. "And Qalb Leader Yabani." The intense-looking man with an equally long black braid inhaled noisily, flaring his nostrils at me as if he'd smelled something foul. All of them had light brown skin, darkened from its typical Khoush tone by the sun.

"We've told them of your suggestion," Chief Kapika quickly said. "That you offer to convince the Meduse to attend a meeting to make peace." He gave me a slight nod and I felt a rush of relief, despite all that had just happened. The Himba Council would be there too.

"We will take the idea to General Kuw and he will take it to the king of Khoushland," Iyad said, looking down his nose at me. "But the Meduse massacred a ship full of our most gifted minds, unarmed students and professors. And all that was left was . . . you. Can you really convince those savages to come and have a rational discussion?"

I don't know when I started shaking, but when I spoke, my voice was vibrating like an Undying tree during a thunderstorm. "You just tried to kill me," I blurted.

Yabani laughed.

"That was an accident," Iyad said. "We thought you were a Meduse."

I felt Dele take my arm. "Breathe," he said into my ear.

I yanked my arm away. I could feel my *okuoko* writhing wildly now. Without *otjize* what must I have looked like? "You shot my friend," I growled. "It's the third time you people have tried to kill it since we arrived here! You agreed to the pact through Oomza Uni knowing you were lying right through your teeth."

"I doubt one dead Meduse is a pact destroyer after they killed a ship full of our smartest and finest," Iyad snapped. "They're barely flesh, anyway."

My vision blurred with fury. "Khoush scholars attacked the Meduse chief, took its stinger, and put it on display in a museum!" I stepped right up to Iyad's face. I am not tall. Nor am I roped with muscle. I barely came to this man's chin and I had to look up to meet his eyes, but he was scared. I saw it in his face. I smelled it wafting from his naked skin. He was terrified of me. I'd seen the Night Masquerade twice, I was Meduse, I was Enyi Zinariya, I was Himba, and I had no home.

"I am Binti Ekeopara Zuzu Dambu Kaipka Meduse Enyi Zinariya of Osemba, master harmonizer," I said. I let myself tree and though I felt calmer, my rage stayed and I was glad. I called up a current and held up my hands to show it connecting to my index fingers like soft lightning. I swirled my fingers and the current coiled into a ball hovering before Iyad's eyes. "I do not want to see my homeland and people destroyed by a stale ancient irrational fight between people who have no real reason to hate each other. When the sun rises, come as you've agreed, to the Root that you reduced to char and ash, where my family lies dead. The Meduse *will* be there and you both will bury this idiocy once and for all." *With the help and power of us Himba,* I thought, angrily. *Because neither of you is reasonable enough to do it on your own.*

I didn't wait for his answer. I pulled in my current, turned, and walked back to Okwu and Mwinyi.

———

The Khoush left. I didn't see them go, but I heard their sky whales take off and felt the dust they blew over us.

Okwu did not die. My *otjize* saved him. Both the *otjize* Mwinyi slathered on its wounds and the *otjize* Okwu had sucked off my skin and *okuoko* when it had enveloped me. Mwinyi, his fingers coated with what was left of my *otjize*, wouldn't stop looking at me.

That night, we stayed in the Osemba House. Somehow, we'd been able to fit Okwu through the dome-shaped door that was wide but not nearly as wide as Okwu. The Meduse were huge but easily compressible, when they wanted to be. Iyad had been rude in his words, but correct, nonetheless. There really *wasn't* much mass or weight to Meduse. Once inside, Okwu hovered weakly beside the well. It was quiet, glad to be near such pure water, its god. Mwinyi took a bucket of it out back and bathed with it. I can't say that I didn't have the urge to do the same, and this disturbed me.

The elders and Dele could not deal with me being *otjize*-free. Thus, after Titi and the other women brought us food and blankets and promised to check on our camel, they left us. They would meet us in the morning. Out back, the Sacred Fire burned, small now and fueled by the bark of an Undying tree, so it would not go out, as long as no sky whale wind turbines blew dust on it. Titi brought me a jar of *otjize* and now I sat on a blanket facing the back door and Sacred Fire, contemplating the large jar on the mat before my crossed legs.

Mwinyi sat beside me and picked up the jar. I let him open it and sniff the contents. "This one and the other I put on Okwu smells different from your own," he said.

I smiled. "Mine was made from clay I dug up on Oomza Uni."

He put the jar back down and turned to me. "Is it an insult if I said you look beautiful with it *and* without it?"

I met his eyes for only a moment and then looked away, my heart fluttering.

"I can see you more clearly now," he said. "Now that I've seen you with it and without. The two make one."

"You're not supposed to *ever* see me without *otjize*," I said. "Only a Himba girl's parents should ever see a Himba girl my age without her *otjize*. Not even a woman's husband will—" I bit my lip and looked at the jar.

"I know," Mwinyi laughed. "But remember, I'm not Himba. Me seeing you with and without it just means I see you. Nothing demeaning." He touched the long matted braid that grew from the middle of his red-brown bushy hair. It was so long that it reached his knees. "See this? The Enyi Zinariya call it *tsani*, a 'ladder' for the spirits. You start growing it at the age of ten. So it's been seven years. A woman isn't supposed to touch it and not even my mother has." He hesitated for a moment and then held it out to me.

I looked at it. "Are you sure?" I asked. "Why?"

"Do you know the desert dogs we met didn't think you were from Earth?" he said. "I think, maybe, I think you're part of something, Binti." His confident smile was faltering now. This was anything but easy for him. I looked at the rope of red-brown hair. Then I reached out and took it in my hands. It felt like my hair, except it wasn't made firm with *otjize*.

"There," I said, putting it down. "Do you feel different?"

"No," he said. "But I am." He smirked and then laughed.

"What's funny?" I asked.

He grinned bigger than I'd seen him grin since we'd left his home. "Honestly, I'm not even sure if you're a human being anymore, so maybe you don't really count."

I laughed, gently shoving him away. We sat there for a moment, gazing at the Sacred Fire. I could feel the darkness of my family's death trying to pull me down, and I scooted closer to Mwinyi. He turned to me and touched my *okuoko* and I didn't push his hand away.

"You shouldn't allow that, Binti," Okwu said from behind us.

Mwinyi quickly let go and stood up. Then he knelt back down, brought his face to mine, and kissed me. When he pulled back, we looked into each other's eyes smiling and . . .

Then darkness.

Then I was there again . . .

. . . I was in space. Infinite blackness. Weightless. Flying, falling, ascending, traveling, through a planet's ring of brittle metallic dust. It pelted my flesh like chips of glittery ice. I opened my mouth a bit to breathe, the dust hitting my lips. Could I breathe?

Living breath bloomed in my chest from within me and I felt my lungs expand, filling with it. I relaxed.

"Who are you?" a voice asked. It spoke in Otjihimba and it came and it came from everywhere.

"Binti Ekeopara Zuzu Dambu Kaipka of Namib, that is my name,"
I said.

Pause.

"There's more," the voice said.

"That's all," I said, irritated. "That's my name."

"No."

This was true but the truth of it made me flinch . . .

. . . I fell out of the tree. From Mwinyi's eyes. My gold ball was floating beside us. Rotating like a small planet. It dropped to my mat.

"Where did you go?" he asked, leaning away from me. "Where was that?"

"You saw it too?"

"It's different when it's human master harmonizers," Okwu said from behind us.

"I know that place," Mwinyi said. "That's the ring of Saturn."

I frowned, "How do you know? I thought you said you'd never left Earth."

"I haven't, but the Zinariya have," he said. "And they gave us the zinariya. I've looked at their memories of space travel; Saturn and Jupiter have always been my favorites. Why are you seeing Saturn's ring? Flying through it like a bird?"

"It's something the *edan* keeps showing me," I said. "Even after it fell apart. Maybe I'm meant to go there."

"Never seen a Himba constantly called to leave home," Mwinyi said more to himself than me. He kissed me again, and this time I leaned forward and took his face in my hands and kissed him back. He wrapped his arms around me and pulled me close and for a while, we lost ourselves in each other. Dele and I had shared kisses a few times when we were younger, but his strong traditional beliefs made him begin to keep his distance as we grew older. And when my friend Eba had asked me to sneak away with her behind the bushes as some of the girls liked to do, I had laughed and said, "No thank you."

Now, I was overwhelmed. There were no taboos or hesitations in the way. And when I pulled my lips from Mwinyi's, his arms still around me, I didn't look into his eyes. "I feel like I'm falling," I breathed. He kissed me one more time and let go. I was leaning on my elbows on the mat, my body throbbing and my mind a swirl of so much, when he stood up.

"I need to go into the desert," he said. "I'll be back." I held up a hand and he took it. "You should remove your sandals and stand outside in the sand," he added. "It'll ground you and that way, you won't feel so much like you're falling. Because you're not."

"That's what the Night Masquerade said to me."

"It spoke?"

I hesitated then nodded. "It said, 'Death is always news. A bird who has flown off the earth and then returns to land is still on the land. Remove your shoes and listen.'"

Mwinyi clucked his tongue as he wrapped his braid around his finger. "I repeat, maybe you should take your sandals off and go stand outside," he said.

I went back to looking at the jar of *otjize* after he left. I picked it up and put it back down. I sighed, unsure. I picked it up and stood up. "Okwu, are you alright?" I said.

"I would tell you if I were not," it said, puffing out enough gas to envelope itself.

I coughed. "I'm going to stand outside near the fire for a bit."

"I will be here listening to the waters below," Okwu said.

The night was cool, but the fire made the area around it warm, even at its decreased size. Its light reached out into the open desert, but where it did not reach was blackness. It reminded me of when I looked out the window while traveling in the Third Fish. Though that blankness was much deeper.

I put the *otjize* beside me and raised my hands. *"Are you alright?"*

I typed. Then I pushed the red words off into the desert. They fled as if blown by a powerful invisible wind, scaling and disappearing over a nearby sand dune in the direction Mwinyi had gone. A moment later, "*Yes. Get some rest. Don't test the zinariya,*" came back to me in his green letters. Then I heard the strange whispers and it seemed as if I saw a planet peeking over the horizon. I looked down, closing my eyes until the whispering stopped. When I opened them, the planet was gone.

Despite Mwinyi's warning, I considered testing my tolerance of distant zinariya. I needed to reach my grandmother and tell her what happened. It needed to be me, not Mwinyi. But if I tried and my still fresh mind reacted badly to the attempt again, with Mwinyi gone I only had the injured Okwu to help me. Okwu needed rest. *No*, I thought. *I'll tell my grandmother when I have some good news. I'll try after sunrise.* Another sunrise in a world where my family was dead. I felt the hot embers in my chest begin to burn. Quickly pushing the pain away, I thought to Okwu, *Can you hear me?* My *okuoko* wriggled gently on the sides of my face and against my shoulders. He was close, so my effort did not have to be much.

Yes.

I sighed, bringing the golden ball from my pocket. I no longer thought of it as an *edan*; I saw it more like a little planet. No reason. It was just what was. And I was floating around it, untethered, homeless. I allowed myself to tree and then called up and ran a current over it and watched it rise before my eyes on the electric blue current, slowly rotating. I reached up and took it in my hands, running the pads of my fingers over its fingerprint-like surface.

I picked up the jar of *otjize*, unscrewed the lid, and dug my index and middle fingers into it. I spread it on my body.

CHAPTER 4

Homecoming

The first class I took at Oomza Uni was Treeing 101. It started the equivalent of seven Earth days after I'd reached Oomza Uni alive and become a hero. It was one of several first-year student classes from all specialties—from Weapons to Math to Organics to Travel, and more. I placed out of it that first day. The class was conducted in one of the large fields between Math, Weapons, and Organics Cities. The dry yellow grasses there had been cut low but still were occupied by hopping ntu ntu bugs, their brilliant orange-pink pigmentation eye-catching in the sunlight. All the students sat in a huge circle to listen to the instructor Professor Osisi, who looked like a tall wide tree with fanlike leaves bigger than my head.

We were all dazzled as Professor Osisi called up ten thick currents at once *as* it told us about the class. After what felt like a half-hour of talking (I was still adjusting to the faster cycle on Oomza Uni), we were split into smaller groups of about six, in which teaching assistants had us each step forward and tree in front of our groups. In my group were two Meduse-like people, someone who looked like a crab made of diamonds, and three blue humanoid types who kept touching my *okuoko* and humming in a way that seemed a lot like laughter to me. None of us spoke similar languages, though all of us spoke in sound.

"My name is Assistant Sagar," our teacher said, a sleek hairless foxlike person with eyes on its snout who stood on two legs at my height. When it spoke, it touched something near its throat and though I understood it, I also heard other voices speaking at the same time, probably in languages the others could understand. I smiled, delighted. The way people on Oomza Uni were so diverse and everyone handled that as if it were normal continued to surprise me. It was so unlike Earth, where wars were fought over and because of differences and most couldn't relate to anyone unless they were similar.

"This is a placement test," Sagar said. "You will step up and face the group and tree as well as you can."

"What if we can't really do it well?" the one who looked like a giant crab made of diamonds asked. It was beside me and clearly agitated as each of its legs kept stamping on the grass, sending ntu ntu bugs leaping this way and that. I grinned again. I could understand it, too! Whatever Sagar was using to communicate with all of us, it connected our group as well. I turned to the group closest to me, which was a few feet away; all I heard were grunts, humming, and a "pop pop pop."

Not one individual in my group could tree with difficulty, let alone with ease. When I took my turn, Sagar said, "Good. At least there's one. And you might be the only one in the entire class today." I was. In a class of over two hundred new students, I was the only one who could tree. This would not have been the case if all the other students on my ship hadn't been wiped out; Heru could tree as well as I could. This added to the other reasons students mostly kept their distance from me. In that group, where we'd all stayed close to each other as we waited to be tested, as soon as I got up there, did what I could do, and then moved aside for someone else to try, I knew I was apart again.

After the last two students took their turns, I looked at the sky above. I'd once read about a phenomenon that happened in the colder parts of Earth when oxygen and nitrogen in the atmosphere collided with electrically charged particles released from the sun. The resulting swirls of green lights were beautiful and strange and though I never wanted to go to a part of Earth where there was snow and intense cold, I'd been curious what these lights would look like. As I stood away from my fellow students I realized that, with so many trying to descend into mathematical trance and call up current, the air had charged. The odd pinkish orange bright sky swirled with green-blue lights. I could even feel the charged air on my skin. I'd stood there for minutes looking up and reveling in the feeling of so much possibility and newness.

Now, in the Osemba House, I awoke feeling like I did that day on Oomza Uni—the hairs on my hands standing on end, the feeling of energy all around me. I opened my eyes and sat straight up. Mwinyi was nearby on his mat and he stirred but didn't awaken. Then I heard it, a rumble from far away and a low haunted howling.

I got up and walked out the back door. Okwu was already there, floating easily before the fire. Its *okuoko* that were intact looked fully healed and the ones that had hanging tips were shorter, the tips having fallen off. But at least they were blue again.

"I thought you didn't like the fire," I said.

"I've grown used to it now."

Warm wind blew off the desert and from afar I could see a flash of lightning.

"It's still far," Okwu said.

"But it's coming," I said. "It doesn't rain much here. But I hope it'll arrive after sunrise." I paused and then asked, "Will your chief agree to a truce?"

Okwu didn't answer for a long time and I began to wish I hadn't asked.

"Meduse aren't the problem," Okwu finally said. "Your council must succeed. And I think you need to be careful."

We left the Osemba House with about an hour until dawn. It was windy and the overcast sky made it even darker, and thus easier to see the occasional flash of lightning in the distance. I shut the door behind me and when I turned, I was shocked that I actually had a reason to smile.

"Oh!" I exclaimed as we left the Osemba House. "You're glowing."

Okwu, who'd regained most of its strength, vibrated its dome. "I took from your lake," it said. "Those snails."

"The clusterwinks?" I asked, gently touching its softly glowing blue dome. The bioluminescent snails lived in the lake and happened to be spawning when we arrived. Okwu had been covered with them when it had emerged from the lake yesterday.

"Yes," it said. "When Meduse spend a lot of time with such things, we absorb their genetic coding and make it our own."

"Is Binti going to start glowing too?" Mwinyi asked. I frowned at him as he snickered.

Okwu's dome vibrated, but it said nothing.

Okwu's glow came in handy. The overcast sky, blowing dust, and the Osemba-wide blackout left the streets darker than normal. With my astrolabe broken, I had nothing to help light the way. Even the glow from bioluminescent flowers on some of the homes and buildings was muted. We walked close to each other, this time completely alone and unwatched as we journeyed across Osemba back to the Root.

With each step I took through my hometown, I wondered what I was walking toward, purposely bringing myself closer to. I'd needed to reconnect with my family after I'd left the way I did and with all that went on to happen, but realistically, it was my own insecurities that brought me running home so soon. When the Meduse anger had come forth, I'd immediately assumed something was wrong with me instead of realizing that it was simply a new change to which I had to adjust. I'd thought something was wrong with me because my family thought something was wrong with me. And now my childish actions had brought death and war. What had I started? Whatever it was, I had to finish it.

The wind blew harder and I was glad for the layer of *otjize* I'd put on my skin and rolled over my *okuoko*. As we passed the group of Undying trees, Mwinyi and I pressed our hands to our ears and Okwu rushed up the road so fast that I lost sight of it. Mwinyi and I stopped, completely in the dark.

"Okwu!" I called. But the noise drowned out my voice. I called it through my *okuoko*. Far up the road between two homes, it stopped.

Just come, I heard it say in my mind. *I cannot be near those evil trees.*

I looked at Mwinyi.

"I have an idea," I quickly said, trying not to look at the trees yards away that were vibrating so fast that they looked like a blur. I relaxed as I focused on the powerful gusty wind and raised my hands and typed through the zinariya as I spoke the words. The equation "$w = \frac{1}{2} \, r \, A \, v3$" floated in red before me, then it began to blow toward Okwu like a flag attached to an invisible pole in front of me. As I watched it, I raised my hands and called up a bright ball of current.

The dusty road, vibrating trees, the storefront across the street, and the people looking out the window from the home beside it were all illuminated by my light. Mwinyi and I took one look at the Undying trees and quickly moved on. Even when we caught up to Okwu, I continued to use my light. And in this way, as we reached the part of Osemba near my home where the Khoush had taken out their anger when they couldn't find Okwu and me, we saw that several of the half-destroyed homes had caved in or toppled because of the wind. This last block of homes and buildings looked like the old images of Khoushland cities and towns during the Khoush-Meduse wars decades ago. Pockmarked walls, blasted homes, crumbled buildings. Sandstone wasn't made to survive war, and stone buildings, like the Root, could be exploded to rubble and even burned.

Treeing helped me clear my mind of worry and the strong light gave me what felt like my last view of Osemba.

━━━━━

The Root had stopped burning.

Now it was just a mound of char, much of the ash blown into the desert by the winds of the coming storm. Sunrise was close and all I could do was stand before the mound and stare. The only person who met us at the Root when we arrived was our camel Rakumi, who had, indeed, eaten all that remained of my brother's garden. The Himba Council had promised to meet us here but it was nowhere in sight. Not even Dele.

"They're just late," I said.

Minutes passed and there still wasn't a sign of them. So to add to my despair and worry, I looked at my home. The wind had blown so much away and revealed the remains—a black foundation of charred wood. The opening to the cellar must have been burned shut. Still holding the ball of current, my mind numb and empty, I stared and stared.

Across what was left of my home, I could see Okwu inspecting the remains of the tent my father had made it—which was nothing but a cracking mess formed from sand heated so hot by the explosion of Khoush weapons that it had become a yellow-black glass. Mwinyi was digging and knocking at the char at the base of the Root's foundation.

"What are you doing?" I called.

"Looking," he distractedly said, pressing both his hands to it now.

I clucked my tongue, irritated. What if he caused the entire thing to cave in? What would he reveal? I shivered. "Mwinyi!" I called. "Please stop doing—"

The thunder rumbled, this time louder, and it was blended with a deeper, more urgent purring. "Oh no," I whispered. Slowly, I turned to the west, dust spraying squarely in my face. The Khoush were here. From Kokure in Khoushland? Further west? The skyline seemed to be crowded with sky whales. They flew smoothly, despite the high winds and charged air.

I spat out dust and blinked my eyes as Okwu joined me, positioning itself in front of me. "No," I said, stepping aside. "This is for peace. If they shoot me, then—"

"You will be dead," Okwu said, getting in front of me.

"Don't be a fool, Binti," Mwinyi said, joining us. He too moved in front of me. "If the Himba Council isn't here . . ." He bit his lip. "Maybe they set us up."

When the ships landed, the number of soldiers that poured out and the sheer amount of artillery that they unpacked was incredible. Within minutes, the expanse of desert was occupied with hundreds of waiting Khoush soldiers standing in formation, several of the sky whales had broken down into weaponized land shuttles, and there were long sticks with black hoops that extended into the sky whose function I didn't know.

"I thought they'd just bring an envoy," I muttered as three Khoush walked up to us.

"They have always been about show," Okwu rumbled in Meduse.

"Translation, please," Mwinyi said.

"They like to show power," I told him in Otjihimba. "Okwu, shall I call them now?"

"You said sunrise," Okwu said. "They will come."

And sure enough, as the sun peeked over the horizon, before the three Khoush members got to us, they stopped and looked toward Osemba. I turned as well. The Meduse ships looked like they belonged in the water. Bulbous and glowing a deep purple blue, they looked like larger versions of the Meduse themselves. I briefly wondered if they were, for I'd been inside one a year ago and it had felt like being inside the body of a living thing, and stunk like one too. They silently landed, the ships' *okuoko* whipped about and their bodies buffeted gently by the winds.

CHAPTER 5

Homegoing

I stood between the leaders of both sides.

I could barely look at Goldie, the Khoush's king. I'd only seen his face on the news feeds and heard the Khoush who came into my father's shop speak of him as the Honorable One. He was a tall stout man with pale skin that looked as if it never saw the sun. His garments were immaculately white, glowing and blowing in the dusty wind.

Flanking his left and right were his military commanders whom he'd introduced as his minister of defense, a plump tan-skinned woman named Lady who had severe eyes, and Commander of General Staff Kuw, a muscle-bound man with a shiny bald head who looked only a few years my senior. I recognized Kuw's name. He was the one Okwu said had set the Root on fire. Even from where I stood, I could feel Okwu's hatred for especially Kuw.

Scuttling behind them was the Khoush mayor of Kokure, Alhaji Truck Omaze. He nodded at me, flashing the same smile as when I'd stepped off the Third Fish days ago. Had he known of the plan to assassinate Okwu even back then at the launch port when things had so nearly gone wrong? If not at that point, he probably knew soon after we left for Osemba. I scowled back at him.

The Meduse chief came with two of its military heads, first-in-command Mbu and its second-in-command, named Nke Abuo. Unlike the clear-fleshed chief, Mbu and Nke Abuo looked blue and opaque like Okwu. Okwu stood between me and the Khoush.

I looked at both groups. Each seemed to be waiting for me to speak. I wanted to crawl into myself. I felt small. I opened my mouth and closed it. The Khoush king was looking at me like I was something useless. I glanced at the Meduse chief, whom I'd last seen while on a different planet, after I had saved everyone, after I'd been so brave. This was Earth, where I was just a Himba girl.

"The Himba Council haven't arrived yet," Mwinyi said, stepping up beside me.

"We're not going to wait much longer," King Goldie said, giving the Meduse chief a hard look.

"Neither will we," the chief rumbled in Meduse.

"It said, 'Neither will we,'" Okwu translated to Mwinyi.

We were all quiet. I glanced at the mound of char; Meduse rage and indignation flooded into me so suddenly that I twitched. The Khoush king was right here, before me. I spoke. "Do you know who I am?"

Goldie smirked and I felt angrier. "Of course I do. You're more dignified and well-spoken than I expected." He chuckled. "And at least I can hear you clearly. Himba women and girls are so soft-spoken."

"Do you know what that mound is?" I asked.

Above, thunder rumbled and I felt even stronger. Before he responded, I let myself tree. My mind cleared and I thanked the Seven for that because of what King Goldie of the Khoush said next.

"Your family harbored the enemy," he said, his smirk dropping completely. "They suffered the consequences." He motioned to where the Root had been. "If it were up to me, that would be a hole in the ground."

I felt my *okuoko* begin to writhe on my head and slap at my neck and back, but I held steady, equations circulating around my head. The golden ball in my pocket was warm and rotating. I took a deep, deep breath, imagining the air filling my toes all the way up my body as my therapist had taught me. Then, as she also taught me, I stepped back from all of them, looking every single one of them in the eye, ending with Goldie. But Goldie didn't even notice.

He turned to his commander of general staff and said, "The Himba are a cowardly people."

Kuw nodded. "They hide when they get scared. Like intelligent, innovative desert foxes."

I opened my mouth to speak, but then closed it. I pressed my lips shut, shaking with anger as I looked around. Where *was* the council? I met Mwinyi's eyes and he mouthed, "Just wait. They'll come." But every second was sending the plan closer to failure. Above, the storm churned in the sky, the thunder crashing now, lightning flashing. I called up a current to calm myself and let it linger around each of my hands. The feeling of the current and the way it drew from the lightning above without drawing the lightning down made me feel powerful. I stood up straighter.

"I will not speak to the Khoush," the Meduse chief said to Okwu. "This is not how we agreed things would go." Then to me, it said, "Binti, where are the men of your council?"

Goldie had completely turned his back on me to speak with his commander and minister of defense. "I only gave this a chance because of my relationship to the president of Oomza Uni. A meeting of men and instead, only this foolish Himba girl is here. We should—"

It was the phrase "foolish Himba girl." That's what did it. In that phrase was condescension, a mockery of my high standing at Oomza Uni, a spitting on my family and the Himba as a whole. And where *was* the council? I didn't care. My family was dead. Everyone kept dying in the ship. I saw Heru's chest burst open again and I felt my *okuoko* writhing as every part of my being filled with rage. Doors deep within me flew open. All of them. All at the same time. My body waved forward, then backward, as I felt the current I was holding expand. Lightning flashed above and something in me decided to do something I'd never done: grab it.

I fell out of the tree. Then *POW!* the current I'd drawn poured into me.

I awoke. I knew something very, very important. I knew that everything depended on that moment. I wasn't sure exactly how, but the destiny of my people was temporarily in my hands.

And so, I screamed, *"I'm the one who called this meeting! This was my idea!"* I faced King Goldie, my eyes wide and wild. He'd whirled around, gawking at me now. Current surrounded me in an electric blue spiral that felt warm on my skin and protective. At the same time, I spoke these words through my *okuoko* to the Meduse chief in my roughest Meduse. My hands moved as if owned by a part of myself that had its own intent and soon I was pushing those same words into the desert. When I did this, my world remained as it was . . . because it was already expanded.

The words returned to me as if whispered from afar. Not in text, but in sound. "You tell them, Binti." It was my grandmother's voice. With my peripheral vision, I saw Mwinyi suddenly turn and run toward the Root.

"I'm not crazy," I said, addressing all. I faced King Goldie as I spoke. "I'm *not* small. I'm *not* foolish." I paused for a moment. "Do any of you even remember why you started fighting? The Meduse tried to drain the lakes? The Khoush massacred a tribe of peaceful Meduse explorers? The Khoushland chief's daughter was kidnapped? If I ask each of you the reason, you'll cite different stories from so long ago that the grandchildren of the grandchildren of any possible witnesses are long dead." I turned to the chief. "What do you want with these lands? Your god is water, maybe there was water when this war began, but this part of the Earth is parched of it now. In my town, the trees had to tell us where to find water so we wouldn't die. Khoushland is mostly desert, while seventy-one percent of the Earth is water! Why not go there? There aren't many humans who live on the oceans. You can frolic in those waters with no trouble. But you'd rather fight and die and kill for a drop of water in a dry land."

I turned to Goldie. "And you Khoush, who *don't* you look down upon? The Himba create technology that allows your whole community to thrive and you repay us by behaving as if we're your slaves. Because what? What makes Khoush superior to Himba? Tell me! Then your egos are bruised when one of us befriends and brings a Meduse as a show of peace. So you try to assassinate it, knowing that it's one of the ultimate forms of disrespect to the Himba, knowing that this will bring war from the Meduse! You took their chief's stinger, just to show you had the power to do it, and you complain when they retaliate."

I took a deep breath.

"I incite the deep culture of the Himba." I looked intensely at both King Goldie and the Meduse chief. "Neither of you know of it and that is okay. The Himba Council members were to do this, but I think they're afraid. I think they're hiding. I'm not. And I'm a collective within myself, so I can.

"Meduse tradition is one of honor. Khoush tradition is one of respect. I am master harmonizer of the Osemba Himba." I raised my hands, the currents swirling into balls in both hands like blue suns. I held one toward Goldie. "The one who represents the Khoush." I held a hand toward the Meduse chief. "The one who represents the Meduse." I steadied myself. I pulled from deep within me, from the earth beneath my feet, from what I could reach beyond the Earth above. Because I was a master harmonizer and my path was through mathematics, I took what came and felt it as numbers, absorbed it as math, and when I spoke, I breathed it out. "Please," I said, the words coming from my mouth cool in my throat, pouring over my tongue and lips. I was doing it; I was speaking the words to power. I was uttering deep culture. "End this," I said, my voice full and steady. "End this now."

As soon as the words had left my lips, my throat began to burn. Lightning flashed, immediately followed by the crash of thunder. The noise didn't shake me, the threat of lightning would never scare me again. I felt it still within me, though it was dissipating now. From my feet and through the top of my head, through the tips of my writhing *okuoko*. I felt as if I were both sinking and levitating. Draining and spouting. That is the deep culture. Never in a thousand years would I have believed it would move through *me*. Never. *If Dele were here to see, he would be on his knees in amazement*, I thought. But he wasn't. None of the council was here.

"Okay, Binti," Goldie said, his voice soft and his face slack with awe as he gazed at me. He nodded. "I . . . I agree to the truce."

The Meduse chief breathed out a great puff of its gas and so did his two comrades and Okwu. Several of the Meduse hovering near the ship did the same. Then the chief spoke to me in Meduse. "I will listen to the Binti. She is right. This fight is useless."

"The war between Khoush and Meduse ends," I said, bringing my hands together. Immediately, both balls of current extinguished, sending a ripple of energy through me that made me stumble back as it all stopped. I coughed, tasting blood in my mouth. Above, the storm having blown itself out, the sky began to clear, sunrise's light.

I smiled as the Khoush king and Meduse chief both went back to their people.

"Well done," Okwu said in Otjihimba.

I nodded to him. It was so quiet now, the wind having died down to a strong breeze and the lightning and its thunder retreating into the sky. I looked around for Mwinyi and didn't quickly see him. I looked up at the sky, a large sliver of sun shining through the dissipating clouds.

"Thank the Seven," I said, my voice rough. "Thank Them for giving me all I needed to do it." I laughed.

When I brought my gaze back down, my eyes fell on a very strange sight. For the third time, I was seeing it: the Night Masquerade. Again, during the day. It stood on the dirt road that led to my home. The road I'd walked down when I'd left home in the dark of early morning. No smoke billowed from its head this time. In the silence, I could hear its drumbeat as it danced, kicking up dust as it shook its raffia hips and raised its long arms. I knew only one person who danced like that.

"Dele?" I whispered, squinting.

I jumped when I heard the shots. At first, I was so focused on the Night Masquerade that I thought they were sharp drumbeats. Then I felt a powerful zap in my *okuoko* as vibration shivered into my forehead, face, and neck. My eyes watered with the pain and when I turned toward the Meduse ships, I saw a ball of fire smash into the Meduse chief.

I didn't hear Meduse voices in my head, I heard a collective shriek. Then I knew it more than saw it, for the armor Okwu had created on Oomza Uni was clear and fit over its body perfectly. Every single Meduse, outside and on their ships, was encased in this armor. Including the chief, who floated back upright, flanked by two of its commanders. Then the Meduse ship began smoothly flying into a battle formation, its movements rippling and fluid like water . . . this was army-scale *moojh-ha ki-bira*. I turned to the Khoush just in time to see one of their sky whale ships explode. More Khoush soldiers on the ground fled.

A rough hand grabbed my right arm and I whipped around to meet the twitchy eyes of General Kuw. "You're coming with us!" he roared.

I looked at my arm, his strong hands digging into my flesh, and then everything around me became a hot blue. I balled the fist of my left hand and smashed it into his face. My fist connected with his teeth and nose and I felt what must have been several of my fingers snap with the strength of it. I brought my fist back and punched him again and he stumbled to the side, letting me go. "Argh!" he grunted, pressing his hand to his face. But even then, he'd brought up his weapon from inside his uniform. *So they'd come to this meeting armed,* I thought, staring at him. Then he brought up his other hand and spread his fingers just in time for a blue ball to explode over the shield he'd activated. I turned to see Okwu flying toward General Kuw and the two went tumbling in the sand.

Pain radiated from my hand now and I stood there for a moment, stunned more by my actions than the state of my mangled fingers. I'd never hit anyone in my entire life. Shuddering with adrenaline, I held my hand up. My middle and index fingers had broken completely enough to show jagged bones. I looked around, dazed. General Kuw was fleeing toward the Khoush ships. Okwu was fighting off barrages of fire bullets with its shield.

It was a strange moment as both the Khoush and Meduse fled toward their armies, leaving me standing there alone. Mwinyi had rushed off while I had been talking to do something I had no time to consider now. Okwu was being pushed back toward the Meduse ships as the Khoush shot at him. I heard Mwinyi yell from nearby and saw Okwu dodge several fire bullets to rush toward me. It came from both sides at once, as the Khoush and the Meduse threw aside what their leaders had just agreed on—the truce.

Who had shot at the Meduse chief to start it all? I will never know. What I did know was that I'd seen the face of the Khoush king when the Meduse chief was shot and it was a face of astonishment and despair. He didn't know; he hadn't wanted this. The rest was reaction. And in their reaction, they all forgot about me. They forgot I was standing there, between their sides as they shot at each other.

Red fire balls and blue searing waves of light flew past me, filling the air. The smell of smoke, incineration, the very air around me began to burn. Rakumi, who was standing where my brother's garden had been, fell as her head was blown clean off. The sound of fireballs zipping past my ears. I coughed and stumbled. Then I felt something punch me in the chest, then my left leg, and then I don't know. I don't know. I screamed. I was flying. The pain bloomed all around me, within me. Now I was moaning, rolling in the dry dirt.

Okwu was on me and everything became blue and muffled.

Binti, I heard it say to me. *Hold on.* Okwu pressed us both to the ground as the world around us exploded. I felt Okwu shudder as something smashed near it and burst into flames. Then it was as if the fight itself began to rise. I saw it happening and at first thought I was falling. But no, it was the ships of the Khoush and Meduse. They were taking the fight to the skies and probably into space.

Just as quickly as it began, it was over. At least, on Himba soil. Not over, elsewhere. I could hear the battle raging high above and something huge crashed to the ground nearby. I could not tell, for Okwu was still holding me inside its body. As Okwu lifted off me, I felt myself fading. I could actually *hear* my blood draining into the desert sand beneath me. My back stung in a distant way. My chest was wet and cool, open. My legs, whether they were just torn up or actually torn off, were gone.

Limply, I raised my arm and let it drop to my nose. I sniffed the *otjize* on it and it smelled like home. I heard Mwinyi calling me as he fell to his knees beside me. He was shaking and shaking, his eyes wild. His beautiful bushy hair covered with dust and sand. But I was smelling home. I closed my eyes.

Death is always news.

CHAPTER 6

Girl

Mwinyi was screaming.

He looked down at her again and kept screaming and screaming and screaming. Her chest was smashed and burned open, bone, sinew, and flesh, red, yellow, and white. Her legs were each a mangle of meat. Her left arm had been blown off. Only her right arm, face, and tentacles were untouched.

Mwinyi had been at what was left of the Root when it all fell apart. He'd turned and seen the Meduse chief and Khoush king both looking at Binti with awe and respect. He'd heard Binti laughing. He'd been proud. He'd seen the leaders walking away. Then he'd turned to what he'd come to see and it had all happened behind his back. By the time he reached her, she was gone.

Okwu floated on Binti's other side, its tentacles touching her torn-up arm and pulling back, touching and pulling back. It could feel the battle happening above, but it stayed with Binti, allowing the others to know that the one who'd become family through war had been killed. They fought harder and angrier because Okwu stayed, because Okwu felt.

Mwinyi looked up, his mouth in an open wail. He was so numb that the sight of the raffia monster running wildly toward him did not startle him. It roared, shoved Mwinyi aside with long sticklike hands, and threw off its head of wooden faces. Mwinyi fell to the side and then stared back at the creature. Not creature, Night Masquerade. The Night Masquerade was mourning Binti.

＝＝＝＝

Dele had forgotten all protocol. Last year he'd been initiated into the secret society through which the Night Masquerade spoke. He'd joined just after Binti had left. Learning the chants from the elder men, taking in the smoke from the burned branch of an Undying tree, and seeing the friends of the Seven had all helped him forget about Binti. Then he'd been tapped for grooming as the next Himba chief. He'd been so proud and felt strong, though he hated the scratchy beard he'd had to grow. Throughout, however, no matter how hard he'd worked to forget her, he'd sorely missed Binti.

Days ago, during a meditation with the elders, the elders had all agreed that Binti should see the Night Masquerade. Chief Kapika had been the one in costume standing outside her window. Dele had hated this; Binti was a girl and she'd abandoned her own destiny. And the elders hadn't even bothered telling him Chief Kapika had decided to show Binti the Night Masquerade again yesterday.

However, last night during the *Okuruwo* meeting, Dele had had a change of heart about Binti. He'd listened to her speak, watched her closely, and realized she *was* the Binti he'd known all his life and she was amazing. The elders were the elders for a reason. Even in their own bias, they'd still been able to see and admit to each other what he couldn't up to now . . . but the elders were deeply flawed, too. Hours ago, he'd joined them in a second meeting, this time in the quiet of the desert a mile from Osemba. Dele had thought they were just gathering to go to the Root as a group. When the elders had all agreed to forgo brokering a truce and to sacrifice Binti instead, Dele couldn't believe it.

And so, he'd stolen the Night Masquerade costume. The moment he put it on, he knew what he was to do. And because when a man wears a spiritual costume, he is not himself, Dele found it easy to go to the Root. And there he placed himself where she would see him, hoping she would be encouraged.

And Binti *had* succeeded. He'd seen it even from where he stood on the road. She'd channeled deep culture! He'd felt the power of it shivering through the ground, into his feet, halfway up his legs like electricity, like current. Like almost all the other kids in Osemba, he didn't know how to call up current. He'd only watched Binti do it over the years, glad the practice wasn't his calling. Now, he was watching her do what only a handful had ever done in Himba history. And she used it to convince the leaders of the Khoush and Meduse people to finally stop fighting. She had truly been Osemba's master harmonizer.

Dele stared down at her face now. So beautiful, though the *otjize* on her face was partially rubbed off, her strange tentacles spread over the sand. Limp. It came from deep within his soul, the keening. He threw his head back and opened his mouth wide, tears dribbling from the sides of his eyes. The horror of it squeezed at his heart. He threw aside the leather gloves that made his hands long and sticklike and tore at the Night Masquerade costume, pulling at the raffia, tearing at the blue-and-red cloth.

━━━━━

Mwinyi stood up and walked away, his blue garments darkened with Binti's blood and his eyes toward the sky. The fighting had moved toward Khoushland and that was best for them.

"Okwu," he called, hoarsely.

"Yes," the Meduse said, floating over to him.

Behind them, the only Himba Council member to show up continued to scream and scream, his voice rolling across the now empty desert.

"I think we should take her into space," Mwinyi told Okwu. "That's where she belongs. Not here."

"How?" Okwu asked. "The launch port is that way, where the fighting is happening. I don't think . . ."

"Not from the launch port," Mwinyi said, shaking his head.

"A Meduse ship?" Okwu suggested. "They will understand. We set our dead free in space too."

"No," he said firmly. "I have a better plan." He paused, shutting his eyes as despair tried to take him again. "I . . . I know exactly where to take her, too. Will you come?"

"Yes," it said.

"They would never have listened to us," Dele sobbed from behind them. He was holding Binti's only remaining hand.

"Is that why you left her to die?" Mwinyi snapped.

"I didn't," Dele said. "I tried. I didn't agree with the rest of them. But I am just an apprentice; I wasn't even supposed to be speaking. But I did. 'We don't abandon our own,' I said. They said she was no longer one of us and then I was told to be quiet. And none . . . none of them believed they could really evoke deep culture. They didn't believe in . . . they had no hope. The chief said the Khoush would never listen to the Himba because they don't respect us." He squeezed his eyes shut at this as if in physical pain.

"But they respected Binti," Mwinyi said. "The Khoush and Meduse. Then they forgot about her."

Dele looked at Binti and started to sob again.

"Come," Mwinyi snapped. "If you want to do something that would have pleased her, come. Okwu, come."

Mwinyi walked to the wooden foundation of the Root without looking to see if they were following. With each step he took, he saw more. It was breathtaking, never had he experienced anything like this before. He could *see* where they were, through his feet. All it had taken was for the one he had come to love so much in a matter of days to get torn apart by two irrational peoples.

He stopped at the place where he'd kicked off his sandals. They lay there like the ripped-off wings of a sand beetle. Okwu hovered on one side of him and Dele stood on the other as they looked down at the charred remains of the Root. Mwinyi breathed a sigh of relief. With his feet he could see much. The zinariya had shown him relatives who had this ability in the past. It was called "deep grounding" and it always kicked in when one "walked far enough."

He held his hands up for a moment, preparing to send word through the zinariya, but then he noticed that already coming in all around him were messages from the Ariya, Binti's grandmother, his parents, his brothers, several of his friends, people. The Enyi Zinariya knew what had happened somehow. He had not sent word himself. How did they know already?

"Just stand beside me," Mwinyi said to Okwu and Dele. How could he explain? So he did not. The storm had awakened it and though the storm had passed, he could still feel it vibrating through his exposed feet. The Root's foundation had been made on the dead root of an Undying tree. At least, they'd thought it had been dead. The inside of one of the roots had been hollowed out and made into the house's cellar.

Like Binti, Mwinyi was also a master harmonizer. And his ability was communication in a different way; he could speak to those who were alive. So just as he'd been able to speak with Okwu in a way that allowed him to locate where it had been hurt and where it was best to slather the *otjize*, he'd been able to speak to the living Undying tree that was the Root's foundation.

Dele looked back at Binti's body, lying there alone, and then at her friend, the desert savage named Mwinyi. His bushy hair was a strange red brown, freed like a dust storm and full of dust like . . . a dust storm. His skin was dark like Binti's, but where he'd never seen Binti's skin tone as a marker of being uncivilized, everything about Mwinyi said savage. And so when Mwinyi bent down and placed his hands on the dense charred wood and the ground began to shudder, Dele shouted, "Stop it! What are you doing?" because whatever it was *had* to be wrong.

Okwu watched Mwinyi closely. The human reminded it so much of Binti. *Harmonizers are the same,* Okwu thought. And from a distance, it felt many others of its kind agree with it. It stayed there and waited.

CHAPTER 7

The Root

A tree with strong roots laughs at storms.

Mwinyi could not remember who said this but he'd heard it often as a child. Never did he imagine the proverb was so literally true. The ground was shuddering as he held his hand to the foundation and repeated over and over, "Let go, please. Let go, let go. Please."

The moment he heard the sound of cracking, he said, "Dele, go!"

"What? Where?" Dele asked. "What is . . . what is happening? What are you doing?"

"Go where the cellar is," Mwinyi said. "You know this house better than I."

"I see it," Okwu said, floating onto the charred foundation.

Mwinyi and Dele followed it. Mwinyi gasped, ran to the spot, and stared. He shut his eyes, as Dele knelt down beside him. Mwinyi could hear the plant's voice in his head now and it was so broad that his head pounded and his vision blurred. It spoke no words he could understand, but there was relief and a sigh. Mwinyi waited as he heard more cracking and then the sound of Dele grunting and pulling and kicking.

Mwinyi held his breath, his eyes closed as he waited a little longer. He saw them with his feet. Then he heard other voices and he sank to the ground, his head in his hands. Binti should have lived to see this. How ecstatic she would have been to know that every single one of her family members was alive and well.

═══════

Dele had lain on his belly, reached down, and one by one pulled them out. Mother, father, sisters, brothers, nieces, nephews, cousins, and even a few family friends. They ran about, jumped and sang and danced with joy. They didn't care that their skin and hair were nearly free of *otjize*. They kneeled and prayed to the Seven. Sobbing and hugging. Binti's father was the only one who could speak through his joy. He explained to Mwinyi about how they'd all fled into the large cellar and when the Root had been attacked and set aflame, something had made it react as one of the family. It enclosed and protected. And inside the Root, there had not only been supplies that they could eat, but pods of water that grew from the walls of the cellar.

"The Root is true Himba," Binti's father said.

Then he asked, "Where is Binti?"

═══════

The sun shone bright now and the war happening over Khoushland and in space just outside of the Earth's atmosphere felt more and more distant. It was not the Himba's war, and so for the time being, they were not concerned. News spread fast about Binti and her family's survival through word of mouth. And now that they were out of the protective cellar, they could reach people with their astrolabes, too. Soon a large crowd had gathered at the Root, yes, now it was the Root, again. They brought joyous jars of *otjize* and baskets of food. Home or no home, the Root had been burned, but its foundation was alive and well and strong, as were those who'd lived in it.

Most feared Okwu, but Binti's father stayed at its side well into the day, forcing people to look at and speak to it when they came to wish Binti's father their condolences. Binti's mother stayed with

Binti at the place where Binti had fallen. She'd placed a red blanket of mourning over Binti's body, as she hummed to herself and rocked back and forth to keep from tearing her hair out.

Over and over, Mwinyi told Binti's family and those who came about what Binti had tried to do and what she died for. Mwinyi watched their faces; all of them looked upon him as if he were a wild man who had something they wanted—especially Binti's older siblings. Still, Mwinyi told of Binti's bravery and the betrayal of the council and answered their questions because they needed to know.

When the Himba Council arrived at the Root, Mwinyi walked away, heading to Binti's mother. Okwu joined him.

"I don't want to hear any of what they have to say," Mwinyi said.

"We should leave," Okwu said.

"Soon. First, let's talk to her." Mwinyi pointed at Binti's mother. She was cradling Binti's head in her lap and humming. The tips of her long *otjize*-rolled locks dragged on the ground, collecting sand. Even covered with old *otjize*, the bright sun couldn't have been good for her skin. Sweat rolled down her face, dropping into an *otjize*-red damp spot in the sand beneath her.

"Mma Binti," Mwinyi said, sitting before her. When he glanced at Binti's face, every muscle in his body tensed up. When he spoke, his voice quivered. "I'm sorry."

"She didn't know," her mother said. "She didn't know her family was alive. She must have felt . . . homeless."

Mwinyi glanced at Okwu, who floated over. "She loved you all," it said. "She fought for you."

Binti's mother looked at Okwu, then nodded. "My husband . . . he was too afraid to see me do it. He thought I was delirious with panic." She frowned and then continued. "When everything was burning above, *I* was the one who woke the Root," she said. She held up her hand and gracefully made a waving motion. "Everything I see fits together, even all this. I see both sides of the equation, the path that leads to the death of my brightest daughter." She closed her eyes and when a minute passed and she still had not opened them, Mwinyi was about to get up. Her eyes suddenly flew open and she was looking intensely at Mwinyi.

"Are . . . are you alright, Mma Binti?"

"No," she whispered. After a pause, she said, "You have eyes like hers."

"I'm a harmonizer," he said.

She nodded, vaguely, looking down at Binti. "You know, those equations that Binti and her father work to create current, I can *see* just by opening my eyes. Binti got some of this, but she has trained it toward current. I have no training, I just see it. At the door, the center of the cellar, then the wall, that was where the spot was. While everyone cowered in the center, moving from the walls where the heat and smoke were coming through, I went to the place directly across from the door. Across the diameter. I could see the line. Do you know plants can do math? They measure what they need to survive and thrive. The Root has survived long.

"The Root had a spot. I could wake it, if I gave from my own life force. We all have current running through us, that's why we are alive." She held up her right hand. The palm was an angry red and covered with crusty blisters. Mwinyi gasped, reaching for her, but she pulled her hand away. "That's how the Root knew to protect its people." She pressed her hand to her chest. "But once it closed, it would not open. You saved us too, Mwinyi."

She took his hand with her uninjured one. Then she quickly let go and her eyes fell back to Binti.

"We want to take her," Mwinyi said, after she'd been quiet for several moments. "Into space. That's where she always said she felt most . . . natural." When Binti's mother didn't say anything, Mwinyi continued, "She once told me that she thought she needed to go to the rings of Saturn; that a vision was calling her there. That's where I think we should take her."

He waited, holding his breath.

"Why'd you come here?" she finally asked, without looking up. "Why couldn't you both have just stayed there?"

Mwinyi sighed and sat down across from her. He looked at her puffy red downcast eyes and then slowly reached forward and took the hand that was not holding Binti's remaining hand. "I didn't want to come," he admitted. "It wasn't safe. And even as I rode out with her, I felt something was off . . . with her." He looked cautiously at her mother. She still looked down at her daughter. He continued. "She's a master harmonizer, but what harmony did she bring? I couldn't understand her. She seemed broken." He held his breath. But now that he had started, he might as well finish. "But Binti was . . . was more than a harmonizer, I realized. There is no word for her yet. I knew she'd do something amazing."

"But she didn't," her mother said, looking up at him. "She failed." Her face was naked as tears ran from her eyes.

"She didn't fail, Khoush and Meduse did," Okwu said, from behind Mwinyi.

"Binti did what she was born to do. Even the most ancient of my clan could not have done what she did, been what she was, carried it as she did, and understand, my people are old and advanced." He waited and when she didn't speak her mind, he continued, "You Himba know us as the Desert People. We are—"

"The Enyi Zinariya," she said. "I know. I married one of you . . . who also was a master harmonizer." She looked down at Binti. "I always knew that she was meant to do something great. We knew when she got into Oomza Uni, though she didn't know we knew. I knew when she agreed to the interview. Her father was so angry when she left . . . but I . . . I wasn't. I understood." She leaned down and kissed Binti on the forehead and then her shoulders slumped. She looked up at Mwinyi, waiting.

"Can we take her?" he asked again.

"How?"

"By neither Meduse ship nor Khoush," Mwinyi said. "Don't worry about that."

"To the rings of Saturn?"

He nodded. "It's where she wanted to go next."

She stared at Mwinyi for a long time and he did not look away. This was part of their conversation and Mwinyi relaxed into it, letting Binti's mother in. When she finally looked away, her tears had stopped and she smiled weakly to herself. "The women will have to prepare her, first," she said. "But, yes. Take my daughter where she wanted to go."

———

Binti's brothers erected a tent around her, so that no one would see. Then the women spent the rest of the day preparing Binti, right there on the spot where she'd fallen. The chief of surgery, a stern woman who'd tied back her waist-length *otjize*-heavy locks, repaired Binti's insides as best she could and sewed up her chest, and the opened wound left where her arm had been. They bathed her with water from the Sacred Well. They massaged her flesh with sweet-smelling oil and then applied Binti's mother's *otjize*. And lastly, one of the seamstresses presented the "homecoming" dress she's sewn for Binti as the other women worked. The long dress was the red-orange color of the richest *otjize*, with a light blue sash that the seamstress refused to explain.

When Binti was ready, she was placed on top of the costume of the Night Masquerade. Because so many had seen it, those in the secret society would need to create a new, different one. And both Chief Kapika and Dele felt that it belonged to Binti now, anyway. Binti was change, she was revolution, she was heroism. She was more Night Masquerade than anyone had ever been. Then the chief called a ceremony and had a girl climb a palm tree and cut a large leaf. The traditional leaf was sent from home to home, though messages about it via astrolabe traveled faster.

The evening was windy again. Another electrical storm thrashed itself out somewhere deep in the desert, but close enough to give the air a tangy charged smell. Dele spoke the words of dedication and love to what was probably all of Osemba. And as he spoke of his best friend, his voice loud and strong, from the west, in Khoushland, the distant boom and crack of Khoush and Meduse arsenal finding purchase distracted many. The darkening sky flickered as the Khoush and Meduse battled in space above.

All the while, Mwinyi and Okwu stayed on the outskirts of it all. These rituals were not for them. Not really. These were not their people and, in Mwinyi's opinion, much of this was done out of guilt. As they'd waited, Mwinyi had spoken with everyone back home and then he'd stopped because they were so angry and disgusted with the Himba and he didn't really want to hear them express what he was working not to feel. He'd only told Binti's grandmother of the plan.

"Take her home," was all she said.

Come evening, everyone had said their goodbyes and all that remained were Binti's parents, siblings, Mwinyi, and Okwu. Boxes of packaged foods, including dates, green plantains, flour, stacks of a dried edible weed, boxes of roasted grasshoppers Okwu liked to eat, and other supplies were stacked beside Okwu. They were quiet as they stood around Binti's body in the dark. Mwinyi walked away from them all and stood on what was left of the Root. It still smelled of smoke here and some of the pieces crumbled beneath his feet as he walked and listened.

Through his rough feet he saw many things of the past, when the Root had stood. He saw Binti's mother singing mathematical equations to a large grasshopper that had flown into the cellar, holding her hand out for it to land, and watching it slowly fold its beautifully decorative wings as if to show her its mathematical pattern. He saw Binti arguing with her sister so many years ago about a dance and her sister laughing and rolling her eyes. He saw Binti's father sneak into the cellar to use the zinariya to speak to his mother.

Mwinyi opened his eyes and took a deep breath. He loved being able to "ground," absolutely loved it. The universe was a singing connection of stories and he could listen to that song anywhere he went now. "I'll never wear shoes again," he whispered to himself.

He looked to the stars and then smiled. It was time. And sure enough, there were the lights. She was coming. He looked to the group; several of Binti's sisters had begun to cry. Binti's father was standing with his head in his hands. And her mother was looking mournfully at Mwinyi.

Shrimplike in its shape, the Miri 12 luminesced a deep purple blue in the night, with pink highlights running around the windows of its front. But this wasn't Third Fish. This Miri 12 was nowhere near as large, barely the size of the Root when the Root had been intact. This was Third Fish's baby, New Fish. She zipped swiftly around them in a large circle, playfully blowing them all with warm air, though remaining careful not to blow dust on Binti's body.

"Praise the Seven," Mwinyi whispered.

He'd called Third Fish last night when he'd walked out into the desert from the Osemba House. The great elephant Arewhana, who'd taught him so much (including how to call large animals from afar), would have been proud. Unlike Binti, Mwinyi hadn't been so confident that things would turn out well with the truce. And so he'd used his harmonizing skill to reach out to Third Fish. The first time had been yesterday, as he stood near the lake. Surprisingly she responded in her deep soft voice. She said she'd help if he needed help, that she was nearby. All he'd have to do was call.

And he'd called. And Third Fish had sent her child to take this sad journey.

The goodbyes were quick.

Binti's brothers had carefully picked up her body and taken her into New Fish. Soft blue lights on the soft ship floor guided them to where New Fish wanted her kept. Mwinyi assured them that this was fine, and no one questioned the ship's decision. In actuality, Mwinyi knew as little as any of them, aside from what the ship told him in its strange voice. But he was struggling with the very idea of leaving Earth, so the smoother and faster this departure went, the better. Mwinyi took one step onto New Fish, stopped, rubbed his now throbbing temples, and put his sandals right back on. Best to deal with his first experience of leaving Earth before anything else.

The room New Fish led them to was one of its upper breathing rooms, a place full of green leafy Earth plants that were just taking root in the newly born creature. The floor here was a soft, almost raw-looking pink and this was where New Fish told Mwinyi they should set Binti. Mwinyi immediately thought of Binti's grandmother's room where she kept so many plants she'd discovered and nurtured. The smell here was wet sand during rare rains, water-filled leaves, the ozone smell after thunderstorms, and the soil Binti's grandmother collected from the bottom of wells and used to pot plants. It was fresh and full of life here.

Okwu had squeezed itself into the room, but moved out of it a moment later. "She loved this place in the Third Fish," it told Mwinyi and Binti's brothers as they put her down. "She said she liked the damp, the warmth, and the smell. All I smell are microbes." Then it left to explore the rest of the ship.

Binti's brothers Omeva and Bena didn't linger either. They clearly wanted to leave the room, to get away from their little sister's body. Binti's mother had to be taken away by Binti's father before the ship took off, for she'd begun to tear at her clothes and had even torn one of her locks out. The sisters had started to keen and sing a mournful song that Mwinyi never wanted to hear again and the other Himba people only stood there staring, still in shock about all that had happened in the last twenty-four hours.

Mwinyi remained in the room for a while longer, then he left, and the door slid shut behind him.

CHAPTER 8

Space Is the Place

"I'm glad to leave Earth," Okwu said. It exhaled a large cloud of gas as it looked out the window.

Mwinyi still clung to the pillar in the middle of the pilot chamber. He had been born and raised in the desert and never had he dreamed of leaving the Earth. He'd been happy protecting his people when they went on journeys across the desert and communing with the various peoples of the desert, from fox to dog to hawk to ant. His life had been simple; however, the moment Binti entered his life, he'd known that simplicity was over.

He would never be able to describe what it felt like to sit strapped to one of New Fish's strangely molded chairs and leave the Earth. Even an hour later, he wasn't able to speak. Okwu seemed to understand this, for it left Mwinyi alone as it hovered near one of the wall-size windows in New Fish's cockpit. Okwu hadn't needed to strap itself down and didn't seem to be affected by the change in air pressure or gravity as the ship balanced out its insides to reflect an Earth-like atmosphere.

When Mwinyi did speak, it was to New Fish.

After? it asked, hours later as Mwinyi slept in the large room near New Fish's top called the Star Chamber. It felt like a vibration on his back that formed words he could understand in his mind.

Mwinyi had chosen this room because its ceiling was all window and he could rest on his back and look into space in a way similar to how he looked into the sky when he went off into the desert alone back home. He'd been asleep on the floor, which was so soft that he didn't need his mat. He rolled over, resting his hands on the purple luminescent floor. "After what?" he said aloud.

After Saturn. After we set her free.

"Oh," he said, his shoulder slumping as it all came back to him. The deep exhausted sleep he'd been in gave him respite from Binti's death and the fact that he'd just left his home without mentally preparing to do any such thing. "I . . . Okwu says we should go to his school. Oomza Uni."

That is far.

"I know."

What do you want?

He sighed. "It's fine. What do *you* want?"

The ship vibrated, the ceiling creaking and the floor flickering with stripes of blue purple and pink. Glee. Mwinyi smiled. *I want to fly*, New Fish said. *Go far.*

Mwinyi lay on his belly, his hands still pressed to New Fish. "Can I go back to sleep now?"

Yes. But . . . no. Will you please tell me about Binti? My mother told me much. You tell me things too.

And so it was an hour before Mwinyi went back to the escape of sleep, as he told New Fish all he knew about Binti. He even told New Fish how much he loved her and finished by surprising himself. He *did* want to go to Oomza Uni. It was far from the home he wanted to return to, but it was where a part of Binti also lived. He told New Fish that he wanted to meet her friends and her mathematics professor. He wanted to see where she collected the clay she used for *otjize*. And when he finally did lie on New Fish's soft welcoming flesh, he slept even more deeply than before and the dreams he had were full of beautiful flashing colors and a soothing hum.

=====

Neither Mwinyi nor Okwu could bring themselves to go into that room. As the days passed and they got closer to Saturn, the idea became less and less savory. For Mwinyi, he could only imagine what her body looked like or how she smelled in that warm jungly room full of plants, soil, and according to Okwu, microbes.

For Okwu, opening that room meant it was time to set Binti free. Neither Okwu nor its fellow Meduse, who were most of the time thirsty with war, wanted to send this peaceful girl human on a journey on which they could not join her. And Okwu couldn't bear to part with its partner. Not at this time, when things had gone so far.

Nevertheless, when the equivalent of three days had passed and New Fish excitedly told Mwinyi that they were approaching Saturn's ring in an hour, it was time to face reality.

It's time, New Fish excitedly rumbled.

Mwinyi, who'd been watching Saturn approach through the star room window, felt his spirits drop. New Fish had been moving and now she came to a stop, hovering in deep space. Waiting. Mwinyi found himself a bit annoyed with the ship's overly cheerful demeanor, especially in the last twenty-four hours. But he said nothing. New Fish was a young living ship, a creature born to travel far and fast, and she was in space for the first time. How could he blame her for feeling free and adventurous?

The walkway to the breathing chamber was narrow and the left side was lined with windows that showed the blackness outside. Okwu led the way.

"I don't know if I'm ready for this," Mwinyi said.

"No one is ever ready for such a thing," Okwu said. "But we will send her on her way to her next journey."

Mwinyi saw Binti's faces in his mind, with and without *otjize*. He felt his heart would break a second time.

"Keep moving," Okwu said.

When they reached the breathing chamber, Okwu went right in. Mwinyi hesitated and then followed. He shut the door behind him. There, among the lovely plants, irrigated by clean waters that ran throughout New Fish to other breathing rooms, was Binti's body wrapped in its red soft cloth, lying on the costume of the Night Masquerade.

"She looks the same," Okwu said and Mwinyi shivered, understanding exactly what it meant. Her body wasn't bloating yet. Making an effort not to look at the unnerving Night Masquerade costume, Mwinyi put the transporter on the floor beside her body and powered it up. Within a second, it shivered and then buzzed softly. Binti's wrapped body and the Night Masquerade costume lifted off the ground.

Mwinyi sighed. "Okay," he muttered, his voice thick. He gave her a gentle push and she smoothly glided toward the door. Mwinyi stopped her, looking at Okwu.

"What?" it said. "We must do this fast." It moved quickly toward the door. The door slid open and Okwu squeezed through. Just outside the room, Mwinyi could see it let out a great blast of gas and inhale it back in. Then it let some out again, as it moved away from the door.

Mwinyi looked down at Binti. He inhaled and held his breath; he didn't want to smell her. He reached down. He had to see her face one more time. He did not care if it was bloated from death or even eaten by organisms that lived in the breathing room. He had to see her, to truly say goodbye. He flipped the red cloth aside. He stared. He let out his breath.

Her *okuoko* were writhing like snakes.

═══

I was staring back.

CHAPTER 9

Awake

I was there.

Then I opened my eyes.

"It's all mathematics," I said.

I don't know where the words came from or why I said them. Mwinyi was staring at me, his mouth agape. "Life, the universe, everything." I turned my head to the side and caught a glimpse of the Night Masquerade I lay on. The costume.

Mwinyi reached a hand forward and pulled more of the cloth off me. I looked down too, as he gasped, jumping up and stumbling back. "*Okwu!*" he finally called. "Okwu! Get in here!"

I looked toward the door where Okwu hovered, just outside the room. The moment I laid eyes on it, I saw it float quickly back, leaving a great cloud of its lavender gas as it went. Then I could hear it puffing it out, sucking it back in, puffing it out, sucking it in.

"Binti," Mwinyi whispered. "What . . . is this really you?" He had tears in his eyes, his lips were quivering. I'd been watching him move about the ship for hours. It had been as if I were swimming, rolling, floating in the tree. Then I was pulled into this place, this ship, and it had embraced me with delight. And I'd seen Okwu and Mwinyi moving about, both of them so sad, numb, and quiet. I'd followed them here and opened my eyes.

I sat up as he stared at me. I touched my left arm. I had a left arm. Mwinyi sank to the floor, his back against the slender trunk of a young tree with tough rubbery-looking leaves growing from a hole in the floor. A tree that looked oddly like an Undying tree.

Home, I thought as I pressed my chest. I remembered most clearly when the Khoush fire bullet hit me in the chest. The punching, then stabbing pain, and once inside me, it had hungrily bitten at me with its fire. I pressed my soft breasts now, beneath the red dress I wore. I rolled to the side and touched the sticklike hand of the Night Masquerade costume. I held it with my left hand, kneading the actual sticks used for the knuckles with my fingers.

I nearly laughed now when I thought back to that moment when I'd stood at my bedroom window staring down at the Night Masquerade that first time. Deep down a tiny, tiny voice in me had wondered if something were wrong with me, if my spirit was that of a man's, not a woman's, because the Night Masquerade never showed itself to girls or women. Even back then I had changed things, and I didn't even know it. When I should have reveled in this gift, instead, I'd seen myself as broken. But couldn't you be broken and still bring change?

I powered down the transporter beside me and it lowered me to the ground. I closed my eyes and said a silent prayer to thank the Seven for Their Mysterious Mystery. Then slowly, my muscles creaking and aching, old *otjize* flaking to the floor, I stood up. I had legs, too. I felt the ship rumble, the leaves, flowers, stems, and branches around us shaking. I felt the ship's voice more than heard it, in every part of me, but especially my chest, left arm, and legs. *"Hello, Binti,"* it said. It spoke in Khoush. Mwinyi looked around and then back at me.

"New Fish is speaking to you, isn't she?" he asked. "I can hear her, but barely."

I nodded.

"Hello," I said aloud, not sure how else to speak to it. "You are New Fish? Is that—"

"Yes. Third Fish's daughter," she said.

"I died," I blurted. "I remember. They had agreed to stop fighting and then something happened and they started fighting anyway. They forgot about me and I got caught in the crossfire. I don't know if Khoush or Meduse killed me . . ." I paused, as more of those moments returned to me. I'd seen flashes of blue and red, felt heat and cold. I'd been shot by Meduse and Khoush alike. "How is it possible that I'm standing in your breathing room looking at Mwinyi. Breathing." I held out my arms to him and immediately he rushed over.

He gathered me in his arms.

"Microbes," I heard Okwu say from the door. It stood in it, filling it up completely as it floated.

"Okwu," I said, feeling my *okuoko* writhe. And for the first time I knew how to do it. I sent the small spark toward it and it popped in a series of blue sparks at its tentacles. Okwu's dome expanded, filling the doorway even more tightly, and then deflated.

"*My mother said it would happen if they put you in my breathing chamber, because I am so young,*" New Fish said. "*That is why she sent me instead of coming herself. She would have broken through the curfew gate they set up for all launch port ships once the fighting started. My mother isn't afraid of her bond to the Khoush. But she knew. And she saw your soul when everything happened on your journey to Oomza Uni. She calls you the 'gentle warrior' and believes our union would bring Miri 12s forward.*"

"Union?" I asked. Again, *another* connection.

"What's she saying?" Mwinyi asked. "I can't quite—"

"Shhh," I said to Mwinyi, still holding him.

"*Come up to my Star Chamber and I will explain,*" New Fish said.

═══════

I sat on the Star Chamber floor looking out the large window before me. This was where Mwinyi had been staying and I could see why. I stared out at the distant Saturn as I drank a second cup of water and finished a bowl of dried meat. The water tasted soily, having been drawn from one of New Fish's wells, and the meat was spicy and tough. It was delicious. I didn't have to ask to know that this was meat someone from my town had supplied for the journey. Goat meat, sliced thin and cured in an Osemba smokehouse.

I had followed Mwinyi up the corridor, marveling at New Fish's young interior design. I soon slowed down, overcome with a thirst and hunger so strong that I felt as if my body were trying to consume itself. By the time we reached the Star Chamber, I'd sat down right there in the middle of the room and could say nothing but "Water," and then when I had that, "Food."

As I ate and drank, things around me cleared and soon I was just chewing on the meat because it was tasty. Mwinyi sat beside me, eating a handful of dates. Okwu hovered near the other wall of windows, chicken bones scattered on the floor beneath it. I'd never actually watched Okwu eat; Okwu liked to go off and eat alone and for a while, I'd wondered if it ate at all. Thus, seeing it consume the roasted chicken it had brought up from storage had been a sight. Meduse eat like delicate old ladies, slowly picking at and drawing in the meat bit by bit with their *okuoko*. Watching it eat had brought me my first real smile since I'd sat up and had a living body to smile with.

"Okay," I finally said, taking one more gulp of water. "I'm listening." I looked at my right arm, flaking the remaining old *otjize* off to reveal my dark brown skin.

"Wait," Mwinyi said. "Before New Fish speaks to you, Okwu and I want to tell you what happened after you . . . after they killed you." He frowned, a pained look on his face. "I can't believe I can say that to you. 'Killed.'" He let out a breath.

"I know," I said. But somehow, out there in space on New Fish, with a Meduse and an Enyi Zinariya master harmonizer, it all seemed so bizarre, what was the added detail of me coming back from the dead? "When one dies, the Seven take you, no matter who you are. You join the whole again. The wilderness. You don't come back."

"Meduse always come back," Okwu said, quietly. "We reincarnate."

"Do you remember the Seven?" Mwinyi asked, ignoring Okwu. "The Principle Artists of All Things?"

"I do," I said. Seeing the shock on Mwinyi's face and the puff of gas that Okwu blew out amused me. They hadn't expected me to say that; however, I *did* remember. "But tell me what you need to tell me."

When he got to the part about my family, I screamed. I jumped up, knocking over my cup of water. I didn't know where to go, so I just stood there. I just stood there. My chest tight, the heart inside it beating strong again. My legs strong. My flesh naked. My *okuoko*, which were now past my waist, vibrating. I pressed my hands against the sides of my face. Then I lifted my dress to my knees and did my village's fire dance, stamping my feet hard to make my anklets jingle. When I looked at my legs, I saw that I didn't have any anklets. I danced anyway, hearing the jingling in my mind.

"I spoke to the Root," Mwinyi laughingly explained as I danced and danced with joy. "And it opened up. And we were able to get everyone out."

"Everyone," I said, stretching my hands toward the window, toward outer space. "No one was hurt?"

"Everyone was well," Mwinyi said.

I whirled around, ran to him, threw my arms around him, and kissed him long and hard. And through my *okuoko*, I threw a blue spark, the size and shape of a large tomato, at Okwu. I jumped back and began to dance again and when I saw Okwu vibrating its dome with laughter, I danced harder. My family was *alive*! My family was *alive*! The Root was alive, even if the house built on it had been burned to ash. We *survive*.

"How?" I asked.

When Mwinyi told me what my mother had said, I stared at him in awe. "She used her mathematical sight?" I whispered. "My mother, she sees the math in the world, she was born with it. That's where the sharpness of my gift comes from. She was never trained, though. She just used it to protect the family during storms, to fortify the house, sometimes to heal you if you were sick. My mother is so powerful." I laughed to myself, tears welling up in my eyes. "I can't believe it! Thank the Seven, praise the Seven, the Seven are great, they make circles in the sand!" *That* was why I couldn't see her during my fevered zinariya visions. While everyone else had moved from the walls to get away from the smoke and heat, my mother had gone toward the danger to find the spot that woke the Root's defenses.

"I've contacted my home," Mwinyi added. "They are sending people to meet with the Himba. Your man Dele will lead the meeting with them."

I paused at him referring to Dele as my "man," but quickly moved on. "Dele was there?" I remembered. "Oh! Mwinyi, he was the Night Masquerade! I saw him! I saw him!" I wrapped my arms around myself, tears welling in my eyes.

"The Himba Council *did* betray you," Mwinyi said. "But Dele didn't. He was there as the Night Masquerade to give you hope and strength."

I listened in silence as Mwinyi explained. This part I had to let sink in. The Night Masquerade was a secret society of men? And Dele was in it? A part of me still rejected this. That first time I'd seen it from my bedroom window, it had looked like a creature, not a man in a costume. And what of my uncle and my father who had also seen it? Did they know of the tradition too?

Regardless, I felt good. About everything. The war had begun again, my home would never be what it was, but this, I understood more than ever now, was inevitable. Change was inevitable and where the Seven were involved, so was growth. My family was *alive*, the Enyi Zinariya were going to meet them and help Osemba *survive* and evolve. And if any people knew how to survive and evolve, it was the Enyi Zinariya. Osemba would change and grow.

Dele was not a harmonizer, but he had come of age with me and he had to have learned something about himself after what happened with the Himba Council. He'd just started his apprenticeship to be the next Himba chief and, rigid and traditional as he was, he'd already broken out of the mold when he believed the council had made a mistake. His love and protectiveness of his people was strong enough to push tradition to grow. Dele was ready for what was coming and I felt good about what he'd do.

It was then that I remembered something else and my heart began to pound like crazy because it had already been three days. There was no going back home with ease. I reached into the pocket of my right hip where I had kept it. I wasn't wearing the same dress, but maybe . . . my shoulders slumped. The *edan* pieces and its inner golden ball weren't there. It was lost.

"New Fish," I said. "Okay, I am ready to hear your explanation." I reached into my left front pocket as I sat down. I felt the edge of something sharp. I grinned as I shoved my hand further in and grasped the golden ball. *"Thank the Seven,"* I whispered. "And thank my family."

"I am young and there wasn't much time," New Fish said to me.

Mwinyi was sitting on the floor, with his chest pressed to it, his arms out as he pressed his palms to the floor. "It's how I hear her clearest," he said when I looked at him questioningly.

I nodded at him and looked at Okwu, who just said, "Tell me when she has finished."

"I don't know much," New Fish continued. *"Most Miri 12s never do this. We don't become more. We are ships because we like to travel, that's what mother said. Until she harbored you. Then she started thinking. Even before Mwinyi called out to her. So she told me about 'deep Miri' and how I had to work it. We have breathing chambers.*

"My mother said that before I was born, my chambers were seeded from her inner plants. Those plants not only produce the gases for us to breathe when we leave planets with breathable atmospheres, but they also carry bacteria, good viruses, and other microorganisms, and these microbes go on to populate every part of my body. But they populate the breathing chamber most passionately when a Miri 12 is new born like me.

"When your body was placed in my chamber, my microbes went to work. You are probably more microbes than human now."

I frowned. "What does that mean? I look and feel like myself. I remember who I am. I was dead, right?"

"That is the 'deep Miri' my mother said would happen. I don't understand it, myself. But they blended with your genes and repaired you, regrew your arm and legs, then pulled you back. There is one thing, though." She stopped talking for a moment and I was relieved. I needed to think.

I was dead. This fact echoed through my brain, ricocheting off the walls and slamming back again and again. *I was dead, I was dead, I was dead.* I remembered joining the Seven. Was I even me now? I was physically more Miri 12 than human. I touched the *okuoko* on my head and my temples throbbed. I raised my hands and typed and pushed the message to Mwinyi with more ease than I'd experienced while on Earth. "Am I still Enyi Zinariya?" I asked. My world stayed steady and there were no voices. I didn't look toward the window to see if there was a tunnel in space or a strange planet bouncing beside Saturn.

"You will always be Enyi Zinariya," he responded, his green words appearing before me in crisp letters. I touched them and they faded away like incense smoke.

"What is Enyi Zinariya?" New Fish's words floated at me in bright pink and I gasped.

Mwinyi gasped too.

"Did she send it to you, too?" I asked.

He nodded.

"*I've absorbed some of you, too, Binti,*" she said. And again, the room lit up with the orange-pink color.

"The Enyi Zinariya are my tribe, our tribe," Mwinyi said. "We got our name from the Zinariya people who visited and changed us long ago." He cut his eyes at me and added, "You might know us as 'the Desert People.'"

"*Oh,*" New Fish said. "*Yes, my mother liked to talk about Binti's dark skin, dense hair, and old African face. She said that may be what gave Binti her fight, desert bloods. We weren't even sure if you were really Himba.*"

"I am Himba," I snapped.

The room became orange-pink again, and this time stayed that way. Mwinyi rolled his eyes and said, "Yes, yes, Binti, you are Himba. No one's taking that from you."

I frowned even more deeply and turned my back to him, for the moment angry and frustrated with too many things to focus on a response.

"Can I ask you something, New Fish?" Mwinyi said.

"*Ask,*" New Fish said.

"If you were only born a few days ago, how come you can communicate so well?"

The ship's room flashed a soft orange-pink so pleasant that I instantly felt less annoyed. It was the same color as the ntu ntu bugs on Oomza Uni. "*I have been talking to my mother for five Earth years and my mother is old, so very smart. A Miri 12 is 'pregnant' when she is near her time to give birth. And birth is not the beginning for us; it's just a change.*"

Mwinyi nodded, looking amazed. "So you have been inside your mother for five years and you two talk?"

"*I've been all over the galaxy with my mother, who was born on Earth. But mostly to Earth and Oomza, since my mother has been doing that route since I spawned. This is why I can speak Khoush.*"

"So you were there when . . . did you know when the Meduse killed everyone on board your mother?"

"Moojh-ha ki-bira," she said. "*Yes. My mother said she and I should stay quiet until we reached Oomza. That was the first time in my entire life that I had nightmares when I slept.*"

We were quiet for a few moments. Then I asked, "What was it that you were going to tell me? You said there was something I needed to know."

"*I may have spoken too soon,*" New Fish said, after a moment. "*You've just woken. You've just eaten.*"

"I'm fine," I said impatiently. "Please, tell it all to me now. I'd rather be shocked all at once. Tell me everything." I was breathing heavily. I'd had a strange feeling as New Fish spoke to me. It was leading up to telling me something big. "Should I let myself tree first? When I do that I can handle any shock, any—"

"*No. Don't tree. That won't help.*"

"Why?"

"*You will see.*"

And then I did.

Suddenly, the Star Chamber, Mwinyi, Okwu, everything was gone. I was in space. Infinite blackness was all around me, except for Saturn, pale and blue in the distance, and the sun in the other direction. The blue-pink bioluminescent light of New Fish seemed to radiate from me. With each second, I became more aware of this and then I began to fall. And as I fell faster and faster, I didn't have any arms with which to flail and I began to panic. I started screaming. I shuddered and my scream came out as a deep groan.

Relax, I heard New Fish say. She spoke in my head. *Just be. You are safe.*

What's . . . what's happening to me? I shouted. Again, my voice was just a rumble. I could feel myself shaking, shuddering. Not myself, not my body. New Fish's body.

Your body too, now, she said.

The word she'd said before came back to me, "union."

Your body is partially me, she said. *That's how the deep Miri brought you back. And in turn, I am partially you.*

As I relaxed, I realized that for the first time, I could do something I'd always dreamed of when I was little. I was in space with no suit, in no ship, and I wasn't dying. This was my chance to do that for real. I let myself be New Fish and noticed that I was just floating. There was no up or down. I felt neither cool nor hot, though I felt a warmth from within and that was enough. I looked straight ahead at Saturn.

The Seven are Great, I said.

They are.

How do I—

But then I was doing it. I was flying forward. I flipped and flew what my body perceived as down. I laughed with glee and flew fast and stopped and flew faster and stopped. The feeling of floating in space made me euphoric. It was such freedom. I was doing a barrel roll when I remembered Mwinyi and Okwu were on the ship and in that moment, something odd happened. I could feel myself gradually slow down. Then I was back inside, looking down at Okwu and Mwinyi in the Star Chamber. Mwinyi was hanging on to a pole, a look of horror on his face. Okwu was simply hovering, now on the other side of the room. Then I was back in my body, sitting cross-legged on the floor in the middle of the room. I looked around, blinking.

"Binti? Can you hear me now?" Mwinyi shouted.

"Huh?" I said, resting a hand on the soft floor.

"You nearly killed us!" Mwinyi said.

"She nearly killed *you*. Not me," Okwu said. "And I caught you. You are fine."

Mwinyi frowned angrily at Okwu.

"Sorry," I said. When I stretched my legs, I had to use some effort because the bottoms of my legs were adhered to New Fish's surface with some kind of mucus. This was why I hadn't been thrashed around like Mwinyi. I pulled some of the gummy substance from the backs of my legs and dress. "Can you become me as I became you?" I asked New Fish.

"*It is not that you became me. I'm a Miri 12, it is how we connect. But no, I would not connect with you in that way. You don't have the capacity.*"

I was too tired to address New Fish's quiet condescension.

"*The final thing I must tell you is that if we were on Earth, because you've taken so much from me to live, you and I can never be too far from one another.*"

I yawned. "Why? What would happen?"

"*I don't know.*"

"How far is too far?"

"*I'm not sure,*" she said. "*When my mother sent me, she couldn't answer every question I had. With all the shooting near the launch port, I was more worried about getting shot down on my way to you.*"

"It's alright," I said, standing up. I didn't have the energy to wonder about this, either. Not at the moment. Plus we were in space and I wasn't going to move away from New Fish any time soon. And where were we going now, anyway? I needed to rest first.

CHAPTER 10

Stones of Saturn

"We're going to go through Saturn's ring," I said hours later, after a long nap. "I'm not discussing it. Then we turn around and head to Oomza Uni, as you planned."

"Okay," was all Mwinyi replied.

Okwu said nothing, nor did New Fish. I turned back to the large window feeling satisfied with myself. I'd been ready to argue with all of them and it was nice to get what I wanted so easily.

After waking from my nine hours of sleep, I'd connected with New Fish again. This time, I did it on my own. New Fish might have been asleep, for I didn't sense her presence at all. It was just me out there as a living ship. I felt the air in my breathing chambers, the strength in my body. I even felt Mwinyi standing in the corner, moving his hands about as he talked to several people in the desert on Earth and Okwu in the room below. Okwu was not talking to the other Meduse on Earth, it was observing. When connected to New Fish, I brought all my skills with me. I considered attempting to tree while connected, but decided against it. The results of treeing were affected by size, and who knew what I'd call up.

As I floated out there in space, enjoying the absolute quiet, I gazed at Saturn. We were near enough to see its shape and rings. Saturn was close enough to reach within hours, even if New Fish took her time. This was when I'd decided we should go.

"My mother says edans *are unpredictable,"* New Fish said now. *"She said yours especially could have its own consciousness."*

But I wanted to see. Had to see. After all I'd been through, I needed to get to the bottom of this mystery. "I don't care," I snapped. "We are going even if I have to hijack you and force you to fly there."

"*You can't*," New Fish said.

"I'll try," I said.

"*Go ahead*," New Fish goaded.

"Only if I have to," I said.

"Ugh, will you both shut up?" Mwinyi snapped, taking his hands from the floor. "No one's fighting you on this, Binti. No need to be like that."

Okwu vibrated its dome and blew out so much gas that both Mwinyi and I started coughing.

I got up and went to the breathing room where I'd lain for days. I picked up the Night Masquerade costume. Then I went down to another of New Fish's breathing rooms. I'd felt this one when I was connected to New Fish. When I went inside, the light in here was very similar to the midday desert sun and when I saw the trees, I knew why. There were ten of them, some were saplings, several were small nearly matured trees, and one of them was fully matured, reaching the ceiling and bending a bit to the side. Undying trees! The saplings looked recently potted inside the flesh of New Fish, and the mature one had roots that extended down into New Fish like nerves. The floor was slightly transparent and I could see the roots going deep. These trees had all been growing while New Fish was in utero.

Not for the first time, I wondered if Third Fish was also psychic. And did that mean New Fish was too? There were other plants here that I recognized from Osemba as well. Plants that were usually peopled with land crabs, lizards, and other creatures because these plants attracted insects and smaller life forms. They attracted life. The floor here was dry, even coated with a layer of sand in some places. I touched the trees' leaves, which were all rough with what the Himba called "life salt," a pinkish grainy substance that healers used to cure and treat all sorts of ailments.

I tasted it now and it invigorated my tongue. When I'd first found my *edan*, my father brought it to his tongue to taste what kind of metal it was. He hadn't been able to identify it, but he'd said it tasted like life salt. I laid out the Night Masquerade on the floor and looked at it. The smiling side of its many-masked head stared back at me. I shivered with residual disbelief that this was the costume of the Night Masquerade, that it *was* a costume. I sat down facing its head. Then I brought out the *edan* pieces and the golden ball.

I brought the ball to my face and looked at its fingerprint-like surface closely. Then I held up my left hand and looked at my fingerprints. Had the print on my left middle and index fingers always matched the ones on the ball? I'd never compared them before I'd lost my left arm, so who knows. But now they matched perfectly and this didn't surprise me. Nor had the presence of Undying trees.

Holding it on the palm of my right hand, I touched my index and middle fingers to their spots on the golden ball and immediately it began to hum and vibrate. "Okay," I whispered, placing it on the floor before me. If it weren't for the sand, the ball would have begun to roll away. Softly, I whispered, "$(x-h)^2 + (y-k)^2 = r^2$" and the equation floated from my lips in a way that reminded me of the zinariya. It was even my color of red. I chose the equation for circles because it was all coming back around and around and around. And the equation stretched into a circle as I let myself tree, surrounding me before it faded away.

The moment I called up a thick strong current, blue like Okwu, the Undying trees in the room began to vibrate too. It was the same way they reacted to lightning storms back home. As I led the current to the golden ball, the trees' vibrations had become so fast and steady that they began to hum. Slowly, the ball rose. It hovered before my eyes, a foot away, and began to slowly rotate.

As I climbed higher up the tree, I thought about the Zinariya. They'd come to a quiet part of Africa, where the people lived very close to the desert. Close and isolated enough that the people in those small communities knew how to keep a secret. And thus, the rest of the world never knew of the tall, humanoid gold people who loved the way the sun reacted with Earth's atmosphere there. They saw this small patch of Earth as a vacation spot and the people they met didn't mind. Their friendship started with a girl named Kande. In many ways, she was like me. What Kande started had eventually made the people in this small town more.

Made the Zinariya more.

They left an *edan*. No instructions. No purpose. But it could make you more, if you let it. I'd found it.

I don't know how long I was watching it rotate, as I climbed deeper and deeper into the tree. Mwinyi would later tell me that he'd been in the Star Chamber; they'd been eating and Okwu had been telling him a story about a Meduse meeting of chiefs long ago that had gone horribly wrong. "We knew you were off somewhere brooding," he said.

The ball was rotating faster and faster now with my current, humming with the trees. The hairs on my arms rose with the charge in the air. My *okuoko* slithered about me at my sides and back, old *otjize* still flaking from them to the floor. Then I was in space!

Infinite blackness.

Weightless. Flying.

Falling a bit.

Catching myself.

Then flying again.

I wanted to scream *and* laugh; I had become something more again. This time, I was so changed that I could fly through space without dying. I could live in open space. I moved through Saturn's ring of brittle metallic dust. It pelted our exoskeleton like chips of glittery ice. It felt pleasant, so I flew faster, resisting the urge to do barrel rolls because of Mwinyi and Okwu. New Fish was quiet, letting me take the lead. This was my mission. My purpose. And it was fantastic.

Living breath bloomed in me from the breathing room where I currently sat, the whirling golden ball humming with the trees. The metallic dust grew thick like a sandstorm and I stopped as some of it whirled before me in a way that reminded me of the golden ball.

"Who are you?" a voice asked. It spoke in the dialect of my family and it came from everywhere.

"Binti Ekeopara Zuzu Dambu Kaipka of Namib, that is my name," I blurted before I let myself think too hard about what was happening. "No," I said. "My name is Binti Ekeopara Zuzu Dambu Kaipka Meduse Enyi Zinariya New Fish of Namib." I waited a few moments and then decided to ask, "Who are you?"

"We are . . ." And for a moment, I heard nothing. Then the sound of their name split and split like a fractal in my mind. It was like the practice of treeing embodied in one word. Their name was an equation too complex, too various and varied to mentally fix into place, let alone put into a language that I was capable of uttering. It was beautiful and my joy in just letting it cartwheel and bounce about my mind was reflected in the color New Fish shined in the metallic storm of Saturn's ring.

When I could finally speak, I said, "You've called me here. Why? What is it you want?"

The rush of debris swirled before me into a funnel shape now.

"Did *we* call you here?" it asked, its voice almost playful.

"You did." I focused hard on the funnel, their name still in my mind vying for attention.

"That ball belongs to a people we've met. They only leave it to be found by those they feel should find them. They pack it between pieces of beautiful metal like a gift."

"What is it?" I asked.

"What do you think it is?"

I could see New Fish's light grow purpler with my annoyance. "You called me," I repeated. "Why?"

"Okay," it said. "We called you, yes. Through your zinariya object."

"I'm here now, finally. What do you want?"

There was a long pause. The dust swirled and swirled and for a moment, I was sure I saw a flash of red-orange light. I didn't bother wondering who these people were or where they had come from or what they even looked like. If I was meant to find out, I would. If not, then I would not. If there was one thing I had learned in all my strange journeys it was that what would be would be and sometimes you wait to see. And this was fine, because at least I'd gotten to the bottom of the question of my *edan* and that odd vision and what was there was just as strange as I had imagined.

"Tell us about Oomza Uni," the voice said.

I was so shocked that I couldn't answer. Then I said, "What?"

"You are a student at Oomza Uni, no?"

"I am, but—"

"That is why we called on you. We want an opinion on the university that comes from someone like us."

"But . . . like you? How am I—"

"We're people of time and space. We move about experiencing, collecting, becoming more. This is the philosophy and culture of our equation. There's no one of our kind there, yet we hear it is the finest university in the galaxy. There is plenty we could learn from there and we'd like to apply. But first, we need a true recommendation of the place from someone we trust. We trust you."

"So you've known I would eventually be . . . what I now am, so you sent for me?"

"Yes. We are many things. What is your opinion of the university?"

"Well . . . I left my home to attend, nearly died on the way, and when I got there, it turned out to be the best experience I ever had as an academic. Excellent professors, excellent students, and excellent environment. It's the perfect place for me."

There was a pause and then it said, "Thank you."

And just like that, the dust and debris of Saturn was simply dust and debris again. A recommendation, that's all they needed. It was so . . . anticlimactic. Not that I was complaining.

For a few moments, I enjoyed the sensation of space and the flecks and larger chunks of stone bouncing off of New Fish's body. Then I had an idea and used one of New Fish's large pincers to catch two fist-sized stones tumbling about. As New Fish, I could "taste" the dust and stones and they had a tanginess that reminded me of the life salt scraped from the leaves of Undying trees and the sandstone from which I made my astrolabe. I stored them in one of New Fish's many outer crevices. When I returned to myself, the golden ball was on the floor, the trees were quiet, and Mwinyi was standing over me, a perplexed look on his face.

"What was that all about?" he asked.

"Not as much as I expected," I said with a laugh as I got to my feet.

CHAPTER 11

Ntu Ntu Bugs and Sunshine

New Fish landed in the yellow grassy field where I'd had my first Oomza Uni class—Treeing 101. The large field was between the Math, Weapons, and Organics Cities, and it was typically vacant. This day, there were a couple Meduse-like people with nets, probably catching ntu ntu bugs to study. The moment we landed, one of them roared and floated off, while the other puffed out gas and watched as a university shuttle glided up and waited for us to come out.

I said nothing as Mwinyi and Okwu moved down New Fish's walkway. In Okwu's excitement and Mwinyi's hesitation, they'd both forgotten. I was fine with this; I preferred to deal with the anxiety on my own. Well, as on my own as I could be now.

"Walk slowly," New Fish said as I paused at the exit.

"I can't do anything else," I said, trying not to think about how naked I was. I had no *otjize* on my skin. The hot entrance into the atmosphere had been different this time because my connection to New Fish made me feel the discomfort of the heat. And the shift from New Fish's internally balanced gravity to that of Oomza Uni's still left me a bit weak and dizzy. The grass was so yellow that it practically glowed in the shine of Oomza Uni's two suns. I could smell the scent of the soil, grass, and the ntu ntu bugs who lived in the grass.

I heard Okwu speaking to someone further out and Mwinyi had taken his shoes off and bent down to touch the ground. His eyes were shut. I began to walk down the walkway. New Fish had said that I wouldn't be able to go far from her because I was technically a part of her now. However, she didn't know what "far" meant. Did this mean I couldn't leave the ship? That I couldn't go more than a few yards? We were about to find out. And what would happen if I went too far?

My feet touched the grass and I exhaled, looking back at the ship. I paused as I gazed upon her for the first time. She was bigger than the Root, but had the same natural grace. I smiled to myself. This was because both New Fish and the Root were alive. She wasn't shaped as much like a shrimp as her mother. She looked more like a water creature I couldn't name; she was bulbous in body that reminded me of the translucent Meduse ships. And here in the atmosphere and sunshine, her purple-pink flesh was detailed with thick lines of gold that rimmed the openings of fins and ran around both her sides. And she had eyes! How had I not known that she had enormous bright golden eyes? When I thought about looking through her eyes at Saturn, I could have sworn that I saw colors I couldn't name. So this made sense. Those glorious eyes looked at me now as I moved away from her, walking backward toward the Oomza shuttle and representatives who'd come to meet us.

"You are alright?" New Fish asked.

I nodded, grinning.

Slowly, I walked to the Oomza representatives, two crablike people, one with a rose-colored exoskeleton and the other green. Both of their bodies were wrapped in blue Oomza Uni cloth. Both had their astrolabes hanging from golden chains at the base of their left fore-claws and from their astrolabes came their cheerful voices.

"Welcome back, Binti," both proclaimed.

"Thank you," I said. "I hope our landing here wasn't too much of an issue. We didn't want everyone to make a big fuss at the launch port."

"It is what it is and we know you do what you do," the rose one said. "And your ship is small and living, so it's good for the grasses."

"President Haras says she can stay here for now," the green one

said. "It would like to meet with you, Okwu, and the Mwinyi immediately."

"Just 'Mwinyi' is fine," he said, looking up from where he squatted with his hands to the soil.

"Mwinyi," the green one said. "We will drive you all. Your ship
can rest, graze . . . does she need something else?"

I looked at New Fish. "Should I? Can I?" I asked.

"I can fly with you."

And that's how we did it. With New Fish flying directly above.
It was Oomza Uni, such a thing may not have been a common
sight, but it probably wasn't bizarre here. Few things were.

CHAPTER 12

President Haras

The Oomza University president's name was something that sounded like the sound of the wind blowing over the desert sand dunes back home. To me, it sounded like "haaaaraaaaaaaaas-ssssss," so I called it Haras. It didn't mind, as long as I prefaced it with the title of "President." I'd first met President Haras at the meeting directly upon leaving the Third Fish, when I pled the case of the Meduse and their violent killing of all but one of the Khoush people on board.

My first impression was that it looked like one of the gods of the Enyi Zinariya (well, back then I'd thought, "Desert People"). President Haras was a spiderlike person who was about the width of Okwu and as tall as me. And like its name, it seemed to be made of wind, gray and undulating here and not quite there. I'd met with it several times over my year at Oomza Uni and I loved its office.

Positioned in the administrative building in Central City, President Haras's office sat at the top of the hivelike sandstone building. Nothing but a great bubble of blue-tinted crystal, the floor was a soft red grass that warmed with the sun. Embedded in the wall opposite the triangular door was President Haras's astrolabe, which liked to buzz whenever anyone walked up to the entrance.

"Take your sandals off," I said to Mwinyi.

He quickly did so, looking around with awe at the blue dome. He was grinning again, something he'd been doing since we'd landed on Oomza Uni. He laughed to himself with glee when he set foot on the soft grass of President Haras's office. "I can hear them here, too," he said. He giggled.

"What is wrong with Mwinyi?" Okwu asked me in Meduse, as we walked toward President Haras.

"He can talk to living things," I said. "And do something called 'deep grounding.' Plus, he's never been on a different planet."

"Will his happiness kill him?" Okwu asked.

"President Haras," I said, ignoring both Okwu and Mwinyi, who was still giggling, and looked at the grass.

"Welcome back, Binti and Okwu," it said in Otjihimba. It stood in the center of the dome and for a moment, it completely disappeared and then it was back. I was used to this, but Mwinyi was not and behind me, I heard him gasp. "Just in time for some rest and then the start of the next academic cycle. You will be staying for that?"

"Yes," Okwu and I said.

"Good," it said. "And my *greatest* welcome is to you, Mwinyi Njem of the Enyi Zinariya."

"I am so happy to be here, President Haras," Mwinyi said.

"You are also the first of your people to be here," President Haras said. "The Zinariya have written research papers about your ancestors and speculated about your people in current times. From what I understand, a group of Zinariya students wants to reconnect with your people. It's been a long time."

When Mwinyi only stared at President Haras with his mouth hanging open, President Haras chuckled. "You are a harmonizer?"

"Yes, Mma," he said. Then he frowned. "I'm sorry. I don't know if . . . do I call you Oga? President? In my village, we have only men and women and some who are both, neither, or more, but all human. At least, since the Zinariya left us long ago."

"What do you call Okwu?"

"I just go with what Binti says," he said. "But in my head, I often call it 'he.'"

Beside me, Okwu puffed out a burst of gas and I looked at my feet smiling.

Mwinyi looked at me and then Okwu, then shrugged.

"You may call me 'Mma,' if you like," President Haras said.

Mwinyi nodded. "Thank you, Mma."

"So," President Haras said, turning and scuttling toward the far side of the dome. The three of us followed. President Haras always liked to walk in circles around the dome as it spoke. It looked up through the top of the high ceiling at New Fish, who hovered just above the building. "Things didn't go as expected?"

We told it everything, me talking sometimes, other times Okwu and Mwinyi. President Haras clicked its forelegs and a few times seemed to completely disappear as it listened, but was mostly quiet and fully present physically. I couldn't help crying when I talked about when the Root was burned and I was sure my family was dead. Mwinyi told President Haras about what he'd seen from afar when I stabbed the owl-like creature's feather into my flesh to activate the zinariya. He'd said it was like something had erupted. "The ground shook enough for small cracks to open up around me and from where the Ariya's cavern was, or at least near it. And there was a blast of blue-purple light," he said. "But it rose and fell like water."

When I'd come back to myself, the Ariya's clothes had been on fire and I'd been horrified that I'd somehow called up current and lost control of it. What Mwinyi described was even stranger. When Okwu told of its killing of all those Khoush soldiers as my home burned with my family inside it, I felt a rush of hot fury and pleasure. My parents had not died, but the Root, a place dearer to Osemba Himbas than even the Osemba House, had been burned down out of Khoush spite. The Khoush did *not* get to walk away free from that. I knew my glee at hearing about the justified killing was part of my Meduse side and it bothered me . . . but not as much as it would have a few weeks ago. I let myself feel it.

As we told it all, we walked and walked the circle of the president's office. Only as I told of my death and New Fish's resurrection of me did President Haras stop walking to ask questions.

"But they agreed on the truce," it said. "Why did they start warring?"

"I don't know," I said. "Someone shot at the Meduse chief and then everything just exploded."

"The Khoush are a terrible people," Okwu said.

I frowned, looking at it. "The Meduse killed my friends in cold blood," I said. "A ship full of unarmed students and professors who'd have been happy to talk things through and help get the stinger back. How different are the Meduse?"

"We acted out of duty, loyalty, and honor, Binti," Okwu said.

I was shaking now, the tips of my *okuoko* quivering and against my back. I was seeing Heru again, his chest exploding. And not for the first time, I wondered if that stinger had been Okwu's stinger. It could have been. At the time, I did not know Okwu very well. My memory could not identify it among the many Meduse committing *moojh-ha ki-bira* right before my eyes. Even when I was later stung in the Meduse ship, Okwu had been beside the chief, but I'd seen Okwu move very fast, it could have zipped behind me in that moment.

"Binti," President Haras said, putting a foreleg on my shoulder. I flinched and it pressed its foreleg to me harder. "Look at the grass. Remember what we say?"

"It grows because it's alive," I whispered, looking at the red grass. "It grows because it's alive." This was a mantra President Haras had taught me to say whenever I was in its office and a panic attack descended on me. The grass I stood on with my bare feet was a deep red like blood, but it wasn't bleeding, it was alive. *Red was not always bad,* I repeated to myself. *I wore red, the Himba wore it,* otjize *is red. When I speak through the zinariya, my words are red.* "It grows because it's alive." I inhaled, exhaled, and felt better. Calmer. However, I didn't look at Okwu.

"Mwinyi," President Haras said. "Do you remember what happened?"

"At this point, I was at the base of the Root," he said. "I'd heard . . . I'm . . . the lightning may have allowed me to hear it without touching . . . I'm a harmonizer, I—"

"Yes, I understand what you can do," President Haras said. "You can communicate with and to living things without necessarily knowing their language. You're a different type of harmonizer than Binti."

Mwinyi looked relieved and nodded. "It's hard to explain to people."

"You're at Oomza Uni, not many surprises here," it said.

"I also, my feet. I can ground, now. Maybe seeing Binti die triggered it."

"That's most likely," Haras said. "Those who bond closely with planets often develop grounding tendencies. You're a born harmonizer and natural worlds appeal to you; it's surprising you haven't been grounding since birth. So you heard something?"

"Yes, I was listening to the Root, realizing that it *was* a root, no, a tree, an Undying tree. Just growing underground, upside down. Binti had spoken and it seemed everything was great. We'd won. I did look up just in time to see the chief shot. But I also saw the Khoush president's face. He didn't look like he knew that was coming. And then he looked a little angry. But I saw his general Kuw, too. *He* looked ready. He ran at Binti."

I blinked, remembering. General Kuw had grabbed me. I'd punched him. Twice. Then Okwu had fought with him, but there was shooting and Okwu had had to shield itself. Kuw had still gotten away. And I had been killed.

"I think there was disagreement among the Khoush," Mwinyi was saying. "I think someone knew."

"Maybe," President Haras said. "Maybe the Khoush president's second or third in command betrayed him like the Himba Council betrayed Binti. Or maybe someone's weapon was too sensitive. Or maybe one small soldier didn't like what she or he was seeing and decided to change everything. We may never know." It looked up at New Fish. "You are not the first Oomza Uni student to be paired with a ship, Binti."

I looked up from the grass to stare at the president.

It crossed its forelegs, shook them, and faded a bit, laughter. "Again, I remind you all that you're at Oomza Uni. There are few surprises here. Most things have been researched, documented, and obsessed over. You will find entire dissertations written about paired people, especially ships and those who travel within them because such pairs tend to be the most traveled and knowledgeable of people. There are paired professors at Oomza Uni." It paused and then said, "We're done here for today. Binti, you'll go to the New Alien Medical Building. It's near here. I've scheduled you to be examined. They'll be able to tell you how far you can go from your New Fish. If you'd like to speak with paired people, just ask."

I frowned. I didn't really want anyone looking too closely at my blood or my body, me. I knew this was Oomza Uni and they had probably seen people like me before, but I wasn't sure I wanted to know the details.

"Mwinyi, would you be interested in testing to get into the university? You're of human age and you'd be the first of your kind here. Plus, it seems you're a master harmonizer, gifted in your own right."

"No," Mwinyi said. He looked at his bare feet and shook his head. "I'm sorry, Mma. That was rude. No, Mma, President Haras. I'm here for Binti . . . and Okwu. I don't want to be a student. I learn best by wandering, really."

President Haras gazed at him for several moments with its many black eyes and then said, "Well, as an honored guest at Oomza Uni, you're free to sit in on whatever classes you like. Maybe you'll eventually change your mind."

Mwinyi smiled and said, "Thank you," though his tone clearly said he would not.

"I'll have to meet with the committee about the Meduse-Khoush War," President Haras said. "It's not our fight, but we are involved. The Khoush Oomza Uni students harbored the stinger that restarted it and Oomza Uni endorsed the new pact and Okwu's visit. We'll meet and discuss, then we will act. If we need you, we will call. But until then, don't worry too much. This fight is old and if the Enyi Zinariya are going to help the Himba, then at least your families will be safe. With you gone, the Khoush will not bother with the Himba, I don't think."

What about when I go back? I wondered.

"Have you reached out to your father?" the president asked.

"I will," was all I said, looking away. *Do they really need to know I'm alive yet? After all that? With what is probably happening over there right now?* I preferred to allow my family to focus on the present, for the time being. And that present meant getting away from the Meduse-Khoush War and opening themselves to the Enyi Zinariya. I felt a pang of guilt for not being there and then quickly pushed it away.

"Ah yes, and we've already heard from the people you met in Saturn's ring," President Haras said. "They've been tested and, oh my, those people have several youths and even a few elders who will make fine students here."

"Really? Already?"

"Oh yes," President Haras said. "They don't waste time when they are sure of something. And they said the recommendation they got made them very, very sure. I suspect at some point one of you three will meet them."

I glanced at Mwinyi. He was grinning again.

CHAPTER 13

Medical

Twenty-five hours later, I walked up the path to the white building. On the front was a symbol that was a combination of individuals (only one humanoid) standing together. Leaving my dorm room, ignoring the stares of classmates, and feeling the sun directly on my skin and *okuoko*, had been extremely difficult. Not only had most people heard bits and pieces of what had happened to me on Earth after a few students overheard a professor who'd just spoken with the president, but I *looked* very different. Without my *otjize*, my dark brown skin was that much more noticeable, compared to the few other human students who were all Khoush. In addition, without the *otjize* covering them, my ten thick *okuoko* were on full display. I was a human with soft transparent blue tentacles with darker blue dots at their tips that hung nearly to my knees now. People associated me even more with Okwu, whom they feared so much already.

My friend Haifa was the only one who'd come to my room and demanded I tell her every detail. And as I had, she'd stared and stared at my face and I'd felt so uncomfortable that I'd begun to sweat and had to tree a little in order to finish. I'd missed Haifa and even in my discomfort, I was happy to see her. However, her staring and the feeling of being naked left me tired.

Now at my medical exam, I felt the same anxious fatigue. I'd considered bringing Mwinyi, but he seemed to be having too much fun running around barefoot and meeting everyone for me to drag him along. Okwu had disappeared into its dorm, telling me nothing but, "Go to your exam. I will be here." As I walked into the building, New Fish hovered above.

———

My doctor was surprisingly a human being, a tall plump Khoush woman who was about my mother's age. She wore flowing black robes and a sparkling earring on each ear that matched her equally green eyes. President Haras probably had made this happen. She towered over me as she held out a hand. "Hello, Binti. My name is Tuka."

I shook her hand and said, "Hello" as I glanced around the small room. It looked similar to the patient rooms back home, though the examination table was much wider, longer, and sturdier than any I'd seen.

"I spoke at length with President Haras this morning," she said. She smiled, looking keenly at my *okuoko*. "You're amazing, my dear."

"Thank you," I said quietly.

"I want to put you through a series of tests—blood, skin, digestive, brain; I want to look at everything. We'll be able to talk about the results in a few hours."

"Hours?" I said.

She nodded. "And yes, I'll be able to tell you how far you and your ship can go from each other."

My heart started racing and I sat down heavily on the yellow chair behind me.

"What's the matter?" she asked, worried.

"I'm afraid of what you'll find."

"We'll definitely find some interesting things, but nothing you can't deal with, Binti. You already are what you are and you're fine."

"Am I?" I asked.

She patted me on the shoulder. "Let's get started. You can stay sitting. We'll test your reflexes."

═══════

Afterward, I was in the waiting room for three hours, too paralyzed with worry to get up and move when a Meduse-like person came and hovered beside me. It was probably worried too, because it puffed out gas constantly and barely bothered to suck it back in. I would have had my astrolabe play some soft music for me, but mine was broken and, unlike my *edan*, its broken remains weren't anywhere to be found when I'd awoken on New Fish. Since I'd died and returned, I'd been able to speak through the zinariya with ease, no more vertigo and no gaping tunnel or strange planet appeared behind me anymore. However, speaking to my grandmother or Mwinyi through the zinariya was out of the question because they'd both just ask me if I'd gotten the test results yet. At some point, I curled up on the blue chair and fell asleep.

I immediately awoke when my name was called and followed the small hovering droid back to the same patient room I'd been in before with Dr. Tuka. She sat on a high chair with a tray on which she had her astrolabe projecting a chart before her eyes.

"Have a seat," she said without looking away from it.

I sat in the yellow chair, unable to hide my shivering.

"So, your tests have all come back," she said, turning to me.

"Please, tell me how far I can go first," I blurted.

"About five miles on land and she can fly about seven miles up," she said. "That's not so bad, is it?"

I smiled and said, "No. Thank the Seven."

"But unless she follows, no more taking university and solar shuttles, okay? New Fish can take you."

I nodded and then asked the question I'd been dreading most, "What happens if we get too far from each other? Will . . . we die?"

"*She* won't," Dr. Tuka said. "But *you* might, if the distance happens very fast and is a lot. But first, there will be terrible pain. It's different for everyone. Just don't do it."

She paused, waiting for me to ask anything else. I didn't want to know anything else.

"Okay, so your DNA is very interesting, Binti," she said. "You're . . ."

"Am I . . . am I still human?" I asked.

"Do you think you are?"

"I mean, well, that's not . . ."

"You are a Himba girl, right? That's what you say you are?"

"Yes, but . . ." I touched my *okuoko* and smiled sheepishly. "Aren't I equally New Fish microbes? Isn't that why I'm alive?"

"Your DNA is Himba, Enyi Zinariya, and Meduse . . . and some, but not much, New Fish," she said. "But your microbes are mostly from New Fish, yes. Your microbes exist with your cells, so this blend is what makes you, you. So you are different from what you were born as, certainly. But as I said before, you're healthy."

I breathed a sigh of relief.

"There's more, however," Dr. Tuka said. "Something you should know."

I frowned. "Like what?"

"Well, at this point, this may not be much of a surprise or issue since you've already spent a year at Oomza Uni, met many people, and so on." She paused and looked at the virtual chart. Then she said, "You're seventeen Earth years old, correct?"

I nodded, but she wasn't even looking at me.

"Have you ever thought about having children?"

I frowned more deeply. "Of course," I said. "For me to do all that I've done and never have children, what kind of Himba—"

She turned to me. The look on her face made me close my mouth.

"What if Okwu gave birth to it?" she said.

"What?!"

"This will happen. Not now, but in time."

"But—"

"And if you were to have a baby, it would have your *okuoko* because Meduse DNA is strong. It bullies its way into all offspring."

"But Okwu and I aren't—" I paused, thinking of who Okwu was to me and then I thought about when I'd kissed Mwinyi.

"On top of this, if you were to have a child, you would pass New Fish microbes to it and there is the possibility that your child would be part New Fish as well. Though no likelihood of the link. Also—"

"Stop!" I screeched, my eyes closed. "Enough. Enough!" There was a ringing in my ears and it was getting louder. My face was growing hot and felt as if something were squeezing my head. I was both falling and rising. "Even my astrolabe broke," I breathed. "The chip is corrupted. I have no documented identity." I giggled wildly and screamed, "What *am* I? I'm so much," with tears welling in my eyes. "I . . . I didn't go on my pilgrimage when I went home. That was supposed to complete me as a woman in my village. Instead, my mere *presence* started a *war*! In my home! *They burned my home!* And they killed me! I died! And then I came back as . . . am I really even me?" I was on my feet now. Pacing the small room. Smacking my forehead.

On the room's counter was a vase full of soft-looking yellow flowers with petals that each looked like bladders of water. I grabbed one and crushed the flower in my fist as I stared at Dr. Tuka, who calmly watched me. The liquid that burst from each petal dribbled down my wrist to my elbow and the room suddenly smelled sweet and earthy. "My past and present have become more and *now my future?*"

I sobbed, throwing the crushed flower to my feet and sinking to the floor. I rested my head in my hands. "I have always liked myself, Dr. Tuka." I looked up at her. "I *like* who I am. I *love* my family. I wasn't running away from home. I don't *want* to change, to grow! Nothing . . . everything . . . I don't want all this . . . this weirdness! It's too heavy! I just want to *be*."

Dr. Tuka watched me, quiet.

"Am I human?" I asked. As I desperately stared at her, as she said nothing, she grew blurry as my eyes teared up more. For the first time since I'd left home, I wondered if I should have left home.

"Binti," Dr. Tuka said. "In your tribe a woman marries a man, and in doing so, marries his family, correct?"

"Yes," I whispered.

"She marries a man chosen by her family and herself, who will provide for and protect her and nourish her being."

"Yes."

"This is the path to respect among the Himba. I read up on them before seeing you. So see it this way: You're paired with New Fish and Okwu, each of whom has a family. Your family is bigger than any Himba girl's ever was. And twice, you were supposed to die. And here you stand healthy and strong . . ." She chuckled and then added, "And strange. There is no person like you at this school."

I sat down again, still shaking from all the information, all the reality. "I'm sorry I did that to your flower," I said. "I don't . . . I don't normally destroy things."

"It will grow another one," she said.

I nodded. "Good."

"Go and study, Binti," Dr. Tuka said, turning back to her virtual chart. "I'm also scheduling an appointment for you with your therapist."

———

The moment I told New Fish that we could be apart for five miles on land and seven in the air, New Fish took off, gleefully zooming up about two miles, then free-falling back to land and zooming large circles around the area. Still, she couldn't return to the field that she'd liked so much because it was over a hundred miles away. Not without me. And I wanted to return to my dorm and lie down.

I'd been so worried and now things were sort of okay. I was okay. Sort of.

There was a small open field near my dorm. It didn't have the tasty yellow grass or the ntu ntu bugs New Fish wanted to taste, and students liked to walk through it on the way to class. But it was relatively quiet and two other living ships stayed there. New Fish approved.

⸻

I closed the door behind me and sank to the floor. Then I quickly got up. I needed to check on the fresh jar of *otjize* I'd mixed last night. I took the lid off, sniffed it, and looked at the red-orange paste. It still looked thin. Maybe another day. Another day of being naked. I sighed, putting it back on the windowsill where the light from Oomza Uni's large moon and tomorrow's sunshine would heat it. I'd just lain on my bed for a nap when there was a knock on my door. Groaning, I reached into my pocket to grab my astrolabe so I could see who it was. Then I remembered that my astrolabe was back on Earth. Broken, probably left in the dirt when I'd been shot.

"Who's there?" I said.

"Open the door," Haifa said.

I smiled and said, "Open."

Haifa stood there grinning at me and behind her stood Mwinyi, who wasn't grinning at all. "Saw him in the lobby and assumed he was coming up here. I decided to show him the way."

"I've been here twice already," Mwinyi said, cracking a small smile.

"Okay, I just wanted to walk with you," she said, batting her eyes flirtatiously at him. "You seemed lonely." From the moment Haifa had set eyes on Mwinyi, she'd been in "love."

Mwinyi laughed. "I appreciate the company," he said, sitting in the wooden chair at my study desk.

Haifa giggled and sat on the bed with me.

"You didn't tell me you were back," Mwinyi said.

"I assumed you were busy with all your new friends," I said with a smirk. "When you had time, you'd come here."

Where I'd had a hard time making friends since coming to Oomza Uni because people were afraid of Okwu, Mwinyi was a friend magnet. From the moment the university gave him a room in the mostly humanoid dorm beside mine yesterday, despite the fact that he refused to become an Oomza Uni student, he'd been incredibly popular. I was there with him when he entered the dorm. He'd immediately struck up a conversation with the dorm's elder, a treelike individual who spoke in a series of cracking and creaking sounds. Somehow, Mwinyi was able to understand it. I watched him relax and give that intense look and then start to make gestures. This dorm elder liked Mwinyi so much that after introducing Mwinyi to practically everyone on his floor, it and several others stayed in Mwinyi's room to help him set up and just to "talk." I'd ended up quietly saying goodbye and heading to my dorm. From the start, I saw that people of all kinds were simply attracted to him.

"What'd they tell you?" he asked.

Haifa looked at me and yet again, I felt my nakedness. I glanced at my jar of still-stewing *otjize* and wanted to groan. One more day. Hopefully.

"Stop looking at me like that," I muttered.

Haifa laughed. "I'm just glad you're back," she said. "Even the Bear said she missed you."

"No she didn't," I said, rolling my eyes. "The Bear doesn't like anyone."

The Bear lived in one of the rooms down the hall. She was mostly bushy brown hair. The Bear and I didn't speak much, but we often sat side by side on one of the large couches in the main room. We'd always shared a quiet bond. I imagined she understood one's need to be covered.

"The Bear was the first to ask me why you'd left for break instead of staying with all of us. She wondered if you didn't like us."

"After we went into the desert that night? Of course, I like you
both!"

"Binti, what'd they say?" Mwinyi insisted.

"I'm okay, Mwinyi," I said. "I can move five miles from New
Fish on land and she can fly about seven miles high."

Before I even finished saying this, Mwinyi slumped in his chair
with relief. I laughed. He stood up suddenly and then seemed unsure of what to do next, as he looked at Haifa and me on the bed.
Haifa looked from me to Mwinyi and back to me. Her eyebrows
rose. "Oh!" she said. She looked at me and pointed at Mwinyi. I
nodded.

"You could have told me," she said, smirking.

"I just got back yesterday. There's a lot I have to tell you."

Haifa got up.

"Tomorrow . . . do you and the Bear want to come with me to
see the Falls?" I asked her. I turned to Mwinyi, "You too, and Okwu.
I've been meaning to see them since I came here but never had the
time." I didn't say the rest of what I was thinking, which was, *Better
see them while I can. You never know tomorrow.*

Haifa kissed me on the cheek. "Of course. It'll be a good homecoming thing for us. I know the Bear will. She loves the Falls with
all those colors."

"Mwinyi?" I asked.

He nodded.

"I hope you all don't mind that we'll have to fly there in New
Fish instead of taking the shuttle."

Haifa beamed and clapped her hands. "Yes! Everyone will be so
jealous. You do know that everyone in this dorm has wanted a ride
on your ship since you got here, right?"

"Really?" I asked.

"Yes," Mwinyi and Haifa both said. Then they laughed.

When the door shut behind Haifa, Mwinyi turned to me. "What else did they tell you?"

"I don't really want to talk about it right now, okay?" I said.

He came across the room to me. I looked down, trying to avoid his eyes. He took my chin and lifted my face. "Are you alright?" he asked. As I looked into his eyes, I felt all my defenses relax. Looking into his eyes was like being a mirror who was looking into another mirror. Universes.

"Everything is going to be fine," I said.

"Everything is going to be fine," he repeated.

He stepped closer, paused, then closer. He took me in his arms and slowly I relaxed and then finally lay my head on his shoulder, turning my head to his bushy hair. Somehow, he still smelled like the desert. I kissed him on the neck and soon found my way to his lips.

We forgot ourselves for a while.

CHAPTER 14

Shape Shifter

In the morning, I sat at the windowsill with my jar of *otjize* in my lap.

The first sun had just risen, shining its lush yellow light into my room. I tilted my damp face toward it, enjoying the warmth as I leaned against the wall. My *okuoko* were wet from the long shower I'd taken, but they dried quickly in the morning light. The transparent blue flesh that they were remained soft once dry, it never grew chapped like my skin when I didn't apply *otjize*. I opened my eyes and they fell on the two large stones I'd had New Fish pluck from Saturn's ring.

After digging them out of the crevice I'd had New Fish hide them in, letting the ice encasing parts of them melt off, I'd brought the stones to my room and spent several minutes examining them. I'd tasted them and indeed they had the same tang as the salt from Undying trees and god stone. Then I decided to test for what I suspected by treeing and called up a complex current. Splitting the current into a treelike shape, I laid it over each stone and watched how the network of current sank through it with control and ease. I smiled widely. Not only would I use these stones to carve out each intricate dial, womb, rete, star pointer, plate, and circuit board, but the astrolabe I would build would be like no astrolabe any Himba has ever made.

I picked up the jar and held it between my palms. It was also warm, as if it had absorbed the sun. I put on my favorite red wrapper and matching top, one of the outfits I'd brought with me when

I'd first arrived on Oomza Uni. The material was soft and worn from many washings and wind faded because I'd gone off into the desert many times wearing this very outfit.

The night of my return, I'd gone to the usual spot in the nearby forest to collect the clay. I'd dug a small hole and marked it with twigs and, apparently, while I was away one of the round-bodied beasts I'd seen a couple times had made the place its rest spot. The top layer of clay was coated with rough black hairs and pressed with hooved footprints. I scraped off this layer and dug out a large clump of the clay. I mixed it with the special black flower oil I still had in my room and then I started counting down.

Now I whispered, "Zero," and twisted the jar open. The smell that wafted out made me grin. I looked at the Night Masquerade costume I'd hung on the wall beside the window and said to it, "Yes. It's ready." I dug my right index and middle fingers into it, my two fingers I'd had since I was born. Then I smeared it on my left hand, thinking hard about the fact that this was the first time it had ever had *otjize* on it. It went on smooth, like something that belonged there. Then I fell into my routine. I always ended with my face.

With a sigh, I dug out a large dollop and massaged it into my cheeks. For the first time in a while, I felt like myself. When I was done applying it to my skin, I started rolling it on my ten *okuoko*, hiding the clear blue with speckles at the tips. Because they were so long, they required quite a bit of *otjize*. As I started rolling the last one between my palms, I heard the sound of metal clinking and then a soft hum from behind me.

Slowly, I turned around. There on my desk, the golden ball and its triangle metal slivers were rising and hovering about five inches in the air. As I watched, the pieces were drawn to the rotating golden ball. They clinked some more as they reattached themselves, trying one shape and then shifting to another. Stellated, square, star, cylinder. I crept over to it, my hand still clutching my last *otjize*-free *okuoko*.

I quickly climbed the tree, grasping at the Pythagorean theorem. I called up a current as I brought my face about a foot from it. The moment I held up my hands, the current softly buzzing between them, the pieces suddenly decided to stick. I actually *felt* the force the golden ball made in order to pull the metal pieces to it. Then the object fell to my desk with a *thunk*.

"What?" I asked, touching the tip of the shiny silver pyramid it had become.

When it did nothing else, I went back to my jar of *otjize* and finished doing my hair. I rubbed a bit more into the five anklets I now wore on each ankle, took a last look at my new *edan*, and then left to meet up with Mwinyi, Okwu, Haifa, and the Bear. When school started back up in a few Earth days, I'd have something interesting to show Professor Okpala. However, for the time being all I cared about was finally seeing the Falls with my friends.

And when we got there, it really was like witnessing a beautiful dream.

ACKNOWLEDGMENTS

Three Augusts in a row, Binti's story came to me. It happened each time I returned to Buffalo, New York, after spending the summer with my family in the south Chicago suburbs of Illinois. In the August of 2016, I wanted to take a break from writing. I didn't think I'd have the ending to Binti's story for a while, years even, and I was fine with that. Then I sat down one evening and the entire story came to me. First the end, then the middle, then the beginning.

Over three days, I scribbled down the plot in the little Ankara cloth-covered journal I'd bought in the Lagos airport. But I didn't answer the call to adventure immediately. I had courses to teach and another novel to edit. I went to South Africa and gazed at the Lion's Head, went to the Arizona desert and followed a Pepsis wasp, I saw the White House while it was still worth seeing, and I had a conversation about microbes with a Ph.D. student during a lunch with the African Cultural Association at the University of Illinois, Urbana-Champaign. When winter break arrived, the moment I took off my professor hat to give the writer's cap that I always wear some fresh air, whatever it is that takes hold of me to make me write descended on me.

So first and foremost I want to thank that thing that grabs, that whispers, that urgently tells. I'd like to thank my Ancestors, who walk in front of, behind, beside, fly above, and swim beneath me. Thanks to my daughter, Anyaugo, for demanding to know what happened to Okwu. Thanks to my editor Lee Harris and my agent, Don Maass, for their excellent feedback. And thanks to my beta reader Angel Maynard, who responded with, "Mind blown!" after reading the first clean draft. And finally, thank you to the rest of my immediate family, my mother, sisters Ifeoma and Ngozi, brother Emezie, nephews Dika and Chinedu, and niece Obioma. Without you all energizing my life, the Binti Trilogy would never ever have happened. I love you all.